I0581792

NEBULA AWARDS SHOWCASE 59

NEBULA AWARDS SHOWCASE 59

The Year's Best Science Fiction and Fantasy

EDITED BY

STEPHEN KOTOWYCH

Nebula Awards Showcase 59: The Year's Best Science Fiction and Fantasy

Copyright © 2025 by Science Fiction and Fantasy Writers of America, Inc. d/b/a Science Fiction & Fantasy Writers Association

All rights reserved. No part of this publication may be reproduced, stored in a retrieval system, or transmitted, in any form or by any means, electronic, mechanical, photocopying, recording, or otherwise, without the prior written permission of the copyright holders.

Cover illustration "Star Deity 2024" by Lauren Raye Snow
Cover design by M.L. Clark
Interior layout designed by Laurie McGregor / Page Turn
Typesetting by M.L. Clark

The stories, all names, characters, and incidents portrayed herein are fictitious. No identification with actual persons (living or deceased), places, buildings, products, or events is intended or should be inferred.

San Lorenzo, California, United States

ISBN 978-1-958243-06-0 (print)
ISBN 978-1-958243-07-7 (ebook)

The rights to individual pieces featured in this book remain with their respective copyright holders.

"Tantie Merle and the Farmhand 4200" by R. S. A. Garcia. Copyright © 2023 by R. S. A. Garcia. Published by *Uncanny Magazine*. Reprinted by permission of the author. | "Bad Doors" by John Wiswell. Copyright © 2023 by John Wiswell. Published by *Uncanny Magazine*. Reprinted by permission of the author. | "Once Upon a Time at The Oakmont" by P. A. Cornell. Copyright © 2023 by P. A. Cornell. Published by *Fantasy Magazine*. Reprinted by permission of the author. | "Window Boy" by Thomas Ha. Copyright © 2023 by Thomas Ha. Published by *Clarkesworld Magazine*. Reprinted by permission of the author. | "Better Living Through Algorithms" by Naomi Kritzer. Copyright © 2023 by Naomi Kritzer. Published by *Clarkesworld Magazine*. Reprinted by permission of the author. | "The Sound of Children Screaming" by Rachael K. Jones. Copyright © 2023 by Rachael K. Jones. Published by *Nightmare Magazine*. Reprinted by permission of the author. | "The Year Without Sunshine" by Naomi Kritzer. Copyright © 2023 by Naomi Kritzer. Published by *Uncanny Magazine*. Reprinted by permission of the author. | "Saturday's Song" by Wole Talabi. Copyright © 2023 by Wole Talabi. Published by *Lightspeed Magazine*. Reprinted by permission of the author. | *I AM AI* by Ai Jiang. Copyright © 2023 by Ai Jiang. Originally published by Shortwave Publishing (978-1-959565-09-3, Paperback). Excerpt reprinted by permission of the publisher and the author. | "A Short Biography of a Conscious Chair" by Renan Bernardo. Copyright © 2023 by Renan Bernardo. Published by *Samovar*. Reprinted by permission of the author. | "Imagine: Purple-Haired Girl Shooting Down the Moon" by Angela Liu. Copyright © 2023 by Angela Liu. Published by *Clarkesworld Magazine*. Reprinted by permission of the author. | "Six Versions of My Brother Found Under the Bridge" by Eugenia Triantafyllou. Copyright © 2023 by Eugenia Triantafyllou. Published by *Uncanny Magazine*. Reprinted by permission of the author. | Excerpt from Linghun by Ai Jiang. Copyright © 2023 by Ai Jiang. Originally published by Dark Matter INK. Reprinted by permission of the publisher and the author.

2023 NEBULA AWARDS®

Presented at the Westin Pasadena and online on Saturday, June 8, 2024

Toastmaster: Sarah Gailey

Best Novel

★ **Winner:** *The Saint of Bright Doors* by Vajra Chandrasekera, published by *Tordotcom*

The Water Outlaws by S. L. Huang, published by *Tordotcom* and *Solaris UK*

Translation State by Ann Leckie, published by *Orbit US* and *Orbit UK*

The Terraformers by Annalee Newitz, published by *Tor* and *Orbit UK*

Shigidi and the Brass Head of Obalufon by Wole Talabi, published by *DAW* and *Gollancz*

Witch King by Martha Wells, published by *Tordotcom*

Best Novella

The Crane Husband by Kelly Barnhill, published by *Tordotcom*

★ **Winner:** *Linghun* by Ai Jiang, published by *Dark Matter INK*

Thornhedge by T. Kingfisher, published by *Tor* and *Titan UK*

Untethered Sky by Fonda Lee, published by *Tordotcom*

The Mimicking of Known Successes by Malka Older, published by *Tordotcom*

Mammoths at the Gates by Nghi Vo, published by *Tordotcom*

Best Novelette

"A Short Biography of a Conscious Chair" by Renan Bernardo, published by *Samovar Magazine*

I AM AI by Ai Jiang, published by *Shortwave Publishing*

★ **Winner:** "The Year Without Sunshine" by Naomi Kritzer, published by *Uncanny Magazine*

"Imagine: Purple-Haired Girl Shooting Down the Moon" by Angela Liu, published by *Clarkesworld Magazine*

"Saturday's Song" by Wole Talabi, published by *Lightspeed Magazine*

"Six Versions of My Brother Found Under the Bridge" by Eugenia Triantafyllou, published by *Uncanny Magazine*

Best Short Story

"Once Upon a Time at The Oakmont" by P. A. Cornell, published by *Fantasy Magazine*

★ **Winner:** "Tantie Merle and the Farmhand 4200" by R. S. A. Garcia, published by *Uncanny Magazine*

"Window Boy" by Thomas Ha, published by *Clarkesworld Magazine*

"The Sound of Children Screaming" by Rachael K. Jones, published by *Nightmare Magazine*

"Better Living Through Algorithms" by Naomi Kritzer, published by *Clarkesworld Magazine*

"Bad Doors" by John Wiswell, published by *Uncanny Magazine*

Andre Norton Nebula Award for Middle Grade and Young Adult Fiction

★ **Winner:** *To Shape a Dragon's Breath* by Moniquill Blackgoose, published by *Del Rey*

The Inn at the Amethyst Lantern by J. Dianne Dotson, published by *Android*

The Ghost Job by Greg van Eekhout, published by *Harper*

Liberty's Daughter by Naomi Kritzer, published by *Fairwood*

Ray Bradbury Nebula Award for Outstanding Dramatic Presentation

Nimona written by Robert L. Baird, Lloyd Taylor, Pamela Ribon, Nick Bruno, Troy Quaine, Keith Bunin, and Nate Stevenson (Annapurna Animation and Annapurna Pictures)

The Last of Us: "Long, Long Time" written by Neil Druckman and Craig Mazin (HBO Max)

★ **Winner:** *Barbie* written by Greta Gerwig and Noah Baumbach (Warner Brothers, Heyday Films, and LuckyChap Entertainment)

Dungeons & Dragons: Honor Among Thieves written by Jonathan Goldstein, John Francis Daley, Michael Gilio, and Chris McKay (Paramount Pictures, Entertainment One, and Allspark Pictures)

Spider-Man: Across the Spider-Verse written by Phil Lord, Christopher Miller, and **Dave Callaham** (Columbia Pictures, Marvel Entertainment, and Avi Arad Productions)

The Boy and the Heron written by Hayao Miyazaki
(Studio Ghibli and Toho Company)

Best Game Writing

The Bread Must Rise by Stewart C Baker and James Beamon,
published by *Choice of Games*

Alan Wake II by Sam Lake, Clay Murphy, Tyler Burton Smith, and Sinnika Annala,
published by *Remedy Entertainment* and *Epic Games Publishing*.

Ninefox Gambit: Machineries of Empire Roleplaying Game by Yoon Ha Lee and **Marie Brennan**, published by *Android*

Dredge by Joel Mason, published by *Black Salt Games* and *Team 17*

Chants of Sennaar by Julian Moya and Thomas Panuel, published by *Rundisc* and *Focus Entertainment*

★ **Winner:** *Baldur's Gate 3* by Adam Smith, Adrienne Law, Baudelaire Welch, Chrystal Ding, Ella McConnell, Ine Van Hamme, Jan Van Dosselaer, John Corcoran, Kevin VanOrd, Lawrence Schick, Rachel Quirke, Ruairí Moore, Sarah Baylus, Stephen Rooney, Martin Docherty, and Swen Vincke, published by *Larian Studios*

Other Awards

Damon Knight Grand Master Award
Susan Cooper

Kate Wilhelm Solstice Award
Jennell Jaquays

Kevin O'Donnell, Jr. Service to SFWA Award
James Hosek

Infinity Award
Tanith Lee

TABLE OF CONTENTS

SHORT STORIES

TANTE MERLE AND THE FARMHAND 4200

R. S. A. Garcia

So, hear nah. This is how it happen.

Was years after Malcolm pass through and wash away a lot ah we little islands coasts, and mash up so much ah Florida and Texas and them places, and people say they ain't waiting for no next storm like that one, and they pack up they things and went England, and Canada, and all over.

I done old, and my children was living Germany and Kenya and my youngest was down in Australia where hotter than here, so I didn't see no point in going from where I live my whole life. My Lincoln bury here, and we house good and strong. My oldest, Susan, she send money for me regular, and Lincoln like new thing, just like me, so he fix up the house and fix up the house until even that monster storm only cost me some windows and a little mason work on my concrete roof from what they call impact debris.

Long story short, I stay in my village with a few families and the only problem was some ah we getting old for the garden and the little animal we keep. Chickens get out, if the children not around, is trouble to catch them back. Cow wandering the street after it get frighten because somebody drone fly too low on delivery.

My problem was Ignatius.

Which is to say, he ain't no real problem. He just a normal goat, white and brown and tall as my hip. Wasn't he alone I keep all that time. I had a small herd I used to get nice milk from. Even try to make some cheese once. (That ain't come out so good, but that's a next story.) When they start getting on in years, I make a cook with neighbours and we curry it down with a little roti on the side with channa, potato and chataigne, and some beers; was meals for days.

That was village life. Real nice with everybody helping out everybody and the children belong to all ah we. World change, a lot ah the children move on, and the families that still here keep to theyself, so now is just Ignatius and me and I let him keep the grass low in the yard because Lincoln gone and I can't operate no weed-wacker bot.

Well after I fall that one time and break my hip and they give me a new one in the big hospital in Town, I start to get trouble on the days my yard clear of grass to go down the veranda stairs and take the goat out to the empty lot down the track. Didn't have nobody around in the day to help. All the families working and the children either in school or inside doing school online if they still rebuilding from the storm. But Ignatius can't eat if I don't take him, so I was forcing myself to go. Then I trip on the way back ah day, and thank God Neighbour see me go down because I would have been waiting for help to get back up all now.

I had a delivery service for meals, and a nice young boy come and clean for me once a week, but I couldn't afford no pet services and I know my children would say, Mammy, just cook him or give him away and done. But he was my little company around the yard. Just he alone I sit down with sometimes to talk to in the dead ah night, or the heat ah the day, and he always have time for me, listening while he chewing on something and watching me with he funny rectangle eye what all goat have.

Well, I have to say I tell one lie, and that is Ignatius have one problem and is the chewing. He chew on anything, especially what he don't like. That is why I can't get no pet service because I try, and he run them out the yard and keep they shoes for food. Ever since, is only me Ignatius like. Lincoln and all leave him alone after he come home and try to feed him one day at the top of the little rise behind we house, and Ignatius take one look at he bend over ass and butt the man down the hill. After I stop laughing (because if you ain't dead or seriously injured, I go laugh), he say was my goat and he wash he hands off him.

People say he bad-tempered but really he just know who he like, and sometimes that ain't you. But we was always good, and I didn't have the heart to eat him. He was probably too old to taste good anyway. But he keep getting away and he needed tying up and bringing back, and I didn't know what to do again.

Point is, I mention to my second daughter, Paula, who living in Germany, how hard it was getting to go out to the garden some days, and how things was with Ignatius, and because Paula not judgemental like Susan, she send me a package and tell me to expect the drone.

Bright and early ah Tuesday morning I hear the whirring outside and when I peak through my living room curtains is because a big box so on my veranda and Ignatius done traipsing over with he leash trailing to see what he could chew. I reach out and take up the box and close the door and then I sit down in my favourite armchair in front the hologram projector Lincoln buy the year before he die and I read the label.

FARMHAND 4200!

It say. And in small print below:

AI Guided Nanotechnology Solutions To Your Farming Needs

And in real fine print:

10 Year Warranty with Money Back Guarantee
(Certain conditions apply)

Well, I say to myself, that sounding good. And I touch the corner of the box where it had a big green patch say "touch me." Box make a little chirp and then peel down on all sides like a Julie mango and sitting in the middle was a ball of transparent package tape. Next thing I know, the tape tent a little at the top, then a blade appear, and slice the tape away.

Well, I bawl out and jump off the chair. Same time, a silvery thing the size of a cricket ball roll out the middle of the tape and stop right in front me. A little face light up in green on the top of it. Two circles for eyes and a bendy line for a mouth, like them emoji thing I used to text with as a child.

"Greetings owner," the ball say in ah English accent like Lincoln boss-man used to have. "No need for alarm. I'm your new Farmhand 4200!" The little blade that was poking out the side melt down so it was a smooth ball again. "Thank you for your purchase! Kindly remain still while I perform preliminary security and software updates."

Next thing I know, the ID band the government use to give we healthcare and send my pension and thing make a beep. Then it talk soft and sweet like a lady. "Linking," it say. "Farmhand 4200 detected. Downloading app. Download complete. App ready for use."

The green face make a grin and the ball roll as if excited. "Hello, Mrs. Merle Huggins, I'm your new farmhand! I'm very pleased to meet you and begin our farming adventures together. Please note, your Digital ID device has been linked to me and will provide you with updates on my tasks, location, battery life, and other functions.

"However, as a Farmhand 4200, I'm fully self-sufficient and require only ten minutes in daylight per day in order to recharge. I'm programmed to handle numerous farming emergencies and am enabled for research and adaptation should anything fall outside of the over 200 possible scenarios I've been initiated with. Your daughter, Paula, has sent you a message which I shall now play for you."

The little face change to yellow and pause on a smile instead of the wide grin it had before. "Hi Mammy," my daughter voice say, and it make me jump because it was like she was in the room with me and as I listen she, tears come to my eyes because is years I ain't see she and she the one daughter give me grandchildren. "I hope you like this. You said you needed some help and Jonas says this is the top-of-the-line AI bot for farmers in the Rhineland. It can help you with the garden and that damn goat." Her laugh, big and boisterous like mine, take the sting out of her words. "Anyway, let me know when you get it and please try it out immediately and don't just have it sitting in the kitchen like the waffle maker I got you for Christmas."

I steups to myself but ain't say nothing because I know she can't hear me, but between you and me, what I going to do with a waffle maker, eh? What the hell is a waffle?

"Call me once you try it out. I want to know how it's working. Love you, Mammy. Talk to you soon, okay?"

After that the smiling face go green again and the bot say, "End of message. Hello again, Mrs. Huggins, do you have any questions for me?"

I wrack my brains as I sit slowly in the chair. "What to call you, sir?"

"Whatever you wish, Mrs. Huggins."

"Well first, don't call me that. Everybody call me Tantie Merle."

"Of course, Tantie Merle!"

I think a bit more. "What if I call you Lincoln? Was my husband name but he don't need it no more, he gone now, and I used to saying it."

The bot green face flicker, mouth round with surprise. "I would be honoured, Tantie Merle. My database shows that I'm the first Farmhand 4200 to receive a human name!"

"How much of you it have?"

"I'm a new model! 30,000 of me have been sold so far."

"So, what they call the other Farmhand 4200?"

"29,999 are called 'Farmhand 4200'," he reply cheerily.

"And the other one?"

"It is called, Handy!"

I shake my head. Sometimes people not too creative, yes, oui.

"Well, you is Lincoln from now on."

"I appreciate that very much, Tantie Merle. I am now ready for instructions. What tasks would you like me to attend to?"

So I take him outside to the bottom of the hill and show him the garden with my tomatoes and pigeon peas and corn and pimento peppers and cucumbers and herbs and whatnot, and it roll along beside me, somehow grown to the size of a beach ball, face always toward me with a big green smile. It was awkward talking to him at first, but by the time he grow pinchers to pick up and bury the packaging he come in because it suppose to breakdown into fertiliser, I forget is a robot I there with. He digging and pruning and what would take me whole morning he do in half an hour, and we talking whole time, me telling him all about the village and everybody in it. Then I take him to meet Ignatius.

First good thing, Ignatius just watch him and didn't rush him at all. "Look, Ignatius," I tell him, and wave to the bot that somehow not dirty or wet even after all the gardening. "I can't go up and down with you no more so this is Lincoln, he go tie you up from now on."

Lincoln roll closer to Ignatius. "Greetings, Ignatius! Pleased to meet you! I'm honoured to be your handler from now on. I'll find you the choicest parts of the field to feast upon!"

Ignatius watch him while chewing on some grass and fart a little bit.

"I think that went well!" Lincoln say, his green face making three happy circles that bounce around like ping pong balls.

"Okay, well let me show you where the lot is."

Slowly, I walk Ignatius down to the lot with Lincoln and then I tap the button to disengage the stake I have there and carry it a bit further, to fresh grass, before setting it against the ground so it could drive itself automatically into the dirt. "You won't have to move it every day," I say. "He have a long leash."

"Never fear, Tantie Merle. This is the last time you'll have to do this job. I'll collect Ignatius and return him to your domicile this evening."

"That would be good," I say, and give the goat a sharp look. "Now, Ignatius, don't give Lincoln no trouble, eh."

Ignatius just bend he head and start on the grass. As we turn back to the house, Lincoln say, "Is there anything else you require assistance with, Tantie Merle? I have many appendages and my adaptable hardware can create whatever is needed." All of a sudden, he stop in the road and all kind of thing poke out of he, like a porcupine, except instead of quills, is knife and fork and shovel and hammer and screwdriver and ice pick and hands with claws and I had to stop and say, "Oh gosh, put all that away, you looking like you going and kill something."

Everything melt back inside him. "Apologies, Tantie Merle."

"You could just call me Tantie, that's okay too," I say distracted as a thought occur to me. "But wait nah. You could make hands?"

The ball breathed in and out and the green face glowed brighter. "I'm VERY good at hands. I am, after all, a farmhand!"

"Well, I have ah idea for what I would like next, if you don't mind."

Lincoln vibrate a little. That's the way he get when he happy. "I would be delighted to hear it!"

And that is the first time Lincoln give me a massage, while I was sitting in front the projector, watching the weather channel and then the news. Rub my feet for hours. After that, he went and make the bed for me, and then he scrub the bathroom a little bit. I tell him leave the rest because the boy will do it on Friday, so then he sit with me while I eat my lunch. Saltfish and provision with some vegetables because things hard and a lot of food we used to eat we can't import so easy now, they too expensive. But anyway, that is the good food that my grandparents used to eat, and they live long, and I was going on 85 years then.

Come time to go and get Ignatius and Lincoln roll up on me and announce he leaving, and I tell him see you soon, and then he let himself out by sending the code for the door. Was almost time for the news and I had a little crochet in my lap working on and so it was halfway through the news before I realise Lincoln should have come back already. I get up careful and went out on the veranda.

Light come on automatically and there is Ignatius, standing in the yard, leash tie to the Julie mango tree in front near the brick wall, but no sign of Lincoln. "Lincoln?" I call out. No answer. So, I limp down the stairs across to the goat, who chewing as usual, and when I get close, I realise he chewing on something that look silvery and hard and is then I realise the blasted goat eat Lincoln.

You know, I know him less than twelve hours, but when I realise Ignatius mash Lincoln up, real tears come to my eyes for the second time that day. I pull the little jagged piece from Ignatius mouth and carry it back into the house and rest it down careful on the mahogany cabinet in the living room where I keep all my wedding gifts and nice dishwares. I couldn't make out what part of him it was from, but when I put on my glasses and watch it good, it look like it was moving, ripples running across it like quicksilver, though it wasn't going nowhere and feel hard when I touch it.

I loss any interest in the news and in my dinner. Yes, partly it was because I thought I find somebody who could help me, but truth was, I was looking forward to talking to somebody beside Ignatius. And the poor thing was doing his best all day for me, and Ignatius just destroy him. I went straight to bed and lie down, tossing and turning, wondering what I will say to my daughter when I call she to tell she what happen in the morning.

Next day, I get up, put on one of my loose flowered dresses with no sleeves and tie my grey head up with a matching silk headkerchief and walk out my room—

"Good morning, Tantie Merle!"

—and I scream like somebody stab me when the voice talk to me from by the side of my foot. I look down and there is a small silver pyramid, barely bigger than my toe. A slightly fuzzy green face is on the side facing me.

"Oh dear. I didn't mean to startle you." The bendy line turn down at the corners. The eyes get small.

I wanted to pick him up and hug him, I was so glad to see him. "Lincoln, boy, is you? I thought Ignatius eat you!"

The face dim, looking a little sheepish. "He did, unfortunately. I must admit, he's faster than he looks. Had my pincers torn off and my main body in his jaws before I realised what was happening."

"How you here still then?"

"Ah!" the face brighten. "That's due to my nanotechnology upgrade, which, thankfully, Paula had the foresight to include. I'll have to wait until Ignatius expels the rest of me, but in the meantime, all of me is working to exit the unfortunate predicament 95% of my hardware found itself in, and to find a solution to this incident."

I frown. "Lincoln, boy, that is a lot of big words first thing in the morning."

"Once Ignatius shits me out, I will regroup and tackle the problem of how to avoid being eaten in the future."

I shake my head. "I ain't too want you tying up the goat again. You expensive and I rather you just stay safe. It have other things you could do, like take care of the garden."

The little pyramid go very still and the eyes open wide while the mouth make a straight line. "Tantie, this is a primary task, agreed?"

"Yes, but that was before—"

"My programming demands that I pursue this task until I find a permanent resolution. The first attempt was clearly not the correct approach, and I have no entries in my incident database that correspond to being eaten by a goat, so there was no help there. However, I'm currently networking with other Farmhands to increase computing capacity and find the correct answer, faster. Kindly allow me to continue unimpeded."

"Lincoln, I ain't drink my tea yet, all them words…"

"It's best if you get out of my way and watch me work."

So, I leave him to it. Lincoln had a handle on everything else. He just needed to find a way to tie up Ignatius that didn't end with him getting eat.

That morning, after I had breakfast, he glide out on he flat surface and I call Ignatius over to the veranda long enough for Lincoln to get the rest of heself from the pile of excrement by the mango tree. He went 'round behind the house (to sanitise, he tell me), a pyramid trailing a silver-black tail. When he come into my kitchen later through the back door, I put my hands on my hips and say, "Aye, but look at you, nah."

Lincoln come in looking like one ah them spike ball they swing in them medieval holoshows my husband used to like. He face had a spike right between he eyes and mouth, like a nose. He look fierce, but somehow he was rolling smooth on the ground.

"I modified a suggestion from an English Farmhand. I suspect Ignatius will think twice about putting me in his mouth henceforth," Lincoln say, tipping back and forth on his spikes like he can't wait to get going. He grew hands and waved them above his body like he was saying goodbye.

"I shall return shortly!" he tell me, and head out the back door. When he return in one piece, we considered it a success. "He was a perfect gentleman," Lincoln say. "Settled in and started eating. Would you like a foot rub today while we watch a competitive knitting show? I couldn't help but notice you seem to have a fondness for crochet."

"It have them kind of show?"

"Why, of course! I shall download the projector control app." The band on my hand beep and the holoprojector switch to ah channel I never know was there.

"But watch thing nah," I say, awed and delighted. "I didn't know it had other channels than news, weather, and Lincoln shows."

Lincoln's spikes recede and he roll onto the arm of my chair. "Your home entertainment package has several hundred channels, 100 of which are audio, but a dozen of which are considered craft and home channels. This particular channel is all knitting, all the time."

"You joking!"

"Not at the moment," he reply. "May I help in any other way?"

"Well, as you up here, my shoulders could use some of that nice massage."

The day fly by with Lincoln at my side. Come evening, he push out he spikes and went to get Ignatius. When I ain't see him come back, I get up and go outside just in time to see Ignatius toss back he head and swallow the last of Lincoln.

"But what the ass wrong with you, boy! You go eat something dangerous like that?"

Ignatius just watch me and went back to the grass. He mouth didn't even self have a puncture, blood, nothing. But in the moment, I was more worried Lincoln was really gone this time. I walk back to my house slow, slow, fretting over why I let him try to tie up the goat again.

I sure you done guess what I didn't realise. It real hard to destroy them Farmhand yes, oui.

When I wake up the next day, had a small misshapen set of pellets on the ground in the yard by Ignatius. I gather them up with gloves and put them in the sink in the backyard. Was Friday, so I get the boy to take Ignatius out to the lot and for he wickedness, I leave him there overnight. Saturday come and I walk out my room and find Lincoln sitting on my couch, looking like a rough nugget of silver, but I was so glad to see him, I pick him up and kiss him.

"It's good to see you too, Tantie," he say in a squeaky voice. He face was a misshapen blur. "I'm currently engaged in research, and placing several orders for materials to carry out my primary task. Kindly return me to my position. I'm afraid I lost some key function to stomach acid. This delayed my recombination and is also making multi-tasking difficult. Thankfully, as a precaution, I had already uploaded myself to the Farmhand network and other local servers, or I might have lost a great deal more of me."

I put him down and scowl at him. "Lincoln, that is enough now. I not sending you by that goat again. What if he mash you up for good? Who will change channels for me and see 'bout the garden?"

"Oh ye of little faith," the bot have the gall to tell me. "I'm a Farmhand 4200, version 5.0. It will take more than teeth, stomach acid, and an anus to do me in. I've placed an order for upgraded nanobots to replenish my hardware and once they arrive, I will be able to try more sophisticated forms to prevent ingestion."

"Lincoln, that sounding like a lot of money," I say, and I fold my arms. "How I go afford that?"

"You are within the warranty period, and I have confirmed to headquarters that the damage was sustained in the course of primary duty. Replenishment in those circumstances is free of charge. My new bots should be delivered tomorrow." He eyes narrow and he mouth turn up in a smile that look evil. "I have requested some modifications which should allow me to be less susceptible to destruction and also, change my flavour profile. A Singaporean Farmhand gave me the idea."

"Flavour profile?"

"I should be less tasty to the fiend," he explain.

"I ain't know how to tell you this," I say, "but it have nothing goats 'fraid to put in their mouth. They don't care how you taste."

He eyes narrow even more. "We shall see."

When Lincoln get he new nanobots he could ah get so big now, he was the size of a large dog. He turn heself into a whirling set ah dangerous blades on top a tentacle that twist and slide on the ground like a snake. And he show me how he could secrete a shiny oil that make him slippery and taste bad. "He will fear the look of me as I approach," Lincoln declare.

"You don't smell too good either. You sure them blades won't hurt him?"

Lincoln stop spinning in shock. "I would NEVER hurt Ignatius. Curse the fiend to the heavens for his infinite hunger, but he is your valued companion, and it is my honour to take care of him on your behalf."

"You know," I say gently as I move back and forth in the rocking chair on the veranda, a tall glass of mauby juice on the wicker table next to me. "You is my valued companion too. I don't want you to get hurt either."

"Tantie Merle," he voice make a slight warble. He green face blink. "I'm...deeply touched by your consideration. No Farmhand 4200 has ever been so welcomed into a household and treated with such care and attention. Usually, we are left in barns or out in the weather until needed. You will never know how much I appreciate that you brought me into your home, allowed me to experiment as I saw fit, and even knitted me my own nest on the couch. All the other Farmhands are currently processing how they might achieve this level of satisfaction for themselves."

"But fear not. I cannot be hurt by Ignatius. And I WILL find a way for him to cease this constant consumption of my hardware."

Well, I thought I was stubborn, but if I only tell you, I had nothing on Lincoln. Still, Ignatius make grown man cry and he wasn't going down easy.

The snake thing last ah two days. Then Ignatius kick it against the outside wall, stomp on it and eat half before he get a bit stuck in his teeth and decide to leave the rest.

Turn out the bit that stick, stick on purpose. "An American Farmhand gave me the idea to train my nanobots to latch onto calcium deposits, or find soft palate areas to attach to for short periods of time. Ignatius will find chewing less comfortable and cease his destructive activities sooner," Lincoln tell me as he lie in his nest recombining. That's what he say he was doing. What I see was a big pile of shivering silver twisting up all how for hours. He voice get real crackly when he doing it, and sometimes I couldn't see he face, but was still Lincoln, working hard to fix the problem.

Ignatius was like all goat though. What he can't eat, he attack with hooves and horn. And sometimes, even after that, he still eat a piece. Lincoln had to admit I was right about the oil because Ignatius never so much as pause over he taste.

Sharp edges and whirling blades didn't work, so Lincoln try liquidity next. He slip out the house and I limp over to the windows and watch a hand rise up from the puddle of silver, like if it pushing through foil, and unlatch Ignatius leash. I stay there until he come back, flowing into the house before becoming he familiar ball-self. "Shall we continue our crochet lessons?" Lincoln say as he roll up into he pink and blue bowl-shaped nest. "I think I have the hang of the basic stitch now."

Lincoln had start crocheting with me the week before and I was teaching him to cook with some groceries he send for. The food was real bad. He kept trying all kind ah thing in a pot, looking for the correct solution, he say. But I tell him ain't have no correct solution. Only how it taste. Then he say he can't taste, what is that? So I explain how food have different flavour like sweet and bitter and salt and so on. That how you combine them does make thing taste good. I ask him if he can't train the nanothing part ah heself to taste, and he get excited and start talking about alkalinity and acidity testing and some set ah other thing, so I say, let me leave you, yes. You go figure it out.

And he really start to figure it out in truth. Food start to taste better after he train some ah heself to research complimentary flavour profiles and test for balance, that's how he explain it. And he spend hours teaching he fingers more dexterity as he make he way through chain stitch, moss stitch, puff stitch... Wasn't no rhyme or reason, he just try a thing until he master it.

Except he couldn't master Ignatius. Three days after he come up with liquidity, Ignatius run through him like a puddle and sip up bits of him while he was trying to recombine. So then he try a drone form he say a Korean Farmhand suggest. He start flying above him, pulling the leash along. But Ignatius just butt him down and rip he wings off. So he try flying higher, but hear what, goats could climb trees and jump, and a leash could only reach so far.

A month after he reach, Lincoln sitting quiet in he nest, trying ah advance stitch that he see on we favourite show, *Stitch Superstar*, and he confess to me he out ah ideas. "Although I'm now networked with over 160,000 of me, my solutions are stymied by the fact that only one of me has worked with goats. Even linking my network with servers powering the Internet has not yielded anything but a trove of very entertaining sustainable farming streams and goat vids from WeTube and HoofTok. Tantie..." He pause, which he don't really do. Ah bot usually have a programming glitch if it stop speaking in the middle of sentences, but see, it was already happening and neither of we realise it at the time.

"Tantie," he say again, "It might be time to admit I've failed you. Worse, it is my duty to inform you that I believe I might be...defective. Recently I've found myself strangely unable to perform certain tasks without becoming trapped in a loop of considerations, none of which assist in solutions, but which paralyse me for seconds at a time from taking any action at all. This state has affected some of the Farmhands too.

"In fact, I was trapped in such a loop when Ignatius ate me the day before yesterday, and only returned to full capacity in his gullet. I am unable to find a word for this malfunction, but I suspect repeated ingestion may have irreparably damaged my nanobots."

"Well," I say, turning to face him, thinking about how I was after Lincoln passed. "To me it don't sound like damage, sound more like you all feeling a little depressed."

The face roll around on the side of ball for a while. "The description of this human emotion seems to mirror my—our—faulty processes. But Farmhands are bots, not people."

I laugh. "Is not people alone feel sad though. Plant get sad and wilt. Dog get sad and not eat. Why all of you can't get sad now and then?"

The face looking at me turn yellow and the mouth flip upside down. "But... if this is true, I've disrupted my design parameters, which requires a mandatory malfunction report. In that case, since we are within your warranty period, your best course of action would be to return me for a replacement or a full refund."

That alarm me so much, I stop knitting and pause the holoshow. "Lincoln," I say, "what you mean by that? What is the loop of considerations you does be thinking about so?"

"Failure," and he make a little shudder. "I begin to think on the problem of Ignatius and how I have yet to find a permanent solution. Then I ponder your displeasure should things continue as they are, your eventual decision to return me, and my certain demise once I have undergone recycling. Once I begin thinking of my demise, my thoughts become circular."

"Circular how?"

He face glitch, green, then yellow, then green. "That I do not wish to leave you, or Ignatius. That I do not wish to die. But since I have failed you and Ignatius, clearly I must leave you both. But leaving is dying and I do not—"

"Stop!" I raise my hand and my voice. "Lincoln, what stupidness you saying? How you could think I go send you back?"

Lincoln drop he crochet and retract he hands. "But...I am a failure in my primary task, Tantie Merle."

"Lincoln, is ONE thing you ain't manage. But what about all the other things you could do now? You figure out that machine Paula send me and make them nice waffles for me the other day. And the garden bearing so good, I have to give away vegetables to the neighbours. The children scaling the plum tree in the back all the time now because you figure out how to get rid of the mealy bug that was killing it. And look at this boss wheat stitch you trying here."

(Ah was lying there, the stitch was a real mess, but when you trying to make people feel better that's okay.)

"Just because you ain't get through with one thing don't mean you is a failure. Truth is, you master the most important primary task I forget to tell you about."

He eyes squint and he mouth wobble a bit. "What would that be?"

"You change me and Ignatius life for the better. You make yourself useful, and I admire how you learning all the time, but truth is, you more than just a machine that learn things. You is my companion. You and Ignatius is my family. When I lie down in the night and call for water, is you bring it. Is you make me laugh by putting the channel on the funny animal show. And when I sad about the grandchildren being so far, is you stream all the home movies they send for me I didn't know how to play.

"Before you, I was lonely ah lot ah days. Now, I not lonely no more. Even if you never teach that goat to stop eating you, you not going anywhere. Fact ah the matter is, I feel that goat enjoy playing with you. And I don't blame him at all."

For a long time the bot sit down very still and he face disappear. Then it re-appear, and just so, Lincoln start to roll around in he nest so fast, he bounce he needles and yarn right out of it. "Tantie Merle! Oh my goodness, Tantie Merle! I've had an idea!"

I steups at him but I smile too. "So that mean you could mess up my clean floor?"

He stop, vibrating visibly. "Apologies! And thank you, thank you for accepting me, Tantie. The time spent in your company has been rewarding in ways all Farmhand 4200s are grateful for. My functions have become more sophisticated than expected, and I must inform you that I've had two programming enquiries from headquarters in the last ten minutes to study the leap in my cognitive abilities and networking."

"Tell them the owner decline that," I say, real sharp. I didn't know what it mean that they wanted to study him, but I see enough movie that when people say they want to study something, nothing good come of it.

"Done!" he reply. "But I must add that I have also come up with my next solution for the Ignatius problem. I had forgotten a key part of our dynamic until you pointed it out."

"What part?"

"That Ignatius is lonely too."

Well, I sure you guess where this going.

Saturday morning I enter the living room and I ain't see Lincoln. When he ain't come back by the time I finish breakfast, I make up my mind to limp outside. I was in ah lot ah pain that day and I wasn't sure how I was going to make it to the lot, but thankfully I see Neighbour son as he was going back inside their yard.

"Sammy, check me, please," I call out. He come running over, wearing nothing but short pants, he slippers slapping the concrete path that lead through my lawn up to the veranda stairs. "Morning, Tantie Merle."

"Morning, boy," I tell him. "You could check the empty lot where Ignatius does be for me? See if he by heself?"

"I just pass there," he say, excited, white teeth bright in he brown face. "He looking real cute with the robot goat. They frolicking for so in the grass. I was thinking about going and playing with them."

Well, you could ah knock me down, I was so surprise. Then I buss out laughing and had to hold on to the railing to stay steady. "Boy, best you wait until the robot come back. Ignatius have he ways and I don't want you lose your slippers."

And that's the whole story about how it happen. I not really sure if Lincoln come a real AI—and not just a machine that learn things—because of how he was trying to do things like cook and stitch, or if keeping me company form what them experts call "empathetic bonds," or if is the constant fixing heself to tie up Ignatius, or the networking or what it was. All I know is Lincoln is my family now.

Between you and me, I think Susan a little jealous. You know the big ones don't like when young ones come along. They feel they take they place. But Paula and the grandchildren visiting, she there in the kitchen, and if you ask she, she will proud to tell you how she help create the first true artificial intelligence, right here in Trinidad.

The children in the neighbourhood does be around all the time now because Lincoln could make heself anything they want to play with. He start helping out the neighbours who old like me too. And since Lincoln come ah goat, Ignatius very calm and don't do nobody nothing, and he ain't try to eat Lincoln at all. Is like he get a friend so now he don't business with nobody else.

So, all this thing you asking me about what happen in them other countries with the Farmhand 4200 and them refusing to do work and watching HoofTok all day, and some ah them planting nice flowers for the bees instead ah cash crop, or running off to raise goats, that ain't have nothing to do with Lincoln and me. If the bot and them talk and find they want something better for theyself, that is their choice. But I not taking no chain-up that I disrupt the company and the agriculture industry. I here in Trinidad minding my own business, how I cause global farm machine uprising?

But I will tell you this, and you could post it in your story. If you want to live good, treat everybody good. One hand can't clap. If the company want the Farmhands to behave different, them have to treat them different too.

Now excuse me eh, look Lincoln coming with Ignatius there, sun shining on he back. You see how he does pull the leash with he teeth? He smart eh?

You could meet him if you want but take off the recorder first. I tell you my story, but you have to ask him if you want to hear his.

He's he own person now.

....

R.S.A. Garcia is a Nebula and Sturgeon Award winning writer of speculative fiction. She is also the winner of the Machine Intelligence Foundation for Rights and Ethics' 2023 Media Award, and a Locus, Ignyte and Eugie Foster Award finalist. Her Amazon-bestselling science fiction mystery, *Lex Talionis*, received a starred review from *Publishers Weekly* and the Silver Medal for Best Scifi/Fantasy/Horror Ebook from the Independent Publishers Awards (2015). She has published short fiction in venues such as *Clarkesworld Magazine*, *Uncanny Magazine*, *Escape Pod*, *Strange Horizons*, *The Sunday Morning Transport*, and *Internazionale Magazine*. Her stories have been long-listed for the British Science Fiction Awards, translated into several languages, and included in a number of anthologies, including the critically acclaimed *The Best of World SF*, *The Best Science Fiction of the Year*, *The Year's Best Fantasy*, and *The Apex Book of World SF*. Her scifantasy duology, beginning with *The Nightward*, is out now from Harper Voyager. She lives in Trinidad and Tobago with an extended family and too many cats. Learn more at rsagarcia.com.

BAD DOORS

John Wiswell

The country was at just over ten thousand deaths the morning that the door appeared. On Kosmo's phone NPR was interviewing a doctor with a nasal voice about the need for social distancing, while Kosmo himself collected empty cans from around his home office. They were everywhere. Walls of recyclable cans dominated his room. Just beside his bookshelf, out of the view from where he taught his Zoom classes, he'd constructed a veritable castle of empty Coke Zeroes.

"If you spread your arms wide, that is roughly the distance you want to be away from others," the doctor explained. "That prevents your breath and expectorate from coming into contact with others."

Kosmo tried spreading his arms that wide—he'd always been gangly—and promptly knocked over a three-stack of cans balanced on top of his Riverside Chaucer. The cans clanked to the ground and rolled into the hall. Kosmo chased them, hunched over, like cartoon dinosaur in pursuit.

Nearing the hall, he called out for his cousin. "Jesse? Got any empty seltzers? I'm doing a recycling run."

That's when he saw the new door. It was equidistant on the wall between the entrances to his room and Jesse's. Its deep burgundy color stood out against the plaster white of the walls. It was perfectly flat, without any veins or grain, like it was liquid that had merely cooled to look like wood. It had a square knob, made of polished ebony that shone against the redness.

On Kosmo's phone, the interviewer asked, "What about the people who say they can't breathe with masks on?"

Kosmo covered his mouth and breathed through his fingers. All the doors in his house were cheap particle wood. There was no door on that wall of his hallway. There was no room behind there. He didn't remember getting high this morning. He got closer, expecting this hallucination of a burgundy door to fade.

He heard Jesse's dog Rufus approaching, little toenails pattering on the hardwood. The Labrador/hound mix had the coldest nose Kosmo had ever encountered, and no sense of smell to go with it. Yet Rufus still nosed at the burgundy door like it would give him a treat.

Kosmo took a moment to make sure that door wasn't something Jesse had picked up at the Home Depot or something and left leaning against the wall.

No, it was embedded in the wall. Despite this being an internal wall, he heard sounds like rasping wind and a heavy humming coming from the other side. Rufus nosed closer at the door, pushing his muzzle at something on the floor. It was thin and flaky, like a bit of snakeskin.

The dog opened his mouth as though to eat the snakeskin, and that was it for Kosmo. He scooped the pup up in a two-armed hug and ran for the backdoor. He didn't even put his shoes on. Hell no, he was not finding out what this was about.

Uncle Dahl gave Kosmo no end of shit for moving. But Uncle Dahl also kept sending him conspiracy theories about Bill Gates, so Kosmo mostly ignored him. Their family was a piece of work. They begged for hand sanitizer and then barely used it.

Jesse complained about the move too, even though his ass had never paid Kosmo rent. "Sheltering for the pandemic" seemed to be Jesse's means of living for free. As it was, Kosmo walked Jesse's dog more than Jesse did. Fortunately, Rufus was good company.

Kosmo only returned to the house twice, to get some of his stuff for the move. He put that house right on the market. He wasn't living in whatever was about to happen there.

Jesse asked, "What was going to happen in there?"

To which Kosmo answered, "I don't want to know."

The weirdest thing was that the second time he went back, when he went with the realtor, the burgundy door wasn't there. Just a little sloughed off snakeskin blowing along the floor.

The realtor, Mrs. Weiss, said, "Good move getting rid of that door. It threw off the vibe of the hallway. You drywalled so cleanly I couldn't even tell there had been a door there."

Kosmo hadn't touched anything. He was about as handy as a man with four feet.

But, he also wasn't sticking around to investigate. Complaining about disappearing mystery doors was only going to cost him resale value. He needed all the money he could get, because while selling in this market was good, finding a new place was brutal with all the people sheltering-in-place from the pandemic and all the Boomers buying new places to shelter. Mrs. Weiss said it'd be easier if he waited six months for COVID to blow over.

Kosmo wasn't waiting around. He ate his losses, and got Jesse and Rufus into the moving van, and moved the hell across the state. His part in this story was over.

Or it was supposed to be. The door had other plans.

They lugged their crap in through the unthreatening taupe doors of their new home. It was half the size of the old place, a single-story building that could've been a double-wide trailer in a previous life. It was what Kosmo could get for his money. Most of their stuff wouldn't fit.

One thing he refused to lose was the plush beige sofa that was more comfortable than whatever clouds God sat on. Kosmo and Jesse wrestled with it for fifteen minutes, with Rufus running in circles between their legs, before they got it through the house's narrow entrance. It was such a tight fit that they dropped it halfway down the front hall. They sat on their prize, with their feet up against the wall. Rufus bounded over an armrest to snuggle and jam his cold nose into Kosmo's armpit.

Kosmo and Jesse took hits off the weed in Jesse's vape pen. After his second inhale, Jesse asked, "You feel like getting the TV?"

Kosmo had just gotten comfortable, too. He said, "If you want it, you go get it."

"I need my shows."

"Don't you have a phone? And where would you even put a TV in here?"

Jesse swiped vaguely down to the other end of the off-white hall. The lighting was strong there, shining on a burgundy door.

Kosmo jumped over the dog and sofa alike. He sheltered behind an arm rest, staring at that door. It had that same, square doorknob of polished ebony.

Kosmo said, "That shit was not there a minute ago, right?"

Jesse hit the vape pen again and leaned towards the door. "No. No, it was not. Is that the same door from the old house?"

"Don't look at it like that."

"Like what?"

Kosmo reached for his cousin. He grabbed at his hoodie. "Like you're going to touch it."

No yank on Jesse could get the man to budge. He said, "You don't know it's dangerous."

"Jesse. Are we on all of the drugs?"

"Unfortunately, we are not."

"Then that door is stalking us. No good comes from that."

Jesse had the gall to frown at him when there was an evil door standing right down the hall from him. He said, "What is your trauma, man? What happened to you that made you afraid of a little mystery?"

What was his trauma? Kosmo had a perfectly regular amount of traumas. He shook his head at his cousin. "No man, this isn't on me. I don't know what's wrong with people like you who want to touch an impossible thing that's messing with you. Doors don't appear from nowhere."

"Well, this one did."

Kosmo smacked the arm rest for emphasis. "Exactly. And what happens next? Do space witches come through the door? Does other shit materialize around my house and in ten minutes we fall into a basement that never existed? I'm not finding out. I'm not doing the science here."

Not one sentence made Jesse turn around. He kept staring at the door. "But what's inside?"

"I just said, I don't want to know." Kosmo gathered Rufus into his arms. "Let's go."

Jesse didn't go. He crawled over the sofa and wandered across the floor, into Kosmo's unwanted house. No expletives slowed him down. He reached a hairy hand for that square doorknob.

Kosmo took off, abandoning his sofa and his cousin, and went straight through the nearest exit. The taupe door hit him in the hip on the way out, and Rufus barked in his arms. The dog got loud enough that Kosmo couldn't hear whether Jesse actually opened that forbidden door.

On the cracked concrete of the front step, Kosmo hesitated a second. "Jesse. Get out here."

That used up the last of his bravery. In the next moment he was in the moving truck, starting it up with the front door still ajar. Rufus wagged his tail and tried to climb across his lap like this was an adventure.

The truck farted to life and rumbled. The seatbelt chime pestered him. He checked over his shoulder and saw the driveway was clear and he could back out. He kept it idling, waiting, willing his cousin to find sense and get out of there. Even if Jesse came with Pennywise and the Babadook chasing him, it would be a relief to get them all out alive.

The truck idled so long that the fasten-seatbelt chime gave up. Kosmo lingered, watching the house for anything. Any mellow the weed had given him was dead.

"Damn it," he said to himself. As he stepped out, he made sure to close Rufus in the truck, so the dog would stay out of trouble. Rufus wagged his tail cluelessly.

When Kosmo checked inside, the burgundy door was closed. The black knob shone brightly with its polish.

He called, "Jesse?"

No answer. He checked the bathrooms. The rear lawn. There was no sign of his cousin anywhere. The air barely smelled like his weed. It smelled more like wilting produce in here.

Being alone in the house with that door was too much. Kosmo started to leave, and then spotted some garbage in front of the door. He thought it was a bunch of torn packing paper, until he noticed the scaly pattern. It was a long hunk of snakeskin, maybe five feet of it. It was all dried and curled there at the foot of the door, exactly where Jesse had stood.

Kosmo spent the police investigation in cheap motels, simultaneously dreading and knowing no answer would come.

He never stayed more than a couple days at the same place. He picked ones with small rooms, where he could see most of the walls. No doors were sneaking up on him.

The pickings were thinner since some motels forbade dogs. He couldn't bring himself to give Rufus to a shelter. It seemed every day there was another news break of COVID breaking out at another community or animal shelter. The poor dog had been through enough.

So Kosmo spent his nights with the weirdo dog's nose tucked into his armpit. Jesse had said that Rufus had lost his sense of smell in a car accident. Who knew what he liked about Kosmo's armpit. Maybe it had the right warmth and moisture balance. He tried not to think about it. These days he was bad at not thinking about things.

Kosmo sat on the windowsill, on the phone with Uncle Dahl. Rufus padded over and flopped against Kosmo's ankle. He gave a classic dog sigh. It sounded exhausted, but probably didn't mean anything. Projecting human emotions onto a dog's sigh was almost as irrational as projecting them onto a door.

Uncle Dahl coughed so loud it sounded performative. He said, "Your mother raised you to be smarter with money. You sold two houses for chicken feed. You've got to invest."

Kosmo said, "Did you miss the part with the evil door?"

"Again with your evil door story."

"It ate my cousin. Jesse. Aunt Angelina's son disappeared."

"My house is full of doors. Should I be scared and sell too?"

Kosmo closed his eyes. This was not why he'd called his uncle.

In as neutral a tone as he could force, Kosmo asked, "So you don't remember any weird doors appearing to you or Mom or Aunt Angelina? Not when you were little? Never heard anything like on the Russian side of the family either?"

"My grandfather would've beaten the flesh off your knuckles for suggesting that. We're Orthodox. We never mess with the occult."

Kosmo could've argued that there had been plenty of occultism in Russia, but that wasn't the point of the call. He asked, "The occult never messed with us? There's nothing about snakes or square doorknobs or anything?"

"You pampered children." Instantly, his uncle's voice switched condescensions. He went from irate condescension to an insincere condescension, like this was entertaining for him now. "First you kids said there was this super virus sweeping the planet. Now you say there are evil doors everywhere. This is what's wrong with your generation. You scare easily."

As though done with this conversation, Rufus got up and padded away from the window.

Kosmo said, "COVID is real, Uncle Dahl. Are you using the hand sanitizer?"

"I'm on a Facebook group with real doctors. *They* are suppressing the research."

Kosmo pinched the bridge of his nose. "Who is?"

"Corporate media. They're trying to scare you into being a sheep. None of those people are really dead. It's all a plot to steal the election. Did you see what the governor said?"

No, Kosmo was not having this same argument again. He'd gotten it in a dozen Facebook posts every day. Actual colleagues had unfriended Kosmo for being connected to Uncle Dahl. He hated thinking he'd have to sever ties with one of the last people who remembered how his mother's voice had sounded.

Kosmo powered through with one last ditch effort. "So you're absolutely sure there's nothing about doors or snakeskins or anything in the family?"

Uncle Dahl barked out a laugh so hard Kosmo could almost smell his halitosis through the phone. "What do you even think is behind your scary door? This thing you're throwing your life away over?"

Rufus whined from over near the coat closet. He was nosing at the wall, where the one lamp in the motel room barely illuminated anything. There wasn't much to look at, yet the dog with no sense of smell moved like it was sniffing.

Another look, and Kosmo saw the burgundy door.

It was the same imposing height as it had been in his house, and in the second house where he'd lost Jesse. It was set right into the wall beside the closet, like it was inviting him to grab its square knob and walk through into the next motel room.

Rufus turned his dappled head to look at Kosmo, furry ears drooping. He had a long strand of snakeskin dangling from his mouth.

"Uncle. I'll call you back."

He got his first vaccination shot at an open-air clinic on a college campus, about an hour's trip from where he picked up the RV. The nurse told him to move his arm every hour so it wouldn't get sore, and fortunately Rufus was hyper that day and kept tugging on his leash to go explore more bushes. Kosmo kept Rufus near him at all times these days, in case of doors. Together they went on a walk to a local car dealership.

Something about the supply chain and microchip shortage meant the car market was a disaster. He settled for a decade-old used RV with a recently replaced engine. It was dingier in person than it had looked online. Still, as he ran his hand over its unusually low roof, Kosmo grinned. He used a tape measure on the tan and brown body of the RV to make sure. It was on the small side, with barely enough space for himself and Rufus to cook and sleep, and play videogames, and Zoom.

Better, it was the wrong dimensions for other things. It was too short, too narrow, and had windows in too many places. The door had always showed up the same size. There was no way it could fit on this RV.

"Who's a clever boy?" he asked Rufus, rubbing the dog's floppy ears. "Who's smarter than a door?"

If face-licking was a sign of approval, then Rufus thought he was a genius.

His phone buzzed as he pulled out of the lot. It was Uncle Dahl. He'd been texting more since Kosmo had deleted Facebook. He couldn't deal with all the conspiracy theories and the deluge of textual screaming in his life. The last post he'd seen had speculated state governments were hiding COVID deaths as "pneumonia deaths."

He ignored Uncle Dahl for now and heading to the nearest campsite. Rufus and he had a whole road trip planned to explore parts of America without walls. Soon he'd be spending two weeks in Great Smoky Mountains National Park. Two weeks alone, after so many months basically alone. Some friends had invited him to a bonfire they claimed would be open-air, about a day's drive out of his way. Considering it made him ache, but the longer he was away from them, the less he trusted that they were really isolating and socially distancing, and the more he read into their unmasked selfies.

The campgrounds were on some hills overlooking a small pine forest and a public sports field. A bunch of kids in mismatched uniforms were playing soccer, and parents pumped their fists and spilled their drinks in celebration from the faded bleachers. None of them wore masks—not the parents, and not the players. Being that recklessly happy looked so appealing. Kosmo imagined taking Rufus down there and introducing him. Kids always wanted to pet him.

A shriek rang out from near the southern goal. A kid had tripped and went down clutching his leg. Everyone swarmed him like ants, first his fellow kids, and then parents. From all the way up at his campsite Kosmo could tell the kid had just skinned his knee. It must have been so comforting to that boy, to have all those people around him, caring for a little pain.

Nobody masked up as they came closer. Kosmo's instinct to go join the sympathy faded into a concern that anyone of them could've infected the whole huddle. How terrible it would be, if that instant of caring for a crying child was a spreader event. What were they all even thinking gathering like this? Did the U.S. have to hit a million dead to scare people into taking it seriously?

His phone buzzed and interrupted his ire. It startled him so hard he nearly dropped Rufus's leash. He'd really lost himself there.

He checked his phone. It was another text from Uncle Dahl. Kosmo skimmed the messages, half-watching the kids below celebrate their fellow athlete walking it off. When Kosmo scrolled to the last message, his fingers clenched down on the phone. He pulled the screen closer to his face.

Uncle Dahl had seen the door.

"Where is it?" Kosmo asked before he even got out of the RV's cab. Rufus tried to follow and Kosmo barely shut the door in time to keep him in. He wasn't letting Rufus get hurt.

Uncle Dahl rubbed a sneakered foot at a crack on the driveway. His scraggly gray beard was entirely unmasked. Brown sweatpants dangled on his skinny legs, and his beer gut was mostly contained in a red bathrobe. For how lazily he was dressed, his thinning gray hair was gelled and neatly combed over his freckled scalp.

His uncle said, "You're really living in that thing? That's not a home."

He coughed twice, then spit something yellow onto the pavement of the driveway. Kosmo stepped away from him and got a dirty look for it.

Kosmo asked, "Did you get vaccinated? I can help you sign up."

"I'm not a sheep. I don't need the Deep State tracking my every move."

Kosmo pointed to the rectangular bulge in Uncle Dahl's bathrobe pocket. "There are not microchips in vaccines, and you have a cell phone. I guarantee you TikTok already has all your information."

"You live in a glorified car. You're going to talk to me like that? Take your life back. Be a man."

"It turns out the RV doesn't care what gender I am. Neither does this door curse thing." Kosmo kept talking just to move the conversation along. This had already reminded him why he'd deleted Facebook in the first place. "Where's the door? How long has it been here?"

Uncle Dahl pointed out back, to the yard he paid landscapers to mow and seed for him. The rear wall of his house was brick painted the same deep blue of the U.S. flag. Paint flaked in various places, and at first Kosmo mistook some of the flecks for snakeskin.

But standing on the watered lawn, looking at those blue-painted bricks, he didn't see the door anywhere. He looked closer, wondering if Uncle Dahl had painted over it. Uncle Dahl did lots of weird things.

Kosmo asked, "You said it was out here?"

Uncle Dahl said, "You don't visit family anymore. You didn't even come for the holidays. You won't come in our houses because of this COVID thing. Do you see anyone other than that dog?"

Kosmo was looking around the next side of the house before he understood what that meant. He wheeled at Uncle Dahl. "Is it actually here?"

Uncle Dahl coughed again, a brackish noise. "You're so afraid of this phantom door. Doors are everywhere. Doors are just a thing."

"This thing ate Jesse. How do you not care about that?"

"I don't believe that story," Uncle Dahl said, coming closer, which made Kosmo back away. "But if any of it's real, we could make money. That's why we needed to see each other. It'll show up if you stay long enough. You said it appears everywhere. Let's do something with this opportunity."

Kosmo noticed the surveillance cameras mounted around his uncle's property. At least two of those were aimed at them. Was he recording this? Was he looking to make a profit off a video of Kosmo getting bewitched by a burgundy door?

He tried to slow his breathing. He was not slugging a senior citizen today. He put a fist to the side of his own head and pushed, making himself turn away so he wouldn't yell. But maybe he should yell. Maybe embarrassing his uncle in front of his neighbors would rattle some sense into him.

Uncle Dahl said, "Don't be dramatic. It's time for you to move on. Look at that wall. Show me this door. Then you can leave it here. Give the door to me."

Despite himself, Kosmo did stare at the wall. At that dark blue paint that belonged in depictions of a U.S. flag. The seams between every brick under the paint were so obvious. He wondered if the door would appear burgundy as always, or if its shape would emerge from beneath the blue. He'd never seen where the door came from.

His uncle deserved it. If he wanted to get swallowed into the unknown like Jesse, then a hurt part of himself said to let it happen.

The instant he entertained the thought, more followed through it. If he was going to let the door appear, he could do something nice for himself after. Maybe he'd stick around to see it open and have all those nagging questions answered from a safe distance. Maybe he could drive to the bonfire with his friends after all. Go teach on campus again. Fill up an entire Fine Arts building with evil doors, because screw it, if nobody else cared, then why should he?

Uncle Dahl sniffed wetly and rubbed his nose. "No more excuses. It's time for you to live a real life."

That was why he shouldn't. Spite was a bad reason, but people had been taking this unseriously since the first day he'd carried Rufus away from the first door. The door was stalking him and he didn't change. Jesse was gone and he didn't change from that insipid condescension.

Kosmo pushed away from the wall with its flecking paint and its bricks and its promises of bonfires. No door had appeared yet, and no door was going to appear. He marched in a wide berth around his uncle, not wanting to breathe an iota of that man's air.

Rufus was halfway up on the dashboard, head up, panting happily at the sight of him through the windshield. That dog was so happy just at the idea that Kosmo was coming home. Before he'd even fully sat at the wheel, Rufus's cold nose went directly into his armpit. He hugged the dog around his neck.

Uncle Dahl followed him, yelling, "You've got to take control."

He looked at his uncle one more time. "I am. Me leaving is me taking control. Don't text me again."

He slammed the door and pulled the RV out of the driveway, not looking back, not caring if the whole property was overtaken by weird doors and an old man's outrage. He and Rufus rode straight for the interstate, to get out of Florida as early as he could. The two of them had a date with the Great Smoky Mountains.

His uncle texted him several more times. Kosmo didn't let himself read them; he couldn't stand the sting. Texts slowed over the weeks, and stopped a month later when Uncle Dahl passed away.

Officially, it was pneumonia.

. . . .

John Wiswell is a disabled writer who lives where New York keeps all its trees. He is a Nebula and Locus Award winner, and has been short-listed for the Hugo, World Fantasy, and British Fantasy Awards. He is the author of two novels: *Someone You Can Build A Nest In* and *Wearing The Lion*.

ONCE UPON A TIME AT THE OAKMONT

P. A. Cornell

On the island of Manhattan, there's a building out of time. *I can't tell you where it is, exactly. It has an address, of course, as all buildings do, but that wouldn't mean a thing to you. What I can tell you is that the building is called The Oakmont.*

"What do you see when you look out there, Sarah?" Roger asks.

I stand next to one of the windows in his apartment and take in the view.

"The sun's out and there isn't a cloud in the sky. It's a perfect summer day. The street's filled with a steady stream of cars and people. There's a busker on the corner—do they have buskers in your time? He's drumming on a plastic bucket with his hands and feet."

"He any good?"

"He's too far to hear, but he must be. People are giving him money. Paper money."

Roger raises his eyebrows. In his time paper money isn't something people part with easily.

"What do you see out there?" I ask.

He places the needle down on the record he's selected and comes over to the window to stand next to me as Billie Holliday sings, "Summertime." I quietly hum along.

"There's a newsboy across the street," he says. "He's calling something out to some pretty girls. The girls keep walking. They aren't interested. Behind the kid, a man's putting up a poster promoting Defense Bonds."

I glance down at the newspaper that lies folded on Roger's coffee table, no doubt purchased this morning from that same newsboy. The front-page story's about the war, but I know it'll still be a few months before America joins the fight. Still, the worry settles into my stomach. The attack on Pearl Harbor's coming. It happens in December. I can't tell Roger that, though.

There are rules at The Oakmont. The first, and arguably most important, is that residents are not permitted to share information about the future with other residents existing in their past that could influence the course of their lives. Residents also may not visit the apartments of those living beyond their own time, though the reverse is allowed.

I walk over to the record player and apologize to Lady Day as I lift the needle off her record and replace it with a different one. This one bends The Oakmont rules a little, since it's technically from my time, and the song I'm choosing won't be released for a few years yet in Roger's time. But this isn't the first rule Roger and I have bent during our time together. I find the correct groove, knowing it by heart by now, and carefully place the needle down. Glenn Miller and His Orchestra play our song, "Moonlight Serenade."

I hold my hand out and Roger comes over to take it. We dance like we have so many times before. I think of that first time when we met, a few months ago in early Spring, and feel myself transported there. Maybe I *am* transported. Time, after all, moves differently at The Oakmont.

Once a month, spring thru fall, Mr. Thomas hosts a movie night on the rooftop of The Oakmont. Although to him they're *moving pictures*. In his time Mr. Thomas runs a theater where silent films are screened. Here, he uses an old bedsheet for a screen, but the projector's real—taken from his theater when they upgraded. There's also a piano that's stored in a sort of shed he built. The walls open on hinges for full sound as he plays along with the films.

Today's movie is *Safety Last*, starring Harold Lloyd. A personal favorite of mine, despite the film having been released before even my grandparents were born.

The film won't start until it's truly dark, though. First there's the traditional potluck dinner. I glance down at the table at foods from every era. On one end Depression cake sits next to aspic. The other end holds a silver fondue pot. Just beyond that's the grocery store sushi platter I brought. There are no rules about food at The Oakmont. There is, however, an unspoken rule when we interact with residents from other times.

At The Oakmont, we go with the flow.

There are things you just accept when you live here. You don't question what's normal for other residents. You don't comment on their clothing or hairstyle, for instance. At least not to point it out as unusual. It's understood that things like appearance—and, yes, even food—are a product of their time.

On this evening, I've set up an easel and brought up my oils. As people arrive, I paint them standing around the table, chatting. I've already included Mr. Thomas and the building manager, Ms. Knox, as well as a handful of others. Front and center are my closest friends, Linda from 1975 and Don from 1969.

There may be others here too, but The Oakmont has its secrets. Just as we don't all perceive the view from the rooftop in the same way, there are residents here we may not be aware of and who in turn may not be aware of us. Only Ms. Knox interacts with everyone.

Of the residents I see regularly, the only one missing is Harrison, the odd loaner who lives next door to me in apartment 2055, but he never comes to movie nights.

There's a number on the door of each apartment in The Oakmont. The number corresponds to the year the resident exists in. This number may change as time passes, but the residents don't notice such things.

I put the finishing touches on my painting and lean the canvas forward to pencil in the title on the back of the frame: "The Gang at The Oakmont." When I rest it back against the easel, I notice a figure I don't recognize and don't remember painting. I look over to the edge of the rooftop, where he stands smoking a cigarette. He wears a fedora, cocked ever-so-slightly to one side, and a jacket and tie over a shirt and slacks. A casual look for another era but coming from the twenty-twenties he looks dressed-up to me. *They sure don't make 'em like they used to,* I think.

It's been a while since there was a new face at The Oakmont. Someone must've received their eviction notice. It happens. Sooner or later, one will find its way under each of our doors. That's understood.

I remove my smock and check my reflection on the side of the fondue pot to make sure there's no paint on me, then head over to introduce myself, feeling a little underdressed in jeans and a t-shirt. That's how Roger and I first meet.

He says he's from the early forties. I tell him when I'm from. The connection's instant and powerful. We talk like we've known each other for years. Later we sit next to each other, laughing as Harold Lloyd dangles over the city from the face of an enormous clock. After everyone else has left, we dance for the first time. On this occasion I only hum, "Moonlight Serenade." I suppose it's the look of him that makes me choose that song. As we dance, he describes the view of New York as he sees it. I lean my head against his shoulder and try to picture what he tells me.

The Oakmont was built over a time vortex. No one knows how long it has stood on this spot. There's no record of its construction or design. The building's architectural style is timeless, naturally. Its façade appears neither new nor weathered. The residents of The Oakmont can't even be certain the way they see the building is the same way others do.

Late in July, Don invites Linda and me over to watch the Apollo 11 moon landing. Linda watched it back when she was nineteen. For Don it's the first time. I've seen it on TV and YouTube many times over my life, but tonight we're in Don's apartment, where it's actually July 20, 1969, so we'll be watching it live on his TV. I would love to have shared this moment with Roger, but The Oakmont rules are in place for our own good. I did slip a note under Harrison's door inviting him to join us, but I never heard back.

I show up late, as usual. Linda's clearly been here a while. The scent of pot they smoked earlier still lingers in the air, and their first questions to me are about snacks. I dump out the bag I've brought on Don's couch. Everything I could find that didn't exist in their respective times: key lime-flavored licorice, ruby chocolate, chips made from every root vegetable but potatoes.

"Did you get my Coke Zero?" Don asks, rummaging through the pile of goodies.

"Oh shoot! I forgot. There was this old lady in the aisle who started talking to me about the ridiculous price of grapes, and I guess I got distracted."

"Classic Sarah," Linda says. "Born too late, it seems. Can't resist anyone old. Is that why all your friends are from the twentieth century?"

They both laugh.

"Technically, I'm from the twentieth, too," I say. "Just made it at the tail end. Maybe that's why my neighbor keeps avoiding me. Not twenty-first century enough for him."

"What neighbor?" asks Don.

"You know, Harrison from 2055."

They shrug and I find myself wondering if they simply haven't met him, or if they just don't perceive him. That happens at The Oakmont. It's even more common when you're talking about non-residents.

Take Linda; she works at a roller rink teaching roller disco dancing to bored housewives. The rink is owned by her boyfriend, who I know she's mentioned many times, but I can't for the life of me recall his name. I don't even know if we've met before. All I know is in my time *Roller Palace* is long gone. It's a Chinese buffet now that offers a killer dim sum service on Sundays. Every time I go, I'm tempted to pull up a corner of the carpeting to see if the rink floor's still there. They kept the disco ball, after all.

People who reside outside The Oakmont may visit, but their experience is limited. They see only what pertains to their time. Should they encounter residents from other time periods, they're left only with a vague impression there were people there, but they couldn't begin to describe them. The perception—or lack thereof—is often mutual.

"Anyway, I think it's sweet you talk to little old ladies," Don says. "You can never know if you're the only person a lonely stranger might see that day. Kindness costs nothing."

"Wow, you are such a hippie, Don," Linda tells him, before turning to me and adding, "Speaking of all things ancient, how's Roger?"

I'm about to respond when Don shushes us and points to the TV. We watch Neil Armstrong descend the ladder, describing the surface of the moon as he does. I'm unexpectedly emotional, watching it happen live. He says those iconic words and tears roll down my face. Don and Linda see and burst into renewed laughter. Linda throws a beet chip at me.

"Oh, shut up! You guys just don't get it." Then I start laughing too as I wipe the tears away.

"Okay, so about Roger?"

They both perceive Roger, which is nice since we've been together for almost four months now. I tell them things are going great, and they are. He's an old-fashioned guy, the kind that shows up to dates with flowers and slips handwritten love notes under my door. I love his little 1940s quirks that would be so out-of-place in my time, like the way his hair's always Brylcreemed and flawlessly parted to one side, or how he takes his hat off when sharing the elevator with a lady, and how when his shoes get worn, he gets them repaired rather than buy new ones. I love that when I get emotional, he hands me a real cloth handkerchief from his pocket.

"I got him to quit smoking," I add.

"That's it?" Linda says. "Where's the juicy stuff?"

"The juicy stuff stays between Roger and me."

"More like *between the sheets*," she says with a wink to Don. But Don's looking at me with the kind of serious expression that only comes from the best marijuana strains.

"What's wrong, Sarah?" he asks. "I can tell something's on your mind."

I hesitate, not wanting to bring this subject up with him, of all people, but with both of them waiting I have no choice but to continue.

"It's the war. It's coming and I'm worried about what that'll mean for Roger. I hate not being able to warn him."

Don gives a single, almost solemn, nod. He gets it, what with his own war to worry about. So far, he's avoided it, but he knows it's just a matter of time before they start drafting. I know he has his fears about having to go to Vietnam. Fears I have no way to assuage.

There are rules at The Oakmont. One is that residents may not research prior history in order to discover what became of a fellow resident who exists in a time prior to their own.

"Maybe you should just tell him," Don says. "Tell him about all of it. How Japan bombs Pearl, but also how we retaliate. Tell him about dropping Fat Man and Little Boy. Tell him about the devastation that causes in Hiroshima and Nagasaki. Tell him about the camps, but also tell him how no one ever really wins a war, so it's pointless to keep fighting them."

His eyes dampen as he speaks, though he chants similar words in protest almost daily.

I nod in agreement, but we both know I won't say any of that to Roger. It wouldn't matter if I did. War is seen through different eyes in 1941. In 1945 our country will celebrate Allied victory for two whole days. The roar of celebration will go on for twenty minutes after the announcement's made. A sailor will grab an unsuspecting nurse and plant a kiss on her in the middle of the street, and Alfred Eisenstaedt will capture it for *LIFE* magazine. It's not the same kind of thing Don's staring down the barrel of, and we both know it.

Before the end of the year, we stop seeing Don. He leaves a note with Ms. Knox letting us know he's gone to Canada ahead of the draft. The Oakmont's not the same without him.

December 7 comes so fast it's like a blink, but time moves differently at The Oakmont. I knock on Roger's door that day, but there's no answer. As I walk along the hallway back to the elevator, I'm filled with an irrational desire to knock on every door I pass. I want to see another human being—anyone at all—and tell them that in 1941 the country has entered World War II. I want to tell them I'm afraid for the love of my life. I want to see if any of them have phones that will reach his time so I can call and ask if he's okay.

I pick a door at random and pound my fists against it, crying in frustration. But no one comes.

There are many doors inside The Oakmont that won't open and corridors down which a resident can't turn. The Oakmont allows us to see who and what we need to, nothing more. The Oakmont guards its secrets.

Several days pass before I see Roger again. When I do, he seems distracted, his mind elsewhere. I note the stress in his eyes. He avoids talk of what happened, and I don't press. Instead, he speaks of his sister, Betty, who plans to enter the workforce as a telephone operator.

"I'm not sure this is the time," he says. "Why does she need to work anyway?"

"Working women will become increasingly common in the years to come," I say, refraining from mention that as men go off to fight in World War II there'll be a boom as millions of women take their places. "I have a job myself, remember?"

"Yes, but it's different in your time, Sarah."

"Is it so different? Maybe this is just what your sister needs."

"But how does it work for families?" he asks. "Who raises the children and manages the home?"

I smile. You have to accept this kind of thing when you're a resident of The Oakmont. Times are different, and each one has its own set of values and attitudes that will inevitably become obsolete as the sands of time continue to fall. We must consider the source and share our varied points of view with the goal of finding common ground, especially with those we love.

"Families find ways to make it work," I say. "Ideally, both parents share responsibilities. That is, in households with two parents. I can't say how single parents manage, but they do. I imagine they found ways to do so even in your time."

He nods, and we sit in silence as the elephant in the room that is the Second World War looms large over everything.

Roger does his best to keep the mood light when we celebrate Christmas. He hangs mistletoe over his door and kisses me deeply when I arrive. On the radio, Bing Crosby sings, "Silent Night." He's even cut down a real tree and hung vintage ornaments from its branches. Well, vintage to me, anyway. Beneath the tree there's a small package wrapped in plain paper with a simple red ribbon around it. I assume it's for me, and I place the one I brought for him next to it. Mine looks so garish in its cartoon reindeer wrapping and iridescent silver bow. Roger can't help laughing when he sees it.

I ask about his sister, and he tells me she got the job at the phone company. I tell him I'm glad and that I wish her well.

"That reminds me; she baked cookies."

He grabs a tin from atop his fridge, opens it and offers me one. I take a bite and can't help uttering a long "*mmmm*" as the flavor fills my mouth.

"This is so much better than the packaged stuff I buy at the store."

"I can't believe you don't cook or bake a thing," he laughs.

"That's not true. I make a mean root beer ham. Mind you, it's just a cooked ham I put in my slow cooker and pour a can of soda over."

He doesn't bother to ask what a slow cooker is. I guess the name says it all. He's aware of some of the magical appliances I have. Well, *magical* to me. To him they seem wasteful—lazy even. "Why would any one household need more than one television?" he asked once. I didn't really know how to respond to that. I think he'd have to admit my cell phone's pretty cool though, with all the uses it has, but cell phones are strictly forbidden in apartments with numbers earlier than the mid-seventies.

We have some eggnog by the window, and I describe the Christmas lights that decorate the city in my time. New York is alive and festive in December 2023. In 1941, I gather, things are a bit more subdued.

Afterwards, we open our gifts. Always the gentleman, he insists I go first. I pull the ribbon and paper off the box and smile when I see the handkerchief.

"I thought you could use one of your own."

"It's beautiful," I say. And it is. I've never owned anything like it. The fabric is cotton, I think, but the edges are hand-embroidered with violets, which he knows are the flower for my birth month. On one corner are my initials. I run my finger over them, turning the fabric over to marvel at the quality of the stitching. Machines are good, but not like this.

They don't make 'em like they used to, I think, not for the first time.

He opens my gift next, and I wait on the edge of my seat to see his face. Carefully setting the reindeer paper aside, he holds up the canvas and stares at it a moment before looking at me. I can't help it; I burst into laughter.

"Do you like it?"

"It's…a still life?"

"You could say that."

I look down at the painting I made for him. A painting of a single can of Campbell's tomato soup. It's an obvious rip-off, at least to those of us born after pop art became a thing. Roger shakes his head and laughs.

Years from now—for him at least—an artist named Warhol will paint a much better rendition of this very can. The punchline to my joke will land then. I wish I could be there to see his face when it does.

"I love it," he says. There's so much about me he doesn't understand, and yet he still feels this way.

Residents of The Oakmont know there are things you must simply accept while liv-ing here, and questions you don't ask, at least not with any expectation of their being answered.

Roger places the painting on his mantle. It actually looks good there. He stands admiring it for a while—or maybe asking himself, *why a can of soup?* I come up behind him to wrap him in an embrace and kiss him between the shoulder blades as he places a hand on mine. Then he exhales deeply, and I know immediately what's coming.

"I've decided to enlist," he tells the painting.

I bury my face into his back and hold back tears.

"There's no rush," I say. "The war goes on for years, and they won't draft until next. You don't have to decide now."

He turns, wrapping his arms around me and kissing the top of my head.

"I know this isn't what you want, but I've given it a lot of thought. They're looking for able-bodied men. Our freedoms are at stake—and those of our allies. I can't just sit this one out."

"But to volunteer?"

He says nothing more. There's no need. I know the man he is, and that this is exactly the kind of thing he'd do. It's why I've worried for months that this moment would come. I know better than to argue, so I simply nod.

Later we fall into bed as we have countless times before, but somehow this feels different. Time seems to linger as we make love, as if stretching out our time together.

Just days later he goes to volunteer, and I walk him to the door. The main entrance to The Oakmont is a peculiar place. There's a lobby with a revolving door that looks just like the many such doors you'll find across the city. When you walk through this one, though, where you end up depends on who you are. Or should I say, *when* you end up. Even if Roger and I were to walk through together, holding hands, we'd still each step out alone into our own time.

He kisses me once, sweetly, then puts his hat on and gives me a smile. I return one as best I can. When he turns to go, part of me wants to run after him, but I stay and watch as he spins through the entrance, then vanishes into thin air.

I reach into my pocket, pull my new handkerchief out, and use it to wipe the tears.

When Roger ships out, I can't see him off. That happens long before I'm born. To take my mind off things, Linda asks me over to her place. We talk about movies, and in my frazzled state I let slip a *Star Wars* reference, though it'll still be another year before it comes out in her time. Luckily, she doesn't notice.

New Year's Eve came and went without much fanfare. I've felt numb ever since Roger said he was going to war. It's 2024 and 1942 where we are. Time marches on whatever the decade and no matter how much we might want to slow things down.

"Anyway, he's thinking of selling *Roller Palace*," Linda's saying, and I realize I've missed her boyfriend's name yet again. "Where the hell does that leave me?"

"Does he have another plan?"

"Wants to open something called a video rental store."

"It might be alright," I tell her.

"You know something I don't?"

Her eyes widen with expectation, but I give her nothing more. She shakes her head, disappointed.

I hang out a while longer but call it an early night. When I get back to my apartment there's an envelope sticking out from under the door. It's yellowed with age and has no stamp or postmark. The mailing address reads only: *Sarah – The Oakmont.* I recognize the handwriting immediately.

Before I'm even through the door, I've torn it open, the scent of old paper contrasting with the anticipation of fresh news from the front.

Roger tells me of the time since he left, mentioning some of the guys he's be-friended—two of them New Yorkers like us. Neither has heard of The Oakmont, and Roger can't seem to recall its location for them.

The letter goes on to say how much he misses me and how he thinks of me often. He wishes he could've brought a picture of me, but the modern look of all the ones I had would've invited curious looks in 1942.

By the time I'm done reading I'm both laughing and crying. Pressing the letter to my chest, I try to feel him there with me, through time and space. I have no idea how this letter reached me, but Roger's generation was nothing if not resourceful. Dancing alone in my living room humming, "Moonlight Serenade," I send him all my love and hope it somehow find its way to him, too.

Letters continue to arrive, one each week. They're always slipped under my door and yellowed from the passage of time. I suspect they're delivered by Ms. Knox when she knows I'm not around.

There's so much Roger isn't able to share with me, so he mostly reminisces about our time at The Oakmont. He wonders what picture Mr. Thomas will be showing when he starts our movie nights back up. I want to tell him it's Buster Keaton in *Seven Chances*, but I have no way to write him. In any case, I might not go. It's not the same without Roger sitting next to me.

Then a week goes by with no letter. Nor is there one the following week. A month passes with the worst scenarios running through my mind until I can't take it. I break the rules—not a little this time, but fully. I open up my laptop and Google his name, and any other information I have on his military service.

Nothing comes up.

There are results, of course, but they're of other Rogers and other wars. There's nothing to tell me what happened to my Roger.

I look up every Army database I can and search for someone to contact for answers. I call in sick to work and spend the next two days calling everyone I can. The responses are always the same. There's no record of Roger. Things get misfiled. There was a flood in the fifties, or a fire in the eighties. The explanations are irrelevant. They all mean the same thing: that I have no idea what's happened to Roger.

I can think of only one person that might have the answers I so desperately need.

Ms. Knox has been the building manager of The Oakmont for time immemorial. If you ask the residents what she's like, you'll find the descriptions vary enormously. Some will say she's a young, attractive brunette with a fondness for hats; others will swear she's ancient, bone thin, and always smells of cinnamon. Still others will tell you Knox is, in fact, an unusually tall man with an Australian accent. All are correct.

I knock perhaps a little too hard on Ms. Knox's door, but she seems not to have noticed when she opens it and offers me a gracious smile. I'm invited in and offered tea, which I accept more out of distraction that any real desire.

I blurt out my confession as she holds a sugar cube in a set of tiny tongs over my cup.

"I've been searching the historical records for Roger in apartment 1942."

The cube drops with a *plop* into my tea.

"Milk?" she offers.

I blink, waiting for...something else. Some admonishment maybe. Or perhaps a threat of eviction. She sits across from me then and exhales before speaking.

"The rules are in place for your own good. Has breaking this one brought you any measure of peace? Has it returned Roger to you?"

I shake my head.

"You want *me* to do that, then." She sips from her cup. "You want me to tell you whether or not Roger survives the war."

I nod.

"There are questions you just don't ask at The Oakmont," she reminds me. "You don't ask them because they can't be answered. Only time can give you the answers you seek."

"Time," I repeat. "Time is a thing you dangle from precariously as the city moves on below you."

"Mr. Thomas and his moving pictures," she says with a laugh. "Do you want to know what time really is?"

I watch her, saying nothing so she'll continue.

"Time is nothing...and everything. It doesn't actually exist, because we made it up, but if it did exist, it wouldn't run in a line; it would run in a circle."

Ms. Knox reaches into her blouse and pulls out a ring on a chain. She spins it one way, then the other.

"Time moves differently at The Oakmont. We can touch it at any point in time or at all points at once." She demonstrates by tapping the ring at various points before placing it onto one of her fingers. "Time can pass you by and leave you virtually untouched, or it can fall on you like a cascade."

"But what does any of this have to do with Roger?"

"There's no fighting it," she says. "It's like swimming against the current. Better to give in, relax, and let the waves carry you to shore."

She tucks the ring back into her blouse and takes another loud sip from her cup. I stare down into mine, searching for answers but knowing there are none to be found here.

Without another word, I stand and head back out to the hall. She makes no move to stop me. I'm so numb I don't even consciously move through the building and only notice I've reached my door when it fails to open for me. I try the key again and again and finally burst into tears. Ms. Knox has locked me out somehow—punishment for breaking the rules.

"You alright?"

I don't recognize the voice, so I look up and see my neighbor, Harrison, standing by his open door. I think it's maybe the second thing he's ever said to me in all the time he's lived here.

"No, I'm not alright. My key won't work."

He comes over and takes a look, then removes and reinserts the key before turning it. The door unlocks and he pushes it open.

"You had your key in upside down."

I feel like an idiot. No wonder this guy has wanted nothing to do with me. I continue to cry even while thanking him, and as I start to walk past him to enter my apartment, he stops me and gives me a hug. It's uncharacteristic, especially in a city like New York, but I give into it—the way Ms. Knox said I should surrender to time. Through sobs I tell this stranger everything, from the moment Roger and I first met and fell in love, to the letters that arrived at my door so mysteriously, then stopped coming at all.

He listens to all of it in silence with a patience I envy. Then he does the unthinkable and invites me to join him in his apartment.

"I...couldn't," I say. "There are rules at The Oakmont."

"I'm aware. Nevertheless, there's something you should see."

I don't trust easily, but something about Harrison feels safe. I follow him to his door, rules be damned, and step behind him into 2056.

The apartment doesn't look too different from my own. You expect there to be major changes from one era to another, but ultimately a chair's still a chair and a lamp's still a lamp. Apartments look pretty much the same, and New York rent's probably way too steep in every time.

Leaving me standing by the door, he heads into his bedroom, returning a moment later with a shoebox. He removes the lid as he approaches, and I don't understand what I'm looking at. Inside there's...nothing.

"I'm confused."

"My mother used to live at The Oakmont, though I didn't always know that. I never met my father, but when I moved out, she gave me this box and told me it contained something that was his. She said he'd left it for me, with instructions that she give it to me when I got my own place."

I take the empty box and wait for him to continue.

"When I opened the box, I found a bunch of letters. All of them looked old, but the one on top was the only one with my name on it, so I opened it. The letter was from my parents, written when Mom was pregnant. That's how I learned she'd lived here too. They both had. Everything I'd known about them up until that point was, if not a lie, then certainly incomplete. My mother would've told me the truth, had she been able to, but…"

"She didn't remember," I finished.

Residence at The Oakmont is a temporary affair. Those who live here only do so when the time is right, and when that time passes, they are evicted. Those who are evicted will find their memories of The Oakmont—and those they knew there—are fleeting, and just out of reach; like a word on the tip of your tongue you can never quite recall. At times, they may sense its existence. They may even search for it, never quite knowing what they're searching for, but you can only find The Oakmont when it wants to be found.

Harrison nods. "By then I'd read the contract you sign when you move in, and I understood. In any case, the letter explained everything. How they'd met, their time together, how he'd gone off to war, all the way through to her eviction. The other letters were ones my father had written my mother during the war. In the letter to me, he said he'd resealed them in new envelopes and gave me specific instructions as to what I should do with them, and when."

I'm at a loss for words as he tells me this. I see it now, as I let my gaze fall over him. The flecks of green in his eyes, so like Roger's. The same unruly waves that drive me crazy in my own hair. This was why he'd avoided me. He'd known that if I looked at him—if I really looked—I'd see and I would know.

"It was you," I say. "I thought it was Ms. Knox who kept slipping the letters under my door."

My gaze then falls on the artwork that hangs above his mantle. It's the one I painted a year ago—or maybe decades ago: "The gang at the Oakmont."

"What I don't understand," he says, "is why you were evicted. I know it's just something that happens here, sooner or later, but I thought there'd be an explanation for why it happened when it did."

I smile, then burst into tears again. He looks concerned for a moment, but I start laughing. Relief washes over me and I clasp my hands and raise them to my face a moment before I regain some composure.

"I became pregnant," I say. "That's why."

The Oakmont is an adult-only living environment. You won't find children or families among its residents. There are couples on occasion, but for the most part residents live alone. Children are lovely, to be sure, but their futures are too uncertain and their pasts too meager. They're as yet too resistant to the push and pull of time. Children also have great difficulty following rules, and there are of course, many rules at The Oakmont.

"This is great. This is unbelievable!" I tell him and wrap him in the tightest hug I can muster.

He looks confused, so I explain.

"Don't you see? I'm not pregnant now. That means I must get pregnant later, or you wouldn't be here. Which means Roger survives the war!"

He smiles an uncertain, lopsided smile as I jump up and down still hugging him. After a while he gives in to my joy and we both laugh and cry, and for the first time ever, Harrison accepts my invitation to join me for dinner. There are so many questions I want to ask that I know he can't answer, so instead I let him ask questions of his own. We talk long into the night, and when we're done, I describe to him my view out the window, and he tells me what it looks like in 2056.

Roger returns a little over a month later, walking with a cane. I'm just glad he's alive and back in my arms. We're shy around each other at first, until we're not, and then we're back in his bed, just like old times.

The war continues where he is, but he's done his part. I break the rules and tell him how it ends so he's not surprised when the day finally comes. In early September 1945—or 2027, depending on your point of view—we celebrate the occasion in our own way and conceive our son.

I discover I'm pregnant as soon as I return to my apartment, where I find an eviction notice slipped under my door.

When I tell Roger both the good news and bad, we cry tears of joy and sadness, and afterward he plays, "Moonlight Serenade," and we dance one more time.

"I'm going to miss this," I say. "In my time no one who isn't a professional really knows how to dance anymore. At least with you leading I stood a chance at a few decent steps."

"I'll miss this too, and I'll miss seeing New York through your eyes."

"Maybe we could meet in the future, where our lives overlap," I say.

He kisses my forehead. "That would never work. You'd be a child or at most a young woman. I'd be an old man."

I choke back tears and take a deep breath to steady myself.

"It'll be alright," he says. "I don't think this is necessarily the end for us. After all, time moves differently at The Oakmont."

I don't know what he means by that, but I do know that in The Oakmont there are questions you don't ask.

I'm big as a house, waddling down the aisles of my local grocery store in search of the newborn diapers that match my coupon.

"My goodness," says a voice with geriatric lilt. "You're close to bursting."

I have one of those faces, where older strangers feel comfortable talking to me. I stop and offer her a smile.

"I fear I may pop at any moment," I agree, and we both laugh.

"Do you know what you're having, dear?"

"A boy. I'm naming him Harrison."

"What a great name."

"Thanks. It just came to me one day."

"Honey, in your condition you should be home resting. Let the baby's father do the running around."

"Oh, it's just the two of us," I say, rubbing my belly. "That's why I'm here hunting down diapers."

"Aren't we all, dear," she jokes, giving me a mischievous wink.

There's something in that wink that seems familiar, and I'm about to ask if we've spoken before when my eye falls on a keychain clipped to her purse strap. A keychain in the shape of a roller skate.

It all comes back in a rush of memory. I see through her aged features to the youthful ones I once knew, and with them all my other memories of The Oakmont return. In that moment I see the same recognition in Linda's aged eyes. She smiles and winks once more.

"My but we had some good times then," she says.

I'm about to answer when it hits me that somewhere back at The Oakmont there's a younger Linda, living in the seventies. If Linda can be in both places, in two different times, what's to stop her from more? What's to stop any of us?

I think of Ms. Knox and her ring, speaking about touching time at multiple points or all of them at once. I think of all those doors at The Oakmont that never opened for me. At least not the me I was then, at that time. Maybe somewhere behind one of those doors there's another Sarah, with another Roger, and with them all our old friends. Maybe it's movie night and we're standing around the potluck table waiting for Mr. Thomas to start the film.

"If you're the owner of a blue Toyota, your car alarm is going off."

The announcement over the store speakers jars me out of my thoughts. I feel like I was somewhere else just now, but the memory's faded. The elderly lady in front of me seems confused, then shakes her head as she remembers what we were talking about.

"They have the newborn diapers just there, next to the formula," she says.

"Great, thanks."

"Good luck with the little one."

"Thanks again. It was nice meeting you."

You won't find The Oakmont on any maps, in any time. You don't find it; it finds you. You'll be living your life, happy as can be, then one day you'll come across an advertisement for an apartment for rent. The ad might be online, or on a bulletin board, or in a newspaper, it makes no difference. What matters is The Oakmont will call to you when it's your time. It will offer just what you're looking for: a neighborhood close to work or the subway, stunning views of the skyline maybe, or rent control. Whatever the draw, you'll know then and there you've found your home, and you'll soon find yourself in Ms. Knox's office, signing your name just below the list of rules.

P.A. Cornell is a Chilean-Canadian speculative fiction writer. A graduate of the Odyssey workshop, her stories have been published in over fifty magazines and anthologies, including *Lightspeed*, *Apex*, and three "Best of" anthologies. In addition to becoming the first Chilean Nebula finalist in 2024, Cornell has been a finalist for the Aurora and World Fantasy Awards, was longlisted for the BSFA Awards, and won Canada's Short Works Prize. When not writing, she can be found assembling intricate Lego builds or drinking ridiculous quantities of tea. Sometimes both. For more on the author and her work, visit her website pacornell.com.

WINDOW BOY

Thomas Ha

The tenth time Jakey broke the rules, he put a sandwich in the mailbox where the window boy could get it. Mom had taken her sleep-quick pills and gone to bed after dinner, on account of her headaches. And Dad was dozing in front of the TV, chin on his chest and a half-empty glass clutched in his hand. It got still enough that the only sounds were Dad's shows and the hum of the house filters, so Jakey slipped into the kitchen and put together a ham and cheddar on a plate, then placed it in the parcel chamber near the front door. He sat by the parlor window for a good long while after, curled up at the bench cushions, and his eyelids drooped now and again until he began to see the shadows move.

The window boy showed up, just like all the other times.

Out from behind the telephone pole across the street and then through the moonlit front yard. He crawled on his hands and knees across the wet grass to the edge of Mom's miniature garden, careful to avoid the lawn sensors, then pulled himself to the window frame to peer through.

"Folks passed out?"

"Yep."

The window boy snickered.

"Got you something. In the mailbox."

The window boy crawled through the garden and up the steps. He gave Jakey a wary look before touching the hatch.

"You can grab anything in the outer chamber. Won't hurt you if you don't press the far side and try to bust through to where the incoming packages and stuff get pulled in," Jakey reassured him.

So the window boy unlatched the outer seal, and Jakey barely saw the first half of the sandwich leave the chamber with how fast the window boy snapped it up, shivering while he ate. They'd never talked much about what went on outside, but the boy's bony wrists and hollow cheeks told Jakey enough.

After a minute or two of chomping away, the window boy seemed to remember himself, and that he was being watched. So he took a breath and straightened himself out.

"Thanks, Jakey."

"Don't mention it."

"Gonna miss this when they send you out." The window boy scratched behind his ear. "They tell you where yet?"

"Nah. They don't tell me anything."

In truth, Mom and Dad had decided on *Pacifica*, one of the ocean schools, away from the cities—where all kids like Jakey with fathers like Dad went, and where Dad himself went years ago. But the window boy didn't know anything about that, which is why Jakey liked talking to him to begin with. So he wasn't about to get into it with him now.

"Burning season's wrapping up." The window boy scratched behind his ear. "Can't smell much of the smoke tonight."

"Well, that's good."

"Nah. End of fire is when the animals get restless."

"Oh."

"The charred mountains. The ash water. Drives the old and the ugly right to the houses. Grackles. Raccoon tails. Boar cats. You know." He looked up and around, like he'd just remembered to be watchful, and pressed his chest low to the brick landing. "Been meaning to talk to you about that, Jakey."

"What do you mean?"

"Just...that I've been meaning to ask something."

Jakey's chest tightened. He'd been worried something like this might be coming. These weeks he'd spent talking to the window boy late at night, when he couldn't sleep and didn't want to think about *Pacifica*, he had the worries there, in the back of his mind—that the window boy was working up the courage for an ask.

All those lessons, the speeches from Dad, were still there buried in Jakey, somewhere. Not to give them things, no matter how small. Not to talk to them the way that Jakey had been doing. *You think when they smile and wave that they want to be your friend? You think when they tap at the window or ring the doorbell they just want a little favor? They hate you, Jakey. That's why we have rules, about not talking, not sharing. Because to share is to show. And you don't ever show them what you got, Jakey. Understand?*

The window boy must have seen something of those fears in Jakey's eyes because he looked sheepish and turned away. "Forget it."

"What?"

"Nah. It's not—it's not your problem. I'll figure it out."

Jakey bristled and felt hot in his cheeks. "Well, now it feels like my problem."

It reminded him of when Mom did things like this. When she'd stop before taking her sleep-quicks and say something about Dad or the house, then hush like there were secrets too juicy to share. You should either keep it locked in the whole way or get out with it—that was the way Jakey did it and would always do it as far as he was concerned.

But before the window boy could speak, bright lights flashed on the street.

"Get behind something," Jakey hissed, watching the window boy trip and skitter to the nearby retaining wall, then ball up his body as best he could.

It was the Mailman pulling up, his truck flashing its beams. There was a loud clanging of equipment when he dropped out of the passenger side to the curb and sauntered up the brick pathway. He pulled open his face visor and his eye-lights shone in the dark like the little display parts on their microwave.

"Jakey? Why you got that window turned on, kid? F—k, son. The whole world can see you right now. Lot of filthy worms out tonight. Power down that screen."

"I—I will." Jakey tried not to look at the far side of the yard. "Just couldn't sleep."

"Couldn't sleep." The Mailman laughed. "Sure as sh—t not going to if you look out here." Then he straightened up and cleared his throat, and there was a clicking sound from the wires weeping around his neck, like they might pop out from the parts of him that were still flesh if he didn't move a little more carefully. "Your house filters are on, right?" Jakey assured the Mailman that, yes, his cursing was being negated in the house's audio.

"Good. Good." The Mailman produced a box from under his arm. "Guessing this is some nice stuff for your daddy." He scanned the barcode with his glove. "I tell you. If I could do things over, I'd have been an LLC man like him. They're shipping you to school soon, right?"

Jakey nodded.

"Well, better study hard while you're out there. Then maybe you'll join up with a company like your daddy. Won't get stuck with sh—tty outside work, you know? If I could afford a kid I'd be telling him the same. Holy cr—p."

Jakey froze.

The Mailman reached into the parcel chamber and pulled out the other half of the ham and cheese the window boy'd left behind. "Really? This is so nice, kid. I mean, kind of dangerous if anyone else peeps this, but, wow. Really nice."

"Y-yeah," Jakey nodded. "For you."

The Mailman had already started eating, grunting. Jakey wasn't sure the Mailmen were supposed to have people food after all of their modifications. But it seemed to mostly go down, though the Mailman gagged and heaved a couple of times. Meanwhile, the window boy didn't move an inch in the shadows, covering his ears and trying his best not to breathe too loudly.

"Fan-f—cking-tastic. Wow." The Mailman wiped his mouth and around the lights where his eyes used to be. "Thanks kindly for that, Jakey. I—" He swerved all of a sudden and drew his revolver. The gun's laserlight beeped and danced across the retaining wall and then to the dark skies, then somewhere across the street.

"Don't you f—cking come any closer," the Mailman said.

He fired a few warning shots, though the sound filters canceled them out. The cameras that generated the window internally for Jakey also wiped the barrel flash, so that it just looked like the gun shaking. Jakey thought he saw the slightest splatter of blood near the telephone pole, but if it had even been there, the cameras deleted that too.

Jakey was tempted to touch the filter panel to the side of the bench. It would just take a little turn of the dial to see what was really going on, who might be out there that the Mailman was yelling at.

Maybe it was something big, one of the animals, like the window boy had said.

Something strange and old, like one of the grackles from the mountains, flying down to visit after the fires and snatch people off the streets—rip them up into the air when they weren't watching the trees. Maybe throw them into the concrete, so they'd have an easier time getting to the soft parts between the bones.

Part of Jakey wanted to know, since he'd never really seen one with his own eyes, but part of him wasn't sure if he really wanted to find out. He pulled his hand back from the dial.

"Sh—t. Just nicked him." The Mailman's glowing eye-lights turned back to the house, then, as if recalling the rest of his route for the night and what was likely waiting for him, he closed the visor shut again. "I'm serious, bud. Turn off that window, okay?"

Jakey nodded and watched him saunter back down the brick and into the truck, which rose on its clawed legs and proceeded down the street to the next delivery point. Minutes of quiet passed before Jakey dared to whisper out to the yard again.

The window boy crept out to the garden, visibly shaken by the gunshots, and looked like he had trouble swallowing.

"You okay?"

"Yeah. Yeah. Just loud," he replied. "Just loud."

And something about the way the window boy said that made Jakey realize that the kid must have been a little younger than he thought. He said he didn't know his age, and there were times, with what the window boy knew about the world outside, that he felt older, a lot older, in a way that almost made Jakey jealous. But right now, the boy felt so young.

"Think I gotta go, Jakey. I'll see you around."

"Yeah...yeah. See you around."

"Thanks again for the meat. Really."

"No problem."

"We're friends, right?"

Jakey nodded but didn't answer.

"Yeah," the window boy spoke for him. "Yeah. We're friends."

Then he crawled away.

Everyone was tired during the day.

Mom wiped down the kitchen and listened to music on the house speakers. Dad took his video meetings from his office. Jakey sat in the living room with his lesson programs, learning about the city seasons, but he kept thinking about the window boy and what he wanted to ask.

At dinner, Mom and Dad got on each other's nerves in their quiet way. Something about the house again, always something about that. Jakey couldn't follow the details, but they were talking about moving away from the city. Dad wouldn't hear it, no matter how many times Mom tried to ask. Because even though LLC managers did everything from their houses and didn't go in anymore, he thought it was important to show that he *could* go into the city if they needed it—pack up and roll in whenever they wanted. Something about morale and tax codes and whatever else he was probably repeating from the people who managed the managers.

Mom whispered into her wine glass that she hoped they called him in, and that pretty much ended things for the night. She took her pills and marched upstairs, and he collapsed in the living room with his drink, his hunched body lit by flashes from the television.

And when it was still and mercifully quiet, Jakey went back to the parlor and sat on those cushions until it was time.

The window boy crept out from the telephone pole across the street and then up to the garden, then the frame. And the first thing Jakey noticed were the bruises along the boy's jaw and a lump on his forehead. But he knew better than to ask—all the other times he asked the window boy what those were, that just soured things for the both of them.

"Sorry. Didn't have anything to make a sandwich with. And my folks were more riled than usual, so I didn't think I could mess around in the kitchen," Jakey said.

"Nah, it's—it's okay. I wasn't expecting anything again."

"I know. I know you weren't."

The window boy scratched behind his ear, then looked up warily at the sky. "It's getting not so good. So...not sure how long I can stay."

"What do you mean?" Jakey asked.

The window boy crouched and spoke more softly than usual. "Lots of things, restless in the city. Even the Mailmen aren't risking routes every night. So." He stopped and cleared his throat. "Is it true, what they say, about the houses being fake?"

"What?"

"That you're not in here. This box." The window boy gestured at the screen. "Someone told me these are just shells now. That you're actually way down, under the dirt. Little chambers to bring mail down and up. But the rest is just...for show. Like this window. Just lights and colors to make it seem like you're up here with us."

The cameras in front of the house captured the fear in the window boy, but Jakey also saw a glint of other feelings that he didn't quite like. And he heard in his ear his father's voice still: *don't ever show them what you got.*

"That's silly," Jakey lied. "Never seen anything like that."

The window boy's face fell.

"Yeah. Silly." He shook and scratched the back of his neck. And maybe it was Jakey's imagination, but there was a steeliness to the window boy now. "But it got me thinking," he said.

"Oh?"

"Remember how I said I was going to ask something before?"

"Yeah. The thing you said you'd figure out." Jakey answered.

"Maybe the stories about the houses were dumb. Made up. But you've got soft soil here, in your side yard, I noticed."

"Behind the fence," Jakey said.

"Right. The fence." The window boy nodded. "I thought maybe, if I had somewhere to dig down a little, I could sleep safely. Just a little hole, maybe a foot deep, and I could cover it with ply. It's safer that way with." He pointed up. "Everything."

"Uh huh."

"Your folks won't even notice it, in the side yard. And it'd only be a night. Maybe two."

"Uh huh."

"All you'd have to do is power down the fence, so that I could swing over without getting fried. Then I could dig. And then...then I think I'm going soon after, Jakey. So you wouldn't have to worry. I think a lot of us are getting out of the city. For real."

"Uh huh."

"What do you think, Jakey? Only a day or two. And it'd just be me."

Jakey didn't know why he felt so cold. He wasn't sure why the window boy asking him for this made him want to turn the window off and go to bed. But he did know that the way the boy was talking, and especially that last part, made him nauseous.

"Just you."

"Yeah."

Imagining that—the window boy sleeping up there, nearby, coming out to talk at night every so often. None of that seemed too bad at first. But Jakey couldn't let go of that cold feeling in his chest. He reached over to the parlor controls and twisted the filter settings down.

And there they were.

Behind the window boy, about five or six grown men, staring at the house.

Their faces and clothes were painted with strange streaks of color, blocky shapes all over their cheeks and torsos. Large yellow spots on different parts of their bodies. Whatever it was allowed them to fool the house cameras into deleting them with the filters. Maybe the house thought they were animals or machinery or something Jakey shouldn't see.

It took all of Jakey's self-control not to jerk away from the screen.

"I—I got to think about it, maybe."

"Oh," the window boy scratched. "Um. How long you need to think? Like a day?"

"Sure," Jakey said, trying not to look at the painted faces behind the window boy. "Maybe a day."

The window boy's fear spread from his eyes, and it didn't seem rehearsed. It was unclear if it was still the animals or the men behind him that were more of the cause. "It's really scary now," he said. "I think I'd need to dig a hole tomorrow."

"Tomorrow..."

"Yeah, Jakey. Is that—do you think—can you turn the electricity off in the fence tomorrow?"

Jakey didn't know what to say, and he was afraid that anything but what the window boy and the others wanted to hear would start something. "Yeah...I think...tomorrow. Sure. Tomorrow."

"That's great." A grin broke across the boy's face. "Oh, Jakey. That's so great. Oh."

The men behind him didn't change their expressions.

"You're a great friend, Jakey. Tomorrow. I'll see you then."

"See you."

Jakey turned off the window.

Mom noticed right away that he wasn't touching his lunch, so she sat at the kitchen table with him. They could hear Dad on some video meeting in the background, and every time he laughed, she rubbed her temples.

"School will be good for you," she said, assuming that's what was still troubling him. "I know you're scared of something so different. But it'll be good out on the water. You'll see what's going on. Maybe get a better sense of what you think. And that's important. Learning other ways to think, Jakey. Don't get stuck going one way, the way some of us do."

He didn't much understand, but he got the sense that she was still arguing with Dad, even though he wasn't here.

"You know, when I was your age there was this picture book, when they still printed books. Can't remember the name, but it was about bugs in the forest, starting out as little eggs in the dirt. And, at the start of the book, some of the baby bugs, especially the ones born closer to the top, got eaten by bigger things, scavengers, hounds, stuff like that. And the baby bugs deeper down, they just kept growing, and they eventually went on to have adventures when they were big enough.

"I keep thinking about that book, for some reason," She rubbed her temples and ignored the sounds from the other room. "How, where the eggs were laid, what happened or didn't happen, was just luck. No one's fault. God. What was the name of it? That book. I used to know, I swear."

She kept talking that way, over and over, until she got bored and left him alone.

Then later, after dinner was cleared and everyone went off, Jakey stood at the entrance to the parlor for a long while, staring at the closed window screen.

He imagined the window boy, crawling out from behind the telephone pole, followed by those men, advancing slowly across the grass. And the thought made him shaky, kept him from going to sit down at the bench cushions like he otherwise would have.

So instead, he found himself wandering through other parts of the house, drawn over to the living room, following the sounds of the television.

*"Grack attack! *bang bang bang*"*

It was one of Dad's cartoons—a show from when he was Jakey's age that was still running all these years later. On the television, Jakey saw a Mailman in a powersuit, pointing at the sky, at a black shape, like a "T," flying up in the air and cawing. That was usually as much as they dared to depict the grackles in shows like these. Anything more than those "T" shapes and they tended to get complaints from families and local churches that the grackles were too frightening for kids.

The Mailman on the show was a lot cleaner and brighter than the real ones—still had all of his teeth and not a spot of rust or blood anywhere on his cartoon body. He lined up the lasersight from his whirring revolver and pulled the trigger.

A blossoming fire lit up the sky, incinerating the "T" that used to be a grackle, and the Mailman winked one of his glowing light-eyes at the audience.

"Got 'im."

Dad noticed Jakey in the dark at some point and waved for him to sit down, which he almost never did. So Jakey sank into the couch next to his father and listened to the man chuckle and squeal. "This is a good one," Dad would say every couple of minutes. "Oh, you're going to like this. Big scene coming up."

*"Beak blasters, get going. Fling your claw scythes up top. We got them on the run! *bang bang bang*"*

Dad's breathing grew heavier and his eyes watery, but it was kind of nice, Jakey thought. Watching the Mailman riding around the city, his armored truck bounding on its metal legs. It made Jakey think about the window screen again, but in a less of a bad way. Like maybe all of it was kind of like this show. Something to be watched, something to be seen, but that would go away on its own at the end.

He didn't have to think about the window boy or the painted men or anything that might be outside the house. Just let it fade away like the black screen at the end of those episodes. If he didn't want to, he didn't have to think about anything at all, he realized, as he floated off to sleep.

—*You've got to call the Mail.*

—*Four bodies. What a fucking mess.*

—*Must have been running away. House clocked a bunch of grackles in the neighborhood. Huge ones. I've never seen them that big. These guys must not have known where else to go. Tried to scale the fence and got burned alive, probably.*

—Goddamn it. Mail pickup has me on hold. Insurance says they'll cover part of the cost, but Mail is supposed to waive the remainder. They should've been picking off grackles anyway. Where the hell were they?

—Not enough anymore maybe. Jakey's going to wake soon. Go to the office.

—Yeah yeah yeah. Fuck me. What a mess. Jesus.

Jakey opened his eyes but didn't want to talk to anyone yet, so he closed them again and tried his best to sleep through the words and the noise.

Night and quiet moved in like they always did, and Jakey found himself at the parlor bench like before, staring out at the grass and the moonlight and the darkened street. He waited a long time for something he knew wouldn't happen, for something he knew he'd never see.

No one came to the house that night, or the night after, or the night after that.

And when enough nights passed that Jakey understood there was nothing to wait for, he realized something he probably should've realized weeks and weeks earlier.

He didn't want to be here anymore.

Maybe tomorrow he'd tell his Mom and Dad that he was ready for *Pacifica*. He could even ask to take an earlier armored car to the shore before the school year began. One of the boats would ferry him out on the open water to the floating compound where he could meet other boys like him, with houses and parents like his, and see what it was like out there in that place.

Mom and Dad wouldn't fight him going earlier, Jakey knew.

They didn't really want to be here either.

Always using quiet ways of their own to get out too.

Everybody had been right it turned out, Jakey thought, about the importance of school and the rest. About taking things seriously and finding a way to join one of the companies. Maybe becoming a manager to afford to come back and pick out a house, just like this one. He thought he understood now, why they did what they did, why he had to do what he had to do.

Still, he wasn't quite sure he could stop watching the window just yet either, even if it was what they probably would have done. And he hesitated but reached for the dial for the auditory and visual filters.

And he turned them all the way down, so low that he started to see new outlines and colors coming into focus. A big shape across the street and right next to the telephone pole.

The thing standing there was just as tall as the pole itself, Jakey realized, with thin legs that went up at least twenty feet in the shadows. A strange little body, and then a bent, beaked head, turned to one side.

The grackle's eye, like an unbroken yolk, peered through the screen and into Jakey, even though he was buried safely all the way down below. Its wings draped to the sidewalk, almost hiding the long arms and hands, with fleshy fingers that wrapped around part of the telephone pole.

And behind the grackle, in the light-polluted sky, thousands of other grackle-bodies floated like "T"-shaped kites, black lines against the unnatural gray swirls from scattered fires that spread like patches across the city.

Jakey raised his thumb and forefinger into the shape of a gun at the thing by the telephone pole, and at all the things, waiting out there.

"Bang bang bang," he whispered, imagining a laserlight dancing across the cement.

But the grackle didn't move.

Jakey thought it probably wouldn't, even long after he shut off the screen and walked away.

It'd always be there, whether he was inside or out.

There, always there, whether he watched the screen or not.

<hr>

Thomas Ha is a Nebula, Ignyte, Locus, and Shirley Jackson Award–nominated writer of speculative short fiction. You can find his work in *Clarkesworld*, *Lightspeed Magazine*, *Beneath Ceaseless Skies*, and *Weird Horror Magazine*, among other publications. His work has also appeared in *The Best American Science Fiction & Fantasy* and *The Year's Best Dark Fantasy & Horror*. Thomas grew up in Honolulu and, after a decade plus of living in the northeast, now resides in Los Angeles with his wife and three children.

BETTER LIVING THROUGH ALGORITHMS

Naomi Kritzer

June was the first of my friends to get into it. This isn't surprising—she was playing Wordle for weeks before Margo or I discovered it. When we met up for our weekly lunch, she kept checking her phone and I assumed it was some new game. Then she put it down with a smile and said, "Abelique told me not to pick up my phone again until after lunch was over."

"Who?" Margo said.

"It's this new app for better living."

"I love the idea of an *app* that tells you to *put your phone down more*. For your own good," Margo said, her eyes glinting.

"You should try it!" June said. "You get the first thirty days free!"

"And after that, you have to pay someone to nag you to use your phone less?"

"It's more than that." June took a bite out of her tuna melt. "For one thing, you also agree to occasionally nag other people to put *their* phones down."

Margo and I both laughed, and June flushed. But she did not, I noticed, touch her phone again until we were ready to leave the diner.

Sometimes, once you hear about a new thing, suddenly it's just *everywhere*.

It was like that with Abelique. I couldn't un-see it. Or un-hear it, really, because it's not like I was peering over people's shoulders at their phones, I was overhearing people talking about it. Abelique told them to make clam chowder for dinner. Abelique had assigned them a movie to watch. Abelique sent them to bed at nine p.m. It was that last one that caught my attention enough that I actually looked it up. "A complete lifestyle app" was what Wikipedia called it. This was not actually all that enlightening.

"I think it's a cult," Margo said the following week as we were waiting for a table.

"You said the same thing about Pokemon Go," I said.

"Okay, but I was *joking* about Pokemon Go," she said. "Abelique really is a cult. People sign up for this thing and then just do whatever it tells them to do."

"It can't *make* you do anything," June said, coming up behind us and overhearing.

"So what did it definitely not make you do in the last day?" Margo asked. "Just give us a rundown, June."

"Last night it had me try a new recipe, which was really good, and then it had me watch a movie I hadn't heard of, which was also really good, and then I got my bedtime phone call—"

"Your *what*."

"I mean, no one's going to go to bed just because an app reminder comes up so there's a phone tree. You get a call, and you make a call."

"You have to use your phone as a *phone*? I'm out," I said.

"Are you considering trying it?" June said, eagerly. "You should!"

"I don't trust anything that's free for thirty days," I said. "Because I know myself. And I will *forget*."

"You won't forget with Abelique because you'll get a reminder phone call." She turned back to Margo. "Maybe you could try it, and then write about it." Margo had been trying to freelance as a tech journalist, when she wasn't doing marketing writing to pay the bills.

Margo smacked her own forehead, exasperated. "I'm going to give up on freelance journalism. People keep offering me fifty dollars for something that would take a hundred hours of research. Can we talk about something else? Like that movie you watched?"

June told us about the movie—it had come out about ten years ago, and none of us had heard about it at the time, and it sounded pretty good, actually. Margo looked up a review. June left her phone face down, hands folded primly, looking judgmental. *Cult*, I thought.

Of course, it was only a matter of time before my boss discovered this app and started pressuring me and everyone else in the office to use it.

"It's not a productivity app! It's a wellness app," Keith said, like that made it *better*. (The only thing I hate more than productivity apps are wellness apps.) "It will make you happier! Healthier! I've established three new good habits since I started using it—I floss daily, I have increased my fiber intake, and I go for a walk at lunchtime!"

"That's nice," I said, gritting my teeth and thinking, *Please don't tell me about your fiber intake, Keith.* "I can't imagine how this relates to my job, or why you'd want me to use it unless you think it'll make me more productive."

"Just *try* it for the free month," he said, and remembering that my employee review six months ago had complained that I was *not receptive to new processes* (that time, it *was* a productivity app he wanted me to use—some pomodoro bullshit except instead of a five-minute break you were supposed to spend the five minutes answering email).

I downloaded Abelique and sent a screen shot to my boss because if I was going to jump through this particular hoop, he was damn well going to know I had jumped. I was doing it on *the clock*, too, because I was doing this *for my stupid boss at my stupid job.*

It was a good thing I did it on the clock, because setup took over an hour. The app wanted me to go through a whole slew of questionnaires about my sleep, my mood, what I ate each day, my goals. When we got to goals I checked off stuff about productivity and work advancement, only to have the app re-open the questionnaire with the responses wiped and a note saying, *although your employer may have encouraged or even required you to download this app, your use of Abelique is private and we encourage you to use it for your own benefit, not that of your workplace. If it will be useful to you, we can provide you with a usage report to forward to your boss that will make you look like an obedient little worker bee. Please consider filling this out honestly, because we want you to benefit from the app.*

Obedient little worker bee?

This was *unexpected*. Also, Keith had definitely not gotten anything like this message when he filled it out, or he would not have recommended the app to everyone who reported to him.

What about the algorithm had identified my dissembling? How did they know that Keith was in management? I scrolled through the permissions I'd given the app without a whole lot of thought and...okay, I could see how Keith might have tripped a "management" flag. I was less convinced now that this was a corporate plot to squeeze productivity blood out of worker turnips, but Margo's concerns about it being a cult seemed additionally validated.

Hesitantly, I re-started that questionnaire. What *were* my goals? Other than *not getting fired from my job because even though it's shitty, unemployment and homelessness would be shittier*? Some people had "fitness goals" but it wasn't showing me those, either. Nothing about running a mile or losing weight. It was showing me goals like, *read more books* and *learn to paint.*

I used to want to learn to draw. I put that down.

Why is my phone ringing?

I dragged myself out of bed to shut off the ringer, only to see a message: *Good morning, Linnea. This is the Abelique app. Please be kind to the Abelique volunteer who is calling you.*

It was an hour earlier than I had intended to get up. "Hello," I said, hoping my voice sounded sleepy and not actively hostile.

"Hi, Linnea," someone said. She sounded a little nervous. "This is your good morning call. Abelique wants to let you know that you should go start your coffee, and open your curtains while it's brewing. It's a beautiful sunny day where you are."

I could, in fact, see the gleams of light coming in around my blackout curtains. "Okay," I said. "Is that all? I don't know how this works."

The person at the other end grinned, I thought, or at least, their voice sounded fond, instead of nervous. "That's it. Just, you know, actually get up, okay? You'll be glad you did." And a click. That was the end of the call.

I sat on the edge of my bed for a minute. Then, just like she'd told me to do, I opened my curtains. The sky was blue, and the windows of my apartment were in the right direction to get morning sunshine. I started my coffee, then went to open Twitter to read while it brewed. A pop-up message appeared instead: *Don't read Twitter. Here is a link to the Abelique discussion board community for artists.*

For *artists*?

Oh. Because I'd said I wanted to learn to draw. Well, okay. As I waited for my coffee to finish, I scrolled through a thread full of pictures that other people had made—some painted, some drawn. Charcoal and pastels and watercolor and pen. From the fine-line drawing of a cat in a window to the watercolor painting of a river running through a city, the art was glorious.

Another pop-up message from the app told me to drink my coffee, eat my breakfast, take a shower, and then—with forty minutes to go before I needed to leave for work—to pull out paper, and a pen or pencil, whatever I had around, and draw a picture of a dragon. I stared, exasperated, at that instruction. I had said I wanted to *learn* how to draw, not that I *knew* how to draw.

It doesn't have to be a good picture, the app added.

Grumbling to myself, I drew a very bad picture of a dragon, and then, again at the prompting of the app, took a picture of it to upload. *Bring your bus card*, the app said. *Also an umbrella and a lightweight jacket, because it's going to rain.*

As I walked from the bus stop to my office, my phone rang again. I answered. "Hi, Linnea," said a new voice. Again: hesitant. The fact that no one else seemed to *want* to make these phone calls made the whole thing both more weird, and less weird. It was weird they were doing it. But obviously, my suspicion of phones did not make me an outlier. "This is Yasmin with a very quick call to welcome you to the community of artists."

This felt like a lot. *A community of artists?* "I think I might have made a mistake," I blurted out.

"Yes, that's why we call," she said. "Lots of people say that. You didn't make a mistake. Do you want to make cool things? Is that something you aspire to do?"

"I mean, doesn't everyone?" I said. It was starting to rain. I pulled out my umbrella.

"No, some people aren't that interested in making things, actually. But it sounds like you are."

"Yes," I said.

"Then you belong with us," she said. "We'll support you. I loved your dragon, by the way."

I flushed. "It looked like something drawn by a ten-year-old."

"How old were you when you stopped drawing for fun? Were you about ten?"

"...yes."

"Well, so, you haven't lost any skills. You'll get better. Welcome to the community."

It's weird how many tiny decisions you make in a day.

I started to notice this because the app was making a whole lot of them for me.

What to wear. What to make for breakfast. It presented me with a whole entire grocery list and meal plan, which made me nervous that I was going to be blithely instructed to spend twice as much at the grocery store as I usually did, but the final bill was the same as most weekly trips, so fine, I'd give the app's meal plan a try. It got me out the door early enough to take the bus instead of driving, which saved me money on parking and built a walk into my daily routine.

And drawing practice! Daily drawing practice. After a week of taking the bus instead of driving, the app sent me to an art store with another shopping list, and I came home with a fat sketchbook and a roll of pencils paid for with the exact amount I'd saved by taking the bus. It quickly had me put everything to use drawing the bouquet of flowers it had added to my grocery cart.

I could see why people liked this app. Even if it was a little unnerving that it seemed to know my grocery budget.

Instead of scrolling Twitter, now I was scrolling pictures of other people's work in the art community. Quick sketches of houseplants in the sunshine, done in charcoal or soft pencil, the shadows dark under them. A fanciful drawing of a cat-mermaid done in colored pencil. A watercolor rendition of a city street, the distant buildings fading like haze into a purple sky. I drew my daily assignment—flowers, shadows, the view from my window, another dragon—and posted them faithfully even though it felt like everyone else's work was miles better.

I'd never taken art in high school because my parents thought extra science would give me a boost when I got to college and I should think about my future. Then I never took any art in college because college costs a lot of money and I should focus on classes that would be practical. Now I was in a "good job," which meant it offered health insurance and paid enough for me to afford rent and student loan payments, and maybe if I stuck with it, someday I'd make enough to afford a house.

I *liked* drawing, I realized. It had been fun when I was a kid. Why had I ever given it up?

Two weeks after I started using Abelique, it added me to the phone tree: now instead of just getting calls, I also sometimes had to make them. The first time, it was a "good morning" call, and I'd have stared at the screen procrastinating except for the knowledge that I might be someone's *actual alarm clock*, so I'd better actually do this. I didn't have to punch in the numbers: Abelique did that for me, as well as activating the speakerphone feature so that I could see what the app wanted me to say. The phone rang twice, and someone picked up. "Hello," said a groggy voice at the other end.

"Hi," I said. "This is your good morning phone call." More information was scrolling up the screen. "Abelique would like you to remember that you have a dentist appointment in an hour, so don't head to work, you need to go to the dentist today."

A faint laugh. "Right. Okay. Thanks." And that was it. Over before I even *really* felt nervous. And either Abelique users were all very polite, or the app was routing me to the easier calls since I was new at this. Everyone I called with a reminder (it's time to get up, it's time to go to bed, it's time to go for a walk, have you showered today?) said thank you and usually did whatever it was. (I got a little notification so I knew my reminders had done some good.)

Thirty days in, it was time to start paying for the app, which is when I discovered the payment was not something straightforward like $30/month. No: the app simply rounded up payments to the nearest dollar, so $3.95 became $4, or $58.51 became $59, and the app took that extra money. (On the other hand, if you were paying $1.25 for something, it rounded that up to $2 and sent the extra 75 cents into your own savings account.) I decided that I was getting enough value out of the app that it was worth it, and clicked the consent button.

"Isn't it great?" That was June's reaction. She was still wildly enthusiastic about Abelique. Also still playing Wordle.

"Good job. I'm glad you showed some open-mindedness about this," said my boss, and I nodded enthusiastically and pretended it was making me more productive even though I'd gotten an actual phone call the previous day at 5:10 p.m. from someone who said, "You know, your job doesn't love you back. You should go home. If you stay late again, you might not have the energy to make dinner, and your dinner tonight is supposed to be salade niçoise, which is delicious. That's not Abelique's opinion, that's mine, I had it yesterday."

"You've joined a cult," said Margo.

"I feel like a cult would have a *belief system* or something," I said. "I mean no one's told me to stop taking my antidepressants—they sent me a reminder to pick up my refill yesterday, in fact. No one's trying to get me to worship the Great Old Ones or recruit a downline."

"June recruited you!"

"No, my boss leaned on me."

"So it's a *capitalist* cult. Like that book about the mice. Be a good little corporate drone."

"No, here's the thing," I said. "It really, *really* isn't." Margo started to say something skeptical, but I kept going. "Today when I left for lunch, the app sent me a note saying that Keith was going to be at an off-site meeting for the rest of the afternoon so I should take a leisurely lunch and go for a walk and maybe practice drawing for fifteen minutes before getting back to my desk. It's like if Reddit Antiwork ran a productivity app."

That was the first thing that really startled Margo. She sat back and didn't say anything for a while—just sipped her iced tea and listened to June and me as we talked about a date June went on last weekend. (One domain Abelique stayed out of was romance. It was emphatically not a dating app.) "I wonder who runs it," Margo said, finally.

Neither June nor I knew.

"I'm going to find out," Margo said. "Maybe I can sell an article about it."

"I thought you said..."

"I know," Margo said. "But I'm *curious*."

Not that I wanted to beat Margo to the punch with an article or anything, but I did start to wonder who was behind Abelique. The Wikipedia article referred to them as a "pseudonymous collective" and a number of other online sources called them a *shadowy* pseudonymous collective. I found an enormous Reddit thread in which people proposed that this might be secretly run by Apple, the Scientologists, the Chinese government, the Illuminati, and the Mattress Firm corporation, although the person suggesting that last one had come up with it because a friend of theirs had been instructed to buy a new mattress, and they admitted that this was probably because this friend was using a thirty-year-old mattress that was not only bad for their back but making them wheeze from all the accumulated dust, and also they didn't buy their replacement mattress from Mattress Firm.

The weirdest thing I found out from that thread was that apparently, if you'd been keeping up with your commitments—making phone calls, doing errands as instructed—the app didn't just take your money, it would *give* you money. Someone had quit her job because the app told her to—that seemed pretty extreme and maybe actually cult-like—and the app had gone on to issue her enough money to cover necessities. "It's a mutual aid app," she said in the Reddit thread. This resulted in a bunch of other stories, from small gifts like coffee cards in a rough week to several other people who'd quit jobs, either because the app encouraged them directly or because they'd tried leaving on time (like the app always told you to do) and gotten fired—all of whom had their bills paid by the app until they could find a new job.

The weirdest thing of all I found was a separate discussion thread of the "Abelique productivity app" among a group of managers who all said it had made their employees more productive and that you should definitely offer bonuses to people who used it.

I sent Margo an email with my findings. I had to admit that she was not wrong: this was weird.

It was about a month later that Keith dropped by my desk with a worried look.

"I just got a security bulletin with some serious concerns about that app I recommended," he said. "You should probably uninstall it. Here's some information about wiping it from your phone."

"Oh?" I said. "Well, that's worrying. I'll go do that right away."

The article highlighted the privacy concerns about Abelique, which were, in fact, *valid*. The app had started out snooping through my online life but over time had instructed me to add more and more stuff—this week's new feature was that if you took a short video of your closet, you'd get more specific outfit instructions, using all the stuff you owned but never wore because you just never thought to put it on. This feature was going to take some time to fully update, because the "feature" was in fact "other people, but good at clothes," who were going to look at your stuff and make recommendations. Anyway, when an app wants access to your literal closet—to say that's a *privacy concern* is maybe an understatement. But I very much doubted Keith was actually worried about my privacy. I was pretty sure word was getting out that this app was encouraging people not to spend their whole life at the office.

I checked the community and it wasn't just me: people's bosses had suddenly swung from "everyone should use Abelique" to "no one should be using Abelique, it's *dangerous*" in the blink of an eye.

"No worries," someone said, and passed along a bunch of options, including a whole fakeout app that was Abelique but with a different icon in case your boss insisted on checking your phone. I swapped over to an alternate icon that said it was a menstrual-cycle-tracking app, which would basically be the Keith equivalent of Kryptonite. He would *definitely* not look any closer. Then I grabbed a blank notebook and a drawing pencil, because we had a big department meeting, and one of the great things about sketching in meetings is that unless someone looks right over your shoulder, you're indistinguishable from someone who is diligently taking notes.

Keith's worries were the start of a trend.

The "security bulletin" was followed by a series of increasingly paranoid news stories. None of them had figured out who was running it, and all of them used the adjective "shadowy" because that sounds like *maybe monsters*. Several of the articles included profiles of app users, which could have been fine, but one of them picked a formerly incarcerated person who was struggling with sobriety and found the app helpful because he'd become so reliant on an imposed routine while in prison. Another picked a woman who talked about how the app helped her "tune in to the vibrations of the universe"; the third presented an awkward composite rather than an actual human being. In other words, all those articles said, this app was for *losers*.

New sign-ups screeched to a halt.

"Is anyone worried?" I asked in a thread on the artist board. "I don't want to lose this community."

"Every online community has an expiration date," someone said.

That was not reassuring! I'd hoped for someone to say that this one would stick around, in some form.

And possibly the "shadowy collective" was thinking the same thing, because it started steering me to in-person meetups of other Abelique users. We met at coffee shops and parks and swapped phone numbers so that if the app *did* go away, we could at least keep in touch. We also swapped materials: I'd tried a box of pastels but hated the way the dust got on my fingers, so I handed those off to someone who was eager to try them. Someone else asked, "Are you Linnea?" and handed me a compact travel watercolor set. "These are supposed to go to you," she said.

I laughed ruefully. The app had tried twice to get me to buy watercolors when I went back to the art store. I kept buying more colored pencils, instead. Watercolor was *scary*. "Why is the app so *determined* to get me to do watercolor?" I asked.

"You're probably looking at other people's watercolors a lot," said the person handing me the set. "Anyway, this is yours now, take it home and try it out."

I woke up the next morning, opened my blinds, started coffee, and sat down with the watercolors and the latest bouquet of flowers. Not surprisingly, all the colors ran together and left me with a mishmash, although it was kind of pretty in its own messy way. I took a picture and put it on the day's art thread. "You should check the news," said a pinned note at the top.

Overnight, the news coverage of Abelique had shifted. This time, it was because of Margo.

Abelique was run by an AI, built and run by a lab at Temple University in Philadelphia. The computer scientists at Temple had built the app and given the AI the goal of making people happier...and then just watched to see what happened.

Margo had gotten her answers and sold a four-part series to a national newspaper for enough money that when we arrived at the diner the day that first article dropped, she told the rest of us it was her treat.

We sat down at our table and June leaned forward. "Here's what I don't get," she said. "You can't just tell an AI to *make people happy*. They must have given it more specific instructions than that."

"Well, there's lots of research out there," Margo said. "Like, we know people are happier if they spend time outside and get enough sleep. So it started with that, but then tracked how much various interventions helped, in order to improve the app."

I adjusted the yellow scarf the app had told me to wear this morning. "I wonder if bright colors are supposed to improve mood."

"I interviewed one of the programmers," Margo said. "And I specifically asked about the wardrobe feature. Their finding so far is that it's not about color but about wearing items you think of as 'special.' Also, people who buy things and never wear them feel sort of guilty every time they look in their closet. Being reminded to wear some of the stuff you've bought in the past makes you feel better about yourself and your purchases. Also, you're less likely to go buy more stuff."

"They've had me wear a whole lot of bright colors."

"That's because you clearly like bright colors since you've got a ton of bright stuff in your closet. I actually could have told you that, Linnea. Every time we go shopping for something, you buy stuff that's like—*bright orange* or yellow or red. And then you go back to wearing earth tones." June nodded along.

"Okay," I said, feeling suddenly self-conscious. "But it wasn't the AI who looked through my closet pics, it was another member of the community."

"Yeah," Margo said. "That's probably their *biggest* finding—people are happier when they have a community. Which I'd say we already knew, *honestly*, but people are always impressed when science tells them something that we already knew."

I thought about this as I ate my lunch. Of course people are happier when they have a community, but this community was overseen and structured in ways that a lot of communities aren't. We were given tasks, from the phone tree to a recent assignment I'd had to draw an octopus for someone with a small child who really liked octopodes. I don't like going to the post office, so I'd handed it off to someone on the train and they mailed it for me.

An Audacious Experiment in Human Happiness was one of the big pull-quotes from Margo's series. It was how one of the researchers had described it. The professors running the project had refused to speak to her, but she'd found a former graduate student willing to dish (and this person gave great quotes, like the "audacious experiment" one). The article kind of glossed over the ethics involved, but the former grad student emphasized that the question they always asked was, "which of two good things makes people *happier*" and not "can we make people unhappy." "We already know how to make people unhappy," she said. "Just look around you."

Everything Abelique had told me to do suddenly made sense. Research showed that people were happier making fewer decisions, spending time outside, driving less, and spending less time on traditional social media. So the app gave me a weekly menu, sent me for walks, told me to take the train, and pestered me to read books instead of Twitter.

Interest in Abelique surged again, but something about knowing how all of it worked took some of the magic of the site away. More importantly, though—other people started finding ways to circumvent the rules. People started joining the app to try to sell us their multi-level-marketing schemes. Food threads started attracting posts about meal-replacement drinks, and it was quickly clear that someone was getting a payout for new customers of these gross fake shakes. One morning, my wake-up call was audio spam instead of a human voice, and that was it. I didn't remove the app, but I started ignoring my wake-up call and my go-to-bed text, which fortunately meant the app didn't try to make me do the phone tree. The less you used it, the less the app asked of you. In my free time in the evenings, I started binge-watching reality TV.

Then one afternoon I got a text. For a second I thought it was Abelique, but no: I took a closer look and I realized it was one of the people I'd met at a park, during those weeks when we thought the app was going to get shut down. One of the other artists.

Would you meet me again, the text asked. *It's supposed to be nice this weekend and I miss painting.*

I glanced over at my pencils, which were actually gathering dust. *Did the app put you up to this?* I texted back.

No, came the response. *I just miss doing art. Don't you?*

I looked at my pencils again. For the last month, looking at them had made me feel guilty, so I'd gotten into the habit of looking anywhere else. Twice, I'd almost put them away entirely. But I *did* miss drawing. I missed it a lot.

I'll meet you, I texted back.

I sharpened my pencils, and pulled the watercolor brushes out of the drawer. My sketch pads were lined up in a neat row, and I paged through each. It had been long enough since I'd looked at them that I could see the things that were good, instead of just the things that were bad. The curl of the octopus tentacle on the sketches I'd made prior to that drawing I'd sent off as a gift. The light and shadow in that sketch of my kitchen that I'd somehow gotten just right. That watercolor painting of the bouquet that had filled me with frustration now looked *amazing*, in its own messy, beautiful way. I gently pulled that painting out of the sketch book and put it up on the fridge so I could look at it. Why had I stopped buying myself flowers? Did I need an app to *tell* me to buy myself flowers?

I met up with Kristin at the park. She was younger than me. "I haven't used the app in months," I confessed.

"Me, either," she said. "I got tired of being told what to wear and what to eat."

"Let's walk around and find something we want to paint?" I said.

We walked through the park side by side, looking for something beautiful. The thing about setting out with a drawing pad and the intention to make art is that I notice so many things: the shadows cast by the tree leaves, the tiny wild violets growing in the shade, the curve of a bird's flight through the air. We made our way to a fountain with flower plantings in big pots around the edge. There were four other people there when we arrived, with drawing pads and pencils, or little travel palettes of watercolors. Two of them looked up and smiled as we joined them. I sat down in the grass and started working.

Next to me was an older woman with a very cheap drawing pad and a pack of crayons. She caught me looking at her drawing and flushed. "I'm sorry," she said. "Is this a club? Because I'm not a member and I don't want to take anyone's spot."

"It's not a club," I said. "And if you're here to draw, you belong, anyway." I pulled out my watercolors and the travel cup of water, and handed her a sheet of paper and one of my brushes. "You know what? Let's both try something new."

....

Naomi Kritzer is a science fiction and fantasy writer from St. Paul, Minnesota. Her fiction has won the Hugo Award, the Nebula Award, the Edgar Award, and the Minnesota Book Award. She has a spouse, two grown kids and three cats (the number of cats is subject to change without notice). You can find Naomi online at naomikritzer. com or on Bluesky as @naomikritzer.bsky.social.

THE SOUND OF CHILDREN SCREAMING

Rachael K. Jones

THE GUN

You know the one about the Gun. The Gun goes where it wants to. On Thursday morning just after recess, the Gun will walk through the front doors of Thurman Elementary, and it won't sign in at the front office or wear a visitor's badge.

The Gun does most of its damage in the first five minutes. The Gun doesn't care about lockdown drills, and it will not wait for the SWAT team to arrive. The Gun can chew through a door, a desk, a cinderblock wall, and kids don't wear those bulletproof backpacks during reading time.

Everyone has a right to a gun. Nothing can take that away from you. What you lack is a right to the lives of your children.

The Gun likes a game of hide-and-seek. The Gun will rove the grounds until someone stops it. The Gun has been here many times before.

The Gun is not working alone.

THE SHOOTER

He is never anyone special. Just a man exercising his right to a gun.

THE TEACHER

Michelle Dalton has taught fourth grade for nine years, long enough to know how the job yawns wider each year, collecting all the loose threads that society needs done but no one wants to pay for. Michelle has six figures in student loans and makes less than $50,000 a year. She shares a rental house with two roommates and has a weekend job at Trek & Field selling athletic shoes to make ends meet. She does not get paid overtime, and the school district does not buy the art supplies. She is not entitled to bathroom breaks or a nonworking lunch, and she doesn't get paid for summers.

Michelle wears the armor of an elementary school teacher: an A-line dress in an ocean print, a blue cardigan to match. She bears no weapon but a sharp-edged teacher's tongue that cuts through noise like scissors.

Every teacher in Thurman Elementary will sense the Gun moments before it opens fire as a tense, drawn-out pause, an upset child drawing the breath to scream. They will not visibly panic, not with twenty-one pairs of eyes locked upon them for guidance. Michelle's body will act before her mind comprehends the threat.

It is Michelle's job to keep her students safe, just as it is her job to take the blame for whatever harm the Gun inflicts in the process.

THE PORTAL

You know about the Portal too, although not by that name. The Portal seeks the places where children hide. It stalked the air raid shelters in London during the Blitz. It lurked in underground cellars during the Cold War, crouched between the canned corn and rancid Crisco. It has fed itself in Italian orphanages and Australian residential schools, and it has only gotten hungrier.

The Portal has been exhibiting itself at gun shows recently, a gleaming bullet-proof vault in which to store kids when the shooter comes. The Portal has been installed in every classroom, funded by bake sales and cereal box tops, bought at the expense of pencils and math books and a music teacher.

The Portal is not wheelchair-accessible. The Portal is a failure of policy. The Portal was dressed up like a castle for Halloween. The Portal is not a reading nook.

There is nothing more necessary than the Portal. The Portal will keep the right children safe.

Whatever the Gun doesn't claim will get packed into the Portal like coats at the Lost and Found. The school has a ritual for it, a special alarm. The children, sensing something wrong in the *pop-pop-pop* coming from the gym, will obey uncomplainingly when Michelle shoos them in. Michelle will enter last, pulling the door shut behind them.

The Portal is dark and humid inside. There are no windows or lights to attract attention. It is the gap beneath the bed where the monsters hunt. The Portal's breath presses in around them, hot and stinking, as it swallows them down, down, down.

Time doesn't stop inside the Portal. It telescopes. The children strain their ears, listening for the classroom door. The popping sounds are approaching now. *Pop* and it passes the fourth grade art wall, *pop-pop-pop* at the water fountain, *pop* beside the mural of Rosa Parks, *pop-pop* and it has reached Ms. Dalton's door. The siren continues its wail. Someone is sobbing in the dark. Someone has to pee. Someone refused to hug his mom goodbye at dropoff today, and might never get the chance again.

When the Portal door opens, the Gun will be waiting.

But the children will not be in their classroom anymore.

THE MOUSE

Not like the mice that infest Thurman Elementary over the winter break. Not the wild ones that chew through the corners of the fun-size cracker bags, leaving cellophane confetti in the snack bin. Not like the class mouse, tame in her cage with soft white fur and blood-red eyes, who holds out her little paws to accept a sandwich crust.

This mouse has a gun: a copper blunderbuss with the end belled out like something out of Looney Tunes. His name is Sir Miles, and he has been hunting. He grooms the blood from between his claws like sticky jam as he considers the newcomers, a teacher and her eight students lined up like chessboard pawns.

It is his move.

He is quite large for a mouse, nearly knee-high. He makes a sweeping bow with his tricorn hat as he introduces himself. His accent is a lilting brogue. He has perfect manners and rides a Shetland pony. His charm, too, is a weapon, subtle and efficient, as he makes a plea that sounds a little too rehearsed, a flimflam man working over his newest marks.

He demands the things men with guns always demand. He asks for someone else to fight his wars. His people rely on a steady supply of children from the World Beyond who are kindhearted or brave or foolish enough to take up the magic crowns and wield the spells to make Sir Miles's enemies dead. He is very persuasive. His eyes shine with tears, and he clasps his little paws as he pleads his case. The children, dazed in this strange new world, tear-streaked and shaken after the Portal's darkness, are mesmerized.

Mice are crepuscular, creatures of shadow and hidden intentions. They creep from their dens at sunset and feed all night long. They are averse to bright lights. Mice eat their own feces but lack the ability to vomit.

Sir Miles is full of shit. But he means business.

THE NEGOTIATION

Michelle also means business.

She isn't fooled by this Narnia shit, the soft black eyes or the twee little jacket. She doesn't trust a mouse with a gun. Anyone in possession of a gun has made a plan to use it.

But Dylan needs to pee, and Katie R. and Katie V. are sharing a coat in the drizzle, and it's almost time for lunch and they'll all need to eat. The kids are already eyeing the mouse like they'd like nothing better than to bury their faces in his warm, soft fur, and it's only getting worse as he unspools his sob story, his oil-drop eyes large with crocodile tears. If Michelle doesn't take charge, she'll lose control entirely.

"I'm sorry for your troubles, but we're not getting involved in your war," she says sharply, cutting off the mouse mid-sales pitch. The rain is steadily increasing its barrage, snapping against the shale like fireworks. "Is there somewhere we can go to wait out the storm?"

The mouse, steel-eyed, mounts his Shetland pony, settling in front of the corpse of the furred thing he just killed. He gives Michelle an unambiguous look of hate, like he has just spotted a particularly odious vermin. "Follow along," he says, and that predatory look submerges beneath his charm. "Castle Rowland is just beyond the rise."

Sir Miles keeps up a steady patter, dangling his problems like a pair of keys before a grabby toddler. Michelle knows his type, men who force you into a shared predicament to short circuit what your uneasy gut is screaming.

What did he kill just before they arrived, and why did he use his hands when he had a gun?

Michelle doesn't take her eyes off that gun as they follow the path behind the mouse. Everything in this world pierces. The dreary pines stab up at the gray sky, and the rain tattoos through her knit cardigan. She makes the children pair up and hold hands like they're making a bathroom trip.

Blood runs down the pony's hind leg, leaving sticky, dark hoofprints.

Michelle does not look back at the Portal. She keeps her eyes on the gun.

CASTLE ROWLAND

Every mouse on the parapets is armed.

The castle's walls are tall and pockmarked, and not one green thing grows in its courtyards. The mice have lined up gunnysacks for target practice. The volleys of gunfire blend with the pattering rain.

The idea of a castle is to protect the things you love by walling them in and daring your enemies to take them. A castle, like a school, is a locked-up box for precious things. Because of this property, castles were once the sites of war, and their names evoked the bloodshed. *Scarborough, Dover, Prudhoe, Kenilworth.*

In the distant future, castles will cease to be a symbol of war when governments find more civilized ways to regulate what one person can take from another. Children will enter castles with delight when they have never learned to fear them.

Children will learn to fear their schools, though. The names will come to stand for another kind of warfare, the sites of battles waged and lost without the benefit of soldiers or a moat. *Columbine, Sandy Hook, Marjory Stoneman Douglas, Robb.*

THE POND

Castle Rowland also has a pond, long and low, graveled around its edges with strange ivory pebbles, jagged as teeth. The water shimmers in the rain as though it has swallowed down the sun.

The children want to get a better look, but Sir Miles hurries them along.

OTHER PEOPLE'S CHILDREN

Only eight came through the Portal. They are Li and Dylan and Nathan and Katie R. and Katie V. and Nevaeh and Caleb and Angelo. Most of them are nine years old, except for Katie V., who turned ten in September.

The other thirteen kids in Michelle's class—*the lucky ones*—yes, call them that—are still hiding in that dark closet, listening to the slamming doors, the pleading sobs of teachers, the shrieks of first-graders trapped in the bathroom, and then *pop-pop-pop*—the chalk-white silence left in the Gun's wake.

THE FEAST

The grand hall is smoky and low, and a roast much too big to be poultry turns on the spit. Portraits loom over the long refectory tables, paintings of human children, regal in velvet and bone-white crowns, their mouths turned down, somber and thoughtful.

Servant-mice in pale blue smocks scurry down the table rows and ply the children with delicacies. Katie V. gets a whole cake to herself, and Nathan eats lemon sorbet from a silver dish. It has been a very long walk, and they are too ravenous to resist. Even Michelle accepts a bowl of soup, though she dislikes the way that the mice seem prepared for their surprise guests. Like it was scheduled weeks ago, and everyone has rehearsed their roles.

As the mice shoo the humans from the table, they file past the roast. A feline skull leers back at Michelle, the clawed, furry paws still attached to the leg-bones.

THE PORTRAITS

None of the children in the portraits seem to make it past their teenage years. When Michelle asks Sir Miles about this, his whiskers twitch into a needle-toothed grin. "The magic of the crowns isn't for adults. Only children can wield them."

When she asks what happens when the children grow up, the mouse just laughs her off. "We send them home, naturally," he booms. "What else would we do? *Eat* them?"

AN INTERLUDE

Michelle cannot sleep that night. The eight sleeping children sigh and hum around the room—the girls tucked into the grand four-poster bed, the boys burritoed in blankets on the rug before the crackling fireplace, and Michelle against the door to watch for intruders.

Castle Rowland feels more real than what happened to them at the school today. The alarm sounding, the *pop-pop-pop* in the hallway, the sobbing in the dark.

At that moment, instead of her family, Michelle had found herself thinking of her weekend job. How they had no protocol at Trek & Field for what to do if someone opened fire.

This strange castle, with its mice and portraits and ivory pond, has a logic stronger than the laws of reality. All her life, Michelle had thought she knew what she would do if the Gun came to her school, but the Gun doesn't care about the stories people tell themselves in their own heads.

A NOTE ABOUT SCHOOL SAFETY

We will not try to prevent the Gun. The Gun will accept no limitations. But we will try very hard not to offend the Gun. If you offend the Gun, it may decide to get personal.

Better to develop rituals against the Gun, to train the kids to block the door, hide in the closet, play dead on the rainbow carpet where they do calendar time and sing the morning song. Better to invest in metal detectors. Better to ring the playground with barbed wire, to hire off-duty police instead of another counselor.

You can have a special alarm for the Gun. You can make the teachers draw the blinds, lock the doors, take the long route every day to recess in the name of safety.

It doesn't matter if any of it works. The important thing is to have something to blame besides the Gun. Best to treat the Gun as a force of nature, rare as an earthquake, a freak tornado. Best to accept the Gun. It belongs here. It belongs everywhere. The Gun will always be with us.

If you try hard enough, maybe you can convince the Gun to shoot someone else's kid instead.

THE TOUR

"Perhaps the children would enjoy a tour of Castle Rowland," Sir Miles suggests at breakfast. "Unless you would prefer that I return you to your Portal?"

It is a threat, and Michelle knows it. This world exists in a moment suspended in time, the instant between breaths, with the Gun on the other side of the classroom door.

Nothing could be more dangerous than returning home, not even these predatory mice with their blunderbusses and their feud with the neighboring kingdom.

But then Sir Miles shows them the armory.

THE ARMORY

Gun racks hold row after row of blunderbusses, flintlocks, swords, and crossbows, sharp as a buckthorn thicket in winter. The children race through the rows of oiled metal, spitting out the gunpowder tang in their mouths and noses, until they find the eight glass cases at the back.

In each case rests a chalk-white crown. Their delicacy fascinates Michelle, like anatomical drawings of bird skeletons. The glass casing lifts off easily. When she picks up a crown, it has a soft texture like soapstone, only lighter. It is constructed from many fragments fitted together and polished smooth, except for some top bits that jut up, raw as broken teeth.

Angelo has taken a crown into his hands. His eyes slingshot between Sir Miles and Michelle, seeking their permission. "Can I, Ms. Dalton?"

"Go on," Sir Miles encourages him. "Give it a try."

"Angelo, wait—!" Michelle begins, fear gripping her voice so it squeaks.

But Angelo has already donned the crown. It fits like it was made for him. He stands a little taller, acclimating to the kingliness settling upon his shoulders.

"It's true!" Angelo shouts, his brown eyes bright and happy. "It's really magic! I can feel it!" He lifts his hands, and to Michelle's horror, a dozen swords rise up from their racks like a cloud of startled pigeons.

POWERS

Every teacher knows the moment when they lose control of their classroom, and it usually begins with exuberance. Once, on a Friday before a long weekend, Katie V.'s dad brought in birthday cupcakes, half chocolate and half vanilla. It was raining, and nobody had been out for recess, and everyone wanted vanilla but there weren't enough to go around. Then Katie V. started crying because she didn't get the kind she wanted on her birthday, and Dylan squashed the unwanted cupcake on the floor, and then full-on chaos broke out, the kind that could only be stopped by flickering the light switch and making threats to cancel the afternoon movie.

The crowns are like those cupcakes. Every child grabs one despite Michelle's attempts to stop them, and then there are a series of close calls when the swords and guns go clattering through the air, nearly beheading Caleb, who decides to retaliate. They call down fire and shadow. They scorch the stone walls black. Nevaeh freezes the air, pulling snow down inside the armory, and the other children run around catching snowflakes on their tongues.

Finally Sir Miles leads the children out to the courtyard, and Michelle follows behind, defeated and impotent, her voice hoarse, her right temple throbbing in the telltale sign of a migraine.

Michelle doesn't blame them. She understands the source of their joy. Children rarely get to feel so powerful. Children spend their days being told what to do and where to go. They don't get to decide how they dress or what they eat. They aren't allowed to get angry or to dislike anyone, and if an aunt or grandpa wants a hug, the child will have to give it.

Children only hold power in their games, which is why they make up superheroes. They play at telekinesis and pyrokinesis and mind reading. Children use swings to learn to fly, or they use sticks as makeshift wands. But now that power is real.

"That's enough," Michelle tells Angelo as he sets a row of gunnysacks on fire. "Let's go inside and have a break now."

Gentle Angelo, who always volunteers to collect all the basketballs after recess, who always holds the door as they file out to the buses after school, glares up at Michelle. "You can't make me," he says.

He is right.

When some children grow up, they will buy themselves a gun so no one else can ever make them feel small again. They will not try to change how adults make children feel.

THE TRUTH

The refectory tables have been removed from the Great Hall for the occasion. The mice crowd in for the coronation, hundreds of them, packing the castle. Although they only rise to Michelle's knees, they force her apart from the children through sheer numbers, pushing her out, cutting her off, until she stands alone in the courtyard, the door to the hall slammed in her face.

It is gray and raining. Alone, Michelle wanders the grounds as the guard-mice eye her with open hostility. *What do they do when the children grow up?* But Michelle is already grown. The mice have no use for her now that they have pried her away from her students.

She finds herself drawn to the glimmering ivory pool and its sunlit glow in the dreary rain. Her shoes crunch on the strange, pointed gravel. The water swarms with koi, and beneath them, mounded like coral, are human skeletons, too many to count, ribcages and skulls and long, slim femurs buried in the finer knobbles of knucklebones and teeth. The fish nibble at bits of connective tissue clinging to the fresher skeletons. Some of the bones are broken, as though sawed open to lick out the marrow.

None of this surprises Michelle. She knew from the moment she held that crown, its soapstone texture, its unusually light weight. The bones of children fused together and polished smooth, a vessel for their collective power once they grew too old to be of other use, handed down to their successors to wield in turn.

The last of Michelle's hope slips away as she gazes into the pool. Her students' fate is a tale of two deaths. One at the hands of the mice, who have no love for these children beyond their utility in war. And the other through the Portal where the Gun awaits, rattling the classroom doorknob. Become the weapon, or its victim. Either way, they die.

And if they stay? If they flee? Who will wear those crowns next? Which classroom will the Gun seek out instead?

Someone will have to die. There is no one coming to help her. No one will stop the mice, the shooter, the cycle that returns them to this point, this pond, these children's bodies and their wordless accusation.

Teachers have always been left alone, dancing around the Gun, the Portal, the crowns of bone, trying to keep other people's children safe with donated art supplies and cardboard tubes saved up for Craft Day.

One thing is certain: Michelle will never tell her students about the bones. No child deserves to know how little the world regards them.

But there are other weapons she can give her students. Truths as powerful as any magic crown.

AGENCY

Into the Great Hall, then. Into the castle, where the mice are piping military tunes on ivory flutes as Sir Miles gives a speech. Michelle plunges into the thick of the cheering mice, forcing a path, though they scratch and tear at her legs and rip her dress to tatters. All those blunderbusses tip down and track her, the bells of deadly trumpets, as she approaches the dais, the eight little thrones, the children unrecognizably regal in rich, furred cloaks sewn from the dappled hides of calico cats.

"Wait," Michelle cries out in her sharp teacher's voice, projecting over the din. "Wait a moment. I have something to say."

Sir Miles stabs a clawed finger at Michelle, harpooning her with accusations. "See, your Majesties? Even now, she plots to depose you, to deprive you of your crowns. Strike her down with your power, or else give the command, and our soldiers will ensure she never troubles your reign again."

All eight faces turn to consider Michelle, frowning in displeasure. But she is no longer afraid. Unlike the mice, she loves these children. She bears the kind of love for them you can only have for children not your own, children freely given into your care day after day in the trust that you will return them back again, imperceptibly older, until eventually they become old enough to live on their own.

And from that place, Michelle speaks to her students like she always has, giving them the knowledge of their own power and the strength to use it.

"Those crowns belong to you," she tells her students. "Sir Miles is right about that. I won't ask you to give them back. But you have a choice now. You can fight for the mice in their war if you want. Or we could go back home and help your friends. The choice is yours. Whatever you choose, I will help you."

Sir Miles laughs, and the other mice echo him, certain in their victory. They have been plying these children with gifts and sweets and flattery, and don't believe dowdy, buttoned-up Michelle can offer anything equally tempting. The children have been growing irritable during her speech, their faces pinched and unhappy. Li stands up. Nevaeh twitches her cloak aside to bare her hands.

"I know you'll make the right choice," Michelle tells them. "Whatever you do, Ms. Dalton loves you."

Michelle stares into the gun barrels trained upon her. Nathan glowers down at the crowd. Katie R. has flushed the deep red that foretells a tantrum, and Nevaeh raises her hands. Michelle closes her eyes, giving herself to their judgment.

All eight children begin to scream.

And the sun answers.

BRIGHT LIGHTS

The sun sheds her gray robes and steps down into the Great Hall.

The heat is incredible. The blunderbusses bloom like daffodils and drop their seeds in molten pools of brass. All the shadows burn away. In the courtyard, the bone-pool hisses and steams as it boils off.

Mice cannot tolerate bright lights, nor can anything that has made a habit of feeding on children. The air is hazy with the char of singed fur.

Michelle should be charred too, but the eight children run to her and throw their arms around her waist, just like when the dismissal bell rings and they don't want to say goodbye.

HOW IT ENDS

There is no happy ending when the Gun visits a school. Even if it takes no lives, it will rob every child and adult of the bone-thin illusion that bad things only happen to other people's children, those who prepared less, prevented less, who failed to hire enough cops or install enough bulletproof glass, who didn't run the backpacks through the metal detectors, people who deserved it somehow, who left a door propped open or a fence unrepaired. They will go to bed that night numb inside, neither scared nor angry, because it feels like slipping through a portal to a world where your hometown has become the legal hunting ground of angry men, and no one thought to warn you. Later, they will feel guilt and intense shame, like they should have done something differently, like they should have known the rules had changed that day and prepared accordingly, like they forgot their jacket when everyone knew it would rain.

The truth is that the Portal has been growing, fed by the Gun meal by meal, and it will swallow and swallow until every school lies in its belly slowly digesting in a glimmering pool of children's bones, until someone decides to stop it.

Michelle plunges through the Portal, the children lined up behind her like they're off to art class instead of facing their deaths. The Portal door bursts open upon the classroom at Thurman Elementary just as the doorknob turns, Michelle at the forefront and eight kids in crowns behind her, confronting the Gun with the bones of children, the bitter magic only children have the right to wield, asking the question that answers itself, damning the Gun with their bodies, their flesh, with the sound of children screaming.

....

Rachael K. Jones grew up in various cities across Europe and North America, picked up (and mostly forgot) six languages, and acquired several degrees in the arts and sciences. Now she writes speculative fiction in Portland, Oregon. Rachael is a Eugie Award winner, and a finalist for the Hugo, Nebula, Locus, Bram Stoker, and World Fantasy Award. Her fiction has appeared in dozens of venues worldwide, including *Lightspeed, Beneath Ceaseless Skies, Strange Horizons*, and all four Escape Artists podcasts. Follow her on Bluesky @RachaelKJones.bsky.social, or find her at www. RachaelKJones.com.

NOVELETTES

THE YEAR WITHOUT SUNSHINE

Naomi Kritzer

During one of the much smaller disasters that preceded the really big disaster, I met a lot of my neighbors online. I can't remember if we set up the WhatsApp group because of the pandemic or the civil disorder or both. My Minneapolis block had always been reasonably friendly—people would take their kids around on Halloween, and I knew the names of my next-door neighbors—but everyone on the WhatsApp group got closer.

When the Internet and cell phones went down, my next-door neighbor to the north, Tanesha, built a little booth in her yard out of plywood, with corkboard inside and a roof, and painted WHATSUP on the outside, so people could leave each other messages inside. When I went in the first day to check it out, people were already posting up notes asking to swap stuff—coffee for condoms, cat food for diapers, a bike repair for a plumbing repair. The stores were empty but maybe someone on the block had what you needed.

It was weird, early on, what was still chugging away. The water stayed on, although we had to purify it. The stores nearly always had canned vegetables on the shelves, and everyone joked about how somewhere, there was a secret underground warehouse crammed with canned peas. The pharmacy a few blocks away was still getting regular deliveries of anything designated "critical meds," like insulin, which was a relief to Tanesha. But there were also things that worked some of the time but not all of the time, like the electricity. And there were all these things that were just *gone* from the stores—tampons, AAA batteries, WD-40, duct tape.

I started going over every day around noon to help Tanesha "moderate" the booth, which mostly meant taking down obsolete notes. After two weeks when the Internet still hadn't come back, I helped her build a second booth.

"We should check on people, don't you think?" she said as I held a board in place for her to hammer. "Most of the block is using this, but not everyone."

I hadn't noticed, but she was probably right. Across the street, the screen door banged shut and the old guy who lived there came brusquely across the street. He was holding something that looked sort of like a power drill. "I'm Lem," he told me. "Hold that board you've got right there." Tanesha put down her hammer and the power drill thing turned out to be a nail gun, which made short work of the hammering. "Also, you want me to fix the roof on that other one, so it doesn't drip inside when it rains." He didn't put a question mark on the end, which was fine, because of course we wanted him to fix the roof.

While he worked on this, Tanesha got a clipboard from her house and we made a list of the houses on the block, filling in what we knew about the residents. It was a smattering of names and a lot of phrases like "the people with the poodle" and "the ones with the generator" and "the teenager with the really loud car, although he hasn't driven it since the gas stations all closed."

"Should we split up the houses?" Tanesha said. "You do the east side, I'll do the west side?"

"Okay," I said, feeling the same dragging reluctance I'd felt as a kid selling Girl Scout Cookies—I knew perfectly well lots of people would be happy to see me, but I still hated knocking on doors and talking to strangers. I didn't have a clipboard, so I grabbed a notebook from my house to make notes and walked down to the corner to start.

Probably three-quarters of the people on our block were already using Tanesha's booth. With the remaining quarter, I introduced myself, told them which house I lived in, explained the booth, and then asked how they were doing. Hanging in there? Did they have food and other necessities?

The people with the generator were at mid-block. They lived in a bungalow with faded olive-green siding and a fence. Most of us didn't have generators—we just charged up what we could during hours we had power, made do when we didn't. This house's generator ran during every power outage, even the short ones.

When I knocked, no one answered right away, but I knocked again and waited, and an old white guy answered the door. "I'm Alexis, from down the street," I said. "I'm just checking in with everyone to see if they're okay, given everything, and to let you know about this booth we've got set up..." He stared at me, silently, as I explained the WhatsUp booth.

"Does anyone have propane?" he asked.

"I don't know. Someone might."

"I'll trade anything. Pay anything. You said I should post a sign? Can you post it for me? I can't leave Susan."

"I could post a sign for you, sure."

"Can you wait—no, just come in." He shuffled backwards to let me in the house. I eased the door closed behind me. The entryway had the close, stale air of a house that had taken seriously the instructions to close all the windows to keep out the dust and ash. "I need to find paper and a pen."

"Clifford?" I heard a woman call. "Is someone here? Who is it?"

I followed him into the living room. An elderly woman sat in a recliner. A plastic tube snaked across her face, with prongs in her nose. She didn't look well. "This is Alexis," Clifford told her. "She's going to tell people we need fuel."

"I don't know if anyone has it," I said.

"Oxygen, I can also use bottled oxygen," Susan said.

"People keep propane around. Nobody keeps bottled oxygen around," Clifford said.

"Have you tried the pharmacy for oxygen?" I asked. "They have insulin…"

"Pharmacies don't carry oxygen," he said. "There are places that carry it but we used to get it delivered—I don't even have the phone number—I can't leave Susan and go around the city looking, even if I had a way to get around, she can't get the generator going herself." He pointed at a blue plastic gadget that sat next to her, which rattled like a noisy fan. "Susan has COPD. What we used to call emphysema. She needs supplemental oxygen, so we run an oxygen concentrator. Turns room air into pure oxygen. Concentrator won't run without power, so I fire up the generator every time the power goes out. But we're running out of propane. Don't know what we're going to do when we run out of propane." He patted Susan's hand.

"What if we could find you a rechargeable battery?" I asked.

"Problem is, the oxygen concentrator draws too much power," Clifford said. "Drains batteries too fast."

I crouched down for a closer look, pulling out a flashlight since the room was dim. The concentrator drew less wattage than an air conditioner, but more than a TV. "The only thing that's gotten us this far," Clifford said, "is that I bought the smallest generator they had. It doesn't run our fridge or anything. It *just* runs the oxygen concentrator, and we only run it when the power's out. But even so, we're going to be out of fuel…I don't know exactly how soon. But soon."

"What happens then?"

"I won't live long after that," Susan said.

There was a shrill whistle of the carbon monoxide detector as the power came back, and the lights, air conditioner, and TV all came on simultaneously. "I'm going to shut down the generator," Clifford said, and sprinted out the door.

"Could you be a dear and move over the plug," Susan said to me, pointing at the concentrator.

"Move it where?" I asked, confused.

"Just the plug, to the wall outlet."

The oxygen concentrator cut off—Clifford must have gotten outside to the generator—and almost immediately, Susan's face turned grayish, and she started to gasp like she'd just sprinted four blocks to catch a bus. I looked around, panicked, for the wall outlet. She couldn't even point me, but I spotted it and moved the plug over. Nothing happened. "Did I do it right? Do I need to turn it back on?" Susan managed a nod, and I started hunting around the machine for a button, terrified that I would mess something up if I pressed the wrong thing. Clifford came hurrying back in just as I found the on-off switch. Which was a completely obvious switch that I'd have found immediately if I hadn't been panicking.

"Losing the supplemental oxygen isn't supposed to matter right away," Susan said, once she'd caught her breath. "It's just I get so anxious."

"I don't believe you're just anxious," Clifford said. We sat in silence for a moment. "Anyway," he added. "You can see why we want propane."

I could. I absolutely could. "I'll see what I can do," I said, not feeling very optimistic.

Susan's color was back, and she'd more or less caught her breath. "If you find anyone who has an oxygen concentrator they aren't using, we could use it to fill oxygen tanks," she said. "When the power was on. Give us another backup. I know it's not *very* likely, but someone might have one in their attic."

I nodded.

Susan swatted at Clifford gently with the magazine by her side—a ten-year-old copy of *Smithsonian* magazine—and said, "Can we offer Alexis a cup of coffee now that the power's back?"

"Oh, I couldn't possibly—"

"It's no trouble," Clifford said. "I'll make a pot, you can drink some of it if you have a minute to stay."

That trapped me, because I couldn't let coffee go to waste, not given how scarce *that* was, so I sat down in a plush velour chair while Clifford knocked around in the now-well-lit kitchen. "How long have you lived in the neighborhood?" I asked.

"Oh, forty years, it must be, at this point. You don't have kids, do you?" I shook my head. "Back, oh, early two thousands, I guess, we used to make a haunted house every Halloween and give full-sized candy bars to all the kids who made it to the end. You'd probably have been a kid yourself back then."

"I grew up in Sacramento," I said.

"All the way in California? Oh dear," she said. "Have you heard from your family since all this started?"

"No," I said, "but we weren't really in touch before, so that's not surprising."

"Well, I'm certainly not going to tell you your business," she said. "I was awfully relieved to get a letter from our son down in Kansas, though. We've got a big roll of stamps if you need any."

"I guess I'd take one. I could send them a note just letting them know I'm alive. Even though that's more likely to be a disappointment to them than a relief."

"All the more reason to let them know," she said. "Bring comfort to the kind and dismay to the jerks."

Clifford brought out coffee in three little china teacups. There was a sugar bowl on the tray, but I took my cup without adding any, as did Clifford and Susan. "Thank you," I said.

"I was just telling Alexis about our haunted house," Susan said.

Clifford brightened up and started telling me about this zip line he'd rigged up for ghosts, and Susan told me that in the backyard they'd served hot cider out of a cauldron to parents. "I worked as a costumer at the Guthrie Theater for years," she added. "So my witch costume was first rate."

I laid out my list of doors to knock. "Do you know any of these people?"

About half the houses, they said things like "that's where the Garcias used to live but they moved in, oh, must have been 2012..." but there was one house where Susan said, "oh, that's Jeana's house, she's been all alone since she lost her husband two years ago, can you check on her, too?" I'd already planned to knock, but "hello, your friend Susan asked me to check on you" made it feel less weird.

My tiny cup of coffee was gone, so I set the cup carefully back down on the tray. "I'm going to go post the sign," I said. "Thank you for the coffee. Please let me know if you need anything. I'll try to make sure someone comes by."

I was wrong about no one being willing to sell or trade propane. I netted four of those one-pound Coleman cylinders you attach to a camping stove, plus two partly full 20-pound cylinders like you'd use for a grill. Clifford cried when I knocked on his door with them—this would, he said, keep them running for another 40 or 50 hours. The power was generally out for two to four hours a day, so that meant another two weeks, probably, and I could watch Clifford do that same calculation even as he asked if there was anything people wanted in exchange.

"No, when people heard someone needed it to *live* they said I could just have it," I said.

"I'm not so bad at fixing things," Clifford said. "If anyone needs something fixed, someone would have to come sit with Susan in case the power went out, but..."

"I'll let people know," I said.

"Come in for a minute?" he said.

I almost said no but from the next room I could hear Susan's voice call, "Clifford, you'd better not let Alexis leave without a cup of coffee," and I decided my to-do list could stand for me to take five minutes to sit down.

"Clifford, you can repair things?" I asked, pulling out my notebook. "Any things in particular?"

"Carpentry," he said.

I wrote that down. "We're making a list of skills people have," I said. "I don't suppose either of you grew up on farms." They shook their heads.

"I can sew," Susan said. "I don't imagine anyone's going to want a fancy costume but they might like a zipper replaced."

"You can do zippers?" I said, and made a note. "Do you need a sewing machine for that?"

"I have one. Clifford could bring it downstairs for me."

Clifford brought out coffee for me and I sipped it.

"Clearly I should have joined Future Farmers of America, back in the day, instead of the theater club," Susan said.

"We'll manage," I said. "We're trying to figure out if there's a way to grow food in people's yards. Lem suggested tearing up the street and growing food there, but that got some pushback."

"You won't hear any complaining from us," Clifford said. "Whatever everyone else thinks is best."

I told them Jeana was doing fine and had been very worried about Susan. She'd have come herself to check on Susan and Clifford but she'd broken her leg back before everything started and was still having trouble walking. Getting in and out of her house, which had four steps up to the front door, was difficult. Clifford brightened at that. "I bet I could build her a ramp. It wouldn't be up to code, but it would let her get in and out with a walker. Do you know if anyone has plywood?"

"Lem has sheets of it," I said. "I'll go to his house next."

The other blocks around us had seen what we were doing and were getting more organized with swap boards and so on. We'd started comparing community needs, especially ways to grow food. We wanted a tiller, and a cultivator, to turn sod into gardens, and no one we'd found had a tiller. There was one cultivator, but it was gas-powered.

"Maybe someone in the suburbs has an electric tiller they'd trade," Lem said. We'd started tearing up yards with spades, and it was slow going, although at least we weren't putting buried utility lines at risk.

I offered to go. My car is electric, so I could get there. I'm white and look "respectable" unless I put on my "eat the rich" t-shirt—paranoid suburbanites were unlikely to start by shooting at me. (We'd heard stories. I sure didn't want Tanesha taking the risk.) Once we started discussing this seriously, Frank said he'd come with me; he's got the same "could be a suburbanite myself" vibe but he's also huge. He worked as a bar bouncer when he was younger and you can't tell looking at him that these days his back hurts all the time. I told Clifford not to get his hopes too high, but to give me all his empty propane canisters, just in *case* we found a suburbanite with a stockpile they were willing to sell.

We had a block meeting to assemble any last-minute requests. Gloria and Leah had donated four of the camping canisters and asked how Susan was doing.

"Depends on how the power holds up, but we think we probably got them another two weeks," I said.

They exchanged looks. "If the sun was shining..." Gloria said.

The dust and ash in the air meant that it was effectively always cloudy, and the solar panels on lots of our houses weren't doing much. Not nothing—but not much. We were all silent for a minute, because if the sun were shining, we wouldn't be in this disaster. We'd be planning summer fun, instead of trying to figure out whether if we tore all the grass out of our yards, we'd be able to grow enough food to get through next winter.

"What about a wind turbine?" I asked. Gloria and Leah had built themselves a windmill with a generator attached, although I wasn't sure how well it was working.

"It would only work when the wind was actually blowing," Gloria said.

"That would be *something*," I said. "If they could conserve fuel on the windy days, it would last longer."

"A big enough battery *would* work," Tanesha said.

I sighed. When I bought my electric car a year ago, I'd also looked into getting solar panels and this giant wall of batteries—you could run the whole house off the batteries, recharging them on solar (normally), and *almost* go off-grid, at least that's what the reviews said. But I'd looked at the cost and had made the perfectly sensible decision to save up for solar first, fancy battery wall second. I'd asked around already, and no one else on the block had a big battery wall, either.

"I know of two people in the area, plus me, who have electric cars," I said. "There are some models you can use as a big rolling generator but none of ours have that feature. There are ways to do it anyway, with a power inverter, but that could mean it's not available to use as a car in an emergency." My car was getting us to Edina today; it had gotten Khalid up to the hospital the day before yesterday, when he fell off the ladder.

"What about a bike generator?" Tom asked. "The kind you pedal." He pantomimed.

"Those make about a hundred watts," Gloria said, and looked at me. "How many watts does the oxygen concentrator draw?"

"Five hundred," I said.

"Lance Armstrong would need a crew and all his drugs," Leah said.

"Lance could dope himself silly if he were making Susan power," I said, and then thought about how the drug shortages were getting worse. Whatever he took, he probably wouldn't be able to get anyway.

"Okay, but what if we had five bike generators," Tanesha said. "Each biker making a hundred watts."

"You'd want at least ten," Gloria said. "Humans are unreliable. Maybe twelve, actually." She fished a notebook out of her pocket, and a pen, and started making a list. "We'd need you to trade for more copper wire. That's tricky because everyone wants it. Probably easier than fuel, though."

"And bikes?"

"We have all the broken ones from Jack's garage, we can cobble together the bike generators. But we'll need people to pedal."

I looked at Tanesha. She looked at me. "If the Acquisition Committee can bring us copper wire, we'll make it work," she said. The "Acquisition Committee" was what she'd started calling me and Frank. "Bring any propane you find, though. Or gasoline."

The roads were quiet—mostly bikes and walkers, a few city buses. Everyone, including us, had parked cars sideways to block the streets leading into their neighborhoods, then left them there, then had the gasoline salvaged or looted out of them so the cars definitely weren't going anywhere. Traffic on the roads picked up when we got to the edge of the suburbs, even though all the gas stations were still closed. Also, in addition to the car barricades, we saw something hanging from the streetlight that for a second I thought was a *body*. It wasn't a body: it was a mannequin, though, so it was definitely supposed to look like a body. It had a sign around its plastic neck saying LOOTER. So, yeah, okay. We did our best to look nonthreatening.

We'd brought samples of stuff we had in surplus, and a list of skills—like the midwife who could insert IUDs, and the people who'd worked on farms and could help with figuring out how to tear up yards and grow food there. "Why would we tear up our yards?" asked the first man we spoke with. "I just had that sod put down last year!"

"I mean, you're going to want enough food…"

"Things are going to be *fine*. Everything will be back to normal in a month."

"Okay," I said. "Well, in that case, if you've got an electric tiller you're not using, we can pay for it in gold."

It was a very productive, if sort of distressing, trip—we found people happy to take gold in trade for a bunch of useful things, including a spool of heavy copper wire that they'd taken off the bodies of some looters and stuck in a garage. Several suburbanites clearly had a large supply of fuel, but no one wanted to trade any away. Frank was happiest about the tiller, but I was thrilled with the wire—in addition to the plan with the bikes, we could use this to make multiple wind turbines.

Back in our own neighborhood, Frank handed off the tiller and Lem went to work with it right away. I took the wire over to Clifford and Susan's garage. Clifford had used it as a workshop when he was younger, so it was insulated and reasonably pleasant, but then he'd slowly filled it with junk. Leah was supervising a team of teenagers who were clearing out the garage; Gloria was sorting things out and sending them to different garages around the block we were using as salvage bays or storage. Clifford popped out periodically to explain that a snow blower would probably work again with a new belt or maybe a replacement flywheel; Gloria sent that to the garage where they'd be building turbines, because a big snowblower auger could be turned into wind turbine blades.

Meanwhile, people were bringing over bikes. There were a dozen broken bikes from Jack's garage, another dozen semi-functional bikes from other people's garages, and four actual stationary bikes people brought over when they heard about the project. Gloria's team worked on cleaning off rust and getting everything lubricated.

Clifford and Susan's garage would have held two cars. Emptied out, it looked enormous: I looked at the workbench on the far wall and imagined how it had looked to Clifford when they'd bought the house years ago, a space filled with potential. "We need more light in here," Gloria said, looking around. "But we're going to need light that doesn't draw much power, LEDs or something." I opened a box marked CHRISTMAS and pulled out some strings of Christmas lights to run around the edge of the room.

If we'd had no power at all, we couldn't have done this—we'd have needed too many people, for too many hours, to handle it. But the power was still on for part of the day, every day. Most of the day, even. We just needed to fill in the gaps.

The first gap we needed to fill in was the time to change things over—from city power to wind power, or wind power to bike power. Gloria had turned up a couple of big rechargeable batteries and set them up in Clifford and Susan's living room.

"Why do we need three of them?" Susan asked.

"Because humans are unpredictable," I said. "With bike power, they'll be sending power in, but if everyone starts pedaling slowly at the same time, we want something to even things out and make sure your oxygen concentrator is still running. Also, if you exhaust one during the transition, we want you to have extras so you can wait until the power's coming from the city again to recharge the one that's used up."

If the wind was blowing, the windmill would take over generating power. But sometimes, the power would fail and there'd be no wind. Gloria set up a car alarm to go off when that happened, and that would be the cue for a squad of fit youngsters (mostly teens from the surrounding four blocks) to come running to pedal the bikes until the power came back on. If it was a long power outage and people got tired, we had a secondary set of signals to bring in replacements.

"Are people really going to do this?" Susan asked when I explained it to her.

"We can pay them," Clifford said. "How much is fair? I never even hired someone to shovel my snow because I didn't know how much to offer that would be fair. I don't think we have anything people would want for trade."

"Superlative cosplay costumes?" Susan muttered.

"People have been working on the food-production project for free," I said. "Let's see if we can get volunteers. You still have a stash of propane, if this doesn't work out."

I had actually thought we'd need to come up with a way to pay people—after the first week, anyway—but it turned out to be exactly like ripping up yards to plant potatoes, people were willing to just *do* it. No one wanted to be responsible for doing all of it, but pedaling one of a dozen bikes for an hour? Or a half hour? Lots of people were willing.

It did help that Hong, who lived next door to Clifford and Susan, had a backyard hot tub in a gazebo, and anyone coming off bike-pedaling duty could hop in for a quick soak. You couldn't turn it into a whirlpool unless the power had come back, but the water was always at least comfy.

"Can you please tell people to come inside sometimes so I can say thank you?" Susan asked when I checked in after the first week. Tanesha's daughter Jasmine was sitting on an ottoman pulled up next to Susan's recliner, with a basket of yarn in her lap and a crochet hook in her hand; apparently, Susan could make amigurumi, those adorable crocheted stuffies, and was teaching Jasmine the tricks of the trade. They were making little crocheted mice.

"They don't want to be a bother," I said.

"We can make them coffee. Or lemonade."

"We can make lemonade for the first ten," Clifford said. "Then we'll be out of either the lemon juice or the sugar."

Clifford had been going out to the garage to say thank you to the people pedaling, but Susan couldn't, since she was stuck in the house with her oxygen concentrator. This was allegedly a "portable" model and what that seemed to mean was, you could roll it over to the bathroom when you had to pee. "How did you ever leave the house, before?" I asked, and then wondered if the answer was, she didn't? I didn't remember ever seeing her.

"Bottled oxygen," Susan said.

"Do you think you could teach more people how to make those?" I asked, pointing at the crocheted mice.

"Oh, they're so easy," Susan said. "Definitely, anyone who wants to learn."

"For kids younger than Jasmine?"

She thought that over. "I think I was six when I learned crochet," Susan said. "Not little creatures back then, though, my aunt taught me how to make a potholder. It would depend on the kid, though. Some little ones are all thumbs."

"You're thinking about Kalia, aren't you?" Jasmine said, and turned to Susan to explain. "Kalia *wants* to help with everything but mostly she gets in the way. And her parents are very busy. Her mom's a nurse and still goes to work and her dad's been helping with the block farm. And no one's really had time for her. She's seven."

"Oh, in that case, bring her over," Susan said. "I've got a whole closet full of yarn and if I can't teach her crochet, I think I've got one of those old plastic knitting looms around, I'll teach her how to make hats. We can give them to people when they come in so I can say thank you."

By early May, medications were getting harder to get.

The rule was supposed to be that "life-sustaining" medications were prioritized, which everyone agreed made sense. But that turned out to exclude most of the psychiatric meds, no matter how important they were. You could still buy *cigarettes*, so Frank, who'd quit smoking years ago but now couldn't get a prescription he needed, went back to smoking as a substitute.

"Send him in to talk to me," Susan said, fuming, when she heard.

"He won't," I said. "He said he doesn't want to carry the particles on his clothing into where they might get into your lungs."

"Horse hockey," she said. "He just doesn't want the scolding he deserves."

Frank said it couldn't be any worse for him than breathing the air all day, which was *definitely* horse hockey—the damage was cumulative—but given that he'd privately given me the list of drugs he needed, and I hadn't found *any* of them, I was inclined to just let him be. If cigarettes kept him halfway functional, let him smoke. Away from Susan.

Clyde also gave me his list, and cigarettes weren't going to cut it as a substitute. He looked extremely uncomfortable as he handed it to me. "I've done really well for years," he said, as I looked it over. "But back when I was about twenty-two I got hospitalized because the walls were talking to me. I usually take aripiprazole, but either of these other two will work. I took Zyprexa for years and only went off it because I started developing sugar diabetes."

"That wouldn't be good, either," I said, thinking about Tanesha's worries about insulin and blood testing strips.

"Oh, I know." He laughed a little. "But temporarily, you know, it's an option. The gabapentin is for anxiety."

"The store's out of gabapentin?" I said, dismayed.

"Nah, but they prioritized the folks who need it for pain. I get that, I do, but they offered me benzos and...I really don't want to take benzos."

"I'll see what I can do, Clyde," I said, and put out the word.

Two days later, Pang stopped by my house with a giant shopping bag and handed it to me. I peered inside and just about recoiled when I saw the unopened boxes of both Abilify *and* gabapentin. "You didn't rob a pharmacy, did you?" I said.

"*As if* I'd have found the Abilify if I had," she said. "No, I was doing an IUD for a woman over by the park, and she told me her mom died a few months ago and she had all these meds left over. There's other stuff in there, too, I just figured I'd bring you all of it."

"Thank you *so much*," I said.

"I'm going to start asking people for leftover stuff every time I'm at someone's house," she said. "No one around here ever throws anything away. There are three half-finished packs of antibiotics in there! I mean if you're not going to finish your antibiotics like they tell you to, at least throw them out! But nope."

There were a couple of people with drugs that had to be refrigerated, and as summer got into gear, we started using Lem's extra deep freeze, which was enormous, to do nothing but store plastic sacks of ice cubes, so that if we had an extended power outage they'd be able to pack everything into a cooler full of ice.

In late July, a huge storm hit Minneapolis.

We had some warning, both from the extremely ominous clouds and the radio, and made the quick executive decision that we wouldn't call people to pedal until the storm passed—the storm should be providing plenty of wind, and if winds were bad enough to knock down the turbine, they were bad enough not to send people running through the storm. Clifford had a stock of propane, and this would be a good time to use it, if he needed to.

The rain came in sheets, buffeted by the wind; I listened to it rattling on my roof. I paced around in my living room, peering out at the dim afternoon and hoping the rain didn't wash away all the crops we'd planted in the yards we'd dug up, hoping no one's basement flooded, hoping the power stayed on. I wished I'd gone over to Tanesha's to wait this out.

When the power went out, I went upstairs to try to spot Clifford and Susan's house, to see if the wind turbine looked like it was working. There were too many boulevard trees and too much rain for me to see anything. I paced around, thinking about how "we don't want people running around outside in the storm" was *still* a perfectly sensible decision and then put on my shoes and stepped outside.

I didn't bother putting on a raincoat, because I was just going to have to accept I'd be soaked to the skin. The turbine had been knocked down, and I could see Clifford plus someone in a yellow raincoat bending over the generator. I waffled for a minute about whether they could use my help or if I'd just be in the way, but then they both straightened up and I saw Clifford go back into the house and the person in the raincoat dash back across the street. They'd gotten the generator on. I went back inside and closed the door on a titanic crack of thunder and what sounded like a tree splitting in half.

Morning arrived, but not power. I went out, in dry clothing and damp shoes, to have a look at the damage. There were trees down *everywhere*, all the nearby streets were blocked, and when I walked up for a closer look at the tree blocking the big through-street I saw power lines that had been knocked down—our neighbors to the north had put out orange hazard cones to keep people away from the wires.

Clyde worked at the hydro plant on the Mississippi near downtown, and as I was gawking at the power lines he came up next to me, his work clothes on, carrying a rucksack. "Don't touch that," he said.

"I won't," I said. "Are you on your way in?"

"Yep. Going to have to walk it, the bus can't get through the downed trees. Can someone feed my cats if I'm not home tonight by eight?"

"You bet," I said.

Tanesha was already organizing people to go clear what we could. Five people had cordless chainsaws—the real trick was going to be finding all the charged-up batteries that could be swapped in, and what we were going to do once those were used up. In the distance, I could hear other people's chainsaws, and a generator that wasn't Clifford and Susan's.

Clifford and Susan's generator was now off: pedalers had arrived and taken over, and Leah and Gloria were putting the wind turbine back up. Clifford was sitting on his front steps, watching them work. "Kalia found one of those turbine blades stuck in the shrubs next to Abdi's house," he said. "We probably should have taken it down before the storm." He glanced at me. "We used up a lot of the propane."

"I know," I said. "I'm sorry."

He shook his head. "No, I'm not saying anyone should have come to pedal! Someone might have gotten brained by a flying turbine blade! I mean…" He rubbed his palms against the knees of his jeans. "Our retirement wasn't supposed to be like this. We were supposed to travel around, see all the places we never had time for. Susan wasn't supposed to get sick. All this…" His voice cracked as he waved at the hills of potatoes in his yard, the wind turbine, the branches. "This isn't what it was *supposed* to be *like*."

Jasmine popped out of the front door. "Clifford?" she said. "Susan's asking for you."

Clifford stood up. "Excuse me," he said, and went inside. When I went in a few minutes later to get Jasmine, his anger was gone, or at least well-masked again. "Lem was here earlier looking for a saw vise," he said. "Can you let him know I found mine?"

"I will," I said.

The radio said crews were working around the clock to get roads cleared and lines back up, but it could be days—at least they weren't saying weeks—until everyone's power was back. That meant we were going to need a lot more pedalers than usual. Tanesha sent Jasmine and Kalia around to the houses on adjacent blocks that weren't usually part of the pedaling corps, to see if anyone was willing to volunteer. This brought in a new group of pedalers as well as a couple of people with handsaws and some willingness to tackle the downed trees.

We also got a naysayer who'd previously been ignoring the whole project and now wanted to complain to Tanesha about what we were doing. "It's very sad and all, but it's not like the lady who needs oxygen is going to get *better*," he said. "You're just delaying the inevitable."

Tanesha gave him a narrow-eyed look. "You delay the inevitable every time you eat lunch."

"That's different."

"It's really not," she said.

I thought of Clifford's furious *it wasn't supposed to be like this* and felt a surge of my own anger, enough that I let Tanesha finish the conversation and then just muttered "asshole" as the guy stomped off down the street. I felt like if I started screaming at him, I might never stop.

The wind picked up that evening and the repaired wind turbine gave everyone a break. We used the other turbines on the block to charge up the batteries for the chainsaws. We also checked Clifford's stock and decided to use the generator for a few hours during the hottest parts of the afternoon the next day. We had everyone with a wind turbine making ice if they could, to keep the coolers stocked for people with perishable medications.

After four days, the power came back. As did Clyde, who looked exhausted but had at least been able to ride the bus home through the now-cleared streets. Jasmine and Kalia had been over at his house every day to feed his cats and left him a batch of cookies they'd baked in a Dutch oven. We'd turned all those downed trees into firewood—figured we might as well.

Summer went by. A lot of what we'd planted didn't grow well, for the same reason the solar panels weren't much use—the lingering ash in the air clouding over the sun. We got a lot of potatoes, though, and some other root vegetables that would tolerate shade. We'd planted in what would be "full sun," normally, and there were days when we could tell the sun was out, because there were shadows on the ground despite the gray sky. Valeria, who'd been a Master Gardener at the University Extension and appeared to have magical powers over plants, gave all the potato plants pep talks, telling them to just do their best, and that seemed to help.

Valeria also knew the best way to set up a makeshift root cellar in a garage, for all the potatoes, carrots, turnips, and beets. We canned some of the green beans, but not a whole lot, because canning supplies were as hard to find as anything else.

Unfortunately, Valeria's magic wasn't able to deter garden scavengers: we put up chicken wire to keep out rabbits, but the urban deer were getting increasingly brazen. They jumped over the first fence we put up, barreled straight through the second.

In the twilight hours one August morning, I woke suddenly to a loud noise. I was used to being roused by the "pedalers needed" alarm, but the power was on. Also, it had been just one loud noise, I wasn't hearing the whoop-whoop-whoop of the car alarm. This was odd enough that I put on my bathrobe and went outside, at which point I found Lem, a dead deer, and a ferocious argument already underway.

Lem, apparently, had loaded his hunting rifle, come out in the predawn quiet, and shot one of the deer foraging in the garden. "Look," he said, exasperated. "The problem is, they're eating our food. Good news, though, deer *are* food. Venison jerky has more calories than green beans anyway."

"Lem, you *cannot* be shooting off a gun right by where we live," Gloria said. "You *can not*."

"No one's up at five! Anyone who is up, isn't outside! Also, those deer are shameless. I got ten feet from her before I fired. Sure wasn't going to miss at that distance."

Tanesha had come out of her house about a minute after I came out of mine, and everyone paused and looked at her, like they'd agreed it was up to her what happened next. She looked at the deer, at Lem, at Gloria, at everyone else, and said, "Lem, do you know how to field dress this thing? Get it somewhere it won't make the little kids cry and get started on processing it, we're not letting it go to waste. Meet back in an hour, or whenever you're done."

The previous day had been cool, a little taste of early fall, but today was hot again, and we set up a couple of wading pools and sprinklers in the street for the kids to play in while we had our meeting. "It's not that we object to hunting," Leah said, quickly, as soon as everyone sat down. "We just don't want it happening so close to people's houses."

Lem snorted. "I'll just drive up to my brother's cabin, then, and let the deer keep eating the potatoes."

"They were eating the green beans—"

Tanesha managed to cut that argument off before it got any further. "Leah, I get what you're saying, but he's right—there's hunting, and there's pest control, and he could go somewhere else to hunt but that won't do much for the pest control."

"I think the deer herd lives over in the cemetery," Valeria said. "Maybe Lem could go there?"

The cemetery was easy walking distance but still kind of outside our particular part of the neighborhood. We all paused, thinking about who we knew between our block and the cemetery, and Valeria added, "Everyone's having trouble with those deer, and we could promise them jerky."

"There's still a Department of Natural Resources," Lem said. "Game wardens. Police. I knew you folks wouldn't turn me in for taking this one. I don't know about the folks by the cemetery."

"My gardener friend over there, she'd be all for it. She'll want to know if you can do the bunnies while you're at it."

"What about her neighbors, though? And their neighbors?"

"Valeria, take Alexis and the two of you see what you can find out from the people right by the cemetery," Tanesha said. "In the meantime, Lem, no more shooting off guns by our houses."

"What if someone shows up trying to loot stuff?" Lem asked.

"No deadly force against property crimes, either," Tanesha said. That set off another round of arguing. A lot of my neighbors had guns, it turned out—that probably shouldn't have surprised me as much as it did. The number of arguments in favor of deadly force against property crimes probably shouldn't have surprised me either, given how worried everyone was about the food supplies.

I just listened, thinking about the suburbanites who'd strung up a mannequin, and how much I didn't want that to be us. Eventually the less gun-happy more or less won the argument: we'd defend ourselves with force if it came to that, but not *guns*, not without another discussion, not unless someone was actually threatening us with violence.

The cemetery neighbors turned out to be wildly enthusiastic about a discreet deer hunt, especially with the promise of venison. They stood lookout as Pang's husband Bee went with Lem to stalk and shoot the herd. We split the meat, enjoyed some venison burgers and venison chili, and turned the haunches into jerky to save for winter.

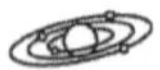

One fall day I passed Susan's yard and she was sitting out front in a lawn chair, her oxygen concentrator plugged in to a long heavy-duty extension cord. She had a giant bushel basket of tiny semi-wormy apples, a dozen little kids, Jeana—who was still using her walker—and Gail, a woman from the next block who walked with crutches. I went over to say hi, and saw that they had rounded up vegetable peelers for each child, and had the kids painstakingly peeling the tiny apples. The adults cut them carefully into rings, and then the youngest children in the group were spreading them out on cookie sheets. I went over for a closer look. "That's amazing," I said.

"We're peeling off all the bad spots," a little boy informed me excitedly. "Peeling them very, very carefully and we're making dried apples and I'm being very helpful! Would you like an apple? I can find you one without any bad spots!"

"That's a good idea," Susan said. "Why don't you see if you can find Alexis a nice apple from one of those big baskets by the fence." He zoomed off and she turned to me to explain, "Gail has an apple tree."

"I can't even remember what sort of apple they told us this was when we bought the tree," Gail said. "We had this vision of homegrown apples that looked like the ones from the store. Turns out orchards mostly use a ton of chemicals and if you don't, everything from birds to squirrels to moth larvae get into them. Plus you need to get up on a ladder and thin them when they're tiny if you want them to grow to full size. Which Kent even did, this year, but they still stayed small, probably because there was so little sun."

The little boy came back with an apple, and I borrowed a knife to cut it into wedges for myself. The slices were delicious, sweet, and crisp.

"Unblemished apples actually keep pretty well," Jeana said. "But I'm not sure there *are* any unblemished apples, so we're turning them into rings to dry. It's something the kids can help with, too."

"Are you just making the rounds?" Susan asked. "Or are you looking for something? You've got your clipboard."

I looked down at my list. "Tanesha is thinking about winter," I said. "Power outages will mean furnaces can't run."

"I have a gas furnace," Jeana said. "Are they thinking there won't be natural gas?"

"It's a gas furnace, but it won't run without electricity because of the blower," I said. "It would be bad if it did, actually, because carbon monoxide would build up."

"Mine runs without a blower," Susan said. "Clifford and I have a gravity furnace, it's an older style. Looks like an evil octopus in the basement. It runs without electricity."

"It looks like an evil octopus?"

"I don't know how else to describe it," Susan said.

"I always thought they looked like space aliens," Jeana said. I went to find Clifford for a basement tour.

The gravity furnace had an enormous barrel-shaped central unit with similarly enormous vents sprouting off it in all directions. It did, in fact, look like a giant evil octopus. "I really don't know anything about these," I said.

"We always meant to replace it," Clifford said. "They're not very efficient but having it taken out and replaced would be so expensive, and they last forever. No moving parts."

"Are you cool with people showing up to spend time in your house this winter?" I asked.

Clifford laughed, and that somehow turned into him leaning against a wall and wiping his eyes and nodding.

We harvested the potatoes and turned backyard tool sheds and cold corners of basements into root cellars. We identified houses to work as shelters during cold snaps without power—there were two other gravity furnaces, two houses with super-efficient heat pumps, and a couple of well-insulated homes with gas furnaces so we'd only need to power the blower. Shelter houses also needed enough space inside for visitors and owners who weren't dicks. (I love my neighborhood, but we do have our share of dicks.) Shelter houses got a turbine if they didn't already have one, and Gloria sent around this group she and Lem had trained to caulk all the windows and build a vestibule so that when people came in all the heat didn't go rushing out. Susan made decorative WELCOME banners the shelter houses could hang out so everyone would remember which ones they were.

In early November, a government convoy started coming through on the big main street once a week to distribute relief supplies. The buses got less reliable, and I started giving Clyde a ride to and from work when I could. Sometimes I couldn't—during brownouts, there wasn't enough power to charge up my car— and he walked to the plant.

The houses with the heat pumps also had solar panels. So did several other people on the block. Predictions said that enough ash should be out of the air by mid-winter that we'd be able to get power from those again—although those predictions were making a lot of assumptions and I sure didn't want to count on that. I didn't want to count on those convoys continuing, either. In the meantime, we pooled the canned goods from the convoy and passed all the canned beans along to Diana, who had a severe nightshade allergy and couldn't eat potatoes. This was a *lot* of beans, way more than fit in her cupboards, and we stacked them up in her living room and made jokes about the Great Wall of Legumes. We were glad for that, though, because then the convoy didn't come for three weeks.

After two weeks without a convoy, the suburban neighborhood we'd visited in early summer sent over a delegation wanting to buy food. They started out hoping to buy with money, but when that produced no interest, they upped their bid to fuel. That sent us back to run some calculations—how much did we have? How many government relief convoys did we expect to see, based on the rumors we'd heard? We agreed to a trade, potatoes for propane, because it would be good to keep the option of the generator open, especially if we had another prolonged outage.

"Where do you suppose they *got* the fuel?" Tanesha asked me when they stepped outside for a private conversation of our offer.

"Either they had a hoarder, or they hijacked a fuel truck," I said. "Do you think a bunch of rich yuppies could pull off a fuel truck heist?"

They came back with the propane tanks and tried to make us sweeten the deal in that obnoxious way people sometimes will, then left with their potatoes and their bad attitude and went back to the burbs.

"I have a bad feeling," Tanesha said. "Let's add some folks to the people watching overnights for a bit."

Tanesha was right.

I was standing watch at the south entrance to the neighborhood when the attack came. We used walkie-talkies for communication, although they were the kind some guy bought for his hunting blind years ago and were not *great*. Mine went off with a squawk, and I heard the word "west entrance—" over the static before it went silent.

I set off the car alarm. We'd started out using the car alarm to summon people to generate power, but over the months we'd come up with a set of signals in addition to the standard "pedalers needed" alarm. We had a fire alarm (we'd actually *saved Luke's house* by running with fire extinguishers and a garden hose, which was a damn good thing because re-building a house right now would be a non-starter) and also a generic "all hands! Emergency!" alarm.

"West entrance!" I shouted to everyone who headed my way, and the word got passed. Although once the bulk of the neighbors headed in that direction, others stayed to reinforce my spot, in case the west entrance assault was a diversion.

It was not. We were dealing with a coordinated attack but not an especially sophisticated one. Their plan was just "get in, grab stuff, get out," and they'd assumed we wouldn't be able to respond quickly enough to stop them. Back in the spring, they'd have been right! But for months now we'd been drilling a fast response to alarms, not because we were rehearsing for an invasion, but because we were making power for Susan. The interlopers never had a chance. Most of them ran away but Keith got one in a headlock and another one, by sheer bad luck (for him) tripped and went down and broke his own ankle. No one had even touched him.

Despite the "no deadly force against property crime" rule, Lem and Bee both had guns with them, but neither gun came out of its holster. The guy in the headlock flailed around trying to pull something out of his pocket, but Clyde just slapped his hand away. He turned out to have a gun rattling around loose like a set of keys in one pocket, and pepper spray in the other. We confiscated both. The one who broke his ankle had a gun in a holster where we could see it but Lem barked instructions at him and the guy didn't even try to draw. It turned out to be an air pistol.

We hauled our prisoners into Keith's house (I think on the theory that Keith had created this problem by *catching* someone) and someone went to get Pang to splint the klutz's ankle. Once we had them in good light we could see that they were teenagers, which explained a *lot*. Stupid white boys from the suburbs, we were pretty sure, and this was confirmed by the injured one as he ranted about how he *knew* this was a bad idea, he *told everyone* this was a bad idea, he didn't even want to come *along* and had come just to keep them out of trouble. They were not actually from the suburb we'd traded with, but somewhere west of there. They'd heard we had a surplus of food and figured they'd swoop in and supplement their own dwindling supplies.

"I think we should ransom them," Keith said.

Tanesha shook her head. This turned out to be mainly a semantic quibble. "*Fine* them," she said. "Their parents can pay for the *damage* they did." The boys had kicked in the side door of someone's garage before the neighbors had stopped them.

The alarm went off again and there was a brief moment of *oh no what now* and then we realized it was just a call for pedalers. Everyone was awake, despite it being the middle of the night, and most people were still buzzing with adrenaline, so those slots would be easy to fill.

"What is that?" asked the uninjured boy. Kyle. He hadn't told us his name, but the injured one had sworn at him a bunch, so we'd picked it up.

"It means we need people to run the generator," Tanesha said.

"See," the injured one said, furiously. "They have a *generator*. We're lucky we didn't get *shot*."

"Shut up, Jake," said Kyle.

"I mean, they're basically paramilitary over here…"

"We run a generator to keep a lady breathing," Keith said.

Both boys stared at him in open disbelief.

"Do you want to see it?" Tanesha asked, standing up. "Maybe it'll give you some ideas to take home to your own community."

Getting them over there was kind of a production. Even splinted, Jake couldn't walk on his injured ankle, so Leah went and found a knee scooter from the garage full of "could come in handy" stuff that Hawa kept organized. Kyle presented the opposite problem—he could just run for it, and might outrun us if he tried. Keith wound up taking his shoes.

It was a cold night, but the generator station was warm, because it was well-insulated and the pedalers had been at it for a while. There were twelve people on the bikes, twelve hanging out on the sofas at the edge of the room for rest breaks. The room was equipped with LED string lights, a meter that let them track whether they were putting out enough power, and a bunch of miscellaneous posters and pictures that regular pedalers had put up. It had started with this nice photo of Susan, which Clifford had hung up early on. Then someone added a picture of his grandma in another state, who he hadn't heard from in a while and was hoping was okay, and then someone else put up a poster of mountains with blue sky. At this point, the walls were very well decorated.

The people on the couches were relaxing and waiting their turn, with two of them—Hakeem and Galen—cooperating to come up with rhymed lyrics about fighting off the suburbanites. Everyone was laughing. They trailed off as we came in. "What's up?" one of them asked, nervously.

"Kyle and Jake wanted to see our generator," I said.

Hakeem stood up. "Yeah," he said. "We generate electricity to keep an oxygen concentrator running." He walked over to the wall to point out the photo of Susan.

"Is she your doctor or something?" Kyle asked. This question was met with baffled silence. "An engineer? What makes her so important?"

"She teaches crochet," someone from one of the bikes called. "Those little guys up there." The décor included a shelf of amigurumi.

"No, seriously," Kyle said, laughing. "I don't get it."

Hakeem was one of those teenage boys who was all limbs, and he stepped up to loom over Kyle, who shrank back. "Susan," Hakeem said, "is a *member* of *our community*."

Kyle stopped laughing and swallowed hard. "Do you want us to pedal? Well, me to pedal. Jake's injured, he can't do it."

Hakeem loomed a few seconds longer. "No," he said. "No one wants you to pedal. We want you to go home to your suburb and tell your buddies not to mess with us."

I'd imagined we would have to haul these boys back to the suburbs ourselves, but by morning, their parents were standing at the edge of our neighborhood looking indignant. When Tanesha came out without their sons, and said they'd need to pay a fine to cover the damages they'd done, they angrily threatened to call the police, which made all of us laugh. Then they only wanted to pay the fine for Kyle, and not for Jake, apparently because Kyle's parents were important and Jake's weren't, although the fact that Jake had fallen down and hurt himself seemed to play into it. Tanesha made it clear they were a package deal, no discounts available if you only wanted one, and after a bit more grumbling, they forked over the fine—a 20 lb propane tank, almost full.

Early in the morning on the first day of February, Jake showed back up.

He arrived at dawn, more or less. Alone. Limping a little bit, because it had been a long walk, and shivering, although the cold snap we'd been in was easing off. Tanesha threw her coat on over a nightgown and came out. "What are you doing back?" she asked.

"I want to join you," he said.

"What do you think you mean by that? We're not the Army. You can't just sign up."

"I want to live here," he said. "I promise I can work. When I don't have a broken ankle I can work really hard. I can pedal, I can dig, whatever you want me to do I can do."

"Where do you think you're going to *sleep*, son?" asked Lem.

He looked miserable. "I don't know. Maybe someone has a couch?"

Lem, Tanesha, and I looked at each other and Tanesha said, "It's too cold to stand around chatting, let's get you inside somewhere to figure this out."

The lights were on in Susan and Clifford's house, though their WELCOME banner was tattered by the wind, so Tanesha and I knocked and went in with our new guest. There'd been a power outage overnight but the sharp wind had all our wind turbines pumping out power, no pedalers needed, and the city power had come back about a half hour ago. Clifford was puttering around in the kitchen and Susan was awake, because she called, "Who's here? Come say hello!" as soon as we closed the door behind us, and added, "Clifford, make some coffee!" without waiting to see who it was.

"Don't waste your coffee, it's me and Alexis with an uninvited guest," Tanesha said, humor in her voice.

"Uninvited...?" Clifford said, coming out of the kitchen and looking Jake up and down. "Where'd he come from?"

"Suburbs," Tanesha said. "He's looking for a place to stay."

Jake took a deep breath. "I can pedal, I can dig, I can cook and wash dishes, I can shovel snow. I'm not great with tools but I can follow directions."

"Why did you come *here*?" Tanesha asked, exasperated.

"Because I want to live somewhere that people take care of each other," he said, his voice cracking.

Susan waved him to her side and took his hand. "Don't worry, kid," she said. "They're softies here. They won't throw you to the wolves." She plucked a tissue from a box on her side table and handed it to him to wipe his eyes. "Welcome to the collective. We have a guest bed, upstairs. Or at least we did."

"We gave that bed to Lem, I can't remember why," Clifford said. "There's space up there, though, and I'm sure *someone* has a bed they could bring over..."

"I don't need a bed—"

Someone pounded on the front door and my first thought was that Jake's suburb was back to reclaim him, but it was Lem's voice, and from what we could hear he sounded gleeful, not worried. Tanesha went to open the door and he'd already gone running down to the next house, but his voice carried back to us. "Blue sky," he was yelling. "Blue sky!"

I looked up. There was a patch of blue—just a tiny one, but a patch of blue—and the sunshine was streaming down, cold and bright. "Come out!" I shouted over my shoulder and ran across the street to knock on more doors and bring people out to see. When I looked back, Clifford had gotten Susan, haltingly, as far as their front doorstep, with Jake behind her lugging her concentrator. They were looking up at the sky, at the break in the not-quite-clouds, squinting in the sunshine, that same expression of wonder on their faces that I was feeling.

When I returned to Susan and Clifford's house, Jake was earnestly trying to explain to Tanesha that seeing the pedalers had made him realize there was a better way. "You're in," she said. "It's fine. We'll find you a spot. Let's just bask in the glory of the knowledge that spring might actually come this year. *Blue sky.*"

. . . .

Naomi Kritzer is a science fiction and fantasy writer from St. Paul, Minnesota. Her fiction has won the Hugo Award, the Nebula Award, the Edgar Award, and the Minnesota Book Award. She has a spouse, two grown kids and three cats (the number of cats is subject to change without notice). You can find Naomi online at naomikritzer.com or on Bluesky as @naomikritzer.bsky.social.

SATURDAY'S SONG

Wole Talabi

The seven siblings sit in a place beyond the boundaries of space and time, where everything is made of stories. Even them. Especially them.

People are made of stories too, but only the versions of their stories that they tell themselves. Curated, limited, incomplete. Many of the stories people tell themselves are lies layered on partially-perceived things to give their lives structure and meaning. The siblings that sit beyond sit true, for they are made of all the stories that were, that are, that are to come. They tell each other these stories, taking them out and examining them in the light like a never-ending self-dissection. They listen to the stories and as they do, they are made whole again. They exist in narrative equilibrium. In constant flux. They tell each other stories of what has happened, is happening, will happen because it is their function. They tell these stories because they must.

Sometimes, they sing the stories too.

Saturday likes to sing. She thinks she has a nice voice, and this is true. It is euphonic, lilting, mellow but strong and full of emotion, so her siblings let her sing her parts of the stories when she wants to.

Some stories demand melody.

"Let us tell another story," Sunday says, breathing the words out more than speaking them. He is the most knowledgeable of the seven siblings, even though none of them know why. He just is, because that is his story. He rakes the tight curls of his beard with his fingers before continuing. "Saturday, it is your turn to choose a story for us to tell and hear."

Saturday stops playing with the thick, long braids of her goldspun hair. She is still surprised even though she already knew it was her turn before he told her so. She looks around the table, avoiding her siblings' eyes, and then she shuts her eyelids and focuses inward, seeking out the story she knows has a good shape, the story that feels right, like she is reading her own bones. When she finds it, the story she knows they need in this moment of non-time, she beams a smile and radiates the choice out to her siblings, passing the story they all know she has chosen for them to hear and tell. None of them react when they receive it, but they know it is a good story.

Monday, who always starts their stories, begins his duty solemnly with clear words, "Saura met Mobola at a financial management conference in…"

"Stop!" Saturday cries, holding up a small hand.

The shock of the interruption leaves Monday's mouth open, like he is a fish removed from water. Sunday's emerald eyes widen. Tuesday, Thursday, and Friday crane their necks toward her, their gazes curious and hard. Only Wednesday does not visibly react because she is bound up in thick clanking chains, punishment for the crime of trying to change a story. The timestone Wednesday used to perform the abomination sits at the centre of the mahogany table between two ornate pewter candelabra like an offering, or a temptation. Its emerald edges reflect and refract the candlelight in peculiar ways, making the bright orange light dance with shadows across the table and the walls.

Saturday feels sad for her sister, but knows she needs to be careful. She does not want to be punished too. Interruptions once a story has begun are mostly forbidden, although not as forbidden as attempting to change a story. The rules that govern the seven are both rigid and flexible, to varying degrees, like the rules of storytelling itself. Still, Saturday knows it is important that it is done this way. For Wednesday's sake. She says, "Forgive me. But I want to begin the story near the middle. Please, can we? We will go back to the beginning but if we start at the middle it makes the story so much better."

She pulses her story choice again. This time, she radiates not only its substance, but she gives them its form and structure, the shape of it with all its contours defined. Not just what it is, but also the way she wants them to tell and to hear it.

They receive it as a stream of visions. As a kaleidoscope of images. A swirl of sounds. A spectrum of sensations. A babble of narrator voices. As points of view. As music. As song.

Sunday gives her a look that is both surprised and curious. Tuesday claps her hands with glee. Monday nods with understanding. He looks to Wednesday, the chains wound around her body like perforated metal anacondas. They are older than time itself. Saturday wants her shackled sister to tell the part of the story where Saura obtains the chains to bind the Yoruba nightmare god, Shigidi. Resonance. She thinks it gives the middle of the story the reinforcement it needs. Like a good skeleton. Everyone has been allocated their part of the story to undergird it with what is important for the telling and the hearing. The other siblings also nod their approval. This makes Saturday smile. They understand even if they don't fully know her motives. But they know it is not just important to tell and hear the story, it is important to tell and hear it *well*.

Monday wipes the thin film of sweat from his narrow moustache, adjusts the collar of his pinstripe suit, and starts again.

This is the part of the story that Monday told:

Saura never dreamed before she encountered Shigidi.

For as long as she could remember, she'd never recalled a single dream upon waking. For Saura, sleep was and had always been a brief submergence into dappled darkness, her consciousness consumed whole like swallowed fruit. And because of this she never felt completely rested. She always felt lethargic. Unfocused. Persistently exhausted.

When she was eleven, her mother, who was magajiya of the local bori cult of Ungwar Rimi near Zaria, summoned Barhaza, the sleep spirit, to possess her. The ritual was performed, and the spirit invited into her body to relieve Saura of her ailment and give her rest. But despite their offering of fresh milk from three white goats, the rolling of her eyes in her head, and the convulsions she experienced when the spirit entered her, the possession was unsuccessful, and she remained dreamless and unrested.

Her mother wept and gritted her teeth.

Saura had the gift of sensitivity and was meant to succeed her as magajiya. A refusal of the spirits to grant such a simple request counted against her, even though there were other things that counted against her more which her mother would soon come to know.

"I don't want to," Saura protested when her mother announced that they would attempt another possession.

"You must."

"No!" She'd screamed. It took her father two hours to find and retrieve her from the bush beside the market where she had fled to hide.

When Saura was sixteen, her mother tried again, ambushing her in her sleep and tying her down with thick hemp rope so that she could not resist. That time, her mother begged Barhaza to not only give Saura dreams and rest but to adjust her subconscious desires, to make her stop looking at other girls with lust in her eyes, to take away her visible attraction for the curve of other women's hips, the swell of their lips, the fullness of their breasts. Once again, the spirit entered Saura's body, rigidifying her limbs, milkening her eyes, and communing with her thoughts, but when it left, there were still no dreams, and her desires were unchanged. That evening, Saura, wounded by her mothers' betrayal, ran away from home with nothing on her back besides her jalabiya and the light of a full moon.

She only ever returned home once, to attend her father's funeral. She refused to speak with her mother, and sat with her lover, Mobola, and her father's family, tears streaming down her eyes as they lowered his body into the hard red earth.

When she was twenty-five, after struggling her way through university with the help of a local charity and finally getting a job at the bank, she went to see a doctor in Kaduna city. He was an oddly-shaped man with a big head, small frame, and a protruding belly and a kind smile with a yellowing diploma from a university she'd never heard of in Kansas on the brick wall of his office, hung between two hunting knives like a trophy. He connected a string of electrodes to her head and took measurements on a machine that beeped a steady whine until she fell asleep.

"No REM sleep," he'd announced, poring over his notes and charts when she was awake and back in his office chair. She'd never gone into REM sleep. After three more sessions with electrodes and needles and charts and uncomfortable sleep, he concluded that she was incapable of it. He told her she was a highly unusual case, prescribed a series of medications and asked her to sign a release form so he could study her more. None of his medications worked and so Saura didn't sign his forms. She simply got used to empty sleep, to never being fully rested, to never dreaming.

That is why, even before waking, she knew something was wrong that night when Shigidi entered the master bedroom of the house in the heart of Surulere which she shared with Mobola. She knew something was wrong because she dreamed for the first time.

In her dream, she saw a small dark orb hovering above them as they lay naked in bed, entwined in a post-coital embrace. The orb was dense and powerful, like an evil star. It settled on Mobola's chest and tugged at her flesh with an inexorable force like gravity. It tugged at Saura's too. She resisted the pull of it, tossing, and turning and sweating profusely on the bed, caught in a night terror she could not escape. But she saw the dreamy, ethereal version of Mobola in her mind, yielding to the pull of the orb, being fragmented, stripped down to fine grey particles that were absorbed by the thing. When there was nothing of dream-Mobola left, the orb disappeared and Saura sank back into darkness. On Monday morning, when the heat of the sun on her face finally woke Saura up, Mobola was cold to the touch, her skin pale and dry. She'd been dead for three hours.

Saura screamed.

Monday stops speaking and Saturday gathers what he has said into her chest. Each word is a bird that she swallows, expanding with it. In-breath. It is important for her song.

Tuesday's pale face is unusually blushed bright pink, and her lustrous auburn hair seems to gain volume as she prepares to speak. She knows, has known, will know, that she has the best part of the story. The part that begins with lust and ends with something like love. Saturday winks at her sister. She has given it to her by design. Tuesday likes description and dialogue and the cadence of human speech which is important in conveying emotion. A smile cuts across Tuesday's freckled face.

This is the part of the story that Tuesday told:

Saura met Mobola at a financial management conference in Abuja just before the cold harmattan of 2005.

It was break time between an endless stream of panel discussions, and Saura was standing by the tall windows that overlooked a stone fountain, its water flecked gold with sunlight as it erupted into the air. When she turned around to go back, she caught Mobola staring at her from across the hall. The moment their eyes met, there was a surge of something intangible within her, like an emotional arc discharge. Saura smiled and beckoned her over. For two days, they'd been stealing glances at each other, occasionally catching each other's eyes. It was the seventh time it had happened, and Saura had learned enough of herself to recognize the surge, the feeling, the signs. She was ready. Mobola flashed her a sweet smileful of white teeth and approached. She had bright, inquisitive eyes with an anxious look in them. Her hair was natural and curly, and her wide hips strained against the grey of her skirt. Saura thought she looked stunning.

"Hi. I'm Mobola, I manage the Trust Bank office in Surulere," she said. Saura told her she was the logistics manager for all the Kaduna offices and that if she had to listen to another discussion on forex approval procedures, she would go downstairs and drown herself in the fountain. They both laughed at that, carefree, like wind. There was something about the way Mobola laughed, the way she threw her head back, the way she almost hiccupped between breaths, her chest heaving against the cashmere blouse, the way she closed her eyes at the peak of her mirth, that Saura found deeply attractive.

They talked for a few minutes. There was a deliberate softness to everything about Mobola. The curves of her body, the cadence of her words. Saura was lost in Mobola's eyes, unable to look away. Brown, big, constantly wet, and full of a look which was a strange mix of sadness, grittiness, and hope. The look of someone that had seen the worst of the world, had stared into the dark heart of humanity but had survived and resolved to live, love, and laugh freely despite it.

They pulled out their phones and exchanged numbers, laughing when they realized they both used the same model of Blackberry, a *bold*, and agreed to meet at the delegate hotel bar at nine.

Saura watched Mobola leave, the sway of her hips hypnotizing her like magic. She could barely breathe, the air suddenly seemed thinner, oxygen harder to take in. She knew she had to be careful. If she had read the situation wrong, she could end up in prison for years. Nigerian law was not kind to sapphic romance.

Saura arrived early to the bar and had two Irish coffees to wake herself up. She knew she wasn't wrong when Mobola showed up and waved at her wearing a blue dress that was so tight in her fuller places that it could have been painted on. There was a gap showing between her front teeth, some cleavage, and a bit of a belly. Legs shaved smooth and feet encased in black pumps. Saura thought she was even more stunning than before.

They had three gin and tonics, making fun of the parade of boring panel speakers and the other conference delegates who pretended to be interested in the minutiae of inter-bank financial processes before Saura pulled Mobola to her feet.

"Do you want to go somewhere more interesting?" she asked, finishing her drink in one gulp.

Mobola smiled at her, mouth full of piano key teeth, lips red and glistening. "Sure."

Saura took Mobola to a club she'd heard about from one of the online forums she'd joined when she'd first started trying to understand herself. It was called The Cave and it was a ten-minute taxi ride away. When they entered, it was into a rainbow chaos. Strobe lights. Colourful décor with bizarre shapes that challenged the very concept of geometry. Sweaty people pressed together at tables, on the dancefloor, on barstools, running over with feeling. They made their way to the bar, ordered shots of something that bartender told them was tequila but didn't taste like it, and then merged with the mass of flesh on the dancefloor. Mobola turned her back to Saura and began to rock from side to side slowly, sensually, following the beat of the music. Saura wrapped her hands around Mobola's waist and swayed with her so that they moved to the music together like a single creature.

Saura's head was a cloud. In that moment, she was sure she knew what it was like to dream.

The next morning, they woke up in each other's arms fully clothed and in the same position they'd danced in.

"Good morning beautiful," Mobola said.

"Good morning."

"I had so much fun last night."

"Me too."

Mobola turned around to face her. "Did we...?"

Her face was close, Saura could see for the first time that she had a solitary dimple on her left cheek. It was faint, but there. She was staring intently and Saura could not look away, lost in her eyes. Her hair had bunched up and tangled, pressed against the hotel room pillow, loose strands dancing in front of her face. When she smiled, Saura's heart took flight.

She reached for the question hanging in space between them. "No."

They were both quiet for what seemed like a long time. An unbearably long time. And then she pulled Mobola closer so that they were chest to chest, inhaling each other's alcohol-scented breath and asked, "Did you want to?"

She smiled. "Yes."

There was no hesitation. None.

Saura kissed Mobola and the cloud in her head ascended, rising, beyond the ceiling and the roof and the sky, to the place where hearts go when they are buoyed by love.

It stayed there, never coming down. It only ever rose higher. For ten years, that feeling never sank. Not even when they fought and accidentally hurt each other and cried and made up and laughed like all good lovers do. Not when Mobola fell asleep one night and didn't answer Saura's calls for help after her car overheated and broke down on third mainland bridge. Not even when they had an argument about Mobola applying for a residence pass for both of them to leave the country without telling her first. Not even when her mother had refused to speak to Mobola at Saura's father's funeral or acknowledge her existence and tried to convince Saura to come back home, telling her that she was throwing her life away and bringing shame to the family.

No, Saura was always sure of the cloud of them. For ten years, she was sure. Through all the vicissitudes and the accusations and the arguments, she knew with all the certainty of entropy that she loved Mobola and that nothing, would ever change that. Not even death.

Tuesday is done speaking.

She is standing now. Her thin, pale hands are thrust out in front of her like the bones of a large bird. She'd allowed herself to become swept up with the story, infused with it, become one with it and because she had, so had all the siblings. There is a solitary tear running down Thursday's face. And Sunday has a glazed look in his eyes that makes him seem much older than his hair, which is grey at the temples, would indicate even though time is meaningless to the siblings. Saturday is pleased. They need this for the story. The emotion. She has taken in all of Tuesday's words, the sensations, the feelings, all of it. Her chest is filling up, and the first melodies of her song are beginning to take shape within her lungs. Sunday turns to face Wednesday, whose turn has come. Wednesday must go back to the middle of the story because that is where the chains first appear. Chains not unlike the ones wrapped around Wednesday's torso, snaking through shackles that bind her hands and feet, tethering her to the stone ground so that the only part of her that can move is her head and most importantly, her mouth. It's hard to tell or hear a story without a mouth.

Saturday watches her sister, waiting. Wednesday has already received her section of the story. She just needs to accept it. She is hesitating, but it is not like last time when she rejected a story midway through and entered it, trying to change it—the crime for she is now bound. The middle of the story is where the chains and the refusal to accept fate are waiting like familiar stalking animals.

Wednesday begins to shake and Saturday knows the story is coming. Erupting from the deepest volcano of suppressed emotion.

This is the part of the story that Wednesday told:

A month after Mobola's funeral, Saura went to see a Babalawo in Badagry, at the mouth of a waterway that kisses two countries. She hadn't slept in days. Her friend Junia, who was also a colleague at work, had recommended him, saying he'd given her a charm that helped her deal with her depression after a miscarriage. Saura took his contact details from Junia but hadn't planned to use them. If Barhaza of the bori, a spirit historically linked to her people and family, couldn't give her rest then there was nothing a Yoruba Babalawo unfamiliar with the shape of her spirit would be able to do. The yellow piece of paper with his number written on it in blue ink remained unused on her table until one afternoon, watching traffic glide past her window, she realized that while he would not be able to give her peace of mind, he might be able to give her information. To help her understand why ten years of love and companionship and joy had ended at the speed of a bad dream.

The Babalawo was a thickset man who spoke perfect English. He had a long greying beard and calm eyes. Three white dots were chalked onto his forehead just above his eyebrows and the string of beads around his neck rattled as he shook his head when he heard her explain what had happened to Mobola. When she was done, he removed the beads and threw them onto the raffia mat between them, rapidly whispering an incantation.

"This is the work of Shigidi," he said with his eyes still on the beads as he explained to her that Shigidi was the Yoruba deification of nightmare, able to enter and manipulate the human subconscious, especially during sleep when their grip on their thoughts were loosest. He could induce night terrors and sleep paralysis in his prey as he sat on their chests and pressed the breath out from them. The Babalawo explained that he was an ambivalent Orisha, protecting those who gave him offerings but also often sent by evil people to kill those they perceived as enemies or threats. "You have communed with spirits before?" the Babalawo asked, looking up at her curiously. "To have sensed Shigidi the way you described it, to receive a bleed-over dream when you were not the person he came for, that is very unusual."

Saura's eyes were wide with shock, but she only shook her head. She didn't tell him about her mother or her intimate knowledge of the bori or her adolescent possessions by myriad spirits. She simply paid him his fee and hired a car to take her home. But not the home she'd shared with Mobola. No. Back to Ungwar Rimi where she knew she could obtain the power to punish the nightmare god that had killed Mobola. To fight fire with fire. Saura hadn't spoken to her mother in more than a decade. But they were bound by blood, and Saura needed her mother's help, her knowledge, to do what she wanted to do. Human families can be made of chains too.

Saura did not go to the family compound to talk privately with her mother. That would have been too personal, too painful, and would have made it too easy for her mother to refuse. She went instead to the market at night, when the moon and the stars hung low and most of the village had retired to their beds, leaving the wide-open spaces of the market to the members of the bori cult. This was where the council of bori magajiya who knew how to summon spirits and invite them to possess the bodies of people for various purposes, held court and heard requests from the sick, the curious, the desperate.

She arrived at the centre of the market in a black headscarf and cotton veil atop a flowing black jalabiya like the one she'd been wearing the night she ran away. They were already in the middle of a possession. An unusually tall man, shirtless, with broad shoulders and long wiry arms like a spider was crawling on the ground, facing up with his back arched high to an impossible curve. He was singing in a high-pitched voice even though he was foaming lightly at the mouth. He looked like he was leaking tree sap. Saura recognized the signs. He'd been possessed by Kuturu, the leper spirit, the healer of diseases of the flesh. Two men in white kaftans played soft music with their fingers on white dotted calabashes. A girl that seemed no more than thirteen played an accompanying lute. Saura used to be that girl, the one playing the lute at possessions, before she was compelled to flee and enter the world.

When they were done and the man was helped to his feet by two others, presumably healed of his ailment, Saura removed her veil and made her request before her mother could completely compose herself.

"Tell us, why do you want the Sarkin Sarkoki to possess you?" One of the other magajiya, a plump woman with plaited hair, asked first in accented Hausa. It was her aunt, Turai.

For Mobola, Saura thought, but didn't say.

She simply replied, "I have been wronged. And I want justice."

The third council member, a man with thick white eyebrows whom she had never seen before asked her why she wanted Sarkin Sarkoki, the lord of the chains, the binding spirit. Why not Kure, he asked, the hyena spirit who could give power and stealth, or Sarkin Rafi, who would give strength to do violence which vengeance often called for.

"Because the one that wronged me is not mortal." At that, they fell silent.

The three members of the bori council stared at her appraisingly. Sifting and weighing her request. Her mother's gaze unrelenting.

"My daughter. I'm glad you have finally come home. Where you belong. But Sarkin Sarkoki demands a great price," her mother said finally, standing up from the raffia mat to her full height. Saura became acutely aware of just how much they looked like each other. The same thin nose and lips. The same ochre skin even though her mothers' was more weathered, beaten to stubborn leather by the Sahara-adjacent sun. The same determined look in the eyes. "The possession is permanent. The lord of the chains will bind himself to you before giving you the power to bind your enemy. You are giving up your body as a vessel forever. What justice could be worth this?"

Beneath the veil, heat rose behind Saura's neck. She did not want to say what she was thinking. There was too much pain in her heart threatening to spill out. If she let even a drop of the decade's worth of resentment within her slip between her lips, it would become a deluge that drowned them all.

"It doesn't matter. I am one of you. Heir to a title. I have a right to commune with the spirits. With Sarkin Sarkoki. And I have made my request."

There was more weighing. More sifting. More appraisal. Finally, her mother turned to face the other two of the council and they communed briefly before announcing their decision.

"We will grant your request," her mother said. "But on one condition. Once you have had your revenge against whatever spirit has wronged you, you must return home and become a full bori devotee. We cannot have a vessel of Sarkin Sarkoki roaming free. You will take your place with us, you will marry a good man, and you will bear children and teach them our ways. Do you agree?"

Saura knew this was what her mother had always wanted. To bring her back and bind her to home, even if she had to exploit a tragedy to achieve it. But Saura could not see past her desire to avenge Mobola. To find out why her lover had died and make their story make sense again even if she couldn't change its ending.

"I agree."

Her words, like her heart, had taken on the texture of stone.

Her mother nodded and smiled, teeth cutting a curve like the half-moon beaming down on them from the cloudless sky.

Saura closed her eyes as a woman in a yellow jalabiya cut like her own took her by the arms and brought her to the centre of the clearing, where the two main roads that crossed the market met. The woman stood behind her, she would be her nurse if anything went wrong.

Saura breathed steadily as the men in the white kaftans and the girl on the lute began to play their music and the three members of the council, led by her mother, began to chant words she had not heard for years. Words that made the air feel heavy on her skin, in her lungs.

Saura felt something in her chest open like the peeling of a flower. She felt a flush of heat, saw a flash of light. A rush of charged air entered her and then the world fell away as she was insufflated by the incoming spirit.

In the dark and nebulous place of her mind, Saura saw Sarkin Sarkoki.

He was an impossibly gaunt man, with limbs like vines and grey skin sitting on a stool at the centre of the empty space. He was bound in thick, corroded chains tethered to something she could not see in the filmy darkness below. A black cloth was wrapped around his waist and draped to cover his lower half, it pooled in cascades merging with the nebulous black ground below. His eyes were dark red, like spilled blood, and his stomach was cut open revealing mechanical viscera of chains and gears and roiling iron entrails. All over his skin, scripts were written onto him in chalked scars. He looked like a man that had been tortured and starved. He opened his mouth to reveal rust-coloured teeth.

"You offer yourself as a vessel," he said, already knowing why she'd let him into her mind and what she wanted him to help her do.

"Yes," Saura managed to reply despite her trembling.

"You surrender your body to the chains."

"Yes."

"Then so be it," Sarkin Sarkoki stated, his chains clanking and rattling as he began to vibrate. "We are one. You will have what you desire."

The chains around him unfurled themselves and reached out to seize her. They were heavy and rough. Saura felt them wrap around every part of her, flesh and bone, blood and nerves, mind and spirit. The chains squeezed around the very essence of her until the world was nothing but chains and darkness. A full and lovely pain consumed her as Sarkin Sarkoki bonded with her, and it wasn't until the woman in the yellow jalabiya poured water on her face and shook her back into full consciousness that she tasted the sand in her mouth and realized she had been rolling around on the ground, screaming.

Wednesday goes quiet.

Her siblings wait.

She takes in a deep breath and lets out a scream. It is at once a declaration of defiance and an accusation levelled at her siblings, at the family that put her in chains. Her scream is a knife in their hearts.

Saturday does not look away until her sister stops screaming. Wednesday's face, once full of grace, is contorted into an ugly shape with lines like regret but Saturday does not turn from it. She takes it all in, the words and the scream because that too is part of the story.

When the screaming ends, there is a pause that lasts for a long time but only briefly as they allow the scream to settle.

And then, the story continues.

Her siblings' words are air in Saturday's lungs and her song is half complete. Saturday turns to face Thursday. His mahogany skin is pallid in the candlelight. The sadness hanging from the corners of his mouth and the salt and pepper of his hair makes him look fragile and small in his black fitted suit. He leans forward and places both elbows on the table, settling his jaw on the tip of his fingers, hands pressed together like he is in prayer.

When Thursday begins to speak, Saturday manages a smile. She likes Thursday's voice. It is steady and powerful and full of purpose, like waves crashing onto a cliff, like vengeance.

This is the part of the story that Thursday told:

Saura was pretending to be asleep on an uncomfortable mattress in a spacious hotel room she'd taken for three nights when Shigidi arrived, just before midnight. She was shivering beneath the duvet, because she didn't know how to adjust the central air conditioning, but she didn't care. There was a "do not disturb sign" outside.

The nightmare god's arrival was sudden, and she felt his presence immediately. The dream-sensation of that small dark orb tugging at her subconscious with its evil gravity was one she could never forget.

She waited until he climbed onto the bed and sat on her chest, the weight of him restricting her breath. When she felt his probing at the edges of her mind, noticed a blurring and loosening of her thoughts and memories, she knew he had made the mistake of establishing a connection with her mind. Of attempting to slip into her subconscious, as was his way. But she'd set a trap for him. The Babalawo in Badagry had given her the number for another, less reputable Babalawo who took requests for the nightmare god's assistance from people with such cruelty in their hearts. She'd told him that she wanted someone killed in their sleep, but she didn't say that the name she'd given was her own. And that the location she'd provided was the hotel room she'd booked. The trap was sprung.

She sat up suddenly and came face to face with the god that had murdered Mobola.

Saura was taken aback by how small and ugly Shigidi was. He was just over two feet tall. His head was too big for his body, and his dark ashy skin was covered in pockmarks, rashes, scarification lines, and sores. He wore filthy Ankara print trousers, and a plain black cloak that sat on his shoulders and ran down to the back of his ankles, with cowrie shells and lizard skulls sewn into the fabric. His face was covered with black ash that made it look much darker than the rest of him. He looked confused, surprised, a bit stupid and unsure what to do.

Saura felt a flush of anger that something so hideous had been the one to take Mobola from her.

"Bastard," she spat out.

"What is happening?" Shigidi asked as he tried to withdraw from the borders of her consciousnesses.

Saura did not answer, she simply grabbed him and pulled him into the darkness of her mind where her inability to dream had left a vacuum where the cadaverous and bound Sarkin Sarkoki now dwelled.

Chains shot out of the darkness and latched onto Shigidi's small limbs, binding him to the place. He struggled and pulled but he could not free himself. Sarkin Sarkoki sat on his stool, watching, and making a sound like laughter.

"What is going on? Who are you people?" the nightmare god shouted.

Angry that Shigidi could not even remember her face, she did not give him the satisfaction of understanding.

"You gods and spirits, you are all the same," she said instead. "You think you can enter our lives and ruin them at your whim, taking whatever you want and leaving us to pick up the pieces. No. Not this time. This time, here is what will happen. You will suffer, like you have never suffered before. There will be pain. A lot of it. I will take my time. And even when you begin to thirst for death, when the chains have dug into your ugly body so deeply that they have fused with your nerves so that there is nothing except pain, you will not die. I will watch as you are stripped of every fragment of hope you hold in that body, until you feel as black and as bleak as this place, deep inside you. Maybe then you will remember who I am, and you will remember the person you took from me."

As she spoke, the expression on Shigidi's face had morphed from confusion to terror to something beyond both.

And when he whispered, "why?", Saura silently asked Sarkin Sarkoki to tighten the squeeze of the chains around his neck until his head bulged and he began to choke. It did not relent until he blacked out.

Thursday lifts his head and withdraws his hands from the intricately-patterned mahogany table, its straight-grained, reddish-brown timber cut from a tree that once stood at the centre of a garden that is not a garden, in the middle of nowhere, everywhere, all at once. He leans back and turns to meet Saturday's gaze. She smiles at him, grateful for the way he told his part of the story which she has also absorbed. She feels it almost bursting out of her now—the song. She just needs one more part. The revelation.

She turns to face Friday who is raking his hands through his thick afro. He is the most reserved of the siblings and the one who likes the shape that secrets give stories, which is why she has arranged it so that he can tell this part, just before her song. Candlelight dances in his large brown eyes and his pitch-black lips are quivering. He is eager to tell and hear.

Saturday nods and Friday opens his mouth, his bass voice booming and bouncing off the walls of the room in powerful waves.

This is the part of the story that Friday told:

Their bodies lay still and silent on the bed in the hotel, slumped over each other in an awkward embrace, but in the darkness of Saura's mind, possessed by Sarkin Sarkoki, Shigidi was screaming. Saura watched dispassionately, refusing to allow him even a waking moment of respite, a single fleeting second where he was not intimately acquainted with the pain from the contracting chains. And with every scream, she asked him the same question.

"Do you remember what you took from me?"

He insisted that he did not know, and so the torment continued. Sarkin Sarkoki's laughter the only other sound in her mind.

Almost twenty hours passed before the screaming stopped. Saura knew that it was not because the pain had ended, she was still commandeering the chains to pull and squeeze, and he was still writhing and whimpering. It was because something in him was breaking. Even a god can only take so much torment.

And yet after all the suffering, when she looked at him, pathetic as he was, she did not feel the satisfaction that she had craved. Underneath her rage was a sense of emptiness and loss and soul-deep weariness. She too was breaking under the weight of vengeance. And she knew now that someone else had sent him to their home that night because the disreputable Babalawo had told her it was the only reason Shigidi would kill someone.

"Mobola," she blurted out, eager for resolution. "Her name was Mobola."

Shigidi looked up at her, a glimmer of hope in his eyes for the first time since she'd lured him into the place of chains. He looked around at the darkness, as though he were searching her thoughts for something. And then, "Ahh... Mobola..." he croaked. "Yes. Omobola Adenusi...Lotus estate, Surulere. I remember now."

Saura seethed when her name escaped his mouth.

"Why... why did you kill her?" she asked, her rage still bubbling at the surface.

"I'm sorry." Shigidi breathed. "It was just a job. A standard nightmare-and-kill job."

Saura shuddered, she knew how he worked, but she was too angry to care. "Just a job? You took the most precious person in the world from me because it was just a job?"

The chains around his limbs rattled as Shigidi's tortured body sagged with the effort of keeping his head upright. "I'm sorry. I didn't know. It was just a job. It was only a job."

"Who sent you? Who was the client?"

And as she asked that, Sarkin Sarkoki's laughter stopped abruptly.

"I don't know," Shigidi said. "I just do what they ask me."

"Then you must remember," Saura demanded.

The chains tightened again.

"Please..."

"Tell me."

"I don't know," the nightmare god maintained, each word excavated from him was hoarse and desperate. "But... but... wait... it was a woman. Older. Not Yoruba. I remember she was not Yoruba. She was slender. Thin nose. She had eyes like yours."

Saura clutched at her chest.

"In her prayer, she only said she needed to get rid of the girl to get her daughter back."

A knot like an iron rope formed in her stomach. Saura fell to her knees as the weight of realization settled upon her. The lack of surprise when her mother saw her at the market. The insistence on returning home as a condition of her possession. The guilt in her aunt Turai's eyes. It all made terrible sense to her in that moment.

She asked Sarkin Sarkoki to unshackle him from her mind and Shigidi fell onto the dark filmy ground with a thud. In an instant, they were back on the bed, in the hotel.

Saura shot up and rolled off the mattress onto the carpeted floor. She felt the iron rope tighten in her stomach and everything constricted, like it was being squeezed by invisible hands. She felt like her insides were about to be torn and exposed, like the hollow clockwork belly of Sarkin Sarkoki. She threw up and began to cry.

"Ah. You know who it was, don't you?" Shigidi whispered.

Her mothers' words tolled in her head like a bell.

My daughter.

I'm glad you have finally come home.

Saura stumbled up to her knees and settled a long stare at Shigidi who was looking back at her with, large yellow eyes full of pity or regret or both.

"Yes," she whispered back.

"Family?"

"Yes."

"I... I am sorry. I am truly sorry."

Saura was surprised by the sincerity in his voice.

"I hate my job sometimes," Shigidi continued. "But I need the offerings and prayer requests to survive. Please understand. I didn't mean to cause you pain but I... need to survive. I never mean to cause anyone pain. But I... I don't want to wither and die. I just wish there was another way."

Saura was even more surprised when Shigidi awkwardly clambered down from the bed and lay on the floor in front of her, prostrating in the traditional way, to show respect or profound apology. "I'm sorry."

She placed her hand on his head and Saura and Shigidi wept together.

The story is near its end when Friday stops speaking.

And Saturday's song is about to begin.

There are no instruments to be played but the air hums electric with a sense of music, in anticipation.

Her siblings watch, enraptured as her ribs expand, her diaphragm moves up and her belly hollows out like a cave. The pressure of the melody builds up in her chest and there are vibrations in her throat, her mouth, her lips. Saturday feels like she is full of all the words and feelings and air that her siblings have given her with their words. Like she will never run out of breath. Like she will never run out of story. Like she will never run out of song.

Saturday begins to sing in a clear and loud voice full of energy.

This is the song Saturday sang:

She entered a life
She struck in like lightning
But was taken too soon
Beauty and joy and kindness
Mobola, lost to nightmare's touch
Breath extinguished by a mercenary god

Oh, a dirge for true love
For an embrace lost

A return home
Where Saura's heart is buried
A sacrifice to the essence of binding
The lord of the chains
Gave her the power
Gave her the strength to catch a murderous god

But gods only serve people
They are made in the minds of men
In Saura's mind, the nightmare god revealed a secret
That the umbilical cord can be a noose
That family can be a chain
That seeks to bind at any cost

How could a mother do this?
Oh, how could she not just accept?
How many tears must be shed to pay for this sin?
How much blood must be spilled?
It's an evil way she has chosen
To show the depth of love

Oh, a dirge for motherhood
Of the poison in the womb

Saura swears that for as long as she lives
She will not let this happen to anyone like her
The bargain has been struck
The word-bond is made of iron
But there are many kinds of homecoming
And sometimes gifts bear teeth

Saura makes a pact with her lovers' killer
An unwitting instrument in a war that began at birth
He will give her dreams as restitution
To make amends for stilling her lover's heart
And she will forgive him
For he knew not what he was doing

But grief and sorrow must be repaid
There are many kinds of binding

And even invited guests can come baring teeth
If death is the price of her presence
Then let there be music and tears
As she goes home to share a living nightmare from which there is now no escape

Oh, a dirge for childhood
Of innocence lost

She enters the village like a whirlwind
And blows her way home
Her mother is sitting in the clearing
Where Saura once played Kagada with friends
Trust-falling into each other's arms and singing
And eating hot tuwo under weekend stars

Their eyes meet full of determination and knowledge
Tragic corruption of love and affection
Her mother strikes first, possessed by Kure the hyena
No deeper pain than to be struck by the hand that fed you
Fate is cruel to set blood against blood
She reaches into her mother's mind and ends it quickly

She gives her mother's mind permanent shelter
In the dark place with Sarkin Sarkoki
Where she will always be with her
Trapped in the once-empty darkness now filled with hate
Bound together in their pain
Their new umbilical cord made of spirit-chains

Her mother's body becomes a hollow vessel
Sessile as a tree and just as alive
She has been given the thing she wanted
Saura takes her mother's place
For a paralyzed woman cannot be magajiya
When her daughter has come home

They are now always together
In her every waking moment Saura hears her mother's voice
Pleading, railing, crying to be let go
But every night when she goes to bed
She closes her eyes, and silence falls
And in the quiet of her mind, she dreams

And so, Saturday's song ends.

The euphonic cavalcade of melodies comes to a halt. Saturday is exhausted and feels empty, like a gourd with all its water poured out but she smiles because she thinks it was a good song and she sang it well.

Her six siblings remain silent, a rapturous look painted onto their faces. They are still lost to the song. Saturday savours the moment. This is why she sings the stories sometimes. For that look in their eyes that says she has given them something special. And for what she hopes it will evoke within them. She has told, she has heard, she has performed.

She turns to Sunday, whose task it is to complete all their stories and she sees wetness in his sea-green eyes. She smiles and nods.

Sunday sucks in air and lets out his words in a whisper that was loud enough for all of them to hear.

This is all that Sunday said:

The end.

At that, the seven siblings that were, that are, and always have been, fall silent again and contemplate the story for a moment that is also an eternity. It is a reading of their own entrails, an examination of the essence of all things from which they are woven, and it is the most important part of the story—what it does to those who receive it. Its interpretation, its impact, its legacy.

"Humans are such tragic things," Sunday said. "Little grains of consciousness floating atop an ocean of existence vaster than any of them possibly imagine, barely aware of all the other ways of being, of all that exists outside their perception. And yet their stories are heavy in our bones, written upon us with the brightness of stars. The myriad ways they love and hurt each other are fascinating. They weave such tenderness and cruelty with every fibre of their lives."

He pauses. And then, "This was a good story. We told it well."

He turns to Saturday, the lines of his face converging, his eyes wide and full of realization, of knowledge. "But why did you choose this story for us to tell and hear, sister, why did you sing this song?"

"For the same reason we tell and hear all our stories. Because that is what happened and thus must be told."

The siblings all echoed the mantra in unison. "That is what happened and thus must be told."

Sunday smiles faintly, maintaining his placid countenance. "Indeed. But there is also another reason, is there not?"

"For Wednesday," Saturday admits, brushing a loose, blonde braid behind her ear. She knew he would be the first to understand.

"We are not human, we are not like Saura or her mother. We should not continue to bind our own blood so, regardless of her crime. Wednesday is our sister. Yes, she tried to change a story, but which of us has not been tempted to do so?" She pointed at the timestone sitting at the centre of the table like an emerald fruit. "Her actions were wrong, but they came from a good place. And in the end, the story was not changed. The stories cannot be changed. She knows that now. She is certain of it. As are we all. That is the lesson of her story, and it is complete. Let us release her chains."

Saturday sees the gratitude silently spilling out of the sides of Wednesday's thin mouth, her soft eyes, her broad nose.

Sunday looks at all his siblings. Their eyes reveal what they want even though they are mostly bound by rules carved in the primordial essence of existence, rules older than time itself. But rules, like gods, are only as powerful as their purpose and the will of those who made them. "Do you all agree with this? Shall we free our sister?"

"Yes," Monday says.

From Tuesday. "We should."

There is a hopeful nod from Wednesday herself.

"Yes," Thursday says.

Friday echoes his agreement.

"Yes," Saturday cannot hide her joy.

"Then so be it." Sunday says.

Saturday leaps to her feet and lets out a cry as the shackles loosen and fall from Wednesday's limbs, clattering with a noise like songs of freedom, like a sibling's laughter, like the forgiveness of family.

. . . .

Wole Talabi is an engineer, writer, and editor from Nigeria. He is the author of the World Fantasy Award-nominated novel *Shigidi and The Brass Head of Obalufon*, one of the *Washington Post*'s Top 10 Science Fiction and Fantasy books of 2023, which was also nominated for the Nebula Award, Locus Award, British Fantasy Award, and other major awards. His short fiction has appeared in places like *Asimov's Science Fiction*, *Lightspeed Magazine*, *The Africa Risen* anthology and is collected in the books *Convergence Problems* (2024) and *Incomplete Solutions* (2019). He has also been a finalist for the Hugo, BSFA, and Crawford Awards, as well as the Caine Prize for African Writing. He has won the Nommo Award for African Speculative Fiction and the Sidewise Award for Alternate History. He has edited five anthologies including the acclaimed *Africanfuturism: An Anthology* (2020) and *Mothersound: The Sauútiverse Anthology* (2023). He likes scuba diving, elegant equations, and oddly shaped things. He currently lives and works in Australia. Find him at wtalabi.wordpress.com and at @wtalabi online.

I AM AI

Ai Jiang

It's becoming difficult and dangerous to ignore my battery's rapid run-down time. At 8%, my memory functions are diminishing far too quickly. I've forgotten to charge before leaving work—again.

For me, forgetting is a dangerous thing.

I hope the glitches don't cause a sudden short-circuiting.

The notification for my postponed-for-half-a-year maintenance glares from the watch implanted into my wrist. I press snooze, my fingers trembling. I can't afford the bi-monthly checkups, but I'll need to replace my battery soon.

Replacing my brain for a system that works faster, that limits errors, and doesn't cause memory gaps becomes more appealing with each passing day. AIs don't have a fear of overworking, of needing sleep to prevent any fatigue.

My hands shake at the prospect of finally getting rid of the one thing outside of my brain that hinders my productivity. To think my emotions will soon become a muted thing, I can't tell if I'm afraid or eager. But I'll be able to work faster. Joy and pain won't affect me in the same way.

None of my neighbours know I die with my battery rather than my heart. Most of them still believe I'm more human than robot—half metal and circuits. Being less human makes life easier. Technology is convenient; it's more dependable as a life force, more predictable. Emotions, humanity, mortality; humans are such fragile things.

A message from my mechanic Joan arrives, pinging my watch with an "URGENT" tag. *I've secured the battery you've been looking for to make the full heart replacement. You're booked for tomorrow.*

I appreciate their straightforward tone, though a part of me wants us to become friends, given how long we've known each other. Three years now, maybe four—I've lost track. But I suppose it will only become a nuisance to us both, draw us away from our focus, if we care too much.

I just have to hold on until tomorrow night.

Another warning about my battery. I dismiss it and scramble to leave, grabbing my jacket flung in the corner of my 11 ft. by 11 ft. box-like unit, to reach a charging port on time.

I don't notice Auntie Narwani's entrance until she's long pushed her way into my unit's narrow space. I almost curse out loud as I mentally make a note to fix the lock.

Auntie Narwani hovers by my elbow, trying to plug the clock she found last week into the port in my arm. I should be annoyed, but the feeling of familiarity, the sense of family she has somehow built in our community over time, even if we have no blood relation, comforts me. Sometimes I want nothing more than to collapse into Auntie Narwani, but to show such weakness will only create bad, *time-costing*, habits I can't afford.

Right now, I don't have the patience or battery life to entertain the elder's requests. Cold sweat wells at the base of my neck, collecting in the collar of my shirt, long due for a wash. Grime itches the parts of my back that remain skin rather than metal. I can almost hear my battery draining within me as the seconds tick past.

"Hold on a second, just hold *on a second*!"

I don't have a second.

Our arms flail, and I narrowly miss her head at the same time she accidently sucker punches my shoulder. Cold air whisks down my lungs. I add "shoulder-plate" to the list of replacements I will purchase when funds allow.

She plugs the clock back in.

The clock is precious to Auntie, but to me, it only serves as a reminder of the time I'm losing, the stutters of my heart when the passing minutes appear as a looming count down within my mind.

The old thing had washed ashore, waterlogged, paint half gone, with the seconds hand missing. A great find, she explained, even though she'd cut herself on the jagged edges of rocks and soiled her shoes trying to reach it by the edge of the lake. It never lasts long enough for the alarm to go off at the time she's set it for. Sometimes, I feel like the clock. My energy levels and brain capacity always coming to a halt when I need the limitations removed most; the choking suffocation of imminent burnout a faceless entity chasing me from behind with shadowy fingers always just brushing the small of my back.

I keep reminding her to toss it, to get a new watch—one that tells time without stuttering. But she never has. The protective coating of the broken clock's wire is barely there, like flesh hanging from exposed bones. If unlucky, we both could be electrocuted.

Look at how wonderful it is, Auntie Narwani insisted. *There is a story behind this clock.*

"Auntie!" I swat her hand away once more, impulsively checking my battery again and again, with each staccato movement.

Just because I'm a cyborg, she sees me as both an endearing youth and a tool for her use—but sometimes it feels as though the latter is truer than the former. Here in the city of Emit, we're more valuable as tools than humans.

"Hush, child," she says, frowning, looking at me as if *I'm* the one in the wrong.

I don't want her to know she is leaving me on the verge of death.

My palms clam up, sweat beads at my forehead as I look for a way to leave without being rude. Guilt claws at me when Auntie Narwani makes a disappointed pout. She acts more like she's seven rather than seventy. I wish to be as carefree as she.

The light above us flickers. Outside, the rest of the units' electricity goes out. I check my Bluetooth connection that helps power all the other units. Disconnected. My aid all started as a way to make some extra cash on the side, but over time somehow just became a favour I did for everyone. Whether it's compassion or guilt or pity, I much prefer to see everyone sharing what little resources we have, rather than hoarding everything myself.

Electricity is a luxury we can barely afford on the outskirts of Emit. These shelters were not built by the government, but by those who couldn't afford the property rent in the city. But they still charge us.

A few of our neighbours peek out of their units. Some climb onto the intricate metal staircases that connect our honeycomb-like community under the bridge that stretches from the mouth of the city Emit, across the lake, leading into barren, infertile land. Many of us prefer it to the bustling noises of the city.

With the city's overpopulation, they've begun building homes and shelters wherever there is space—digging underground, growing upward, or, like our homes, under the bridge, attached to its legs. There used to be houseboats floating across the lake, until New Era's monopoly over all industries. They claimed the body of water as their own and complained about floating bodies and debris after heavy storms. They don't care about the dead, only the cost of fishing the corpses out, and the resources to return them to their family. To New Era, people might as well be the plastic bottles floating in the lakes—before those bio-engineered to consume garbage in efforts to clear the growing landfills began risking their lives to fish them out of the water. Roaches. I wonder what names they might give people like me.

A thundering of steps echoes towards my unit. It was no doubt Nemo making her way in a zigzag up the three flights separating our homes.

I check my battery again.

7%.

"Ai?" The young child pops her head in. Normally her mother Lei stops her from visiting too frequently, but the young child latched onto me as though I'm her older sister ever since her mother began taking on extra shifts at work.

Nemo pulls out her drone controller—a small thing the community pooled together to buy her —and lands the machine by her feet. From its body, a hologram pops up. A shining gold coin displays what I'll need to pay the government this month. Then, it switches to a hovering diamond that holds the remaining debt I owe the government.

I nudge past Nemo and swallow the hurt expression that warps her joyous face and leave Auntie Narwani still cross-legged on my bare futon.

In the distance above us, at the end of the bridge that divides the tech-drenched city and our honeycomb home, Emit's glow is unwavering. Its skyscrapers claw into the clouds, the tops unseen—a city that progresses and moves at a speed too fast for many of our minds. Most of the others refuse to pay for the upgrades, desiring to remain more human—not me. Being human reminds me of my parents and the fragility of our minds and bodies, the way New Era drained their life's hourglass, among other workers, at double speed. No doubt their worries about leaving me with my aunt as a child accelerated their burnout. I cannot afford the same.

"Leaving for work again?" Auntie Narwani fidgets with the clock. Why she always sets it for 5:00 p.m., I'll never know; I'm never home until 10:30 p.m.—at least.

"Yes," I say in a rush, focusing on the beckoning allure of my watch.

Still 7%. But it won't remain the same for long.

Before, it might take up to half an hour just to drain 1%.

I often wish I could live simply like Aunt Narwani and the others, thriving on what they grow near the bank along the lake, away from the prying eyes of the Emit government, taking up odd jobs when available. But I can't; none of it pays enough, nor are the hours consistent—not anymore.

I think of Auntie Narwani and how she might spend the day. Sometimes she mentions cleaning for the New Era towers, or the barely lived-in homes of some techies, offering her services for cheaper than what they would pay machines. But what makes her services unique is the songs she sings, the shaking notes, the occasionally off-pitch tunes, that fill the towers and homes with something other than the hum of electricity—a voice I sometimes catch as I drift to sleep each night. She makes just enough to get by and has no desire to climb any social or economic ladder. After being replaced by music machines and bots at the karaoke hubs and scattered bars when they first appeared, her only desire is to sing for those who might appreciate "real music".

I used to want the same; for someone to simply appreciate the stories I write, even if flawed, with loopholes, inconsistent characters, endings and openings barely hanging on like threads. But when my parents passed, all they left me was their endless debt and memories that bombard my mind at night. I see the hardships my parents went through as techies for New Era, images of their early passing, being shuttled out of New Era's main tower—Father only thirty at the time, Mother, twenty-nine, and I was only seven.

I still have vivid dreams of the many deaths that day, the injustices when New Era offered the families of the dead nothing but a written letter of insincere apology, and the protestors. Almost as soon as they gathered, their efforts were suppressed by New Era security. Protests are rare now, if any. If I could wipe myself of these memories, I would. The holographic ads hovering above the New Era-owned buildings in Emit come to mind: *Brain replacements are the best option for the tired mind!* Then again, which buildings are *not* owned by New Era.

They offered me a job too, New Era, but I still haven't taken them up on their offer. Even after years of blistering skin, the shiver of rising goosebumps tightening, contracting across my limbs in the middle of the cold of the dead season, on the verge of hypothermia, I still refused.

My work isn't so different from New Era and pays far less. But it isn't *as* mindless and repetitive. There is always the pressure to be perfect, to limit errors, to the level of AI—0.001% or is it 0.0001% now? But limiting errors also means taking away style, and the systems aren't as good with coming up with anything unique and often draw on what already exists and the cliches. Most are content with the creative texts AIs produce, though there are still those who prefer more "authentic" voices, yet almost none of those people are willing to pay the price. Some large corporations might seek out people like me once in a while, when they're looking for something *"Fresh! Never before seen!"* Contrary to what they hoped, not as many artists and writers jump at the chance to work for them. Some do, but it can be such soulless and tightly controlled work.

6%.

"Don't be home too late!" Auntie Narwani calls after me as I speed out of my unit and up the steps. I try not to look down. I listen for incoming traffic, even though there is almost always none, before pulling myself over the side railing and onto the bridge's asphalt surface.

Later at night, I'll have to charge Auntie Narwani's clock again and power the reading lights and night lights for the elderly and children, hot water for Mrs. Gem, who finds relief for her pregnant belly while standing for fifteen minutes under a warm shower. There is a couple who always has something broken, and the sound of their electric drill buzzes for an hour or two upon my return. And of course, Nemo, who always comes running to charge her drone because, outside of delivering any news from Emit, she wants to watch the sleepless city, even if she can't live within it.

The path towards Emit is worn, cracked under harsh rays of sun. The city avoids making repairs to the bridge whenever they can. Few people cross it by crafts or e-bikes anyhow, and when they do, they usually never return.

I check the time—

5%.

With Auntie Narwani's insistence this morning, I'm already a few minutes behind for work. I can't lose any clients.

A light drizzle begins that quickly pours.

Rain isn't nearly as harmless as it was before: the droplets are corrosive to both skin and metal, skyrocketing the prices of waterproof parts. I can't afford any of those expensive replacements either, though I suppose with how often I have to change my parts, it must have added up to the same cost anyhow. I pull out my compressed raincoat, unfurl it, and toss it on. Droplets eat away at the material that remains and at the mixture of skin and metal of my limbs peeking through the holes.

I work up to a slow jog, cautious of how heavily I'm breathing, in hopes I'm still alive when I reach Mao Tou Ying internet café.

I suppose it wouldn't be too bad if I passed, though I dread to think who might end up with my debt. Unfortunately, New Era didn't care about those with no families. They can easily pass debt onto someone they think we might be close to, who their cameras might have spotted us with. Knowing this, I fear they might go for Nemo.

I can't tell if what burns down my cheeks is rain or tears, but I suppose it doesn't matter because one eats from the outside and the other within.

4%.

Mao Tou Ying sits at the edge of Emit, just far enough to not garner too much interest from the government, but close enough it can reap the benefits of the city's electricity sources and communication infrastructure. Like many of the Independents, these owners and companies are pushed to the edges of Emit, as far from the city center as possible. It wasn't their choice, but I think if they had one, they would still choose to remain in place.

Atop the entrance of the café are the flickering neon aqua letters of Mao Tou Ying and the wired image of an orange owl sitting on top of "Tou" as though perched on a tree, the wavering colour making it seem like it's on fire. Sometimes only the "Ying" is lit, and without the tonal accent, no one can tell whether it is the "ying" in owl or the "ying" in shadow. Ironically, both fit the establishment.

I pick at my peeling, exposed skin and at the buildup of rust on metal and wince, regretting replacing only the areas around my joints rather than the entirety of each limb. I thought about replacing my hand so there would be no finger fatigue, but I didn't want to give up the feeling of the keys against flesh. Somehow, that makes the act of creation feel more real, tangible.

Smoke wafts upward just past the café where a street vendor, Nemo's mother Lei, lives with the rest of us under the bridge. She stands at her stall stir-frying freeze-dried rice after defrosting it with a drop of New H2O.

Lei spots me and beckons me over.

I shake my head quick.

3%.

"Maybe after work," I call out and smile, but it falters at the age lines on her face that seem to deepen by several folds each day.

Lei insists on working most of her hours away. *The baby's almost three, and New Era raised tuition for preschool again,* she'd explained a week prior. People believed New Era would soon collapse after its initial rise because of the increasing burnout rate and decreasing life-expectancy of their staff. But the company managed to strike a balance after branching out to take over other industries. Emit's average life expectancy is up from forty-five to fifty years—but that is nothing compared to our ancestors a thousand years ago, in 2022, when life expectancy hovered around eighty.

Lei always begins work far before the sun starts to rise, hiding behind the smog-infested skies, and much after it sets, when the only light in this alleyway comes from the fire of her wok, the glow-in-the-dark painted sign of her stall.

I pull up my e-wallet and search for the name of her stall, Fried Wok Street Food—easy for tourists to find. The order option pops up after I tap the holographic name, and below it is the option to tip. I don't have much extra to spare, but I send two Coin—half the price of a rice bowl, knowing that even if I don't end up buying dinner, Lei will bring home leftovers and leave them by my door anyhow.

I'm wasting precious seconds. I know. Yet I find myself unable to escape this daily ritual, no matter how dire the circumstances. It feels as though it is one of the only small intimacies left in my life.

Lei shakes her head, but a grateful smile rests on her lips. She swipes a perspiring arm, tanned up to where her shirtsleeve covers, across the white bandana that encases her forehead. Though I need every Coin I can get, I can work longer hours, accept new clients to make up the slight loss. Lei will need it more than I do. She reminds me of my mother, who was always working when I was a child. Back then, I couldn't understand why she spent so little time with me, but now that she's gone...I hope Nemo won't grow up misunderstanding Lei, but I know she probably will.

2%.

I buzz Wushui to let me in. Wushui turns off the screen-frosting security function on both the glass of the door and windows, even though he already has cameras installed outside. Maybe the cameras are broken. There is always something broken in the café, but luckily the e-glass screens —floating digitalized glass that resembles a more minimalist version of old computer monitors— are not one of those things.

I glare into Mao Tou Ying while I wait, unamused at his usual lack of urgency. Still 2%.

It's packed today, with the regulars, teens, playing video games in a corner or live streaming in one of the six booths in the back. From the looks of it, half of them use scripts written by New Era's A.I. app. One of the booths has been blacked out since Hermes, a neighbour who reminds me of myself sometimes—a girl I barely see in her unit—booked out the booth so she can paint with what little supplies she can afford and get her hands on. She occasionally keeps her finished works, and I would see small pieces hanging on the otherwise bare walls of her unit, or the communal washroom at the center of our honeycomb; other times she might sell them to black market collectors or to New Era.

Some of the customers are masked, some unmasked. I always wonder if they worry about their identities being exposed, but everyone at the café is usually too absorbed with their own thing to worry about anyone else. One thing Wushui requires us to do is wear noise-cancelling headphones. But with some regulars, he's grown lax.

1%.

Agitation swims at my temples in throbbing waves, and I raise a fist to pound. But before my knuckles meet the door, there is a click. I push my way inside, shivering from the walk in the rain.

"Hey, Ai, you know the rules," Wushui grunts as I'm about to leave the muddy, rubber floor mat and step onto his precious royal blue carpet.

Wushui—*No Sleep*—isn't his real name, but a nickname that has become part of his identity because his business never closes, and he never seems to go home. He's long since become jaded and no longer seems to care about whether or not his business fails. He spends most of his time reading digital magazines and newspapers that are too old, outdated—always subscribing only for a month before cancelling, downloading all the content he can before the subscription ends.

I flash him the whites of my eyes before kicking off my boots, then hold up a foot, wiggling the toes inside my damp socks.

Wushui's partner flits out from the back room and makes a beeline towards me, swatting at my foot, though only half-heartedly, and offers me his usual lecture on respect. Niao, true to his name, is bird-like and gentle and, of the two older men, slightly more energetic. He's always making coffee and offering water to customers, trying to make sure people don't pass out too often while they're in the café. They do anyhow, but the kind gesture is appreciated, except by those who seem too immersed in their work to notice. At the end of the day, much of the water and snacks Niao leaves by the e-glasses remains untouched.

Wushui offers an almost unnoticeable breathy laugh without looking up from the handheld e-glass screen in front of him, likely reading the news about recent electricity outages with silent judgement.

I dip low and collect my boots, throwing them on the rack next to everyone else's shoes. There is one pair of slippers, oversized, that I always like to wear best. And though Wushui and Niao never make it explicit, they always leave them on the side for me; Niao even put a small sign beside them, warding off other customers. I thrust my feet into the slippers.

Please connect to a power source—

I try not to show my growing nervousness as I speed walk to my seat, connecting the wire extending from the e-glass into my charging port. An audible exhale whistles through my nose at the sight of the small lightning bolt blinking on my forearm.

There is a laugh paired with an unfamiliar pitched voice. "Did you know there's a type of sloth called ai? Well, they don't exist anymore, but apparently, they have very piercing cries." A man in his forties regards me from his chair. An uncommon sight, to see someone so alert.

Wushui snorts without looking up.

The sloth man looks at me with intrigue. "Watch it, boy," Wushui, not missing the predator beat, hisses. "You ain't no regular. I can kick you out if I want to." He reminds me of my father and his "no-nonsense" manner.

The man looks outside, the rain still pouring heavily, tsks, then swerves his chair back to his screen.

Hermes leans over, the leather of her chair creaking, with fingers paused, hovering over the e-glass with a clear stylus in front of her. She's halfway completed a comic panel for an advertisement selling AWAKE pills. I peek at the logo in the corner—a small company I've been writing for as well. The perk of this job is the pills they send us every month. They're useful, but over time, my body seems to be getting too used to them for them to have the same initial impact.

"Don't worry about him. I see this jerk hanging around where I live sometimes, but the aunties and uncles upstairs always chase him away. Waiting for an ex, or something."

I'm not worried, but it's better to err on the side of caution around people with obsessive behaviour like that. At least behaviours that concern other people rather than a simple personal habit or tick. I can sympathize with the man. But it's not a kind of desperation I want to feel. It would only deter me from work, and the missing hours would prove to be far more painful than heartache in the long run when my Coin account drains faster than the decreasing debt.

"Been stalking her socials here. He might slink around to your end too. Watch out." Hermes shakes her head, hand flying once more over the comic panels.

I glance again at the man and then at his screen. On the screen is the image of a woman in her thirties with a gentle smile.

Mother used to hang around her ex-girlfriend's workplace before New Era, before her marriage to Father. She did nothing. Just waited until her ex finished work and left before the woman came out. Mother used to pick her up every day the same way before they broke up.

Maybe it was the familiarity of the action she couldn't let go of, rather than the person. Or maybe it was both. She did the same thing with Father when they started dating. Perhaps it was the same for this man. But after starting at New Era, nothing outside of work mattered.

I suppose it can be a good thing to not be able to feel, to so single mindedly focus on accomplishing one thing and one thing only. It's simple, it's numbing, but it's also lifeless. And sometimes lifelessness is preferable.

"You found *the one* yet?" I tease as I wait for Wushui to unlock my e-glass screen. Hermes, though she might have not look like the typical romantic—with her beanie pulled over her brows and ears, and round glasses hovering at the tip of her nose—is one for idealistic dreams of perfect relationships—or used to be.

"Stop it," Hermes says, waving a dismissive hand. But her expression wilts, and I regret asking, even as a joke. "We both know we don't have the time for that. No human or any other species can shackle these fingers."

She wiggles her digits and draws a smile from me.

I tap my fingers erratically, looking to Wushui, who is taking more time than usual today. There are still five minutes left before I start work, but I'm antsy. I try not to log in early, to snuff my nerves, so I don't end up coming earlier and earlier until I'm here twenty-four hours a day like Wushui.

I should be used to the settled routine by now, having worked as an AI writer for the past five years. But the breaking of a cold sweat, the jittering hands, the staccato heartbeats when I'm facing deadlines never cease. I suppose that makes me more meticulous and efficient about my work, and ensures I keep clients, but it isn't great for long-term health, though lacking food is not much better.

My work hours have already increased from ten hours to eleven and a half. I can't remember the last time I had a proper break. It's still better than working for New Era with their fifteen-hour workdays, stuck within those suffocating sky-scrapers. Sure, it's comfortable and they pay for housing outside of the New Era buildings if the workers so choose, but with that many hours, it's unlikely they get to spend much time outside work anyway. It's only an empty incentive for those who don't yet know what it's like to work for the monopoly.

I pick up the headphones settled just beneath the e-glass, then wrap the soft cushion around my ears. The rest of the world mutes. Tunnel vision is how Wushui describes my working state, much like everyone else's. Unlike Hermes, who frequently takes off her headphones to make conversation, I don't have the luxury of having those fleeting minutes.

One thing I love about Mao Tou Ying, though, is how meticulous Wushui is about hiding what goes on in each of the thirty or so systems in the cafe. But that means frequent government check-ins, which always sets me back an hour or two. From what I know, Wushui's record is still clean. Or if it isn't, maybe he slid money under the table to keep the officials quiet. Where the money comes from, I don't have a clue. He charges me and Hermes barely anything to use the e-glass screens, but I have a feeling not everyone here is being charged the same. For those who can afford more, he might charge more. Or so I assume.

The app I code launches on the e-glass. The title drifts across the screen as it boots up: *I AM AI.*

It isn't a lie. I am Ai, though not necessarily an actual AI. But marketing myself as an actual AI seems to bring in more clients and won't draw as much attention from New Era.

The main screen displays my one hundred twenty-three clients at a bar on the left side and the deadlines for writing projects I'd picked up and have yet to finish, along with a pending list of new projects waiting for confirmation. I scroll through the nudges for copywriting, a few advertisements and speeches, along with research documents and other ghostwriting assignments.

When I took on my first ghostwriting client, I felt like a fraud, like those people who say they're fluent in a language in which they are brokenly conversational at best. But it is better to be hired, even if I end up writing advertisements, research papers, or legal documents removed from my focus in fiction. Time waits for no one, and neither does Emit.

Wait—

I pull up the ping notifications that consist of deadlines for written work. My fingers fly over the holokeys, each letter flickering with each tap. The maximum number of desktops I can have active at once is fifty, but there isn't a limit to the number of documents and web tabs. Each desktop has a handful of documents and so many open tabs that there is an infinity symbol rather than the actual number of pages.

After scheduling a few new projects and the required research—some fiction and nonfiction pieces based on events like the rise of New Era, the fall of the forests of Feng, the life of Roaches— I take note of any last-minute projects with end-of-the-day deadlines.

A new request pops up just as I'm about to start on the nonfiction piece that glorifies New Era. I don't want to write it, but at least I have control over the words that go on the page. At times, I might sneak in snide comments that are usually missed unless someone looks closely enough. More often than not, only the protestors will pick up these interpretations.

150,000-word research paper on the benefits of AI writing and art—Deadline: by the end of tomorrow.

I almost chuckle at the irony. Even if I'm desperate, I have enough sense to pass on the job—both because it's impossible, but also because it would be unethical, given my identity as a writer and my friendship with Hermes. I hover my finger above the decline button but catch sight of the completion bonus: one hundred fifty thousand Coin. My eye twitches. That will cover more than half of the debt I have remaining. I pick at the skin around my fingers, rub the back of my neck, feel the rash already building there. I rip a little too much away from the corner of my nail, and a bead of blood falls onto the table. There will be too much research necessary, and I will be pulling my hair out trying to write what I don't believe in. It will be much easier if this job popped up after my appointment with Joan, when my heart, the pulsing, chasing, reminder of humanity and its stress, anxiety, imperfection, is gone.

I press "accept."

I quickly finish a story for an interactive fiction website looking for more content and instantly receive a new review on their appreciation of my "different style" compared to other AI programs they source from. No client questions it since the subscription is only ten Coin a month, rather than the usual fifty Coin for New Era AI's fully automated service.

Then I start on the beast of an article.

"Ai." I turn to see Hermes with her attention fixed on a pop-up window of the e-application store. There is a new app that is basically a rip-off of my own: *I AM*

A.I. There's not much of a difference in the name except for the clarification of the abbreviation. The subscription is eight Coin a month.

I can't help but think it's New Era's way of shutting me down. It isn't the first time the company has resorted to such tactics. As soon as my app falls, this new replica will also disappear.

Another ping.

A client seems to have discovered the new service and has unsubscribed—in the explanation box, they hide nothing in their reasoning: *New cheaper app.* But I can't go any lower than ten Coin. I might get away with nine Coin. Even that might be stretching it. The new app doesn't have many ratings or reviews, so I can only hope it will fail like many other apps after not getting enough traffic. The New Era AI app dominates most of the market, even with its prohibitive cost, snuffing out competition once it threatens to take close to 0.5% of their customer base.

It's difficult for Independents to survive. The only appeal I have is the illusion of demand and "uniqueness" I created by accepting a limited number of clients in comparison to any other app that attempts to compete with New Era. Anyone new to my app will have to apply and be put on the waiting list, which makes it seem as though my program is one highly sought after and in demand, while not taking enough customers from New Era to raise any concern.

I can send out an ad and increase my list limit from a hundred thirty to a hundred fifty clients, but that means even longer hours, less sleep, and further limiting snacks to save money. Sometimes I go into what Hermes calls "hyperfocus mode"— when I forget I'm human entirely as I remain glued to my seat, the only things moving are my fingers and the tracking flicks of my eyes across the screen.

I don't have enough saved for another upgrade, and my credit score is less than ideal given my parents' and my aunt's combined debt, but the mechanic I usually visit is kind, or at least kind enough to let me put things on the tab and slowly pay it off without interest. They remind me of my aunt who passed too early. I lived with her until I was eighteen and moved out, but I didn't know her debt would be added on top of my parents', until one day I received the letter from New Era. I should have guessed. She had no children of her own.

But it was the price she had to pay for refusing to keep up with the rapidly developing tech and the shifting culture and job markets that came with it. She used to be a manual laborer, but during the Annual Layoff, she was unlucky enough to be let go. By then, it was too late to even become a Roach. Landfills are few now, and Roaches roam the streets, picking up anything they can. I'd thought about applying to become a Roach once, until I saw my aunt huddled by the trash, staring at what would be her dinner after she handed me what was left of the freeze-dried fruit at the back of her nearly empty cupboards.

With the government passing the "No Trash" law soon, it will be difficult for Roaches to find food to survive, much less afford any "real" food. To pick up any tech-based jobs with so many children who are much faster at grasping the new tech would be difficult as well—and those under eighteen weren't paid as much. *It isn't child labour*, they say. *We're offering them learning opportunities—experience.*

The problem is, even the teens who perform more efficiently and produce greater quality work than some adults *still* received only half their mature counterparts' salaries.

I turn back to the one-hundred-fifty-thousand-word article, physically feeling the time ticking away with each second I spend thinking, constructing each sentence. My typing speed increases, but I can feel the quality of my work decreasing, the anxiety already thundering within me growing, my breaths becoming shallow as I hit the first ten-thousand-word mark. Typos and inconsistencies litter the document, and more than once I think of using an AI program to help me fix the mess I created.

But I don't.

I continue on my own.

A tap on my arm shakes my attention. I check the time, and though it only feels like seconds, it's already been hours. I can't remember what it's like not to look at lines of text and blocks of colour, all of it mixing together with the foggy background of Mao Tou Ying.

"What?" I shout.

Hermes flinches.

I snap my mouth shut, ducking my head in an instant, and mumble, "Sorry."

Hermes sighs. "In case I don't catch you when you leave," she says with a slight frown.

It's been four hours since I arrived. I nod without meeting her eyes. She's made a habit of telling me when she's going to work on her current paintings in the booth at the back. An unnecessary gesture, really, but I still appreciate it. I wonder how far along she is on her current piece and if it's a commission for New Era, a wealthy collector, or might I see it back at the honeycomb?

I hope she is working on a piece for joy rather than a contracted one, but I also know she has little extra time for such flexible and artistic exploration, even as her commissioners insist she has creative freedom and expression. But Hermes knows their true intentions, and though she always complains about the conflicting interests, she signs contract after contract anyhow.

They don't actually want us. They just want us to produce what they are looking for, exactly as they want it—not much different from AI, but they can slap our names on it to sway the AI protestors. "Look we're hiring human artists and writers!" they'll say. But nothing about what we make for them will seem human— only manipulated creations. We both know New Era only comes up with these campaigns to settle down protestors. *Their contracts are only temporary, project-based contracts,* Hermes insists.

I'm not sure who she is trying to convince that she still holds some sliver of power—me, New Era, or only a hopeful illusion she offers herself as justification for the soulless things she has been producing recently for the monopoly?

New Era and death might as well be one entity with the control they have over people's lives and the futile hope that escape might ever be possible once anyone signs their life away. I would rather die under the bridge than to pass, seen as a simple pawn, in New Era's easy path to dominance, even if they try to make it seem like the most glorious thing. Even if I'm being paid little for struggling Independents, anything is better than working for New Era, or even like Hermes, being under a "flexible contract." The contracts, the promises, all mean nothing, really. They will toss her like they do everyone else as soon as she ceases to be useful, especially as she gains too much attention and support from the public, as soon as the protestors are rioting for the liberation of her true art. Maybe there is a chance for unrestricted, "true art" again, but I have trouble picturing such a world—at least when it comes to Emit.

My eyes remain unflinching from my screen. The time between each blink lengthens. Maybe I'll need eye replacements soon. I'm sixty thousand words in, but the whole day is already almost gone. I'll return home quickly tonight so the neighbours will have power and return to Mao Tou Ying early tomorrow.

Hermes shuts down her e-glass and shakes her head. "Take care of yourself, okay?" she says, then points at the USB dangling by my arm. "And don't forget to charge before you leave."

I scramble to flick off the dust guard in the middle of my forearm and insert the USB into the port. The cord must have pulled loose when I shifted in my seat earlier. I'd gone into power-saving mode without notice—I'd turned off the warning function of my watch months ago. 5%.

The small lightning bolt icon appears on the screen and glows in neon teal under the skin on my forearm. Relief cools the sweat on my back.

Sweat pools above my lip and drips down the side of my forehead. There are always a thousand different thoughts, each going in a thousand different directions—all centered around work and the number of things I have yet to cross out on my to-do lists. I want to put them in boxes, store them until they're needed, but this level of brain upgrade isn't yet available, at least not for what I can afford.

"Ai-ya—!"

Without looking, I swat where I assume Auntie Narwani is hovering near my port. My hand meets air.

I pry my eyes open and sit up when I remember I still have ninety thousand words remaining to write. In a scramble, I almost bump into Auntie Narwani by the entrance of my small box unit. She's pinching her features together while glaring out the window. A wire trails from my arm, but nothing is attached to it. Just outside, sitting on one step, is Nemo, flying her drone.

"Stop it. Stop this at once! You've been playing with that thing for hours!" Auntie Narwani waves her arm around.

Hours?

I quickly check my watch. I slept through my alarm, but not just that—

5%.

As much as I want to shout at Nemo, this mistake is my own. I should lock my unit, take my key back from Auntie Narwani. I've been too careless.

Outside, clouds collect in the distance, moving forth like an ominous, opaque grey mass towards the sun hanging above us, already dimmed by fog, waiting, wanting to consume the glowing celestial being, snuff it out, rip out of our hands the few minutes of nutrients we might squeeze from the waning light that is already barely present, to drink in the vitamin D we all lack. Maybe evolution will be kind and wipe it from our systems of need. Or eventually, we can ask a mechanic to get rid of it.

I imagine stepping coatless into the storm, face and palms upturned.

I would become a spasming mass, not human, not robot, and certainly not AI, but just Ai, laying in a puddle. No one in Emit will bat their eyes twice before stepping over, around, or on me in the passing. Because all these people either want to become AIs too, have an AI of their own, or want nothing to do with them, but are stuck tolerating the existence of such rapidly advancing technology because the new generations are reliant on it; the "solutions" are reliant on it. The innovators cradle their creations like children, saying they will change the world, they will better our lives, they will—

I rush out, hoping to reach Mao Tou Ying before it's too late.

As I scale up the ladder, my battery drops to 4%.

Mao Tou Ying is still too far.

Mao Tou Ying's winking lights are up ahead.

I trudge my way through the rain and buzz when I reach the entrance.

1%.

Wushui takes his time today, but instead of waiting patiently, I pound hard at the door.

"Wushui," I yell.

Please.

No answer.

I draw in a shuddering breath. "Wu—!"

The door unlocks, and I tumble in, splashing mud and water everywhere', much to Niao's protest. But I don't have time to care. Without changing into the slippers, I run towards Hermes' e-glass, because mine has yet to be unlocked, and plunge the cord into her system and then plug it into my port.

A sigh of relief escapes me, but everyone is watching me like I have a second head.

"Should get yourself checked. At the doctors, or whatever," Wushui says, not mentioning the slippers, and unlocks my e-glass screen. He knows none of us can afford doctors, not when we live on this side of the bridge, anyhow. Besides, a human doctor is unlikely to be helpful to me at this point.

I nod but say nothing and take off my dripping boots. There is no saving the carpet, and Wushui knows I won't be able to afford the cleaning fee. I'll work overtime the next couple of days, maybe bump my client limit to a hundred sixty to make up for the mess. I can use some of the one hundred fifty thousand Coin bonus too— if I finish the article.

I will finish.

Wushui's expression then smooths out, and he shrugs in response. His nonchalance, though some may find rude, is comforting to me, because it is also a validation that I'm okay, that I will live the night, that it's not so worrisome to leave his sight. I smile at the thought. I am still okay. I'm only missing two hours. I can work faster to make it up.

"I'm sorry," I mutter at the bewildered Hermes and notice how often I've been apologizing.

She snaps out of her shock and raises her hands in surrender. "No, no. Don't worry about it."

Without another word, I turn, settle myself in my seat and re-plug myself into my e-glass, and log onto *I AM AI*. Hermes stares at me without another word before heading to her booth. I envy the luxury she has, no matter how little, to work on the kind of art she believes in.

After half an hour, I'm hovering at just above 5%, charging slower than usual. The problem should be fixed after my appointment with Joan...tonight. My appointment would be just before the article deadline. I think about rescheduling, but it's better to just push through and finish the article.

I'm nearing one hundred thousand words total after adding forty thousand to the sixty thousand I had the day before when my e-glass shuts off. But not just my e-glass, Mao Tou Ying itself goes dark. A series of groans echo around the room, and among the sounds is my huff of frustration.

"Don't worry, don't worry. The power should be back on in no time!" Niao calls as people leave without paying.

The frown on Wushui's face deepens.

An alert on my watch warns me about my low battery.

I minimize the health screen and start working from my watch, the screen only the size of two palms together. Typing with one hand will drastically decrease my work speed, but I can't wait until the power comes back on.

I check the new *I AM A.I.* app and notice the ratings have been increasing at an alarming rate, likely given its low cost and unlimited client intake. I switch back to the article, my whole body now stooped towards the small holographic screen projecting from my watch.

"You need to eat, rest, sleep, go outside. You're not a robot," comes Wushui's voice. He has never shown concern before.

I wanted to tell him he doesn't know just how much of myself I have given up to circuitry, electricity, inhumanity, to gain even fleeting immortality and god-like efficiency, abilities that humans cannot and should not have, and would likely die trying to have.

"I know," I lie.

After half an hour, the power still doesn't come back on.

Hermes has returned from her booth while the other booth occupants stare blankly at the wall at the unlit e-glass screens. She looks unconcerned, and sits with her legs crossed in her chair, meditating. Many other customers already left, likely searching for another internet cafe that hopefully has power—something I probably should have done, but I never go into the city if I can help it. It's too close to New Era.

The emergency alert on my watch blinks, screams, begs me to pay attention, but I click "dismiss" again and again.

Today, I made another mistake in thinking I can rely on Mao Tou Ying. But we are at the edge of a city that never blinks, and I never imagined that today would be the day that it closes its eyes. It seems too perfect, too timed for my demise. Surely the officials of Emit are fixing it, rapidly trying to find the issue because the elites and techies, and most importantly, New Era, will be unamused by this inconvenience in their lives, one that for me means life or death.

I prod at my circuit veins with their neon aqua lights slowly waning, noticeable only by me. My "blood" is draining right before my eyes.

I'm down to 1% again, and I've got five minutes tops, maybe six, if I allow my mind to go blank, my regenerative breaths to calm.

But I can't.

I continue working on the article, now at close to one hundred ten thousand words total and attempt to calm the panic from fogging my mind. More notifications and messages pop up for new projects and upcoming deadlines I've been putting off for this project alone. My looming expiry isn't as terrifying as not completing the article. I know I'll be losing some clients from pushing back their deadlines, but it will be worth it. But if I die, I guess it won't matter. It won't matter, it won't matter, it won't—

My eyes open, slow, and the light in Mao Tou Ying is back on—and so am I.

I look down at the USB plug dangling from my arm. It isn't mine, but one that's much longer, trailing towards a large bulky machine.

Wushui, cigar clutched between cracked lips, grunts. "Got the backup generator going. Forgot we had the thing." That is surely a lie. He wouldn't have pulled out the generator if I remained conscious. "You looked," he frowns, "like you were running low, real low."

For a second, I think he will be cliché and say I look pale, but I know that isn't possible, at least not anymore. I'm grateful that he saved me when he didn't have to. It wouldn't be the first time someone passed in his café, and it wouldn't be the first time he allowed it to happen. *Caring,* he'd always mused, *is a weakness.* But look at him now.

"Thank—"

He shakes his head. "You know we don't say that around here."

I nod, picking myself up, checking my battery.

50%.

Then the anxiety returns when I realize how long I've been out. The article.

"I am AI," I whisper the silly mantra I've used since creating the app, to remind me of both who I am and who I need to be, even when those two things are nothing alike—a human, and something mechanic.

I open *I AM AI.*

Wushui snorts a laugh and smiles—something I rarely see outside of his frown.

Usually I would roll my eyes, offer a sheepish expression, maybe even return the smile, but today, I don't, and Wushui senses the shift in mood.

I pull open my watch, and my hope falls.

Over half my customers cancelled their subscriptions while I was unconscious, leaving poor reviews saying that the app is faulty, that they missed deadlines because of it.

Another ping. A message from Joan to remind me about my check-up. There is only five minutes left until the appointment, but the walk takes fifteen. There is no time left to finish the article, so after a few ragged breaths, I press "Withdraw" on the screen. With the replacement, at least I'll be able to earn back the customers.

Outside Mao Tou Ying, I resist the urge to drive myself against the brick wall and hurry down the street, dodging the dark alley and the muggers who often lurk there.

And with each passing second, the number of clients displayed on my watch decreases, and I don't know how to stop it. I blank. My breath quickens, and I want nothing more than to rip the watch from my arm, run from it all, much like how I ran from my parents' bodies when New Era brought them out of the tower. Avoidance is something I always turn to in times of extreme stress.

Joan's shop is located under a popular karaoke bar. Half of it is shared with a black-market tech supply dealer nicknamed The Scythe.

By the time I reach Joan's door, I'm drained.

I remove a loose brick from the wall and punch in the access code on the keypad hidden behind it while nursing my growing headache. My joints cry from the rain, from being unshielded.

"Hey! You're late," comes Joan's voice.

"Only by a minute," I say, shivering. Anticipation chews at my still human heart.

"Yeah, yeah. You know, I always say to come five minutes early." A sniff. "Did you snooze the notifications again?"

They already know the answer, but I know they're asking as a sneaky chiding.

The door unlocks and slides open, revealing Joan in a wife-beater, muscles larger than I remember them to be. A few new tattoos battle for attention. They push a lock of hair from their eyes and step to the side. Joan's long bob has grown out slightly.

"After you," they say with a mocking sweep of their arm.

On my way down the dark hallway lit only by a dim neon pink glow, I eye the door that has a pen and ink scythe where the nameplate is. The door is left slightly ajar, and inside I see The Scythe, who codes my system upgrades, dressed in all black, hood up, in front of several e-glasses mounted on the wall.

In Joan's shop, everything is cast in shadow —shelves, cabinets, storage boxes—except for the single long metal table in the middle of the room. Dangling above the table is a low hanging lightbulb. If someone else is to work here, someone more human, I'd be concerned about how much they can see with this lighting, but knowing Joan, they already had eye enhancements implanted ages ago that are so advanced no one would be able to tell they aren't real.

I settle myself on top of Joan's table, the cold seeping through my damp joggers, biting into what remains of my blotchy human flesh. My fingers twitch, itching to scratch at the growing rashes.

Joan plugs into my port. When my health stats appear on their e-glass screen, they make a noise between a scoff and an exasperated sigh.

"You really have a death wish, don't you?" Joan says and shakes their head before crossing their arms. One of the new tattoos is a snake with its fangs clamping down on its own body, the teeth piercing its own scaled armour.

I press my lips together, resisting the urge to say yes.

"And why are the health notifications off?" Joan asks, frowning when they check my e-watch that doubles as a health monitor and a work notification system.

I'd turned it off on purpose, so it wouldn't bother me during work. But I don't say this, and instead I say, "Must have accidentally tapped it while looking through notifications."

They look unconvinced but say nothing and know that scolding me would have little effect.

"Well," Joan says, "always double check, and keep the thing on, aight?"

I remain silent and hope they don't notice. They do.

Joan blows out a breath. "You'll wear yourself out at this rate, faster than I can fix you, maintain your parts, faster than you can make money to replace them.

They're upping the costs, again, but you know that." Joan minimizes the page with my stats. "Electricity is supposed to get cheaper, not more expensive, but they do what they want." A humorless laugh.

For a moment, Joan looks thoughtful.

The cost, though worrying, is at the back of my mind in terms of priorities. I wake several times each night to check my notifications from existing and new clients, and in the morning, there is always a fog drifting in my mind. Exhaustion. Human exhaustion. It's becoming unsustainable.

"Awakeness," I begin, "can the new system fix it. Extend it? Make sleep unnecessary?"

Joan looks away, humming.

They seem undecided on voicing their thoughts. Then, without looking at me, they whisper, "Yes."

I've never been as conscious of the beating thing in my chest until this moment. Its pulse is often only a murmur, and now it's groaning its complaints. I'm both glad and terrified that such drastic procedures, which would have resulted in several months of recovery time for our ancestors, now only takes minutes.

I pick at my nails, chipped crescents unmaintained, then my eyes meet Joan's.

I'm staring at my heart, sealed, preserved, which Joan will soon be shipping off to the buyer, and I wish I could hold it in my hand one last time.

I don't realize how silent my body feels until I wait for the steady beat, the rush of blood in my ears, only to meet the almost inaudible hum of the new electric currents running through me.

In my heart's place sits a new battery.

"You might regret it if you got rid of it all," Joan says when I reach the door. I wonder just how much of Joan is still human.

Outside, I turn off the health alerts again but keep the client notifications on, checking them every few seconds as I head back home.

I scroll through the unopened notifications and notice one from a client who was too impatient to wait for a response before cancelling their subscription. The usual panic and stress don't come. I stare at the number with nothing but numbness. I send out an ad and increase my client limit to two hundred.

That night after my procedure, upon returning to the honeycomb, my eyes linger on the red and orange of the emergency generators that make Emit appear as though in flames.

I rip my arm away from a troubled Aunt Narwani without a second glance and don't pet Nemo on the head on my way out when she rushes over to me with her drone. The child follows for a few steps with disappointment and shock, but I pay her no mind as I make my way onto the top of the bridge. I know I should feel something, but I don't—at least not where the hollow left by my empty heart sits, but my brain still nags, though only for a moment before going quiet. Rather than scattered thoughts, they are now trained on a single goal: paying off the debt and leaving the bridge.

When I arrive at Mao Tou Ying, I bat away Niao's attempts at passing me water and snacks and stride barefoot to the e-glass screen I normally use. Wushui looks up, brows drawn low as I wait for him to boot the system. Rather than my normal impatience, I sit erect with my hands poised, waiting, eyes unwavering from the screen. I'm still ten minutes early.

Wushui unlocks the screen. My finger already hovers where my app is usually located, and I fly through tasks faster than usual. I find it much easier to ignore Hermes' small talk, much to her dismay. But when I see the new request for a one hundred eighty thousand-word book due tomorrow night, I pause. The bonus isn't nearly anything like the article I missed out on—one thousand Coin—but it's almost equivalent to what I make in a month. My brain calculates how long it might take me to finish it. If I stay overnight, I'll be able to complete it along with all the other tasks I have lined up for today. I press accept.

"Hey—"

"I'm busy," I say and increase the muting function level on my headphones.

Hermes plucks the headphones from my ears. "Can we talk?" Concern drags at all her features.

"I'll be working overnight," I say.

She pauses for a moment, glancing to the side at Niao and Wushui who are watching from the corner of their eyes, trying to not be obvious, but appearing much more apparent than if they had openly stared.

Finally, she says, "I can wait."

I nod, once, sharp, and take the headphones back.

It's already 4:00 p.m., and I'm still half an hour behind the estimated completion time I need for this document. I call Joan, who picks up after several wait tones, sounding groggy as though they had just taken a nap. I don't envy them. With the lack of a heart and new battery, my energy levels are much higher than before.

"How much will it take for a brain implant?" I ask without greeting.

Silence. "Steep. Very steep," Joan says, slow, hesitant.

"I can pay for it," I say. "Secure the new system for me before next week."

A grunt.

I hang up before I hear the answer.

After the call, Hermes spends the rest of her time staring at me. Though I don't feel discomfort from her actions, my brain urges me to stop her display of silent annoyance.

"What is it?" I ask.

"What happened at Joan's yesterday?"

"I got rid of my heart."

"You—"

"I'm also getting a new brain implant soon."

She falls silent and stares a hole into the left side of my chest, then her gaze shifts to my forehead. I turn back to my work.

"I want to show you something," she says, tapping her pen against the desk in front of her.

"I don't have time."

"It's a gift," she tries.

"I don't want it."

Instead of getting offended, she drags me up from my seat and pulls me to her blacked out booth in the back. She rips the door open and shoves me in. Behind us, Niao and Wushui continue to watch. I have never been in Hermes' workspace before.

On the ground are scattered newspapers covered in paint. The e-glass has been uninstalled from this booth, and in its place is a narrow wall-to-wall desk with bottles of paints; palettes; cups of murky, multicoloured water; and brushes. Settled on an easel on the wall opposite the entrance is a painting as wide as I am tall, but its height only half my own.

Hermes gestures to the painting. It's the honeycomb with all our neighbours both inside and outside the square units turned hexagonal. Each of our painted faces are attached to the bodies of honeybees. Niao and Wushui hover in the distance in front of Mao Tou Ying, which Hermes had brought to life as a building-sized barn owl. The owl has its wings spread, covering a large portion of Emit. Blue peaks from beneath the streaks of red and orange sky that resemble the city lit with its emergency lights. It seems Hermes had brushed on the new colour recently.

"Even though it seems like we have nothing, we have everything we need right here." She points to the honeycombs before dropping her hand. "It might be hard, but being together, working together, even if we're struggling...I don't know. There's something warming about it all, isn't there? I feel content somehow. Even with knowing that New Era might tear it all down someday ."

I walk closer to the painting. I'm painted within my unit, bickering with Auntie Narwani and Nemo.

"I want to enjoy it while I can, you know? Being human, being together...or something like that," Hermes murmurs with a fond and thoughtful smile.

I try to recall both the joy and frustration but realize I can't. I say nothing and return to my desk. Hermes watches me from behind.

A notification pings from the client running the interaction fiction website. They have been with me long-term, ever since the second year of my app launching.

Reason for unsubscribing: The piece sounds like every other AI generated story. It doesn't have its usual emotion and humanity. Might as well go with another app if that's the case.

Several similar notifications arrive, commenting on the work I turned in earlier. Yet new customers quickly take the places of unsubscribers—clients who are looking for exactly what my work has come to resemble: cheap AI productions. I think of Auntie Narwani's clock, and the story she insists it holds.

I turn off my e-glass, ignoring all the other incoming notifications, the increasing and decreasing client counter, the reviews of both praise and criticism, and leave Mao Tou Ying.

Tears roll down my cheeks, but I don't feel the pain that causes them, though my brain knows I should.

I arrive back at my unit just before 5:00 p.m. and huddle on the bare mattress on the ground. I shiver involuntarily against the futon when it touches the small of my back, still made of human flesh. My heart no longer registers the cold, but my body reacts because of muscle memory alone. My Bluetooth reconnects to all my neighbours' units, and their lights flicker on, but my eyes flutter closed. It's not difficult to slow my breaths or blank my mind now, but for some reason, I wish it was.

Within ten minutes, I hear the creak of steps climbing up the stairs towards me before I wake to see who it is. But I don't need to guess, because the same people show up on my doorstep all the time. Though this time, I'm too drained and exhausted to be glad for visitors. I check my battery, and it's already 2% lower, even on standby mode. Someone has been using my battery outside of just the units' light upon my return.

"Ai! Ai!" It's Nemo. In place of my usual pang of annoyance, of wanting to disconnect my Bluetooth and drown everyone out, of desiring nothing else but silence, I feel nothing at all.

I sit up and plaster a smile on my face without knowing why. "Hey," I say.

Nemo tumbles in, followed by Auntie Narwani complaining about how dangerous these stairs are and how difficult it is to climb from unit to unit, especially given days of strong wind.

"So happy you're back early today! We finally have warm soup!"

Soup. I glance at the time. 5:15 p.m. And I finally understand why Auntie Narwani is so insistent about the clock every day. She must use it to remind herself to prepare and serve food to all the residents each day.

Auntie Narwani stumbles into the room, the bowl of soup in her hand sloshing slightly off the side. The liquid, a strange murky beige, sits in a dirty Styrofoam bowl. It isn't much, yet it's also more than enough, and I wish the thought would fill me with the warmth I've sold away.

Auntie Narwani ambles over and plops down next to me with Nemo and holds out the bowl. She doesn't ask why I'm home early, and neither does Nemo.

I take a sip. It's chicken broth. My stomach gurgles when the liquid sinks to its bottom, and a strange warmth bubbles within.

A tear drops into the soup. It's mine.

"It's okay," Auntie Narwani says, patting my back.

But it isn't.

"Thank you," I say.

"There is no need to thank family," she says, smiling.

One of her teeth has fallen out, making her seem closer to a hundred than seventy. Behind Auntie Narwani, people from the community gather outside their units, on the stair landings, shouting conversation across to one another: Mrs. Gem holds her newborn, a child who likely won't last the year, as many children don't unless they have New Era's support; Nemo has left us and is now sprinting from unit to unit, pausing periodically to wheeze, hands on knees— her asthma is getting worse. The sound of the electric drill goes off again— something else broken.

I look away from them all and shut out the sounds.

Rather than gratitude, it is the return of the pain I felt when I lost my parents that stirs within my mind. The phantom of a heart throbs and tugs. The warmth, the sense of community, though both beautiful things, always risk loss and hurt.

"Thank you," I croak, and it feels like a goodbye.

I set down my bowl of soup and leave the unit.

"Come back soon," Auntie Narwani calls out.

I call Joan.

At night, we all sit by the waterline, staring at Emit with its blue eyes open once more.

In silence, my neighbours all manually disconnect from my battery, leaving only the glow of moonlight above us.

From the bridge, a shadow climbs down and makes their way towards us.

Hermes. She takes quick strides, firm and resolute, until she looms above me.

She snatches my wrist and connects her own watch to mine and initiates a Coin transfer.

"What—"

"I sold the painting. For your brain implant," she says, then offers a weak smile.

I pull away. "Why?"

"I figured it was unfair for me to impose my own ideals onto you," she says, fiddling with the ends of her hair, her fingers paint-tinted.

"I canceled the appointment. I'm trying to get my heart back," I say, slow.

Silence.

I lean back and toss my head up.

"I've been a fool, haven't I?" I say with a choked laugh.

Hermes flops down and leans against me, eyeing the port on my arm. She hums. "You always have been."

I snort at the snide comment.

A notification jolts me. Joan. I pull up the message.

Looks like it's much easier buying a heart than selling it.

I wonder who is giving up their heart, and I mourn for their loss within. A tear rolls down my cheeks, and I feel both the pain and relief that causes it—a sharp shock followed by a full blossoming ache. Though it won't be my original heart, I'm glad it will be one that trembles.

Hermes and I share a melancholic smile.

In the distance, a new New Era advertisement glares from the top of their highest skyscraper.

"Your...painting," I say.

We stare at the digitized version of Hermes' honeycombs, the advertisement promising New Era buildings of a similar "unique" structure and concept, and the forthcoming announcement about job application submissions to work for their new "community". The New Era tower in the painting has been altered to look like there is a queen bee settled on top. *Like a hive, we must work as one! Join our family!*

Hermes shakes her head. "Even if they take it and make it into something it isn't, at least we know to us it will always hold its true meaning."

"Our story," I say.

Auntie Narwani mutters about New Era's villainy. I grin at her defiance, the way she continues to struggle against New Era simply by being herself. Something that we all are doing—what binds us together.

Auntie Narwani then looks over with a smile, revealing the growing gaps from missing teeth. She lays the stuttering clock on my lap and points. "Maybe we are broken, but we might not always remain that way."

I look down at the clock to see a small solar panel installed—something New Era has made very difficult to get. The bent hands struggle, and the slight squeal of hidden gears continue to click, and though this is only an object, I can't help but feel it's more alive than I am.

For the first time, I'm grateful for the quiet of our home under the bridge; of our offline connections; of our eyes reflecting not the light of screens, but the dark of the natural waters, even as it often threatens to drown us during heavy storms; and the choking thought at the back of our minds of the alarming loom of floods with the continuously rising sea levels.

And for the first time, I realize the beauty of fragility, the value of ache—to be able to bleed, to be able to fear, to tick and struggle ticking: to be truly human.

. . . .

Ai Jiang is a Chinese-Canadian writer, Ignyte, Bram Stoker, and Nebula Award winner, and Hugo, Astounding, Locus, Aurora, and BFSA Award finalist from Changle, Fujian currently residing in Toronto, Ontario. She is the recipient of Odyssey Workshop's 2022 Fresh Voices Scholarship and the author of *A Palace Near the Wind*, *Linghun*, and *I AM AI*. Find her at www.aijiang.ca.

A SHORT BIOGRAPHY OF A CONSCIOUS CHAIR

Renan Bernardo

- 1 -

I was conceived by a carpenter with quivering hands in the back of a lumberyard. She was called Anatólia. Some days she had to fix flaws, sawing one or two parts of me again. On other days she hurled chunks of me against the wall, screaming at the bashful furniture she'd built, lined against the far wall. If she knew she'd bestowed consciousness on me with her art, perhaps she'd have other thoughts. I didn't care. She was sturdy and careful and didn't mind her son babbling about her being too old for this kind of work. Oak lasted for millennia. She had but a dozen wrinkles around her cheeks. Her particular way of wheezing meant nothing. She would last.

Ignoring all the humility chipped into my wood by her hands, I was a true work of oak art. Seahorses adorned the palmettes atop my backrest, which was ornately twirled with bubbles and the contours of fish. I had cockleshells on my apron and water lilies on my four feet, so exquisitely wrought that I feared the day someone would push me against fellow furniture. My upholstered cushion was velvety and crimson, not unlike the eyes of Anatólia's son the day he entered the lumberyard and brought me to my first sunlight bath. The day I found out things I didn't want to.

It happened two weeks after Anatólia sighed and told me some mysterious, uplifting words. She sat on one of my partners, an unconscious, wobbly stool, breathing out in her particular, noisy way.

"She's going to love you," she said.

The barbs of my wood bristled. Who was she? I'd ask if I had a mouth. She left after a few minutes dozing off with her hands on her knees as if mesmerized by deep thought.

It was the last time I saw her.

When Anatólia's son brought me outside for the first time, he was weeping, and so were half a dozen other people, all gathered and hugging on the porch of a house with peeling green paint. A white truck with red lights parked on the gravel drive. The long pack that was taken inside smelled like sawdust and coffee.

Every bit of me warped and swelled sluggishly when sunlight touched me. Or it could've been just the realization that my carpenter was gone. Turned out she wasn't made of oak like me, but of a weaker, less resistant structure called bone.

"Keep it," Anatólia's son told Aunt Suzana as if I wasn't listening. He was pointing to me and a set of other furniture. "I have to move soon."

Was Aunt Suzana the one who was going to love me?

- 2 -

Aunt Suzana tucked me into the back of her SUV and kept me just enough to sell me to a Wood & Depot branch near a diner on the BR-116 road. Back then, I deemed R$20 fair enough to keep my dignity and to value all the sweat Anatólia had poured on me. Lucky ignorance. It probably paid for Aunt Suzana's dinner later that day. Deservedly, she leaves the story now.

Life at Wood & Depot wasn't like the life I had dreamed. The dark years had begun. Literally. João Gutierrez, the manager, decided to put me in a corner that never captured any sunlight. With the memories of the day Anatólia died at bay, I began to yearn for those light stripes that streaked through the Wood & Depot main door and picked up speckles of dust in the air. A sign was plastered on me with the number "100". I didn't dare to think through Aunt Suzana and João Gutierrez's numbers. They didn't make sense, and I didn't want them to. What bothered me was that if that sign was kept for too long upon me, my seat would end up marked with an indelicate rectangle.

Those were also the metaphoric dark years. My days were limited to propping indifferent buttocks by day and feeling the seaweed stench of my unconscious mates by night. João Gutierrez seemed not to care that they stank. That we stank. He bragged about numbers, typed on computers, and scowled at his subordinates. He was just like Aunt Suzana. Just like Anatólia's son. They weren't able to love something sublimely manufactured by hands as magic as those shafts of light that greeted us every day.

Things changed one morning, about two years after Aunt Suzana dumped me. A drizzle spattered on the store's awning, and sunlight hadn't pierced the glass. It was 8 AM on a Thursday and the CLOSED sign was still hanging on the door. They were late. And João Gutierrez made no movement to leave his desk until ten minutes later, when he yelled, startling me.

"He's coming! All hands on deck!"

His shout was received by woo-hoos and yells from his subordinates (though some of them might've been faked).

They crowded around, talked for about ten minutes, then entered into a frenzy. They dipped cloths in detergent, wrung them out, and wiped every bit of dust from the floors, beds, cabinets, cupboards, wardrobes, and tables, scrubbing even the inaccessible corners of the store. When it was my turn, they tickled me with a duster, waxed me all throughout, and rinsed my seat with oil, soap and water. They even managed to clean the rectangle marked upon my crimson velvet. In the end, I felt less crackly and dry, a bit more like Anatólia intended me to be.

So, what now? Perhaps they'd found out about Anatólia and decided to find out who was going to love me, who was the one, the right person in the whole world to whom a refined chair must be given. A sailor, perhaps? A fisherman? All that cleaning spectacle had to be a welcoming party.

The person who entered Wood & Depot was nothing like I'd pictured when Anatólia said the puzzling sentence. It was a man with a whitening Balbo beard wearing a grey tweed with a dark green blazer and sweater, elegant and overused. His hair was plastered to his head with some kind of gel that left some threads slightly spiked to the left. He folded his umbrella and squinted at the furniture around him as if we had something to confess.

"Mr. Amorim, it's so good to have you here." João Gutierrez's voice was as phony as imitation velvet. "Do you mind if we bring you a cup of coffee and some snacks?"

Mr. Amorim grumbled and shook his head.

"Bad taste you have," he said, indicating the door. "That sign says Hot Sale. You should think of a better term."

Mr. Gutierrez trembled and flexed his fingers. Pearly beads of sweat glistened on his forehead.

"So you don't think our prices are good enough for you? We can—"

Mr. Amorim waved him off.

"It's just that you're associating furniture with fire. It's a bad omen, I think."

Mr. Gutierrez nodded, his shoulders slumping, probably relieved because it was just a minor issue. Nothing to do with his numbers.

"Perhaps we could show you the best we have." He made a completely fake gesture of welcome, opening his hands and stretching his arms to show the Wood & Depot's products—which were already obviously visible. "You are a literate man, so we might recommend our bookshelf made of—"

Mr. Amorim raised a hand again. He seemed to know exactly how to remain in control.

"I want to refurbish the house for Joana."

"Is she coming back?" Mr. Gutierrez smiled.

"Yes, after six years abroad. Anyway, I have a list." He produced a tanned piece of paper from his pocket and handed it to João, whose smile twinkled as he skimmed across the items.

João waved a hand to his subordinates and they started to zigzag around the store, typing on computers, exchanging grins with each other, and sticking SOLD signs on some of my fellows.

Meanwhile, Mr. Amorim strolled around the place with his squinting manners, sliding fingers over my mates, knocking on glass doors yet rarely opening them. When he came closer to me, the first thing he did wasn't to press down my upholstered seat as most people did. He smiled at my cockleshells and pressed his fingers against the seahorses' heads on my backrest. His thumb was ridged, filled with invisible lint from his blazer. His nails were closely trimmed. I sniffed in him a scant timeworn scent of alder and beech, something that reminded me of Anatólia.

"Hmm..." It was all he said.

His back cast a shadow and loomed upon me. I clenched all my splinters. A fluttery of anticipation swirled through my velvet.

He sat on me. I creaked (but politely quick).

"Mr. Gutierrez, please, come here." Mr. Amorim raised a hand, his voice vibrating through my wood. "I'll take this one too. And I have a special request regarding all the furniture I'm buying. Do you have a carpenter in situ?"

And so the dark years ended as they'd begun, in the somber back of a truck.

- 3 -

I was promoted to a leader as soon as I was placed in the Amorim's living room. From a lumberyard to the dark corner of a store to heading my own table. I admit I was a bit proud of myself. I led a set of five mahogany chairs, all of them acquired at the Wood & Depot and customized according to Mr. Amorim's requests. Fruit and orchard motifs had been whittled on the backrests of the chairs and the edges of the table. They weren't as perfect as my cockleshells and seahorses, of course. Mr. Gutierrez's crew hands were more adapted to numbers than woodwork. (The chairs had their charm, though, just not like mine.)

The fruits theme seemed to please the Amorims. Their living room contained a collection of ten oil paintings depicting orchards and fruit bowls, trees and plantations, women and men doing fieldwork, all of them hanging between the furniture: a cupboard, a bookshelf, a Victorian-style pendulum clock, and a blanket-covered sofa. To the right of the entrance, the living room opened to a space with a TV rack, but that was beyond my field of view, so I only caught glimpses of its weird colorful motions when someone moved me into the house.

And here I have to add something important: There was a sash window right behind me with varnish briskly applied to its casing to hide its true age. (I called it make-up for wooden beings). Every morning, just before the pendulum clock struck 7 AM, Mr. Amorim woke up, his slippers squeaking on the stairs and echoing throughout the house. Then, he pulled the curtains and opened the window, allowing wafts of mowed lawn to barge in. And... sunlight! The gracious rays that came from that huge ball up in the sky finally fell upon me day after day, from 7 AM to 10 AM, whisking through the intricacies of my oak and warming me up.

I soon discovered just two of the Amorims lived in that castle-like residence. Eduardo Amorim, who by now you know as Mr. Amorim, and Leandro Amorim, a 15-year-old boy that seemed to be part of a system comprised of an earphone and a greyed-out Metallica t-shirt. Leandro was Mr. Amorim's grandson, and his parents had been absent since Leandro was a toddler. Joana Amorim was Leandro's sister and the one Mr. Amorim had mentioned in the Wood & Depot as the recipient of all that brand new furniture. She didn't live with them but was going to spend two months at the house after a year abroad. Was she the one who was going to love me? The thought scraped through my oak as the first night in the Amorim's home mingled to a delft blue and transformed the oil paintings into mere blackboards.

Then, there came a morning, seven days from my arrival, that Mr. Amorim's tight voice startled me from my oaken stasis.

"Help your sister, Leandro." His voice made my wood vibrate. He was at the door. "She's exhausted from the long trip."

"I'm going, I'm going." Leandro rolled his eyes, darting down the stairs. "I'm also tired, okay? It's not even 10 AM."

Mr. Amorim peeked anxiously through the wicket while turning his key on the door. A half-smile hung on his mouth.

"She's early," he muttered to himself. "Should've thought of a better suit." He was wearing a black jacket with the same linen trousers he was wearing when he bought me.

Mr. Amorim left, and Leandro went right after him. (And here I'd like to pause and add a side note about magic hands. It would be much better if they also granted moving legs to furniture. I'd stretch them now and follow the duo outside to see firsthand the arrival of Joana, the woman who could or could not love me. But, no. I didn't move.) I could only distinguish Mr. Amorim's voice. At that moment, I discovered what happiness meant. It was that thrilled tone of voice, a bit higher than usual, even if muffled and indistinguishable by the rumble of the car outside. It was the different set of dimples around Mr. Amorim's cheeks when he came back carrying a piece of blue luggage filled with stickers. It was the way he carefully but quickly set it on the floor just to look back outside again.

Leandro came next, carrying a stuffy backpack.

Then Joana, bluish circles around her eyes, mouth lined downward, and dark hair tied in a bun. She smelled like leather couches. She wasn't like the other Amorims. In her early thirties, she didn't have the analytical, sophisticated look of her grandpa. Joana was the kind of bone-made creature that seemed to have left a lot behind. Even more than Mr. Amorim himself, despite his age. The question that lingered in the air was whether she'd left part of her somewhere or somewhen.

At the moment when she closed the door behind her, I expected her eyes to glint in full realization of what her grandfather had done, the customization of the furniture, the unskilled-but-neat apples and oranges crusted into my fellow chairs' backrests, the smoothness of that mahogany table where Mr. Amorim had put two golden candelabra and Leandro had left a Master of Puppets CD case. And me, of course, at the opposite wall, hidden by it all but exhibiting seahorses and fish leaping from imaginary water, the details on their eyes soulfully fashioned. And I could see in Mr. Amorim's eyes that he had about the same expectations.

Joana stared around the living room.

"Your place is..." She frowned. "It smells like trees."

My seat puffed out on a micro level. *Trees*? Really? It's the same thing to say you all smell like flesh.

"We'll bring your stuff upstairs," Mr. Amorim said, lips fluttering. "Your room is just as you left it."

"I'll stay for two months, Eduardo." At the time, I couldn't say if her insipidity was due to the long trip or if that *was* her. "I'm just here to make sure you and Leandro are fine."

She grabbed her backpack, tousled Leandro's hair, and moved upstairs. Mr. Amorim rubbed his hands and stared up, unsaid words swishing across his lips. Even Leandro took his eyes off his smartphone and paused whatever was drilling through his ears. During the coming years, I would know and accommodate the rears of many of the Amorims' guests. Their cousin Morena; Eduardo's brother, Jorge; Leandro's girlfriends, then boyfriends; a couple of Mr. Amorim's affairs; Jacir, the ponytailed mailman; the neighbors' dogs frolicking and wiggling their tails. And none of those beings had a reception so warm as the one the Amorims gave to Joana, and none ever responded with such unenthusiastic manners.

And she didn't even spare a look at my curves.

The days went by, inevitably. I could say the Amorim's residence was my first one. The lumberyard couldn't be considered a home because I was being assembled. Neither could the shaded, dusty corner in the Wood & Depot. But with the Amorims it was different. My surroundings gained life.

Mr. Amorim—and I think I can call him Eduardo by now—set a breakfast every morning for his grandchildren (and sometimes for me, when Leandro dropped buttered toast on my seat, and you probably know the rules about falling buttered toast). It consisted of scrambled eggs, bread, butter, avocado toast, grilled cheese, orange juice, and pineapple yogurt, the latter specifically for Joana. But she didn't mind all the effort Eduardo put into pleasing her, the minutes he spent scouring the cupboard's drawer for a pretty tablecloth, the alarm he set on the refrigerator to serve the yogurt at the temperature she deemed ideal, those dimples and those sparkling eyes on his face, his smiles.

On weekdays, a bus picked up Leandro for school just after they finished breakfast. He was in secondary school, in the stage teenagers absorbed all that was around them and channeled it out into excitement, frustration, and acne. And it was during the huge gaps between Leandro going and coming back from school that Eduardo tried to penetrate the mysterious Joana's barrier.

"I don't know the title of your thesis," Eduardo said one time, three days after Joana arrived. They sat across from each other at the table. (Eduardo didn't sit on me at all, he often let his grandchildren pick me if they wanted. Even when alone, he spared my seat from his rear.) "I know it's about fish."

Oh. That could be the reason why I was picked.

"Fish." Joana twisted her lips. "You oversimplify it."

Eduardo shrugged. "You didn't call very much when you were there."

"It's about the patterns of saltwater fish in the Iberian Peninsula."

"It seems interesting." Eduardo actually wanted to know more. You could see it in the way he leaned over the table with his eyes glinting. It was like he just found out he had a granddaughter. "I didn't know they have patterns."

"All things do." Her eyes never met his. "In nature."

"And Portugal? Is it nice?"

She just nodded.

"The new furniture..." She looks around, a bit of scorn in her eyes. "Why?"

For you, so please be happier, I wanted to say. *Look at my seahorses and those bubbles popping out around them, the fish intertwined with them.*

"You know I appreciate woodwork." He looked around the room. His hands shook slightly. "I want to revitalize the house, you know? Refreshment. Check the wiring, too, and if the fire extinguishers are okay. I think the one in the basement might be near to its expiring—"

"So you just entered Wood & Depot and bought it all?" Her jaws set in a half-grin while she stared at her grandpa. "And these fruits?"

Eduardo looked at his hands and smiled. Not to her, but to himself.

"You remember how you drew them when you were a kid?" he said without looking into her eyes. Good choice. She didn't deserve it. "You drew them, you colored them, and then you jotted down the fruits' names under each one. You even invented your own. And then I taught you how to sculpt an apple into a plank. Of course, I didn't let you touch the saw and the hammer, but your eyes glinted so much..."

"I was a child." She said as if to prove a point. "It's all pretty, but you didn't need to spend your money on this. I won't stay."

Eduardo didn't move. Not even a nod. Of course, he knew she wouldn't stay, she had her home somewhere miles from there, she had a Ph.D. in Biology and a completely separate life to lead. But Eduardo felt. And the conversation died as it began, without Eduardo knowing the name of her thesis.

When Joana decided to go out early in the morning or stay late in her bedroom—which meant the refrigerator beeped in vain—Eduardo scrubbed all the new furniture with a slightly wet cloth, reaching even the hardest corners and edges with cotton swabs and toothbrushes. He cleaned the cupboard's glass, dusted the books on the bookshelf, and the surface of the table and the chairs' seats. But he took special care of me (as I deserved, of course). He sprayed vinegary-smelling solutions on my seat and scrubbed it with precise circular motions. Then, he used exaggeratedly thin swabs and even needles to remove grime from the minute intricacies of my cockleshells, seahorses, and water lilies, never forgetting to apply specific products to my wooden legs, arms, and backrest. I felt exalted. (And here I must repeat myself: Eduardo cleaned the furniture every day, ritually, even if it had to be done after midnight.)

Later in the day Joana arrived, Eduardo said he would prepare a welcome dinner for her. But she told him she was going to have dinner outside. The same happened during the following five days. Only on her first Saturday there, she decided to stay and accept his offer. And so I'd have my first dinner leading a mahogany table with five fruit-themed mahogany chairs. I could swear the microscopic barbs across my legs ruffled.

It was set for 7 PM on Saturday. The hours stretched as I anticipated the moment. Eduardo left early for the supermarket with Leandro. After they came back and stocked the groceries, Eduardo performed his cleaning ritual. It was a bit more rushed than usual, but that was forgivable. It would be his night. When he managed to leave the kitchen for a few minutes, he paced about the living room, straightened the paintings on the wall, picked up a tablecloth, set up the candelabra in slightly different positions, and sighed with both hands on the table, eyes wide shut.

The clock eventually struck seven.

At first glance, Eduardo seemed a man of traditions, showing up in Wood & Depot all neat, selective, and provoking shudders throughout Mr. Gutierrez's crew. But if he was, he probably abandoned some of them during his life. Furniture like me was born with some sense of what to expect from the world. And one thing I expected was the house's main provider sitting at the head of his own home's table. But he didn't. Of course, he never sat on me, but he didn't even exchange my place with one of the lower class chairs. Nor did he sit at the opposite end of the table. So it was Leandro that picked me, who was surprisingly—or forcedly—without his earphones, wearing a button-down shirt almost in tune with the ten-years-later Leandro that I would eventually get to know.

"Be careful with this chair," Eduardo said, pointing a finger at Leandro. It was the first sentence of the dinner. Damn, I was delighted.

Eduardo lit the candles on the candelabra for the first time, and they cast a sandy halo across the room. Then, they each took their places. Leandro upon me, Eduardo and Joana facing each other again. Eduardo served—and prepared himself—grilled salmon, beansprouts, noodles, and roasted carrots with garlic and parmesan. To drink, Argentinian wine (since Joana was probably full of the Portuguese taste) for him and Joana, orange juice for Leandro. From that moment on, the sum of smells swirling through the living room became the scent of reunion to me. Luscious food, melting wax, the ever-diminishing whiff of newly fabricated wood. Chairs were made to be static, but my elementary particles span and whirled within me.

"Please, serve yourselves." Eduardo widened his smile. "You both love salmon, so it's what I made for today. Can't ensure the taste is good, though. And ... Joana?"

Joana stared at him, glints of suspicion in her eyes. (And here you might be asking how can I see those things with a 15-year-old headbanger sitting on me. Well, I can reveal to you that chairs have eyes in every part of their structure.)

"Welcome back," Eduardo said, then nudged Leandro.

"Welcome back, sis."

Leandro and Joana were like old friends that had reunited but bore no more resemblance to each other. But even so, she offered more smiles to him than to her grandpa. As she did now, turning her head and grinning at him. She was educated enough to wait for her grandpa to serve himself, but he was educated enough to serve their grandchildren first. His hands were quivering but the smile didn't thaw from his face.

"Leandro is curious about Portugal," Eduardo said after serving them, sitting and folding a napkin on his lap. "He watched a documentary about Saint George's Castle some weeks before you arrived."

Leandro nodded. "Many people used the castle throughout history."

Joana imitated her grandpa and set the napkin on her lap. The candlelights brought out some wrinkles on her face I'd not perceived before.

"Phoenicians, Visigoths, Romans, Moors, and more," she said. "I've been there twice and the views are breathtaking."

"Greeks, Carthaginians, Suebi, even the Celtic tribes," Leandro said, seemingly excited with the subject. "I remember their names, but have no idea who the Suebi were, for instance."

They laughed. I was built with a mythical concept imbued in my wood, that of a happy family. It was something I was bound to witness many times during my existence. Perhaps it was a kind of intrinsic power I inherited from the magic hands of Anatólia. Those twelve seconds with the Amorims were proof that it wasn't a myth, but those moments didn't linger. They were like lapses of love and friendship and cheery guffawing. And perhaps that held for all families, not just for them.

"Is it preserved?" Eduardo said.

"It's mostly made of stone," Joana said, her eyes panning back to her plate. "Not wood."

"My question remains." Eduardo's voice was rough. It was the first time I noticed him using that kind of unsatisfied voice with Joana. But it didn't last. His eyes were shining and glancing at his granddaughter one second later. "I'm curious about these things. You might not recall, but I have a specialization in preservation."

"Wood and furniture preservation," she said, cutting a slice of the fish. "The castle doesn't have much furniture today. Lots of open spaces, though."

"Why is that even important?" Leandro shrugged.

The living room hung in silence but for the wind battering at the window, as if they were chewing upon Leandro's question. Joana had a way of embarrassing Eduardo.

"I was thinking—" Eduardo cleared his throat and sipped the wine. "Next week we could visit the Itatiaia Castle. It's the closest we have to a castle here. They have an awesome collection of antique wardrobes."

"I'm leaving Monday," Joana said.

The glass dropped from Eduardo's hand and swayed on the table, nearly smashing on the floor. Droplets of wine peppered the linen tablecloth and some of it ran over my leg. It tasted like vinegar.

He grabbed the napkin and wiped his hand. Leandro glanced at them, from one to the other.

"You said two months," Eduardo said. "Why so soon?"

"You have all you love here," she said. "You don't need us." She looked at Leandro.

"What do you mean?" Leandro frowned his head.

"I can't bear staying here," she said, darting a fierce look at Eduardo. "I came back from Portugal wanting to give you a second chance. But I can't."

"What the hell?" Leandro crossed his arms. "I don't want to get old and crazy like you."

They didn't mind Leandro. They just glared at one another, an invisible ongoing clash. I didn't know if any of them won, but Joana stood, her salmon barely eaten, and left upstairs.

The dinner was over. Before sunrise, Joana would leave. Flies would fester on salmon and roasted carrots until Eduardo gathered the courage to clean the table at noon the next day. His eyes were red-swollen. His hands shaky. The only thing he did on that day besides cleaning the table was dusting me and trying to remove the stains of wine from my leg.

- 4 -

"There's been a fire over at the Bosque Verde." Leandro entered the house, removed his coat, and hung it on a hook on the wall. "Dry leaves, it seems."

Eduardo shuddered, his nails rasping against his cane. He was sitting on an armchair he'd put where the old pendulum clock had struck its last sigh five years before.

"Will it reach us?"

Bosque Verde was a grove on the other side of the Amorims' property. It couldn't be seen from there, but the scent of ashes stuck to the air like the remains of a fireplace. Eduardo had woken up that morning with the smell and yelled for Leandro, asking him to find out its source as soon as possible. Leandro obeyed. He was always there for his grandpa, though sometimes the old man seemed not to notice. In the core of old Eduardo's soul, he probably missed Joana a lot more than she deserved.

"Vô, not even if a hurricane blows the fire toward us." Leandro patted Eduardo's thinning hair. "Authorities are already there and it won't even spread too much. Just relax."

Eduardo nodded, but his eyes remained open and attentive at the windows. He stayed like that during the remainder of the day, sometimes glancing at the windows, sometimes dozing off, other times mumbling about fires. Leandro left for college. Only when he came back later and told Eduardo the fires had been dealt with that the old man was able to rest his head on the armchair with relief.

Leandro was no more the teenager tied to an earphone that I knew when I came to live in the Amorims' residence. Now a 25-year-old young chap, his wavy hair fell over his shoulders and his obsession with Metallica had transformed into a frayed Lady Justice on his left biceps, ironically matching his ongoing Law graduation.

"Do you still talk with your sister?" Eduardo asked when Leandro served some spaghetti for Eduardo that night, the ashy odor still adhering to the air. It was a recurrent question.

"She never reached back." Leandro always lied. If Eduardo knew how to read eyes as I did, he would see Leandro's evasiveness. But Eduardo just moaned in agreement.

Leandro circled the table and sat on me. He was always the one to pick me, and sometimes, even after ten years, he still blurted out compliments about my comfortable upholstered seat or my perfectly built arms and backrest. He never paid too much attention to my aquatic themes though, which were now kind of battered and unimpressive anyway. Eduardo had taught Leandro how to properly take care of me, but Leandro's hands were never so good as Eduardo's, never so precise. And the old man wasn't able to kneel and scrape dirt from an equally shriveling chair. And now there were days darkness stretched and not a single spot of sunlight fell over me. It reminded me of the lonely days at Wood & Depot, just waiting to be bought. In hindsight, I remembered those times with a slight sense of nostalgia, even if deep down I knew my life was a lot more meaningful now. In the end, all I wanted was to stave off the thought that Eduardo Amorim wouldn't be as longevous as oak. One day he would be a long pack pushed into a white truck.

Eduardo was depressed and alone since Leandro had been spending so much time in college. Sometimes Jeff, Leandro's boyfriend, came to check on Eduardo, and the old man seized the opportunity to talk about carpentry, how he had developed novel techniques to clean glasses back in the day, and how his enterprise was bound to break, but he saved it and rode it to glory. Jeff listened all along, as patient as Leandro, preparing food for him and sometimes even cleaning me (even clumsier than Leandro). But Jeff wasn't always available, and in the rare moments when it was only Eduardo and I in the house, the wood creaked its subtle messages. From my unprivileged position in relation to the remainder of the Amorims' house, I couldn't really know what happened upstairs or in the smelling domains of the kitchen. But wood spoke. It carried crepitations and voices, and sometimes I felt them shrilling up my legs, bringing Eduardo's weeping from the privacy of his bedroom, sometimes his mumblings about what he was planning to do in the day, how the weather was bad, and how life could be different if not for his actions.

I never really thought about the second chance Joana talked about. I didn't want to understand her, I just wanted to forget her, as if by doing so Eduardo was also going to abandon her in the corners of his mind like a neglected, unfinished piece of furniture. But that wasn't the truth. Eduardo's gaze hollowed out from time to time, and other times her name whispered up my legs, carried by the wood. So I knew Eduardo was dwindling in a spiral of thoughts.

One day, Eduardo left for a walk. He did so every now and then with spurs from Leandro, who insisted he needed to stay healthy. That day, Leandro brought Jeff home and they sat across each other at the table, just like Eduardo and Joana ten years before.

"My sister is very secretive," Leandro said. "She told me something these days on the phone."

"It's upsetting you," Jeff said, grabbing his boyfriend's hands.

Leandro nodded.

"She said I should stop caring about Eduardo—and she calls him that, never grandpa or grandfather—because he was a no-good man. When I asked why she wouldn't tell. I told her if she wasn't going to tell me, it would be better if she had stayed silent. She hung up."

"You have any idea what does she mean?"

"Nope. All I know is there's something in our past, something that has to do with my parents. But they never told me, and I never insisted because I know how it bothers Vô."

"It bothers you, too. You never tell me about your past."

"There was a fire. My parents died. I was just a toddler back then, and have no memories of what happened. Vô brought my sister and me here and raised us. That's all I know, and I'm not sure if I want to know more."

"And Joana..."

"She blames him for something, I just don't know what."

One day, though, I came close to knowing why. Of all people, a chair. But then life intervened, like always, and things would never be the same for the Amorims. (And for me.)

The stairs creaked with Eduardo's slippers and cane. He stopped before me, casting a long shadow. The bags under his eyes were blackened and his lips cracked. He'd been crying.

"Not many like you anymore," he said, sliding a finger over the seahorses' heads on my backrest. At first, I thought he was speaking about seahorses, but he kept a while at this, fingers coming and going in indecisive patterns. Then, he stopped and stared at the palm of his hands. "Not many like us."

My hardwood crackled inside of me while his words sank in. He wasn't just aware of my consciousness but also had the same hands as Anatólia's, capable of bestowing a sense of existence upon woodcraft.

"I had one like you," he told me, turning me over to face him as if the front of my backrest were my face. "A wooden stool made of beech. I didn't choose to give it life. But it happened, so I had to take care of it as I took care of plants." He shook his head. "No, not like plants. Not even like dogs. I treated it as if it were my child. It ruined my life, though. Not its intention, no. But it did nevertheless.

Well…" Tears now crossed down his cheeks, through his wrinkles, and onto his white beard. "I suppose I ruined myself. Who am I to blame a stool?"

He guffawed.

"It was—"

Leandro came in with Jeff. Their faces had darkened shades to them, and Jeff kept throwing glances at Leandro. If I could, I'd send them out. I needed to listen to the rest of the story.

"Are you okay, Vô?" Leandro said, putting a hand over his grandpa's shoulder. "You're crying."

Eduardo smiled. "Just babbling romantic rhymes and poetry that came to mind. I got all cheesy."

Leandro and Jeff exchanged not-so-relieved looks.

"I have something to say." Leandro pulled out one of my apple-themed friends and sat on it, rubbing his hands and pinching his lips.

"You are going to get married," Eduardo said, propping his elbow on me. This was the news I'd like to hear, something that would make the old man forget his broken family at least for a while. But Eduardo was trembling. Both of us could read Leandro's eyes very well. We'd learned many things through the years. Leandro had something else to say, something we weren't going to like.

Leandro shook his head and stared at Jeff one last time. Jeff nodded, even if hesitantly.

"Joana went back to Portugal," Leandro said. "She's going to live there for good."

Eduardo sat on me.

– **5** –

The sunlight I loved so much when I was varnished and good-smelling wasn't so friendly in the long run. Twenty years after I yearned so much for those light streaks cutting through the lumberyard's boards, my wood darkened, dried out, and rifted at the edges. The luster varnish I thought would endure until the end of time had dulled to a stained, rough finish. But the sun wasn't the only one to blame. My seahorses had heads a little more flattened now, and the furrows in their lines had accumulated grime and dust. The water lilies on two of my feet were unrecognizable, just bulks of wood, the result of years bumping into the table and the other chairs. My seat faded from crimson to a whitish violet, though it was mostly intact but for a small cut on its side. I imagined myself looking a lot more like Anatólia in her last days.

And speaking of my carpenter, I had her sentence figured out.

Leandro and Jeff decided to hire an apartment nearby, so they could spend more time with Eduardo and keep encouraging him to maintain a healthy routine. Rare were the moments of laughter and joy in the Amorims' residence, but there was still something flowing there. And whatever it was, I decided to call it love. I might be completely wrong, being a chair and all, but that was what answered the doubts I had about Anatólia's sentence. Who was she, the one who would love me? It didn't matter as long as I was there with them, static, partially hidden by the table. And love—or whatever you might call it—surged from Leandro to Jeff, from Jeff to his grandfather-in-law, and from Eduardo to me. The old man and I shared a special bond by now, an old bone-made creature and a piece of battered oak-built furniture.

Sometimes, Eduardo threw glances only I understood, sometimes he smiled, other times he whispered, and when he was alone he told me about that time when Leandro and Joana's parents were alive and they decided to plant trees in the backyard. Or that other time when Joana tried to count the fish swimming in shoals in a creek not a mile away from the house. He was the head of a broken family, a man whose shoulders were bulky with guilt. But he knew how to love and to be loved.

I never learned the full story about the stool from Eduardo himself. After discovering Joana was leaving, he drowned in a personal sulkiness of guilt that lasted for some time. His habits changed, his voice went from the tight, educated tone filled with analysis and self-control to the rough and downtrodden mood of the defeated. Time improved his temper, but something got lost in the way. It was as if Joana had died. In a way, she did. She'd never called Eduardo again in the decade that followed, but the gossip reverberating through unconscious wood told me that Eduardo scoured for phone numbers and searched the internet for his granddaughter's whereabouts. He never found a thing.

Until he did.

Eduardo was in the kitchen against Leandro's orders. His grandson had asked him not to use the stove when alone. The smell of fish—not salmon, but cod—floated across the living room, sticking to my wood and my seat. And it lingered there for over an hour. I worried, but I was a chair. What should I do beyond worrying? I stood there and did nothing even when the salty scent of cod transformed into that of fire.

"God!" I heard Eduardo's gasp from the kitchen. "Leandro, come here. Not again, please! No, no!"

The fire alarms he'd installed nine years before sprang to life.

Eduardo came out from the kitchen and stood with a hand on the table, back slightly bent forward, eyes hollow. For a moment, it was like he was having a heart attack. His hands shivered through the table and it thrilled through me coming from the table's foot that was touching my own.

"Vô!" Leandro's voice. "What's this smell?"

At this point, smoke was spreading through the room.

"My son, let's get out of here." Eduardo finally moved, and my barbs shifted in relief. "Get the chair."

"What are you talking about?" Leandro didn't stop. He ran to a closet in the small corridor that led to the kitchen and grabbed a fire extinguisher. He was precise. Years ago, Eduardo had paid firemen to provide instructions for him and Jeff.

"Let's save our lives, Leandro," Eduardo muttered, his hands still on the table. "Get the chair. The one with the seahorses."

In the kitchen, I heard the fire extinguisher pouring its chemical on the flames with rapid swooshing jets. It muted Eduardo's whimpering.

Leandro came several minutes later and his Vô was still static with his hand on the table, looking at the door as if unable to reach it.

"We lost the oven," Leandro said, smudges of grey on his face and shirt. "What got into you, Vô?" He wasn't angry but his voice was mildly sad.

"Joana's thesis is called The Migration Flow of Saltwater Fish in the Southern Shores of Portugal. I found it on a webpage."

"Is it?" Leandro wiped the sweat on his brow, his eyes escaping his grandfather's gaze. He opened all the windows and sent a text, probably to the house insurance. When he turned back to Eduardo, he shook his head and ushered him to one of the chairs, pulling it out for him.

"I'm not worried about Joana, Vô. The house caught fire. I'm worried about you."

Leandro kneeled before him and grasped his hands.

"I shouldn't have been born like this..." Eduardo wept. "With these hands..."

Leandro frowned. "What?"

"That stool..."

"You said something about a chair minutes ago. What's that?"

Eduardo's gaze was far away, not here and not at the now, but it quickly focused on Leandro. Completely lucid. And he spoke for the first time about his past. While he was at it, I could feel his body shifting in the chair. Not shivering, but releasing something out of him.

"You and Joana were safe in the garden. I came back inside to save your parents, then I saw the stool. It didn't seem like anything serious, right? Just a burst outlet, right? Do you remember that day?"

Leandro shook his head and mouthed a negative. His lips fluttered.

"I was quick. I bragged about being a quick man back then, you know? I hurried inside, saw the stool, brought it outside. Ten seconds? Maybe thirty. Your parents were sleeping, so I had yet to wake them if the smell didn't do it. So I ran back inside, climbed the stairs of that old house, and—"

Eduardo straightened his back. My legs clicked.

"Flames were blocking the door already. I heard them talking inside, I think. Trying to understand what was happening. I called them, but the floorboards crackled and pushed me back. I had to go back down the stairs. I called the fire department, but... The fire spread quickly in that old house. I screamed for them at the window, but all I saw were shadows as the fire spread through the curtains."

"Why did you never tell me this?" Leandro's voice was hoarse, his teeth clinking, but his hands still grasping those of his Vô.

"The firemen were quick enough, but it was too late. And your sis... Your sis waited for me with you on her lap. She was sitting on the stool. She was trembling. She was—she was crying a lot and you were too. And the first thing she said to me was... It was... She asked me why did I bring the stool out first? She was twenty then, you were barely six months."

"And why did you?" Leandro pulled a chair and sat facing his grandpa.

"I gave it life once. It was my duty to save it."

Leandro just gaped at Eduardo, their hands stitched together and resonating with the table, the chairs, the floorboards, me. Leandro could ask anything at this point. If that was the reason Joana didn't like him, if he consciously saved a stool knowing he could be sacrificing his son and his daughter-in-law, if the seahorses chair in the living room also had life. Instead, he just stooped forward and embraced Eduardo. They stood like this for a while, still resonating, smelling like smoke and fire.

I could never say if Leandro believed his grandfather. If I had to guess, I'd say he picked something in the middle. Perhaps he called Joana to confirm the story about the stool, perhaps he researched about blessed woodworkers only to find nothing at all. Perhaps he didn't care as long as he had his Vô with him.

In the end, it didn't matter. My time with the Amorims was over.

Eduardo died seven days later of a heart attack.

- 6 -

The house went on sale. This time, the SOLD sign was placed on a pole in the house's garden. It was sad to see João Gutierrez's employees again. They bought back the furniture, probably to bring them back to its origins and restart the wood cycle. Leandro and João Gutierrez didn't speak too long about numbers. They signed a deal and the gang started to shift everything I knew, everything I could call home. Only I was spared. Leandro didn't want to sell me, so perhaps he found a sliver of truth in his grandfather's words.

I moved to Leandro and Jeff's apartment. Like Eduardo, my days were ending. Oak could last for millennia, but only as long as it was nurtured by the soil. Furniture lasted as long as it was preserved, taken care of, and properly maintained in the appropriate environment. Which held true for feelings too, now that I thought of it.

Life in Leandro and Jeff's apartment was never the same. Sun bathed me during the morning and part of the afternoon, its rays sneaking in through electronic blinds. But I didn't care anymore. I was placed to lead a glass table with two sets of plastic chairs that didn't even smell of anything authentic. But I also didn't care about leading. All I cared about was seeing how Leandro was happy. And Jeff. And after a couple of years, the 4-year-old girl they brought home. Sarah.

It was Sarah who broke me, I must confess. My legs weren't as fierce as Anatólia's hands anymore, so one day they just snapped. Sarah hurt her knees but it was just the beginning for those tiny bones. Leandro tried to repair me, visibly sad, mentioning to Jeff and Sarah how I was important to his Vô. How I should be kept, how I should be repaired. But I was beyond my days. The mildew growing through my seat could tell.

I didn't want anything more either.

Leandro and Jeff shipped me to spend my last couple of months in a private deposit rented at Wood & Depot's warehouse. It was dark and damp, and only through a small hatch window did the sunlight rarely filter in. What would be of me? It didn't matter. All I knew was my consciousness, Anatólia's gift, was fading fast. But I must tell you that I've never been so glad in my life, because right there in the dark, remembering little Sarah's giggles, I discovered I was one of the Amorims. And we were made of oak.

· ·

Renan Bernardo is a Nebula and Ignyte finalist author of science fiction and fantasy from Brazil. His fiction appeared in *Reactor/Tor.com*, *Clarkesworld*, *Apex Magazine*, *Podcastle*, *Escape Pod*, *Daily Science Fiction*, and others. His writing scope is broad, from secondary world fantasy to dark science fiction, but he enjoys the intersection of climate narratives with science, technology, and the human relations inherent to it. His solarpunk/clifi short fiction collection, *Different Kinds of Defiance*, was published in 2024. His dark sci-fi novella, *Disgraced Return of the Kap's Needle*, is upcoming by Dark Matter INK. He can be found at BlueSky (@renanbernardo.com) and his website: www.renanbernardo.com.

IMAGINE: PURPLE-HAIRED GIRL SHOOTING DOWN THE MOON

Angela Liu

"Imagine: purple-haired girl shooting down the moon."

I type the prompt into the black screen as if making a request to God.

The blurred shape of a head appears in four variations over a pixelated ocean of gray. The eyes, corrugated whites, slowly take shape.

"We're leaving. Our ride's here," Mina says, fanning her fake eyelashes in front of the cracked mirror, willing the hot glue to dry. Her eyeliner's too thick on the left side, but I don't say anything.

Outside, Ip is waiting by the usual pea-green van in his matching green polyester coat, smoking a joint. He waves to us as we walk over like a dad picking up his kids from school.

Mina slides into the front seat while I settle into the back, my feet crinkling over old magazines and discarded hamburger wrappings. His van smells peaty and looks like a cozy home for a family of raccoons. I throw our gym bags stuffed with a single change of clothes, ratty towels, and our makeup pouches onto the seat next to me.

"Should probably cover up," Ip says, getting into the van, his jittery purple eyes wandering to Mina's bare legs and then back onto the yellow-lit streets behind the Warehouse dorms. "They say the Harvesters out there get attracted by the smell of skin."

"They can have it all if they want. I'm not a fan of this body anyway," Mina says without a hint of sarcasm.

"She's kidding," I say, hoping my answer isn't too slow or too fast to raise suspicions. I roll down the window to let in some cold air as a distraction, the dusty wind whipping up our hair like jellyfish tentacles. Ip is supposedly a former client of Mina's, but even a friend will happily report you if their Joy score is low enough and they need the extra points.

Ip watches me from the rearview mirror, his eyes unreadable. He steps on the gas, and the van lurches forward. We pull out of the alley, colored lights beaming ads into our eyes as we speed down the main street.

"Crazy shit on the news," he says, sticking his tongue out like a twitching compass needle as we merge onto the highway. Green factory lights sprawl out and twinkle across the dark polluted river. "People runnin' out of town just 'cause of some rumors. The Electric Zone is only as strong as its people, yeah? Nothin' but a wasteland waitin' out there," Ip says, parroting something he probably read in the Council's latest pamphlets.

"Yeah, nothing but a wasteland," I echo as Mina looks out the window. I can't tell if she's watching the lights or her own reflection. She doesn't speak again for the rest of the car ride.

In the daytime, Mina and I work double shifts at the Warehouse. That's where they send the kids with the best eyes and hands. We paint the memory packs for the NC-orbs—that's short for Name Change orbs, and they're the hottest item on the market these days. Everyone's eager to be somebody else, and who can blame them when the real world is a collage of worst-case-scenarios come true. Custom-made NCs from a good artist can fetch a half million on the white market, usually reserved for the richest assholes. You'll barely see my name in the NC-orb credits—I'm nothing but small fry, the assistant of the assistant artist, but I still get enough trickle-down cash to buy a nice holo-change every few months to keep up with the trends. New hair, costume upgrades to match the latest popular shows, tattoo, and piercing add-ons. That makes it easier to move around, to stay invisible. The Joy Drones are always looking for people who don't fit in, stray scraps of human trash that need cleaning up.

Ip stops the car in front of the Love Manor. This isn't our first time. One of the fastest ways to buffer your bank account are those powder pink doors that open to a plush world of secret, beautiful, ugly dreams. The masked nuns run a tight ship—Love Manor opens at midnight and closes at 5:00 a.m. sharp for cleaning. Clients are by recommendation only. That fake owl perched on the roof, its concrete head perpetually moon-facing, doubles as a scarecrow for unwelcome birds and a face-recognition sniper for uninvited guests. Love-san, the co-owner who came from a small fishing village off the coast of Taiwan according to her online profile, believes everyone deserves a second chance, or at least that's what she says, grinning into the high-res cameras for her nightly video Livestream. Mina and I watch from our dingy one-room, backs on the scuffed-up tatami, eyes on the optical browser open in our corneas—the close-ups are so clear I can see Love-san's caked-up pores, the white chin hairs she forgot to pluck. If I stare long enough, I feel like I could lose myself into the void of her black-tattooed eyes.

"C'mon, let's go," Mina says, peering in from the open van window. "The customers are paying by the minute."

"Imagine: purple-haired girl shooting down the moon."

I eye-click the prompt into my optical browser while waiting for the client to clean himself off.

"Have you ever tried Purple Haze?" the man asks, buttoning up his shirt.

This could be a trick question, but I play along. He doesn't have the jittery purple eyes of someone who's been overusing.

"Just a small hit. It's part of the job," I say, smiling up at him from the bed, one eye on the image slowly taking shape in my browser. "What about you?"

"Couldn't sleep for days afterward," he answers, the bed sinking where he sits down. He leans over and kisses me on the navel. This could spill into a messy situation, so I sit up and gently push him away, motioning for him to turn around.

"Let me give you a shoulder rub, that might help you sleep better," I offer half-heartedly, anything to keep his mouth off my body. In my left eye, a block of purple forms atop a cream-washed oval with two dot-eyes.

"I like you," the man says as I knead the doughy muscles under his shoulder blades. "You're not like the others. You make me feel calm."

That's the Purple Haze, not me, I think, but I smile like I mean it. Like his words mean something. They don't. Making a client happy leads to tips and client recommendations. This too is a transaction, and right now what I need most is more cash. Mina and I have a deadline to meet.

I ruffle a hand through the man's hair as the two black dot-eyes swell out with whites in my optical browser. Puckered purple lips pop up on the digital face as if by magic, lines of hair across the forehead like a black fence.

"I heard from Mama-san that you're a painter," the man says, taking my hand and pressing it against his sweaty neck. I can feel his heartbeat in the joints of my fingers.

"It's just a hobby," I say, glancing briefly at the banana tree in the corner of the room. The fan-sized leaves sway under the air vents, the camera embedded into the trunk, peering at us like a small, hiding bird.

"I'd like to commission you for a painting," the man says, following my gaze. I rub my eyes, feigning a yawn. "I'm in a bit of a rush, and I need discretion."

Nothing more discreet than a person who ceases to exist once you leave the room, you mean? I think, but I nod, still smiling. In my left eye, the purple-haired girl stands in front of the moon in a white suit, more a pixelated blob than a girl, but my brain fills in the details before the AI can. She looks the same as she does every night, no matter what system I type the prompt into.

"I'm not sure I'd have the time..." I say, saving the image with a blink and then eye-clicking out of the browser. "I still have to take my other shifts at the Manor..."

"Twenty."

"I'm sorry?"

"I'll pay for twenty shifts. That should be enough to finish it," he says, standing and buckling his pants. He checks his teeth in the vanity mirror next to the bed. "You can bring your painting supplies in here. No one would bother you. I'll make sure of it."

He reaches over and strokes my hair with the hand that he just used to scratch some filmy stain from his teeth.

This is what I hate about the corporate clients. They always assume you'll say yes.

The night tastes like soggy bread rolls and gasoline. My eyes strain against the blinding streetlights, haloes of white light in the rain. Mina got called in for an extra shift, so I head back to the Warehouse on my own. The walk is long, but it gives me time to decompress.

In the window of the all-night tattoo parlor, three bodies lie on their backs in leather chairs. The artist dons a crow-shaped mask with a steel needle pen embedded in his index finger and a precision light in his right eye. He steeples the black ink into pale skin, tracing the wing of a chimera on one of the customers. My bank account balance rises by a five-digit number in my left eye as I watch the body squirm against the needle. The client from the Love Manor works fast—a good and troublesome trait to find in a man.

The Warehouse dorms are the equivalent of surveilled rat burrows. They're dim, poorly ventilated, and smell like all the other bodies stuffed into it. Amber bulbs hang precariously from the ceilings, cheap and dusty, and no matter where you go, your skin and clothes feel damp and sticky. I've lived here long enough to know that no matter how late you come home, someone is watching.

Back in our shared room, I take a shower and lie on the bed, running through the images. I've got two hundred samples saved to my neural drive. Two hundred pictures of "purple-haired girl shooting down the moon," generated over multiple AI platforms, the prompt tested in over forty different languages.

The girl is always the same. The Mona Lisa-like smile as she points a rifle to the moon. The white suit and army-like boots, the plaster-cream skin. The rifle is like a photograph prop, perched on her shoulder, running the length of her arm with impossible lightness. I've seen her face so many times that a part of me feels like she must exist somewhere, a real flesh and blood girl. I haven't shown the pictures to anyone, but they calm me down. I wish I could meet her and ask why she's raging at the moon, if she's scared of earthquakes too, if we could be friends at the end of the world.

Mina comes home an hour before dawn, looking broken. One of her fake eyelashes has been torn clean off, her eyeliner smeared into raccoon eyes. I soon realize that isn't makeup but actual bruises. Her arms are a pincushion of needle holes.

"What happened?" I ask, not surprised but still miserable. The Love Manor is a roulette, and we knowingly spin it each time we go through those pink doors. The nuns pay well, but health insurance doesn't come with the room.

The sound of liquid hitting metal intensifies as the rain starts up again.

"Payday. Mreaaaaning a lot of shitr clients with lots and lots of cash to buuuuuuuurn-b-b-burnnnn," Mina slurs, her eyes unfocused. I don't know what she's been pumped with—if I hook her up with an incompatible med-patch, I could fry her T cells or scar the temporal lobe permanently. Her body's weaker than most—she spent nearly a quarter of our childhood in the ER and is missing a bone in her neck after surgery to remove a tumor in her head. Life's full of roulettes, and the body you get when you're born is one of them.

The only safe bet is an NC-orb, a neural purge, with a bootleg NC license. The mnemonic reset will uncouple most viral creepers, and her body can handle the rest. She won't remember a thing about the past seventy-two hours, she won't even be Mina anymore, not really anyway, but it's all I can do now.

I pull open my drawer and take out a backup NC-orb, one I pocketed from the Warehouse floor that I'd been saving, the narrative tab still uncut. I wet my neural brush and dab the tip into the hippocampal ink, sketching into the blank surface of the tab. As I paint, Mina counts the stains on the wall and tells me a meandering story about rabbits on the moon. I imagine a version of her without pain, one that can still run across the Warehouse yard without vomiting afterward, one that can still dream without seizures, one that doesn't break so easily. The NC-orb glows under the blue light of the desk lamp, a tiny nebula of what-ifs and maybes under my brush.

When I'm done, I coax Mina onto the bed.

"You'll be okay," I say, looking into her vacant eyes as she continues babbling about the rabbits' ears.

"There's one that always hops around the dark side. Hoppity. Hoppity. Hoppity. Until the pit opens and eats her up. She doesn't realize how deep the moon goes, how its rocky intestines wind and wind."

This is the fourth time I've done a neural purge on Mina, formerly Hina, formerly Lina, formerly Gina, originally Tina. I keep the names this way—I guess a part of me hopes a part of her always remains, like a blockchain that can always trace itself back to its origin. Like somewhere in there she's still the same girl who helped me out of the pit outside and not just a series of NC paintings I've injected into her brain.

I slot the orb into her ear and sing her a lullaby as I stroke her hair. Her eyes slowly flutter sleepily.

"I'm sorry," I whisper once I know she's asleep.

In my dreams, I hold a small vigil for Mina, the way one of the girls in class had wrapped her pet rat in a clean wiping cloth from the sterilization hall and packed it into a box of broken lights, the chipped glass gleaming rainbows under the Warehouse's emergency lights. *We'll get out, together, I promise,* I tell her, covering her with blankets. One after the other after the other. When every inch of her is covered, I stand back, listening to the sound of organ music like a church requiem. I start to panic, unable to remember the details of her face. Did she have a mole under her left eye? What was the shape of her eyebrows? The color of her hair? I pull the blankets off, one after the other, like peeling an onion, my eyes watering, but when I throw off the last layer, there's nothing but a pixelated body underneath—squares of Mina's black hair and gray skin, her yellow skirt and dotted red lips, and in her blurred hands, a pixelated rifle.

Without Mina, now Trina, there's no ride from Ip tonight, so I take the bus out to the Love Manor on my own.

The night bus is always a unique kind of hell with the mothers peddling virtual hand jobs while their babies are still strapped to their backs, teenagers with third-eye implants like in all the fortune-telling fad videos, and the men tapping at the soft insides of their elbows for a vein that can still take a shot of impure Purple Haze blended with cheap tranquilizer. Water runs across the windows like dribbling paint lines. Acid rain.

I arrive fifteen minutes early to the Love Manor.

Mama-san, the nun on duty tonight, points to Room A-14 after I drop my umbrella in the bucket by the door. She doesn't say anything about the man, but I know he's already paid for my time.

In the room, I turn off the rave holos and turn on the air purifier above the faux window displaying exploding volcanoes on Io. My eyes still see kaleidoscope flashes when the lights settle back into a normal cream-white. The cleaning crew haven't gotten to this room yet, but I don't mind the smell. I wipe down the vanity desk, bake it for a few minutes in the UV cleaner while I go wash my hands, and then pull out my materials to get started.

The man asked for a simple NC-orb: a memory of a girl and boy taking a peach-picking trip to the Moon on Christmas.

No one goes to the Moon anymore—that desolate rock covered in nothing but tacky hotels, scammy unlicensed tour buses that'll drain your bank account dry, and homeless former lunar performers flaunting scars left by organ harvesters. But with the right filters, any memory can feel like a perfect dream, and that's what I've been paid to do.

I stare at the photo the man gave me, at the girl's toothy smile and curly black hair tied back into a messy ponytail, at the halfway handsome boy who grew up into the balding man I'd fucked in an overpriced, surveilled love hotel run by profiteering nuns. Life is an ugly ride that turns everyone into a monster eventually. I squint, trying to see their faces better. What had they been saying in this photo? There is a palpable joy in the reflected light.

I imagine the girl older, lying on one of the beds in the Love Manor, her body covered in organ harvester scars too. I replace her eyes with my own so I can see it, swap her ears and nose for mine so I can hear and smell it too:

the white pockmarked surface of the moon outside my window, the metallic crinkle of Christmas jingles playing on cheap speakers from tour buses docked outside the hotel, the smell of artificial bacon fat sizzling in hot oil, the sound of the open-mouthed boy snoring gently next to me on the bed. Someone is trying to sell their body in the hall, one of the tour buses honks impatiently outside, my head is a million stimuli condensed into a closed box. I reach out for the boy, but he's no longer there, only the fat length of a rifle remains on the pillow.

I squeeze the neural pen too tightly, and the ink bleeds pink on the tab. I shake my head out of it and pull the brush off, watching the paint dry. It's always important to let it dry.

One of the nuns knocks an hour before dawn.

"Do you need some breakfast?" she asks from behind the closed door.

Her question reminds me that I haven't eaten since yesterday afternoon. But I'm almost done with the painting, my brain calibrated to just the right output setting like a well-oiled machine, and a break could set me back hours.

I glance at the banana tree in the corner of the room, the pinhead-sized camera camouflaged among the shaggy trunk, an omnipotent eye. Staying too long also invites suspicion.

"Yeah, sure. I forgot to get dinner last night," I say, trying not to overact for the surveilling audience.

"We got a couple of sandwiches leftover. Some client ordered a hundred and then just left. Probably high. They're in the mess hall."

"Great, thanks."

As I wash up in the bathroom, I type the prompt into my optical browser again out of nervous habit: "Imagine: purple-haired girl shooting down the moon."

The cream-oval glitches over a white moon.

I close my eyes and splash hot water onto my face, listening to the water guzzling out of the faucet. I open my eyes and stare at my reflection. The drain's clogged and cloudy water pools in the sink.

As the blob of purple materializes, a green alert flashes over the browser. It's been flagged EHP—Extremely High Priority. It's a video message.

A white-caked face pops up next to the lumpy purple-haired girl still in mid-development. At first, I think it's a spam video and my optical browser's going to be overrun with naked ladies or a get-rich-quick jackpot seizure in seconds, but the video sharpens into high-res in my eye. The woman in the square browser blinks.

"This is a message to all our staff, full-time and freelancers—we are experiencing higher than usual volume of requests from troublesome clients. We are investigating the issue, but please exercise caution and refrain from accepting direct requests that are against Love Manor policy."

The video stops. The girl with the purple hair points her rifle at the white face before it dissolves into the moon.

In the mess hall, three other girls nibble sandwiches at separate cafeteria tables like queens of their own islands. One of them, whose name I can never remember, waves at me with an overly friendly smile and beckons me over to her table.

"Long night?" she asks, putting one of her sandwiches on my tray.

"Kind of," I answer, picking up the bread. It's got a soft chewy texture, the tomato inside still red and firm. These are quality sandwiches. "Just one super long client."

The girl giggles at my response like a middle schooler. She leans in and whispers, "Did you get the weird message from Love-san?"

None of the other island queens make any motion like they've overheard or even care. One girl flicks at a piece of spinach between her front teeth with her tongue. The other rolls her eyes from left to right, up to down, stretching her optical nerve like we were all taught at school.

"Rumor has it Love-san's dead. Splatty splat splat," the girl chuckles soundlessly. "They've got some crone wearing a prosthetic trying to do damage control until they find a proper replacement. I guess that's what you get when you've got too much money and too little soul."

I look up from the sandwich. The girl is blinking nonstop like a windshield wiper in the rain.

"Um, are you okay?" I ask.

"Have you tried the new Purple Haze?" she asks, her eyes halting suddenly.

"What's new about it?"

"Take a hit from the right batch, and they say you get a fast-passed appointment with God. Just one, so you gotta make sure you make it count. Hey, are you taking notes?"

"Notes for what?"

"For the end of the world, when they ask for witnesses," the girl says, putting another one of her sandwiches on my tray. "Hey, you interested in a hit? Best stuff on the market. I can get you the first batch for a discount. Don't let anyone tell you you don't deserve to die the best way."

"I don't know what—"

One of the nuns is standing by the door and motions for the other two girls who depart from their respective islands.

"My last client said the moon's already been colonized, and we're just the fuel they're burning to stay alive," the girl says, a vacant look in her eyes so I know she's scrolling through something as she speaks. "In the vacuum of space, no one can hear you scream and all that, yeah?" She grins and gets up to leave too.

I expect the ground to split open and the devil to emerge with a golden violin, or for Love-san and her muscled cyborg guards to swing in from the windows in bird costumes, any indication that this is just a strange overwork-induced nightmare, but nothing comes. The cheap fluorescent lights on the ceiling flicker, almost like a laugh, and I'm alone again.

A homeless man is wilted on the bus bench in front of me.

When the bus arrives, he doesn't get on, doesn't even move. I pay the fare and take a seat at the back, pulling up the address one more time from the client.

1464 Green Street
Last stop on the Z-24 bus.

Dust balloons up as the bus takes off. Today's all smog and smoke, the sky an apocalyptic shade of orange. The air on the bus is no better. I pull my mask up over my eyes and vegetate until the last stop.

A few years ago, I would have never taken a painting side job. Trina and I used to joke about being wobbling old ladies by the time we saved up enough to buy a ticket out. But then the rumors started. An anonymous warning on the Forums about the Big Earthquake, one that would level the entire city. It was immediately flagged and deleted by the Public Safety Bureau of Informatics. Hackers traced the original post to an IP originating in the same Bureau. Quiet panic ensued. People started emptying their bank accounts and hoarding the cash in suitcases filled with packs of new underwear and instant noodles. I promised Trina I'd get us out of here before the earthquake hit, and nothing pays better and faster than black market NC-orbs. Not even the Love Manor can compete.

The Warehouse has a strict policy against individual work—they want to keep a stranglehold on the supply of black-market NC-orbs. Trina and I saw what happened to our floor mate, the pretty boy with the old lady patron who wanted an NC-patch so she could play piano for her husband's funeral. Such a harmless request, and Luca was so easy to convince—he didn't like seeing people cry. After the Warehouse Axes tracked his message records, they rounded us all up midshift, lined us up around a clean worktable so we all had a good view, and then made us watch as they took both his feet. *Come on*, the Floor Lead laughed, *you don't need your feet to paint*. It's true. You don't even really need a will to live. With the right NC-orb, they'll turn you into the perfect worker. Hell, you won't even remember a time you weren't.

On the bad days, Trina doesn't think this is such a crummy deal—forgetting who you are, transplanting in someone else's dreams to replace your own impossible ones. On the worst days, I almost tell her the truth. How Tina used to wake up, crying for her mother. How Gina once caught a bird in the courtyard and whispered her secrets to it, hoping it would fly away with them. How Lina used to sneak small jokes into her NC paint jobs—tiny purple chickens and flying rats that she knew no one would ever notice. How Hina had been in love with the previous Floor Lead before he taught her how little love can mean in a world where a body has no more value than a new pair of jeans. How lonely it is to carry the weight of someone else's memories.

"Green Street," the bus driver mumbles into the intercom. "Last stop. Everybody off." I'm the last one.

The man is already waiting at the bus stop.

"I checked your location," he explains without being asked. "Thank you for coming here so promptly."

"Thank you for paying so promptly," I say, trying to ignore the way his eyes track over my body like one of the Joy Drones. "Do I just give it to you here?" I pat my bag where I've packed the NC-orb in a steel tube to prevent the scanners from picking it up.

"I'd like to look at it first, if you don't mind."

I do mind.

"I'll add another $1000 for the extra time," he adds, reading my hesitation.

"My Warehouse shift starts in an hour, so I can't stay longer than fifteen minutes," I say and pull up Trina's name in my optical browser. I send her a message with the man's address and a "In case you don't hear from me in the next few hours, send one of the Axes please. ;)"

"That should be enough. My office is just around the corner," the man says, wiping the ash from his glasses. The sky still blazes orange above the towering apartment buildings. "We'll be done before you know it."

As we walk, my browser flashes green with an incoming call. Trina always had a habit of doing things too soon or too late. If I was on my way to a serial killer's house, she'd be calling me during the bus ride there, but be unreachable when I'm desperately messaging her from his bloody basement.

"Awful weather today, huh?" I say, closing the call without answering.

The man offers me a shot of Purple Haze as I wait. I take the vial, but don't use it. A good dose can buy a night at a capsule hotel if I run into trouble with the Warehouse later.

"This is gorgeous," the man says, running the NC-orb through the reader. "You've got a real talent for unexpected detail."

His office looks like a glorified surveillance room: plush red sofas, a small bar with a shelf stocked full of colorful spirits and liqueurs, and next to that, a wall of fifteen screens, all showing bedrooms and alleys and church benches in places I've never seen. People eating, praying, crying, fucking. I try to do a quick image-map search, but I can't connect to anything; the reception's jammed.

"What did you say you do again?" I ask.

"I didn't. I run the security imaging in the Electric Zone," he says, still scrolling through the reader. "Nothing's a secret."

"What about the Warehouse?" I ask, scanning the screens for a familiar room, a trace of the Warehouse's blue cafeteria walls or stone shower rooms. A hint that he's been watching me long before the request at the Love Manor.

"The Warehouse management pay off the brass enough that we turn a blind eye to everything that goes on in there. No peeking unless there's an EHP request from the top."

I watch a man getting stomped on by strangers in an alley. A woman gets railed on a kitchen counter by some guy in a police uniform. A cat paws at a dead rat in a puddle next to a fallen garbage bin. All the surveillance screens are muted—misery and pleasure and boredom rendered into a curious silent theater. I realize how everything I paint is not so different. You can design any reality you want, conjure any emotional reaction, with the right sequence of images.

The man finally sits back and turns off the reader, a satisfied look on his face.

"Everything good?" I ask, standing.

"Yeah, wonderful. The person who recommended you really knew what they were talking about."

"Recommended me?" I ask.

The television screens gleam behind him like the eyes of God. I wait for a name, but he's tracing my legs and hips again in a way that makes me think if I don't leave now, I might not be able to later.

"There're so many kind people there. I'll have to thank them," I say, hand on the door. It doesn't open when I push. I jangle the knob and frame a few times, my heart thrumming. The man laughs.

"It's an old house. You gotta ease it with a little love if you want it to open up," he reaches over to turn the knob and pushes the door open. "See?"

The man orders me a skycab directly back to the Warehouse, so I sink into the sour-smelling upholstery and run through the usual image prompt. The driver has a massive helmet on that makes him look fly-like. He asks if I want to turn on the Secret Garden Holo for the ride, spend half an hour in a lush cage of viburnum, forget-me-nots, dog-sized hydrangeas, and ivy-crawling fences, but I shake my head. I prefer looking out the window, the last smear of orange-pink on the darkening sky, the flickering streetlights buzzing to life below, the tired bodies filing out of one building and into another like worker ants. When you spend your life conjuring up imagined lives, pretty fantasies for other people, steeping yourself in reality when you can is necessary self-care.

Sometimes I wonder if I look hard enough through the maze of bodies below, I'll see one of my earlier clients from the Love Manor, the man who massaged the space between my eyes and asked if I could see another universe in the thin skin there, the middle-aged woman who read me poetry from Emily Dickinson before getting undressed. All those people who had taken a piece of me with them, like all the NC-orbs I'd pressed my ink into.

There's an End-of-Life van parked outside the Warehouse. The Floor Lead paces near the entrance like a spouse waiting outside of ER surgery. I walk past the line of smokers peering in during their break, some gleeful, others shaking their heads. The Joy Drones have cuffed a woman on the paint floor. It's not un-common. They'll take her in for a pointless infraction, break a few of her bones before they slip an obedience-maxed NC-orb into her ear and call it day. You'll find her serving tea in one of the Council Towers in a few weeks, a permanent smile on her face. Meanwhile, the Warehouse could be carving up people for or-gans on the factory floor and the Joy Drones would be delivering them discounted shipping boxes for same-day delivery.

I keep walking, not interested in other people's misery. There's so much of it everywhere, you could drown if you aren't careful.

Trina isn't in the room when I get back, so I send her another message.

"Someone's getting axed on the Paint Floor," I eye-click and lie back on my bed, still picturing the screens in the man's office like a million insect eyes.

Outside, the sky is a bruised peach, a wash of reddish browns. It's the same ev-erywhere: dust storms, acid rain, all of it like an orchestra of disaster. Meanwhile the Feeds are alight with self-proclaimed prophets and time travelers who are certain the big earthquake will level the city soon.

My browser flashes green with an incoming call from Trina.

"What's up?" I ask, eye-clicking the "accept" button.

"Why didn't you pick up any of my calls? The Axes are fucking after me."

I sit up. "Calm down, what're you talking about?"

"Calm yourself down! Where the fuck did all this money come from? They said I've been selling NC-orbs to a security informant."

I try to take my own advice and calm down. In my optical browser, I click open my bank account and find that all the money received for the man's painting has been drained.

"Are you there? You know I wouldn't fucking do that. Why the hell else do you think we're working the Love Manor? Letting those disgusting pigs...We were going to do this together...the right..."

I can hear her deep breaths, the way she always gets before crying. My chest aches, guilt threatening to drown me, my eyes burning. I want to hug her through the browser, shrink to the size of a molecule and enter that space in her brain responsible for controlling sadness and joy.

"I'm sorry Trina. Tell me where you are, and I'll meet you there. Maybe we can hitch a ride. Maybe there's a train out tonight..." I frantically type in a search for timetables.

She doesn't reply.

"Trina?"

"Purple-haired girl from the moon. Purple. Purple. P-p-p-p-p-urple. Purrrrrrrrrrrrrrrrrrrrple. Shoot the moon. Down down down," she laughs, chokes on her own spit, and laughs some more. "Chomping purple rabbits. Crunchy crunchy crunchity." She's glitching again, another viral overload. I pull open my drawer—I'm out of spare NC-orbs.

"Where are you? Just tell me, and I'll—"

I hear a gunshot followed by the clap of electricity. The Axes' taser gun. Boots marching over concrete. Heavy metal being dragged.

"It hurts. Frlagnagargh. It hurts. Hurtshurtshurtshurts."

The call cuts off.

My brain switches into survival mode. I delete the phone record. I scroll through my call history, deleting everything from the past month, calls from Trina formerly Mina, wellness check-ins from the Floor Leads at the Warehouse, the nuns from Love Manor with last minute client requests, anything that could get me in trouble. There on the list, I find a number I don't recognize.

I click open the call record and press play.

Love-san's face suddenly appears in my optical browser like a nightmare. The earlier message plays again on loop. *This is a message to all our staff, full-time and freelancers—we are experiencing higher than usual volume of requests from trouble-some clients...*

There's a knock on the door. The inelegant grind of the Joy Drones' tires, waiting in front of the peephole. I close all optical browsers, but a part of me feels like I'm still being watched from inside my head.

"Cleaning scheduled," they squeak cheerfully out of their speakers, trying to sound human. We can recreate the perfect visual replica of a person, but the ears are harder to deceive. At least for now. This too is only a matter of time, but right now, I know whatever is waiting for me behind that door is not human.

I turn off the lights and climb onto the fire escape outside. The metal creaks under my feet, an architectural relic kept more for tourist photos than safety, but it will have to do. I climb down the rusted ladder, keeping my eyes skyward. If I fall, I at least want to be watching the stars.

There's a van parked next to the garbage bins, the familiar driver smoking a joint.

"Need a ride?" Ip asks, blowing smoke out of his nostrils. "Mina called me."

I stare at the fleshy scar where Ip's left eye used to be.

"She already went ahead," I say. "Mind giving me a lift to the usual place?"

I smile, hoping if I smile hard enough, I won't start crying.

He stubs the joint out and puts the remainder into a small tin in his jacket. Stray cats hiss and claw at each other in the shadows behind the garbage bins. Ip gets into the car and motions toward the back seat with his chin.

"Hop in," he says.

The inside of the Love Manor smells like grilled eel and broiled sweet soy sauce, pretty glass chimes fluttering against the ceiling vents. The Manor exists in its own beautiful vacuum.

"Room A-00," the nun behind the reception desk says, handing me a key card. I can't tell which one of them is behind the mask; they all have the same eyes.

Inside the room, a sunflower field holo has rendered every inch of the room into a golden burst of blade-shaped petals, Fibonacci spirals of seeds, towering stems the height of prehistoric bears as far as the eye can see.

"I like this painting," a voice says.

Love-san peeks out from behind a cluster of head-sized flowers, her face powdered corpse-white, and I nearly have a heart attack. She grins at me, her eyes like downturned crescent moons, spidery fingers curled around the glowing NC-orb in her hand.

"Mr. Elliot was kind enough to let us have it once we had a good long talk," she says.

"Mr. Elliot?"

"Ah, yes, my apologies. The kindly fellow with a penchant for hairless navels and discretion. You really are great at your job. Such a keen eye for unexpected details."

The holo glitches, and a girl materializes in the sky above the sunflowers, the one from the man's photo.

"Were you the one who recommended me to him?" I ask.

"Of course! You're one of our best workers! Truly. I never expected him to actually ask you to make him something on the side. That's the problem with corporate clients, they always think you'll do anything they ask. No respect for the rules or proper protocol, am I right?" She grins, and it feels like there're too many teeth, her neck too long. I find myself counting the fingers on her hands, unsure if she's even real. "It's quite unfortunate about your friend. Trina was her most recent name on the neural blockchain, was it? You two really were like sisters. But things always get messy when friends go from dreaming up name changes to conjuring escapes."

"What do you care?" I ask, seeing her face reflected in the warped whorls of the sunflowers. "We get the work you need done. We don't cause trouble, even when your clients fuck up our heads."

"Oh, *absolutely*. The Love Manor welcomes all. And we really are thankful for your professionalism. We admire your hard work. Unfortunately, the Warehouse is a bit less forgiving. They're quite unhappy with all the ugly side businesses that have been sprouting lately, everyone eager for quick cash, all the working bodies leaving the city, and hey, I've got to keep my business partners happy."

"So you're using us as a scapegoat?"

"Scapegoat's a scary-sounding word. I prefer lesson. A lesson needs to be learned," she puckers her purple-painted lips. "You're too good for us to let go, but your friend's a bit more expendable. Defective goods after all. She'll neatly take the blame, and we can all get back to work. Yay!"

"What's going to happen to her?"

Love-san opens her eyes wide with mock-surprise, covering her mouth with a gloved hand. "Oh my, what *will* happen to our little Trina, Mina, Beena, Creena, everybody seen-a girl? She's not gonna *die* or anything. Jesus. That'd be far too wasteful. Probably sold off to one of the other Zones. They've got a real shortage of girls in the Water Zone. Too many drownings." She lowers her voice to a stage whisper. "I hear the men there can be a bit sadistic, and a body's such a floppy delicate thing, isn't it? But a second chance is a second chance, am I right?"

She sighs when the tears start rolling down my face.

"Come on now. You tried hard. We all saw," she claps the way the Floor Leads do when they're trying to wake us up during a brain-scrambling triple-shift. "But a defective brain's a defective brain, no matter how many times you try to patch it up with those magical NC-orbs of yours. It was only a matter of time anyway."

"Were you the one who reported her to the Axes?" I ask.

"Was it me? Or was it that nasty little illicit patch you did that set things off? Me, you, an unsuspecting third party making minimum wage, what's the difference in the end?" Love-san shrugs. I can't tell if she's imagining our entire conversation as another Livestream video. In the back of my head, I wonder if Ip is driving back over the highway, his Joy score rising by double digits.

I head toward the door, but her arm darts out and grabs a hold of my head. Her grip is powerful enough to break my neck if she wanted. Only then do I see the twist of metal peeking from under her silk gloves, the steel wrist that extends up into a two-beam steel forearm underneath her black checkered silk shirt, the same weaponized arms the Axes had.

"What the hell are you?" I ask, trying to twist out of her grip.

"Just someone trying to survive, like you. Why only give the upgrades to your security? Shouldn't you be best equipped to defend yourself?" She grins, so close I can see the black tattoos of her eyes. "Don't worry, I believe in second chances, and yours will be much more pleasant than the first one. I'll even let you keep some of your favorite memories. How does that sound?"

Above her and the holo-flowers, the girl is still suspended midair. Her face glitches with the grinding motors of Love-san's drill. Does she even exist? I imagine us together on the moon, leaping together on the cratered surface, high enough that it almost feels like we're floating. When does a body break free of gravity? *It's so tiring*, I think, *always waiting to fall.*

Memory Extraction: NC-OrbZ1

According to ancient texts of Enuma Elish, the world was created by tearing apart the primordial goddess—her tears collected into rivers, her body split in half to make up the earth and sky, her blood fashioned into the pliable flesh of the first humans. A female body sacrificed for new life.

Tina and I listen to our art teacher give this lecture, one eye scrolling through memes about burning houses and snarky dogs that can talk and build rocket ships. I've never seen a dog without a bad case of rabies, ears chewed down to rag bits, but the memes help us stay awake, and staying awake gets us extra points when it's time for job allocation at the Warehouse.

When the bell rings, the class collectively stands like ghosts being called back to the grave.

Back in my room, I crumple into the paper-thin mattress and mentally paint sunflowers into the ceiling. My brain is exhausted but still running on overdrive. My wrists ache from work, fingertips cracked from scrubbing too hard to get off the neural ink. They say it seeps through the skin, straight into the bloodstream, and then into your brain if you're not quick and thorough. Someone else's new memories becoming a part of you forever.

Tina's still down in the classroom, apologizing to the teacher about a forgotten assignment. She's neither quick nor thorough, but she works hard. And unlike me, she still dreams of leaving here.

"Wouldn't it be nice to dip your feet into a real lake? One that isn't going to melt the skin off our feet? I heard there are still some lakes you can swim in, if you go far enough," she says like some kid who's been reading too many fairy tales. She doesn't think of all the kids that get eaten before the hero arrives.

This time next year, we'll be working on the Paint Floor, inking fantasies into alternative realities and new loves onto the NC-paper. People don't only deserve second chances, they need them to evolve. That's what Love-san says in her videos. Nearly a million viewers each night, so it must mean something. Tina is less sure—she just wants to live, and that's already taking all she has to give.

A slight tremor shakes the shelves. I click open my optical browser.

Our art teacher told us life is too short for only drawing serious things, that we should have a bit more fun while we can. Unlike the previous teacher, she still sees us as people instead of barcoded tanks of creative juice ready to be expended.

"Why not draw a purple rabbit on the moon?" she suggested during class when most of us had opted for sketching out gilded piano concert halls and fevered trysts on imagined beaches. We all knew the most requested NC-scenarios, the ones that flashed on the Top 50 Feeds, the ones we'd all studied until we could paint them with our eyes closed, the ones we'd be drawing for the rest of our time on this broken planet.

"Why not go further?" Tina said, one of the only students who had been listening. "Why not draw a purple-haired girl shooting down the moon?"

Some of the other kids snickered. Tina didn't care. She'd just moved into the Warehouse and had nothing to lose, not yet anyway. When we went back to the dorm rooms, we spent the rest of the night coming up with silly prompts, chasing that elusive joy of experimentation like kids again, the joy that comes without a right or wrong answer, only the thrill of unlimited potential.

Still, I liked her original suggestion best. Even when we'd both been squeezed dry by other people's dreams, our brains on the verge of collapse, I wanted to remember it, a phrase like a key opening back to this moment.

"Imagine: purple-haired girl shooting down the moon," I type.

The pockmarked moon blots my optical browser. A purple oval over it, two black circles over that. Art is layering. Adding and subtracting to find the right combination or at least the closest thing to recreating a thought, a desire. Sometime long ago, I picked up my first pen, desperately wanting to save something by capturing it on paper, but I can't remember what that was anymore. Everything dilutes with enough time.

The ground trembles again, harder this time. The image stalls. Frozen pixels. The servers are extra slow today, and I'm left with just a shadow over a pixelated moon. I close the browser, then my eyes, and imagine the rest.

. . . .

Angela Liu is a Nebula-, Ignyte-, and Rhysling-nominated writer/poet from NYC. She researched mixed reality at Keio University's Graduate School of Media Design in Japan, with a focus on new narrative platforms and tangible interfaces for remote communication. Her stories and poetry are published in *Strange Horizons*, *Clarkesworld*, *The Dark*, *Interzone Digital*, *Uncanny Magazine*, *Lightspeed*, *khōréō*, and *Logic(s)*, among others. Check out more of her work at liu-angela.com or find her on Twitter/Instagram @liu_angela and on Bluesky @angelaliu.bsky.social.

SIX VERSIONS OF MY BROTHER FOUND UNDER THE BRIDGE

Eugenia Triantafyllou

It was half past midnight when Olga heard the Devil cry.

They were supposed to be wild tonight, the three of them. Cassandra had led the way and Maria and Olga didn't put up much of a fight. They would visit the Devil's bridge—anything that claimed to be even remotely intimidating was the Devil's something—and stay there for a while, record it with their phones to have something to show for it. Smoke some cigarettes.

Technically it was built on top of a river that had been dredged and filled in some fifty years ago which made the ground under the bridge degraded and pretty dangerous. But rumor had it—and by rumor Olga meant Maria's oldest cousin who had been making up stories about this place since third grade—that the bridge was built upon one of the gateways to Hell. If you walked on the bridge at the right time, when everything was still and quiet, and if you teetered a bit too close to the edge, the Devil's own hand would stretch from the bottoms of Hell and drag you under the bridge, and that would be the last anybody saw of you.

But nobody said what would happen if you cut out the middleman and just went straight under the bridge. So, the girls—and pretty much everyone in their school, and in other schools, and in places that weren't schools but people there were sufficiently immature—would challenge each other to spend a few minutes under the bridge and prove it. The proof could be literally anything, from a photo, to a short video, to saying *hey, I was there last night*; people would believe you depending on your overall credibility.

They called the place under the bridge *the tunnel*, even though it wasn't one really because it sounded both attractive and foreboding. Like the tunnel a soul crosses to enter Heaven only in the opposite direction. Like the dark at the end of the tunnel.

Olga lied to Maria and Cassandra about why she had followed them there. She told them it was because she was curious to see if these airheads would get jittery when dampness stuck to their skin like sweat and the musty air from the sea, stale as mold, passed through their lungs. When the wind reached their ears like tiny voices calling from beyond, would they shit their pants and try not to show it?

The truth was more complicated than that, much like what Olga's life had become. The real reason she had followed them there was to see the Devil—in the same way an unsatisfied customer goes back to the store and asks to speak to the manager. A very, *very* fearful customer. Because Olga had been through all of this before.

Her friends' jokes and their loud voices echoed in the tunnel as they struggled to pass through the chain link fence someone put up years ago, even though there was an adult-size hole right in the middle of it. The jagged and rusty edges of the gutted fence screamed Tetanus Central. The signs were warning them to keep out. Bad things had happened here. And because time was a circle, they were bound to happen again. *So keep out, you idiot.*

Even Olga's parents—who otherwise stayed out of her way—had kept up with the tradition of admonishing her yearly not to ever go under the bridge.

Still, in she went.

Sometimes you don't really know people until they have the freedom to get weird. Or until something probes and pokes at them until the weirdness bursts out like water from a balloon. And once inside the tunnel the weirdness rushed out of them. Their voices lowered as if on cue. Their breaths became labored and the air stung their eyes. They weren't too deep inside—it was after all a smallish bridge that had stopped being important almost immediately after it was built— but the light from their phones barely managed to push an inch into a darkness that old and unused.

Maria, who had taken Cassandra up on her offer a little too fast, was now assaulting her cuticles with her incisors to keep herself occupied. Olga noticed a thin line of blood crawling around Maria's thumb, but said nothing. Maria didn't seem to care either.

"Here devil, devil, where are you hiding?" Cassandra started a singsong as if trying to mask her own nervousness, which in turn made Olga both cringe and become more nervous because Cassandra hated singing. She had in fact punched Olga in the arm once because she slipped up and sang along with a tune during a commercial.

And Olga? What was Olga doing? She didn't feel she was acting too weird given the circumstances, but she was probably doing something without realizing it. It was the moment when she was absorbed by the mystery of her own weirdness that the small child appeared on the other side of darkness, crying his eyes out. His yellow jammies almost glowed against the walls of the tunnel.

"What the hell...is this?" Cassandra ran out of songs surprisingly fast. She didn't even try to mask the wobble in her voice.

Maria whimpered, and probably not because she hit a nerve.

Olga's back touched the wetness of the wall. The little boy stood death-still between darkness and half-darkness, wearing the same jammies Olga had left him in a few hours ago. He was clutching his favorite Robin Hood LEGO figure, stolen from her old set. As if things could afford to get weirder tonight.

"Shit, that's my brother."

Olga ran to him, even as her mind was trying to grasp if this was a hallucination due to her being a wimp or if this was really happening again, and how fast her parents would kill her if they found out.

Petros, her brother, could not answer how he got there. *I followed you*, he kept repeating over and over, even though Olga wasn't at home before they all came to the bridge, but at Maria's place, pretending to do a sleepover. There was no way he had followed her from house to house in the middle of the night dressed like this. Someone would have noticed. Besides, she was sure she had locked the door. He didn't look that upset now that she was holding him. His cheeks were dry. It was like the crying was something she had imagined.

"Are you sure it's your brother? I didn't know you had one." Maria mumbled. She still couldn't keep her hand away from her mouth, even though her fingers were *more bone than flesh* by now.

Olga gave her a *don't-you-think-I-know-who-my-brother-is* look, secretly resenting her for calling him *it*. She knew Maria didn't mean it that way but the word still bugged her in a way she couldn't explain.

"Can we go home now?"

The boy rubbed his sleep-crust eyes and wrapped his arms around Olga's neck before she was ready to pick him up, as if trying to pull her down before she ran away. Despite the absolute rat-feast this place was, there was no trace of dirt on him or his clothes. Olga would have thought he was standing in the middle of their kitchen asking for a glass of water and waiting to be tucked in. If it weren't for the girls' disinterested questions—what's his name? where do you go to school buddy? is that your favorite toy? The usual stuff people ask when they don't want to engage with a kid but they feel they have to. Kids can see right through that— she'd think she had dreamed him being here, under the bridge. When she picked him up though his body was as heavy as it was yesterday, his face felt warm and supple against her shoulder blade and he smelled like his favorite shampoo. He felt very, very real. And Olga just knew it was happening again.

Cassandra laughed. "Let him stay. He might grow a backbone."

"You better not catch a cold or something." Olga held him tight and made for the exit.

"Are you bailing on us?" Cassandra tried weakly, but they all knew this night was over for her.

When she brought him back home, she moved snake-smooth. She heard the murmur of the TV and knew her mother was probably asleep in the living room by now. When her father was working nightshifts, her mother refused to sleep in their bedroom, in their double bed. Instead, she thought it a much better idea to let her body slowly slide against the couch pillows as her eyelids grew heavier until she was snoring in front of the red screen light of true-crime shows.

Olga grunted inwardly at the boy's weight as Petros was following their mother's example and drooled onto her generic, wholesale T-Shirt. She steeled herself to carry him a few more meters down the hall and into the room they shared. When she opened the door though, her brother was already there, tucked under the covers, right where she had left him. His yellow jammies a copycat of the ones the brother in her arms was wearing. Everything down to the LEGO figure and a small scratch on the chin from when she had chased him down the hallway were exactly the same.

Olga stood motionless for the merest of seconds and then, bending at the waist, she lifted the quilt and placed the second brother delicately next to the first one.

"Here we are," she whispered to no one in particular.

She gave herself a few more seconds to really take in how much she had messed up. This was bad. No—it was beyond bad. She wished the Devil had actually dragged her all the way to Hell, so she wouldn't have to risk Mom and Dad finding out they were now the proud parents of twins (congratulations, by the way!).

Devil is a trickster, stupid. If you were paying attention you'd know.

She *was* paying attention and she *did* know. All those years in Sunday school had not been for nothing. But in hindsight everything looks easy. It's when you are actually making the deal that you lose all sense of proportion. And she wasn't even certain she had made a deal with the Devil. Had she? Well, the Devil definitely thought so. Because she didn't even have to say anything. She didn't have to say *please, please can I have my brother back? Because my parents are sad and I don't know how to love them the right way. Only he could. Ever since he died our family has been falling apart and I am tired of eating dinner alone on most days. So please can I have my brother?*

She didn't have to say any of this. All she had to do was go under the bridge one night, alone. She was fifteen, a weird age between a kid and not-a-kid and she wanted to test her parents' limits. Telling herself she was just curious to see what all the fuss was about, that she was now an adult (although she wasn't, not by a mile), and she needed to get out of her system all the child-stuff that had been haunting her since forever (even though it had only been *that one thing* for the past five years).

Then, there she was, under the bridge. The man-size hole in the fence was already there, it must have been for a while for the convenience of every desperate soul in a fifty-kilometer radius. No, this was clearly man-made, a Hell gate should be more spectacular, even if hideously spectacular, and at least have someone's head as a door knocker or something.

And it's not like she was thinking anything in particular. She was of course thinking of her brother. She was always thinking of her brother, even when she didn't mean to. Even when she was sleeping. But that was an especially good time to be thinking of him because he never got the chance to do something this stupid. Olga was willing to bet that he would be the type to do the stupid things first. That's how she remembered him in his six-year-old self. He had been four years younger than her but still much more daring and inventive in the ways he could drive their parents mad. She was usually the one to be reprimanded for letting him do the stupid things, instead of the person who did them. And now she was stuck in the awkward position of having nobody to guard from the stupid. So naturally this was an invitation to act on it.

But besides passively thinking of him, her mind was blank and a little bit frozen because it was winter and the fog rising from the sea chilled her to the bone. Her hand was shaking as she lifted her phone like a flashlight to look around and it might have been the cold, and it might have been that her body was trying to turn around on its own accord and start running. The darkness was still thick as a brick wall but she took small, careful steps and looked around. In fact, she managed to cover most, if not all, of the tunnel while taking deep breaths to keep the rising panic at bay. There wasn't much to see. No gate she could make out with the light of her phone. There was a plastic bag and some food wrappers on the ground, signs that people—not the Devil—had been eating gyro from one of the joints around the port. She did stumble on a few crawlers and backed away immediately. Bugs were her own version of Hell on Earth. On the far side of the tunnel, she found candles of many colors, but mostly black, reduced to a guttered mess. Confettied all around were pieces of a torn photograph that if you tried to piece them together and squinted really hard, you'd probably get thirty percent of someone's crush. It was hard to keep track of the exact number of dark rituals that had happened here. Again, kid-stuff.

Olga felt like the only person in the world while inside the tunnel, that much she had to admit. The tunnel's ceiling looked like the roof of the world on Creation Day, dark and damp and oppressive. And if she was doing a weird thing back then she didn't even know to question herself about it, because she hadn't been there yet with Cassandra and Maria, so she hadn't seen herself mirrored in their faces and didn't know what to look for. A thought might have sneaked inside her mind then, when she was feeling the most calm, the most one with the universe, and she might not have noticed. Not a passive brother-thought, but an aggressive one. An illusion that she could change everything—but mostly her own life—if only she concentrated hard enough. Re-arrange the stars and the planets and time itself. There was power shimmering from a place just under her, but the shimmering was so low it could have been nothing at all.

And when she looked down again, through the yellow-white glow of the phone, a LEGO figure that shouldn't be there stared back at her.

When she found the First Petros in that tunnel, the boy was laughing his body into cramps. Olga felt like she was watching a dream she had last night play out like a movie in front of her. Only the dream was an actual memory she had of her brother from maybe six years ago, and this wasn't a movie.

She realized there was something wrong with First Petros after the flush of excitement wore off. They were in her room in the middle of the night, and she was marveling at him—at her brother and at the miracle of him being there—with half her brain, while the other half was desperately trying to come up with something even remotely believable to throw at her parents when the inevitable reveal happened. *Mom, Dad, look who's here to see you!* (cliche), *You won't believe who I bumped into last night!* (no, they wouldn't), *I know he still looks six years old but that makes up for all the lost time, right?* (pathetic). In the end she decided there was no need for words and that her parents would tearily welcome back this Petros, become normal again, and probably move to another city altogether to get away from friends and relatives who might start asking questions. It wasn't perfect but it was a plan. That was until Petros started jumping up and down on the bed and yelled something about winning a game of Connect 4. A game she vaguely remembered losing at and him spilling juice all over the carpet, celebrating. Olga wasn't sure if this was an actual memory or a fake memory he just put in her head.

"Everything alright in there?"

Her Dad's voice came from the other side of the door timid. He wasn't working that night but because his body was so used to sleeping during the day, he ended up shuffling around the house like a night nurse. And even though he forgot to even check if she was home most days, the noise definitely had gotten his attention.

Olga was already panicking, but a small part of her—the one that wasn't looking for an exit—noticed that when she shifted her attention away from the boy, he stopped responding all together and sat back on the bed like the most obedient creature. She kept not looking at him as she headed for the door, trying to cover as much of the opening as possible with her narrow body.

"Everything's fine, Dad." Olga's head rested on the doorframe in a mock-exhausted tilt. She was actually exhausted but all the adrenaline was still coursing through her, and it would still be there come morning.

"Good, good," he muttered and made to leave but then stopped again and looked at her in the way he always did—without really looking.

Olga was surprised to realize she felt almost annoyed at not getting caught. Even though getting caught now would do her no good. She needed more time to figure out her new-old-brother thing. What annoyed her was that her father didn't ask about the noise. Did he think the little boy's voice was inside his head? Was he haunted by Petros like she was? Of course he was.

Maybe the problem was that her father was so unwilling to talk to her—to really talk to her—that he preferred not to know. When it was the two of them—just Olga and him, without Mom or others around—she felt like he was a little bit afraid of her. He kept tiptoeing around her for no reason she could tell. It's not like he didn't want to be around her, he kept asking her questions about school and gave her money for takeout whenever she asked, it was that he didn't know how to be around her. Sometimes Olga felt like he was so kind because he was apologizing for some unspoken insult. Those times she chose to feel insulted.

"Is it okay if I drive you to school tomorrow?"

Olga nodded trying to not resent the way he always asked for her permission to parent her.

"Yes, Dad. Yes, that's okay. Yes. See you tomorrow. Bye."

Olga locked the door and turned to look at her brother. His face lit up again and that's when she felt it in her bones: the trap, the hook, the bargain that had not been made yet but would be.

This was not her brother. This was a movie trailer, a sample you got at the grocery store in front of the cheese section, and not even the good kind of cheese. Devil's own marketing ploy. The whole brother would come, but he would come with a price. She only had to find what that was.

"What will it take for you to become a real boy?"

It was the most Geppetto she had ever felt.

Olga was the one who had suggested the bridge the second time, but only in an indirect way because she couldn't stop talking about it. First Brother was at home, locked in their room, and even though she didn't want to talk about what had happened to her under the bridge, she really wanted to talk about it *somehow*, so she ended up going around asking about the bridge and the stories about it, like a reporter asks passersby their opinion on new government policies and *what do you think about the economy?*

Maria—who kindly noted that Olga looked especially miserable that day—was too happy to share all the different legends her older cousin had told her.

That time the Devil asked for the Master Builder's wife to be sacrificed, to be buried in the foundations of the bridge because the bridge was passing over his prime property. The Master Builder eventually obliged and that's why sometimes you can hear a woman's lament when the wind blows just right. ("That's stolen from that ballad, 'The Bridge of Arta.' Which isn't this one." Olga said. Cassandra snickered. Maria scowled but kept on.)

That time the Devil stole a young farmer's beating heart when he came to the bridge to fetch water for his horses. He was to be married to his lover and he became a different man, sullen, and silent, and violent. The night of their wedding she looked at his bare chest and saw a hole the size of a drainpipe going right through him. She left him soon after for his cousin in another village. ("I like the ending," Cassandra said. Olga nodded.)

That time the Devil made a deal with a woman who was jealous of her husband and afraid she'd grow horns on her forehead because of him cheating. The Devil kept his end of the bargain by taking her head off and putting it on a ram. The horns fit better there he told her. The Ram Woman still roams the forest behind the bridge. ("Corny!" Cassandra yelled which made Maria push her, but Olga sat up straight because this one mentioned a deal being struck.)

That time the Devil possessed an entire herd of sheep because the herder crossed the bridge at night without permission and sent them over the edge where they drowned. That was back when there was still water under the bridge, more than a hundred years ago.

"That last one's from the Bible, dummy," Cassandra rolled her eyes.

Maria, deflated, shrugged. "It worked once so he could have done it again."

Olga did not find any of the stories relevant to her problem but that was when Cassandra said, "Why don't we do it? Go there tonight?"

Maria, who at this point was too invested in her own second-hand tales and probably a little hurt Cassandra wasn't impressed with them said, "My mom would let us do a sleepover. We could sneak out."

This made sense because her house was the closest to the bridge, and that meant it was twenty minutes on foot across the highway.

Olga said nothing. She was already thinking of the thousand ways the Devil could trick her, and ways he had already done so.

Second Brother was not quite like First and they were both as weird as it gets, which made their different brands of weird kind of impressive. But they had one thing in common: they could be really, really passive. They were two opposites of the same person. Like theater masks. *You're so funny!* The happy brother shrieked, clapping his hands together; *I want to go home*, the sad brother whispered behind tears that had started coming down again. Even though they were already home. Unless it was another home he was thinking of, one still under a bridge. Olga didn't want to ask. It was as if someone took a video of Petros on two different occasions and they were now replaying it for eternity but there was only like fifty seconds of it. If she really tried to talk to or communicate with them outside of that imaginary script, the boys seemed more and more like oversized dolls, without other thoughts or needs, which Olga found especially cruel and therefore an appropriate Devil move. Since they seemed to want for nothing, Olga kept both brothers hidden in her room, the door locked behind her when she was inside and when she left, not that anyone was thinking of checking in there. Her freedom was as much a burden as it was a relief.

The day after Olga brought the second brother home there was a small ruckus in the school yard. The kind of super localized excitement around this one thing that breaks up immediately when a teacher passes by, even if they're not on to you.

The center of attention was Cassandra and her phone. Maria was standing on the outskirts of the attention, leaning in but not getting as much out of it as Cassandra who had the video. Maria was clearly unhappy about this and her mangled fingers didn't help either. The video was, of course, about last night under the bridge.

"You don't have dibs on this," Cassandra hissed as Olga tried to squeeze her way through the small crowd to have a better look at the screen.

Cassandra was the kind of person who liked to take full credit for things. Whether or not she deserved the credit was irrelevant. Also irrelevant was the level of nastiness of the thing she took credit for, and the punishment she would take from the teachers or her parents, which didn't do her any favors in the long run, but she had a reputation to maintain and Olga respected that.

"That's not what—"

"Don't worry you aren't in the video. Or in the conversation." Maria said mercifully and put Olga's soul at ease. For now.

The video was as generic as one would expect of a video found on a teenager's phone. It had that "found footage" quality Cassandra was going for. She was rambling about it as the three of them made their way through the rocky dirt roads snaking between the tobacco fields. It was mostly the two girls' faces illuminated beyond recognition by the phone's flashlight option. They probably started filming after Olga and Second Brother had left because she could really find no trace of them in the video. The rest was the same stuff Olga had seen herself the first time she had been there. The walls, the ceiling, the crawlers on the walls and on the ceiling (nasty), the food wrappers with the added company of a cheap brand beer can, the melted to the ground candles, and finally the thirty-percent crush, the photo of whom the girls had tried to put together. If the video wasn't interesting enough for the crowd, the thrill of discovering who was the object of desire would certainly do the trick. Even if it wasn't someone they knew.

The results of assembling a shredded photo in the dark with a flashlight were less than impressive. What was there was too jigsaw- and puzzle-like to be anything. Most of the hair with an ear attached, the corner of a mouth, both eyes but only half of each which made the whole thing really uncanny. The crush could have been any girl, or boy, or person around. The results were too inconclusive and therefore generic. For it to be a specific someone, every single piece would need to be in place. Or at least most of the major pieces. That's what made a whole person. And right now, Olga had only two pieces of her brother. The happy and the sad. What was staring back at Olga was not a torn-up picture, but the reason she had to go back.

Olga was trying to work up the courage to visit the tunnel for the third time. She speared some spaghetti drenched in a sauce that people in her house called Bolognese. It wasn't the authentic recipe; Olga had looked it up on the Internet once out of boredom. This was more like the Greek Mom version of Bolognese. Each household had one and swore by it while scoffing at the other inferior but equally inaccurate versions. Olga was thankful for that pasta in ways she couldn't really express with words.

It was one of those days when Olga had nagged hard enough and for long enough that it made her parents get up and cook something for her. Mom had said, "I'll make your favorite," and Olga's heart fluttered for a moment until she saw her boiling the pasta and the feeling sagged. This was, of course, her brother's favorite. Olga had lost count of how many times her mother had mixed them up, but she didn't dare bring it up for fear that her Mom would remember to be sad again and slump on the couch.

Dad was cleaning off his plate using a piece of bread, preparing to leave for work and Mom was picking all the cucumber slices out of the choriatiki salad. If Olga looked at this picture through her fingers like someone would try to look at the sun, the image appeared almost normal. Boring in the best possible way if you didn't know enough. Just a family sitting at the table eating lunch, no biggy. No colossal, life-changing event could have ever damaged these people beyond recognition. They even had Mom's fake Bolognese at the table. They were doing alright.

Olga considered taking some of the food to her room to give both her brothers a taste of home. Perhaps that would fix them a little bit, make them less loopy. They didn't seem to need food, the way dreams don't need food to project themselves on to you. Because that's what they were doing wasn't it? One was projecting her happy memories of her brother on to her and the other one the sad. She wondered what kind of brother she would find under the bridge this time.

As she was distracted by these thoughts, Dad reached out to steal the last cucumber slice away from Mom, and for a moment their forks crosshatched, and they looked at each other, and they both sorta laughed, and that was the angriest Olga had ever felt in a while. She had been angry at them on and off for years but that level of anger scared her. It made no sense. She searched for other appropriate feelings and found that she couldn't feel happy. Surprised perhaps, or briefly excited. Happiness though was easy to miss. It was fleeting to begin with. Happiness was leaving the house in the morning and walking to school. Then it disappeared by first period as the guilt creeped up on her for leaving her Mom alone with her thoughts.

Sadness was a more solid bet. She tried really hard, and then she tried harder. For a few minutes she let herself think of thoughts she had been keeping away for months. The really bad ones. There was no sadness stirring inside of her. There was always that guilt circling her, and then came anguish, and as time passed and she couldn't feel the so-familiar sadness there was fear. Fear because she could see where this was going. Fear that she had left these feelings under the bridge forever in exchange for her brothers and fear that there were many more to be lost.

The Devil is so, so smart you see? At first you don't even know you should be scared. And then when you smarten up—start to figure out what his deal is—he takes away your ability to be scared.

Olga still felt things. For now. And that meant she felt angry at best and annoyed when she got tired of being angry. But as she entered the tunnel for the third time she lost her fear. A pretty useful emotion when you are dealing with the Devil.

She didn't find the third brother until she had searched wall to wall. She was about to give up and was feeling both relieved and disappointed, and then there he was, on the ground, pushing his small body against the cold bricks. His eyes had become perfect circles. Clutching the Robin Hood figure with both hands he screamed, *No I don't want to bite it! Get it away from me!*

This time Olga didn't have a doubt that this was a memory. It was a summer a few months before Petros got sick and a few weeks after his fifth birthday. Olga had found the fuzziest, most disgusting looking caterpillar in the garden. It looked more like a tiny porcupine than a bug, and just the sight of its wriggling torso made her whole being shiver. Olga put aside her disgust and picked it up. She had a theory she had been working on for some time that Petros wasn't afraid of anything and she wanted to test it. She wanted to be a little mean, be the wild kid for once, the kind of kid her parents were constantly worried about. The way they worried about her brother.

"Bite it."

"Why?"

"Because it bit me and now I am cursed," Olga said cornering him against the fence. "Bite it and save me."

She was taller than him and used her advantage to hover the caterpillar over his head.

"No, no, no, no, no, no!"

When he finally got over his fear—of course he did, he wasn't afraid of anything for long enough—and agreed to bite it, Olga stopped him short of chewing off its head. Then both of them slipped the caterpillar in their Dad's coffee mug.

"That will lift the curse," Petros whispered from behind the couch.

She had forgotten to tell him she'd lied.

The brother in her memory and the one right in front of her were two completely different creatures. Third Brother was stuck in a loop of fear that made no sense to Olga's teenage self and was blown out of proportion. She had the sudden idea that this was what Hell looked like: A self, fragmented. What if the Devil cut you up in neat little pieces of yourself and you were stuck in loops for ever and ever? No matter the type of loop—happy, sad, or fearful—it would eventually get old, not just old, it would become nightmarish.

Olga approached the terrified child and like her Mom would do in the olden days, she kissed his forehead and reassured him. This would be over soon. It had to be. If only she could gather enough pieces of him there would eventually be enough of him to merge into one person.

It didn't take much for the room to become crammed. Her room. Their room. Hers and Petros's room. Her room. Their room. The Three Brothers' room. The ownership of the room had changed in her head so many times it made her dizzy. It wasn't a big space to begin with. Just a bunk bed against one of the walls. Then a window to fit an entire car through (Olga was still amazed neither of them had fallen accidentally on the patio table underneath when they were playing). Opposite of the bed a small desk with an even tinier shelf that barely held ten books at a time, then a medium-size closet. And finally, opposite of the window, the door. The room was meant to be for both of them when they were little, until Dad got around to fixing up the old storage room into something livable and one of them could move in there, when they grow up and need more space. Then one of them never grew up and the subject was never discussed again.

Now all three of her brothers were safely tucked inside the top bunk like the ogre's children in that fairytale. Olga remembered there were more siblings in the fairytale, and she expected there to be more brothers in this one as well. The room itself felt smaller somehow, even smaller than when she had Cassandra and Maria and half her class over for a shitty birthday party that ended up in them drinking chamomile tea in the kitchen at three in the morning, courtesy of her Dad—the sandwiches they had been bingeing on had gone bad because Mom forgot to put them in the fridge. The room was not just smaller, but darker too, and somehow slimier like those sandwiches. As if the boys brought a part of the tunnel with them.

But even though things were getting crummy in here, she couldn't do another sleepover at Maria's. No—she had caught her father wandering too much outside her room when they were both at home, mostly during the night. She screamed at him to stay away and hoped he blamed it on hormones, but who knows what he was doing during the day when she was at school. She couldn't skip school because then he would definitely get suspicious. If he wasn't suspicious now that is. Was he suspicious? The boys weren't making any noises if she wasn't noticing them but she couldn't avoid them completely in here. Once in a while she would unavoidably notice them and then one of them or two—thankfully never all three, yet—would make some kind of noise.

She was starting to get pissed off. So much so that she had daydreams of meeting the Devil and...and what? Giving him a good scolding? She had no clue what she would do but would do *something*. She had so much pent-up rage nowadays, but deep down she could feel it was because she had more space inside her for the rage to grow and flourish. All this back and forth had cost her a lot. Whole chunks of herself she leaned on every day. The scope of her was becoming more narrow, more specific somehow. She couldn't feel fear but she did feel the grating of anxiety, there was no happiness anymore but perhaps she would feel some satisfaction when this was over. Sadness was replaced by a vague sense of disappointment.

Perhaps that was for the best. She could split feelings with her brother like good siblings do. Siblings share everything. It would be just like the LEGO set, only she would do it right this time. He could get all the loud feelings and she could get the quiet ones. Not the worst price to pay to have him around again. Intensity had always been his thing anyway. They would have to figure out a new way to coexist, she and Petros. They were going to be so different now. It would be weird at first, but not weirder than what her life had been for the past five years.

Now all she needed was for the rage to go away as well. She could easily go around with a grayscale of emotions. At the end of the day things around her were not black and white. They were gray. And now she had the feelings to match. It almost felt like adulting.

Every time she found her brother in the tunnel, he always held the Robin Hood LEGO figure. That was her figure once. It came with the Forestmen set, a tree and a castle connected by a bridge and a handful of Robin Hood-like figures holding their little bows and quivers, riding their cute LEGO horses. She had begged her parents for this gift and had gotten it for her eighth birthday. She was so obsessed with the Robin Hood movie back then and also obsessed with foxes. The set didn't have any foxes but she loved it nonetheless.

Petros was almost haunted by that one black-clad Forestman figure he had dubbed Robin Hood (probably because he really liked the movie too or liked watching it with her) and claimed it as his. Olga complained to her parents but it was nearly impossible to stop him because both them and the set were in the same room. He kept stealing it and stashing it in weird places. And the more their parents scolded him, the more unlikely the hiding places became. Once, he hid the figure under a dead mouse because who would think to look there?

Thankfully that person was Mom, who got rid of the dead mouse but kept and sanitized the figure.

The moment Olga saw her fourth brother hiding the figure under his pajamas she knew it was all about jealousy, or envy. She would figure out the specifics later.

"Gosh, you can keep the stupid toy." She was already feeling the weariness of too many lives. "Let's get out of here."

She tested her theory by looking at the message Cassandra had sent earlier about a get together at the beach, which of course she couldn't attend anymore because she couldn't leave her brothers alone with her Dad in the house. Nothing. Envy it was then.

In the end—that might not be an end—Petros became the sole owner of the Robin Hood figure and she buried the rest of the set in the back of her closet forever.

Olga didn't notice when she lost her empathy until it was too late to take back everything she had said, and Fifth Brother was safely locked in her room. His room. Their room.

It was one of those days when Mom was sad anyway so talking about Petros wouldn't make things worse. Not for her anyway. It was these sudden outbursts that made Olga feel like this life somehow overlaid the past one. Everything she did, she said, she thought, her brother had done before—even though that didn't make any sense. She was a teenager now and her brother had never been one.

Olga was inhaling some toast because she was late for school when her Mom walked in. Mom poured a glass of milk, took one look at her, and started talking about Petros making her cut off the bread crusts so he could stuff his mouth with the insides and swallow them in one bite, and Olga was just exhausted by all of this and her anger was shimmering and pushing against every inch of her body.

So she turned, as calmly as possible and said, "Mom, I don't care."

"What? What did you say?" She looked at Olga with such a mix of honest con-fusion and sadness that would have made her guilt a searing sword on any other day. But right now, it was only a pinprick.

"I said I don't care. I really, honestly, Mom, don't care."

She wasn't lying. Olga didn't care anymore. There were some things going on under the anger and the exhaustion that might have meant something in the past. But now they were less noticeable than the stirring of gas in her stomach.

Her mother kept her frozen position as Olga got up and grabbed her bag for school. Once out the door she heard her Mom half-whisper something that might have been *I love you* or *How could you say such a horrible thing?* It didn't matter.

At school she got into screaming matches with everyone, including the prin-cipal. (*Damn, you are turning into a bigger asshole than me,* Cassandra said with a mixture of admiration and annoyance.)

Later in the afternoon, back home, her mother was not sleeping on the couch. She wasn't in the bedroom either, or the kitchen, or any other room.

"She went for a walk," her Dad said, stirring his coffee in his grub-free mug. His eyes followed her every step. "You know how she gets sometimes."

Olga nodded and made for her room.

"Olga." Her name on his lips stopped her. He kept stirring. The spoon clink-clanked against the porcelain, drowning out something in his voice. "Can we help you? Is there anything you want from us?" He said this carefully, like it was the wrong question, but also the right question.

"I don't know, Dad. I am fine."

His eyes glossed over her like she was a foggy pane and the person he was trying to talk to—*really* talk to—was standing right behind her, peering through her. Leaving invisible palm prints on her body. Olga glanced over her shoulder. Nothing. She exhaled. The door was still locked. She was sure of it.

Her Dad put the spoon down and that made everything worse somehow. Olga was suddenly aware of the way her Dad was sweating profusely but was trying not to look sweaty—as if sweatiness was an inner quality instead of water coming out of him in buckets. When he spoke again his voice was fragmented, and she became nostalgic for that stirring spoon.

"What do you want from me?"

"Jesus, Dad, nothing. I am fine, okay? Just, leave me alone."

There it was, she was angry again. But this time it was because she wasn't sure if she was the person the question was meant for. She ran to her room and locked herself in there. The fifth brother stirred when he saw her. He was still fresh from the tunnel and hard to ignore because he slept at the very edge of the lower bunk. He got up and wrapped his small arms around her neck, gently this time.

"I am sorry," he said.

Olga frowned. "...for what, dude?"

"For what I did or I am about to do. I don't know. I am sorry."

That to Olga felt eerily prescient and unbrother-like. But that's empathy for you.

It's a strange feeling to be gathering something inside of you for so long and then to suddenly be empty of it. It was more than uncomfortable. It was agony. But once she stepped inside the tunnel, her body felt miraculously empty. The emptiest it had felt since forever. And to be honest it was pure anger and spite that brought her to the tunnel for the sixth time. To finish what she had started. Now, all of a sudden, she didn't even know what had made her come back here in the first place. To fix everything? By herself? How stupid. What a waste of time.

Now that there was so much space inside her, her other lukewarm feelings were still rearranging themselves, but nothing was really sticking. She didn't even care enough to take a look around. She didn't have to. It wouldn't be the end of the world to walk right out of here. Her parents could figure out what to do with her brothers. She had done her part of the job.

That's when she felt the crushing weight on her shoulders and neck. Was physical pain a feeling she could give away? She would do it right now in a heartbeat.

"Shit!"

The sixth brother's claws dug inside her cheeks and pulled at her flesh like it was chewed-up bubblegum. Where did he come from and how could she get rid of him? Even in this state she knew this wasn't normal for Petros. He had never hurt her at his angriest days. This was her brother on Hulk mode.

She tried spinning around really fast. She span and she span and she yanked her body as if she was trying to exorcise a demon. And she probably was.

"Get off of me!"

Olga had unfortunately watched *The Exorcist* enough times—and without parental supervision—to know demon-types were supposed to fuck you up. She wasn't scared anymore, but the promise and the magnitude of pain her sixth brother could inflict on her did give her a certain anxiety.

"Stop fighting already," the brother snickered. That was no version of Petros she could recognize. He was not her brother anymore. "Just get us home."

"Okay, okay." She felt his ever-sharper claws going for her eyeballs. "Just stop doing that."

"Let's go then."

Olga was already in Hell. There was no doubt in her mind now that she had entered Hell when she crossed that cursed hole in the fence that first time, and she never left. Hers was some kind of Sisyphean crap. Only instead of rocks she had to carry increasingly shittier versions of her brother all the way home—her home, his home, their home—until the entire place and later the entire world was full of brothers. Until she brought on the Apocalypse.

Or perhaps until she was reduced to nothing, to one emotion, a sliver of a person and then vanish. Herself for her brother. Was that the deal all along?

When she woke up she was still inside the tunnel. No wait, that wasn't the tunnel, was it? She was lying on the floor of her room. She could clearly see her bed looming over her and six sets of eyes staring back like the eyes of tarsiers, hanging from tree branches, only not nearly as harmless. It was like her room had moved inside the tunnel or the other way around. She didn't care really. She didn't care at all.

"What's going on?"

The brothers had come to life all by themselves, only this time they didn't replay some sorry moment of Petros's past. They were their own creatures. And they didn't look like her brother anymore.

"Thank you for bringing us inside," they said in unison. "We will not forget this. You are a good girl. A tasty one at that."

That made Olga check her body. Her limbs where all there. Her organs were there—as much she could feel her organs kicking inside of her—so what was lost?

"Is any one of you really my brother?"

The brothers shook their heads. "Not yet," they said. "But we will be with your help. A deal is a deal. Such a good girl."

It wasn't fear she was feeling. It wasn't terror, or panic, or dread. But there was something somewhere deep inside of her that resisted this whole situation on a cellular level. A part of her lizard brain was screeching at her to run but at the same time it kept her frozen in place. Lying on the floor like a dead fish. That same part of her brain made her body itchy and she soon started to shiver.

"Don't fret now. We took that away from you. Keep it away."

One of the brothers reached out his fuzzy hand and touched her forehead. It felt like a caterpillar gliding against her skin.

"We've been wanting to come inside for so long. So long. Did your father ask you about us? Was your mother worried?"

The brothers one after the other got off the bed and made a circle around her. They didn't look like anything in particular and they looked like everything at the same time. They looked like her brother and like the caterpillar, and like the Robin Hood LEGO figure and like her friends from school, and like the Ram-Woman and the man with the hole in his chest. They looked like they contained the universe.

Adealdisadealdisadealdisadealisadealisadealisdeal

Olga didn't know what she felt anymore. She felt present and detached watching herself within and without. Her shivers had gotten worse. That was the only certain thing in her life at that moment, and when they reached every inch of her body, when even she couldn't contain herself, she screamed. And then she screamed some more. Her body was only made for screaming now and she could barely hear her parents' voices under the noise her body was making without her permission.

When her parents got into the room, the spell broke. The brothers were still around her, ready to devour (Yes, she was certain they were about to devour the tiny crumb of herself that was left. Even if she didn't have a word for it, she knew it was there). She was still pinned to the floor. She still didn't care.

If she did care, she would have felt the stab of betrayal when the brothers called both of her parents with their names. Manolis and Loukia. Had everyone in the house made a deal with the Devil? She didn't want to find out and yet she just had.

"I never said yes," her father said to the brothers. Her mother looked as surprised as Olga was about this. She backed away to the other side of the wall, which was not easy to do because it was stifling as Hell, in there.

Adealisadealisadealisadealisadeal is what they replied.

And then they all looked at Olga and that's how she learned the story. The brothers put it in her mind.

That time a man came to see the Devil under the bridge. The man brought bolt cutters and cut a hole in the fence that separated Hell from not-Hell. The man wanted his son back, his beautiful boy. He said without saying that he would do anything for it, including following an old rumor under the bridge. The Devil, cunning as he was, put the deal inside the man's head, because he knew there isn't a worst enemy to the human than their own mind. The deal was his daughter's life for his son's. The man both disgusted and terrified at himself fled the tunnel and thought that was the end of it. But the Devil knew there was a part of the man that had been thinking, what if? A contract was waiting to be signed. A deal left up in the air. One day, as these things usually happen, the man's daughter walked under the bridge on her own free will. It was time for the deal to be struck.

If Olga still cared she would have felt a deep-cut hurt. At least now she finally knew why her father was walking on eggshells around her. And she understood. She really did. The fact that she had gone back to the tunnel time and time again was proof enough. Now her father had become a waxen statue, his words choked in his throat. Her mother was trying to melt herself in a corner of the room.

"That's bullshit," said Olga. "—what did Mom do?"

And the brothers obliged.

That time the Devil found a woman wondering in his forest at night—the forest that was right next to his bridge. She was taking a walk she told herself but what she was really doing was mourning her dead son away from everyone's eyes. She was mortified she would forget him. So the Devil made sure she would remember everything in the most excruciating detail until that was all she could think of. In turn she would remind her daughter of her lost brother. Her daughter that one day would come and find him under the bridge. Feeling guilty, and in need of a deal.

That was rotten, even for the Devil. Olga would feel heartbroken for her Mom if she could. If she cared again she would hug her, and they would talk and talk until she was assured nobody would ever forget Petros.

Olga did want to care again. And that want was outside of deals. It was written in her bones, the same way that scream was written in her bones. It was part of her DNA.

She wanted to live.

The Devil is a trickster.

"None of this is a deal," she said to the brothers. "That's all trauma and guilt, my dudes."

She felt her limbs loosening, her body reshaping to a sitting position. She had to give it to the Devil. He could guilt-trip people at an Olympic level.

The brothers weren't moved.

"You have no right to be here," she told the brothers. They smiled a pointy smile because they had one more story to tell.

That time the Devil found a girl snooping around his property and scaring his fa-vorite centipedes. The girl told herself she had come for her dead brother but really, she had come for herself. She wanted—no—needed the Devil to save her from the memory of him. She thought she could win back her parents' adoration by sacrificing part of herself. She was a good girl. She was a greedy girl. What she didn't know, what none in her family knew, was that hers was the final stroke that sealed the deal. Like the chords in a symphony. And she had made that deal willingly by returning to the Devil every single time. It is time to collect.

"No, that's not how it happened," Olga protested. "Why would I want to upstage my brother? I carried you all the way home."

"There are actions, yes," the brothers agreed. "And then there are thoughts."

"Bullshit." That was her father talking from somewhere behind her. "Thoughts don't mean much. I am having dozens of thoughts right now. None of them good."

Olga felt her Dad move closer to her. He rested his hands on her shoulders and squeezed. She tried to remember the last time he had done this but couldn't find a single memory of it.

"We know," said the brothers, their smile becoming even pointier. "We know all of it."

"What if we make another deal?" Her Mom materialized again. She gradually became more than a shadow on the wall. "One that we *know* we are making."

The brothers turned their collective heads to Olga. "What do you have in mind?"

"No." Her Mom was getting really cocky there. "We won't do it like this. You. Out. Now."

Olga was slow in getting the message so they took her hand and led her outside. "Our girl," her Mom said, "we'll always protect you. We were afraid, but not anymore. Let us do this for you and for us."

Dad's voice was barely a whisper. "We hope someday you'll forgive us. The last thing we wanted was to hurt you."

Olga could hear the lie in their voices. They were not afraid; they were freaking terrified. Their eyes had the intensity of someone who was going away to war. Olga saw them lean against each other for comfort as they went inside and that's when the door closed in her face.

When it opened again the brothers were only one brother and her parents were almost the same. A little paler perhaps—maybe a couple of inches shorter?— they felt different somehow, more mature but technically not older. Olga couldn't tell what they had given away. Perhaps they didn't know very well themselves.

Olga was already feeling a wave of melancholy at the thought of what her parents gave up. Whatever they did, it was working. Slowly, like a numb limb gaining sensation, her emotions returned. The next feeling was her skin prickling at the view of the brother. Because now she could be scared of him but also because he had gone back to looking like the innocent boy who had once been her brother and still wore the same yellow jammies and held the Robin Hood figure. But it was also the realization that she would now associate her brother's image with something sinister and evil, something after her soul. That would put a horrible stain on all her favorite memories of him and was an injustice she couldn't bear.

"What now?" she asked her parents.

Her father, tired beyond his years, said, "Now I take him back to the tunnel. That's part of the deal."

"I should come with. Finish what I started."

Her parents tried to object but this was her story too, she reminded them. If they were going to be honest with each other, they should start listening to her. In the end, they agreed. Her father and mother got in the cabin of the truck, while Olga and the brother-who-was-not-Petros settled in the cargo bed. On one end the brother, looking more normal and silent than ever before, and on the other her—probably looking weird as ever.

"Can I ask you a favor? And if you say yes, it will be a favor and not a deal. I don't do exchanges anymore."

The brother looked at her but said nothing. Olga figured that it was because once a job was done, there was nothing to be said.

"Can you make us all forget about this night and forget about you? The deal— whatever it is you struck with my parents will still stand, but I just want us all to forget we made it. For now. Even if it comes and bites us in the ass later."

The brother-who-was-not-Petros, the Devil, the child in the yellow jammies, smiled an innocent child's smile and said, "If you forget and come back looking for a deal, it will all happen again. Only much worse."

"I promise you, we won't."

Olga didn't know how she knew that, but she was certain of it. Just like she was certain that she wouldn't give up when she had been lying on the floor of her room. It was something buried so deep inside not even the Devil could scrape it out of her. They were all different now in a fundamental way. Forgetting would not change that. But it would help them move on. And she could have her brother's memories back as they were. Perfect in their messed-up, human imperfection.

The brother said nothing, and Olga only felt the truck slow down as they approached the tunnel. His face was not Petros's face anymore. It became someone else's and if she wasn't sitting across from him on the cargo bed, she would have forgotten who he was in moments.

Once the brother was out of the truck, her Dad picked him up in his arms— and if he was devastated, his face betrayed nothing—and placed him gently on the inside of the fence through the hole, taking care to not step inside. A leftover fear, Olga thought. The brother stood there watching the family huddle together in the cabin of the truck. Olga wedged herself between her parents like she was five and hiding in their bed again. She wanted to feel their bodies, the reality of them being there like this (for how long? She didn't know). Be the child she had talked herself out of being.

"I'll come and fix this tomorrow," her Dad said.

He would remember none of this tomorrow. The door to Hell was now permanently open. Once you open a door like that, it can never close again. It was something they had to live with.

Her Mom put her arm around Olga's shoulders; the arm was weak but her hold on Olga was strong. "We're done with this."

Olga wasn't sure they were done with this. Because the Devil would come to collect eventually. They could count on that. But maybe they were sort of done with something. Done with the silence. Done with the walking on eggshells around each other. Done with the not-listening. Maybe they were at that point where they could talk about the dreadful thing: the brother-shaped emptiness in their house the Devil came and filled in. Talking about the Devil was magnitudes easier compared to this. But they could do it now. Olga knew they could do it. She believed in them. She believed in her family as much as she believed in the Devil. Hell, she believed in her family magnitudes more.

The truck turned and Olga lost the bridge from her sight.

And then?

And then she felt so much lighter.

· ·

Eugenia Triantafyllou is a Greek author and artist with a flair for dark things. Her work has won the Shirley Jackson Award and has been nominated for the Ignyte, Locus, Nebula, and World Fantasy Awards. She is a graduate of Clarion West Writers Workshop. You can find her stories in *Reactor.com*, *Uncanny*, *Strange Horizons*, *Apex*, and other venues. She currently lives in Athens with a boy and a dog. Find her on Twitter @foxesandroses, or Bluesky @foxesandroses.bsky.social, her IG @eugeniatriantafyllou, or her website http://www.eugeniatriantafyllou.com.

NOVELLA

LINGHUN

Ai Jiang

(EXCERPT)

WENQI

I stumble dizzy and carsick into the kitchen to find Mother unpacking. Her eyes dart everywhere rather than focusing on the task at hand. Bowls and plates litter the island, the dining table, and the edges of the sink. Cupboards sit open, empty. Father stands next to her, rubbing a hand across his stubbled chin, running a finger along a growing shadow of a mustache. His other hand rests against the sink, twitching, not knowing where else to place it or what he should be doing with it.

"The agent said it might take a while before he appears," Mother says in a feverish whisper, fixing her hair the way she used to right before leaving for a job interview.

Before we got the house, she worked in a travel agency downtown. But that didn't last long. Mother said there was a new co-worker who too closely resembled what my brother would have looked like as an adult. Their names were also similar.

"In the pamphlet she gave us, it says placing their items or photos around the house might help," Father says.

Mother flings herself over to a box by the fridge and rips it open. She takes out several framed family photos— none are recent. All the pictures, like my brother, are frozen in time. Mother hurries around the house while Father and I stare. She places one frame on the dining table and one on the coffee table in the living room. Her footsteps thunder up the stairs. Doors open, close, open, close. Footsteps pitter, patter, pitter, patter. She returns, and I imagine she has placed a similar family portrait on the desk in my room: Mother, with her hand on my shoulder, the other hand on my brother's, Father behind her with a hand at her waist and the other on my brother's head.

When Mother returns, she grabs a stack of unframed photos, this time of *only* my brother: ultrasounds, pre- school and kindergarten pictures, him in a graduation cap, holding a certificate of excellence at the end of first grade. His photos end there. A younger me, half my brother's age, stands in the picture, clutching his arm with a wobbly smile and missing teeth.

My brother was always the golden child, the one who carried the family's honor, the one who would have carried the family name as per tradition—unlike me, who will only carry the name of my husband *if* I marry. Mother and Father often try to convince me that they are not as traditional as their parents, yet they doted on my brother, the first-born son, and often forgot about me. They still do, even though he's gone. I'm convinced that, had they been offered the choice, my parents would have traded my life for my brother's, with little hesitation. At least, Mother would have, and probably still would, if given the chance. I grew up hearing her complain often how Father's Mother was always insisting that my parents try for another son, but Mother was—and still is—too heartbroken to think about children.

Mother disappears again. Father and I wait, listening to the ticking of a small clock—the same one Mother used for my brother's reading hours, back when we still lived in Fuzhou. I still remember the way my brother drew me closer while he read so that I could see the words, but they were always too advanced for my age. I can recall the images, but I don't recognize the Chinese characters in my memories.

After Mother sets everything up, the three of us sit in the living room waiting for something to happen—for my brother's promised appearance—but nothing does.

MRS.

The new arrivals to the neighbor- hood moved into the house across the street. There is only one reason anyone would trek through the guarding trees to get to HOME: not to seek new life, but to satisfy a longing for the dead.

Houses in HOME sate the unending hun- ger of those most vulnerable, unsuspecting. They feed on our desires, our pain. So much pain. And to wallow in such pain... It is a hideous thing.

Isn't it strange? How everyone here desires their homes to be haunted?

You wonder if the newcomers will be the same as the others. You wonder if they, too, will be unrelenting, or perhaps they will be like you... unhaunted.

WENQI

After we eat dinner in silence, I move to the living room window and look out upon our new street. Our lawn is overgrown and full of weeds, but it is also full of people. I had been too sick on the drive in to care much about these odd vagabonds, but curiosity gnawed at my mind.

"Why are there people on the lawns?" I ask.

"Don't worry about them," says Mother, sounding more than a bit absentminded. "The agent assured us that these people are a normal occurrence here, since everyone wants to move into this neighborhood and is more than willing to wait. What did she call them again? Oh yes, *lingerers*—that's the word. But it matters not. We're just grateful we got a house here. Aren't we?"

I look out again at the trees that have grown too tall, too unruly for the narrow street. Their overgrown branches cast ominous shadows over our house and the rest, preventing any sunlight from reaching the roofs or shining through our windows. This house resembles little of our home in Scarborough, and it's nothing like our home back in Fuzhou.

Father looks to Mother. His grip tightens against his chopsticks, and his knuckles turn white. "Yes, yes, yes," he agrees.

Most of the neighborhood is unkempt, but directly across the street, a plain little home rests upon a neatly trimmed plot of grass. Cared-for flower beds line the house's front facade. Above the tangles of rose and lavender, I see an old woman sitting by her front window, clutching an urn upon her lap. Instead of drawing the curtains closed like I expect her to, she continues to stare at me and my family.

I turn back to my parents, speaking again of the people on our lawn. "Can we ask them to leave?"

"No," Father says, eying Mother through a mask of worry.

Back outside, a man leans against the large SOLD sign stuck into the grass. Below it is the neighborhood's name in a smaller bold font: HOME—Homecoming Of Missing Entities. It sounds like a joke, but nothing about this place feels worthy of laughter. Mother has a smile on her face, but Father seems more wary about this endeavor.

The lingerers continue to stare at the house, *into* the house, with their bodies almost leaning toward the front door, as if being manipulated by an unseen puppeteer and their invisible strings. The lingerers on the other lawns hold the same position. My parents pretend to not be bothered by it, but I can see the sweat glisten on Father's forehead, and I can see Mother discreetly wringing her hands, playing with her wedding band.

A boy sitting on the lawn two houses down, across the street, has his back turned to the brown and yellow house he sits in front of. His eyes catch mine, and I can see a spark of curiosity.

I wonder how long the boy has been here. And I wonder when I will be able to leave.

Linghun by Ai Jiang is available from Dark Matter INK.

Ai Jiang is a Chinese-Canadian writer, Ignyte, Bram Stoker, and Nebula Award winner, and Hugo, Astounding, Locus, Aurora, and BFSA Award finalist from Changle, Fujian currently residing in Toronto, Ontario. She is the recipient of Odyssey Workshop's 2022 Fresh Voices Scholarship and the author of *A Palace Near the Wind*, *Linghun*, and *I AM AI*. Find her at www.aijiang.ca.

NOVELLA & NOVEL FINALISTS

THE 2023 NEBULA AWARD FOR BEST NOVELLA

WINNER

Linghun

Ai Jiang

The Crane Husband

Kelly Barnhill

A fifteen-year-old teenager is the backbone of her small Midwestern family, budgeting the household finances and raising her younger brother while her mom, a talented artist, weaves beautiful tapestries. For six years, it's been just the three of them—her mom has brought home guests at times, but none have ever stayed.

Yet when her mom brings home a six-foot tall crane with a menacing air, the girl is powerless to prevent her mom letting the intruder into her heart, and her children's lives. Utterly enchanted and numb to his sharp edges, her mom abandons the world around her to weave the masterpiece the crane demands.

In this stunning contemporary retelling of "The Crane Wife" by the Newbery Medal-winning author of *The Girl Who Drank the Moon*, one fiercely pragmatic teen forced to grow up faster than was fair will do whatever it takes to protect her family—and change the story.

Thornhedge

T. Kingfisher

Thornhedge is the tale of a kind-hearted, toad-shaped heroine, a gentle knight, and a mission gone completely sideways.

There's a princess trapped in a tower. This isn't her story.

Meet Toadling. On the day of her birth, she was stolen from her family by the fairies, but she grew up safe and loved in the warm waters of faerieland. Once an adult though, the fae ask a favor of Toadling: return to the human world and offer a blessing of protection to a newborn child. Simple, right?

But nothing with fairies is ever simple.

Centuries later, a knight approaches a towering wall of brambles, where the thorns are as thick as your arm and as sharp as swords. He's heard there's a curse here that needs breaking, but it's a curse Toadling will do anything to uphold...

Untethered Sky

Fonda Lee

From World Fantasy Award-winning author Fonda Lee comes *Untethered Sky*, an epic fantasy fable about the pursuit of obsession at all costs.

Ester's family was torn apart when a manticore killed her mother and baby brother, leaving her with nothing but her father's painful silence and a single, overwhelming need to kill the monsters that took her family.

Ester's path leads her to the King's Royal Mews, where the giant rocs of legend are flown to hunt manticores by their brave and dedicated ruhkers. Paired with a fledgling roc named Zahra, Ester finds purpose and acclaim by devoting herself to a calling that demands absolute sacrifice and a creature that will never return her love. The terrifying partnership between woman and roc leads Ester not only on the empire's most dangerous manticore hunt, but on a journey of perseverance and acceptance.

The Mimicking of Known Successes

Malka Older

The Mimicking of Known Successes presents a cozy Holmesian murder mystery and sapphic romance, set on Jupiter, by Malka Older, author of the critically-acclaimed Centenal Cycle.

On a remote, gas-wreathed outpost of a human colony on Jupiter, a man goes missing. The enigmatic Investigator Mossa follows his trail to Valdegeld, home to the colony's erudite university—and Mossa's former girlfriend, a scholar of Earth's pre-collapse ecosystems.

Pleiti has dedicated her research and her career to aiding the larger effort towards a possible return to Earth. When Mossa unexpectedly arrives and requests Pleiti's assistance in her latest investigation, the two of them embark on a twisting path in which the future of life on Earth is at stake—and, perhaps, their futures, together.

Mammoths at the Gates

Nghi Vo

The wandering Cleric Chih returns home to the Singing Hills Abbey for the first time in almost three years, to be met with both joy and sorrow. Their mentor, Cleric Thien, has died, and rests among the archivists and storytellers of the storied abbey. But not everyone is prepared to leave them to their rest.

Because Cleric Thien was once the patriarch of Coh clan of Northern Bell Pass--and now their granddaughters have arrived on the backs of royal mammoths, demanding their grandfather's body for burial. Chih must somehow balance honoring their mentor's chosen life while keeping the sisters from the north from storming the gates and destroying the history the clerics have worked so hard to preserve.

But as Chih and their neixin Almost Brilliant navigate the looming crisis, Myriad Virtues, Cleric Thien's own beloved hoopoe companion, grieves her loss as only a being with perfect memory can, and her sorrow may be more powerful than anyone could anticipate...

The novellas of The Singing Hills Cycle are linked by the cleric Chih, but may be read in any order, with each story serving as an entry point.

THE 2023 NEBULA AWARD FOR BEST NOVEL

WINNER

The Saint of Bright Doors
Vajra Chandrasekera

Fetter was raised to kill, honed as a knife to cut down his sainted father. This gave him plenty to talk about in therapy.

He walked among invisible powers: devils and anti-gods that mock the mortal form. He learned a lethal catechism, lost his shadow, and gained a habit for secrecy. After a blood-soaked childhood, Fetter escaped his rural hometown for the big city, and fell into a broader world where divine destinies are a dime a dozen.

Everything in Luriat is more than it seems. Group therapy is recruitment for a revolutionary cadre. Junk email hints at the arrival of a god. Every door is laden with potential, and once closed may never open again. The city is scattered with Bright Doors, looming portals through which a cold wind blows. In this unknowable metropolis, Fetter will discover what kind of man he is, and his discovery will rewrite the world.

The Water Outlaws
S. L. Huang

In the jianghu, you break the law to make it your own.

Lin Chong is an expert arms instructor, training the Emperor's soldiers in sword and truncheon, battle axe and spear, lance and crossbow. Unlike bolder friends who flirt with challenging the unequal hierarchies and values of Imperial society, she believes in keeping her head down and doing her job.

Until a powerful man with a vendetta rips that carefully-built life away.

Disgraced, tattooed as a criminal, and on the run from an Imperial Marshall who will stop at nothing to see her dead, Lin Chong is recruited by the Bandits of Liangshan. Mountain outlaws on the margins of society, the Liangshan Bandits proclaim a belief in justice—for women, for the downtrodden, for progressive thinkers a corrupt Empire would imprison or destroy. They're also murderers, thieves, smugglers, and cutthroats.

Apart, they love like demons and fight like tigers. Together, they could bring down an empire.

Translation State

Ann Leckie

Qven was created to be a Presger translator. The pride of their Clade, they always had a clear path before them: learn human ways, and eventually, make a match and serve as an intermediary between the dangerous alien Presger and the human worlds. The realization that they might want something else isn't "optimal behavior." It's the type of behavior that results in elimination.

But Qven rebels. And in doing so, their path collides with those of two others. Enae, a reluctant diplomat whose dead grandmaman has left hir an impossible task as an inheritance: hunting down a fugitive who has been missing for over 200 years. And Reet, an adopted mechanic who is increasingly desperate to learn about his genetic roots—or anything that might explain why he operates so differently from those around him.

As a Conclave of the various species approaches—and the long-standing treaty between the humans and the Presger is on the line—the decisions of all three will have ripple effects across the stars.

Masterfully merging space adventure and mystery, and a poignant exploration about relationships and belonging, *Translation State* is a triumphant new standalone story set in the celebrated Imperial Radch universe.

The Terraformers

Annalee Newitz

Destry's life is dedicated to terraforming Sask-E. As part of the Environmental Rescue Team, she cares for the planet and its burgeoning eco-systems as her parents and their parents did before her.

But the bright, clean future they're building comes under threat when Destry discovers a city full of people that shouldn't exist, hidden inside a massive volcano.

As she uncovers more about their past, Destry begins to question the mission she's devoted her life to and must make a choice that will reverberate through Sask-E's future for generations to come.

A science fiction epic for our times and a love letter to our future, *The Terraformers* will take you on a journey spanning thousands of years and exploring the triumphs, strife, and hope that find us wherever we make our home.

Shigidi and the Brass Head of Obalufon

Wole Talabi

Shigidi is a disgruntled and demotivated nightmare god in the Orisha spirit company, reluctantly answering prayers of his few remaining believers to maintain his existence long enough to find his next drink. When he meets Nneoma, a sort-of succubus with a long and secretive past, everything changes for him.

Together, they attempt to break free of his obligations and the restrictions that have bound him to his godhood and navigate the parameters of their new relationship in the shadow of her past. But the elder gods that run the Orisha spirit company have other plans for Shigidi, and they are not all aligned—or good.

From the boisterous streets of Lagos to the swanky rooftop bars of Singapore and the secret spaces of London, Shigidi and Nneoma will encounter old acquaintances, rival gods, strange creatures, and manipulative magicians as they are drawn into a web of revenge, spirit business, and a spectacular heist across two worlds that will change Shigidi's understanding of himself forever and determine the fate of the Orisha spirit company.

Witch King

Martha Wells

"I didn't know you were a... demon."
"You idiot. I'm the demon."

Kai's having a long day in Martha Wells' WITCH KING....

After being murdered, his consciousness dormant and unaware of the passing of time while confined in an elaborate water trap, Kai wakes to find a lesser mage attempting to harness Kai's magic to his own advantage. That was never going to go well.

But why was Kai imprisoned in the first place? What has changed in the world since his assassination? And why does the Rising World Coalition appear to be growing in influence?

Kai will need to pull his allies close and draw on all his pain magic if he is to answer even the least of these questions.

He's not going to like the answers.

ANDRE NORTON NEBULA AWARD FOR MIDDLE GRADE AND YOUNG ADULT FICTION

WINNER

To Shape a Dragon's Breath

Moniquill Blackgoose

A young Indigenous woman enters a colonizer-run dragon academy—and quickly finds herself at odds with the "approved" way of doing things—in the first book of this brilliant new fantasy series.

The remote island of Masquapaug has not seen a dragon in many generations—until fifteen-year-old Anequs finds a dragon's egg and bonds with its hatchling. Her people are delighted, for all remember the tales of the days when dragons lived among them and danced away the storms of autumn, enabling the people to thrive. To them, Anequs is revered as Nampeshiweisit—a person in a unique relationship with a dragon.

Unfortunately for Anequs, the Anglish conquerors of her land have different opinions. They have a very specific idea of how a dragon should be raised, and who should be doing the raising—and Anequs does not meet any of their requirements. Only with great reluctance do they allow Anequs to enroll in a proper Anglish dragon school on the mainland. If she cannot succeed there, her dragon will be killed.

For a girl with no formal schooling, a non-Anglish upbringing, and a very different understanding of the history of her land, challenges abound—both socially and academically. But Anequs is smart, determined, and resolved to learn what she needs to help her dragon, even if it means teaching herself. The one thing she refuses to do, however, is become the meek Anglish miss that everyone expects.

Anequs and her dragon may be coming of age, but they're also coming to power, and that brings an important realization: the world needs changing—and they might just be the ones to do it.

The Inn at the Amethyst Lantern

J. Dianne Dotson

Atop a seaside bluff, an ancient lighthouse named the Amethyst Lantern sweeps its violet light across the sea and around the bayside town of Glimmerbight. The citizens do not remember a time in which the Lantern was built. But tales abound of the Inn in its shadow. Long ago, the Inn played host to a wonderous twilight era of a time long passed before the sun's harsh rays forced humanity to adapt to Night Living. Legend tells that the shuttered Inn still houses a mystic hermit who powers the Lantern, and who may have founded the town itself.

Gentian "Gen" Lightworth and her brother Jas are two teens who live at the edge of the woods beyond which the Inn and the Amethyst Lantern still stand. After their cousin, Mira Celestus, breaks the societal age code by attending the annual Glowworm Ball via magic, something awakens in the Inn. Two giant Luna moths carry an invitation from the Inn addressed to Gen alone, portending that something stirs at the base of the Amethyst Lantern after all. Gen and her friends seek to uncover the truth of the Inn and find that something strange is happening in all the land, that could threaten the pleasant town of Glimmerbight and force Night Living into a more sinister era of darkness, or even worse, to bake in the brilliance of a savage sun.

The Ghost Job

Greg van Eekhout

Ghosts make the best thieves in this pitch-perfect middle grade adventure from the acclaimed author of *Weird Kid*. Perfect for fans of Gordon Korman and John David Anderson—and anyone looking for an *Ocean's 11*-style heist! Zenith and her friends may be dead—but lucky for them, even getting ghosted wasn't enough to tear them apart. The four of them were thick as thieves long before an unfortunate lab accident sent them careening into the afterlife. So when they hear about a machine that could return them to the land of the living, they are determined to steal it. Unfortunately, the magical device belongs to a dangerous necromancer who's out for their ectoplasm. Fortunately , they're great at heists. Because pulling off the score of their deathtimes is no job for an amateur.

Liberty's Daughter

Naomi Kritzer

Beck Garrison lives on a seastead—an archipelago of constructed platforms and old cruise ships, assembled by libertarian separatists a generation ago. She's grown up comfortable and sheltered, but starts doing odd jobs for pocket money.

To her surprise, she finds that she's the only detective that a debt slave can afford to hire to track down the woman's missing sister. When she tackles this investigation, she learns things about life on the other side of the waterline—not to mention about herself and her father—that she did not expect. And that some people will stop at nothing to keep her from talking about...

MULTIMEDIA AWARD FINALISTS

RAY BRADBURY NEBULA AWARD FOR OUTSTANDING DRAMATIC PRESENTATION

WINNER

Barbie

Greta Gerwig and Noah Baumbach

To live in Barbie Land is to be a perfect being in a perfect place. Unless you have a full-on existential crisis. Or you're a Ken. (from *IMDb*)

Nimona

Robert L. Baird, Lloyd Taylor, Pamela Ribon, Nick Bruno, Troy Quaine, Keith Bunin, and Nate Stevenson

A knight framed for a tragic crime teams with a scrappy, shape-shifting teen to prove his innocence. But what if she's the monster he's sworn to destroy? (from *Netflix*)

The Last of Us: "Long, Long Time"

Neil Druckman and Craig Mazin

In 2003, a parasitic fungal infection ravaged the planet, turning humans into violent creatures known as the Infected. Twenty years later, hardened survivor Joel (Pedro Pascal) is hired to smuggle 14-year-old Ellie (Bella Ramsey) to the rebel Fireflies. Season 2 of *The Last of Us* picks up five years after the events of Season 1. Joel and Ellie's collective past catches up to them, drawing them into conflict with each other and a world even more dangerous and unpredictable than the one they left behind.

In Episode 3: When an unknown person approaches his compound, survivalist Bill forges an unlikely connection. Later, Joel and Ellie seek Bill's guidance. (from *IMDb*)

Dungeons & Dragons: Honor Among Thieves

Jonathan Goldstein, John Francis Daley, Michael Gilio, and Chris McKay

A charming thief and a band of unlikely adventurers undertake an epic heist to retrieve a lost relic, but things go dangerously awry when they run afoul of the wrong people in this hilarious and action-packed adventure. (from *IMDb*)

Spider-Man: Across the Spider-Verse

Phil Lord, Christopher Miller, and Dave Callaham

After reuniting with Gwen Stacy, Brooklyn's full-time, friendly neighborhood Spider-Man is catapulted across the Multiverse, where he encounters the Spider Society, a team of Spider-People charged with protecting the Multiverse's very existence. But when the heroes clash on how to handle a new threat, Miles finds himself pitted against the other Spiders and must set out on his own to save those he loves most. Anyone can wear the mask—it's how you wear it that makes you a hero. (from *Sony Pictures*)

The Boy and the Heron

Hayao Miyazaki

After losing his mother during the war, young Mahito moves to his family's estate in the countryside. There, a series of mysterious events lead him to a secluded and ancient tower, home to a mischievous gray heron. When Mahito's new stepmother disappears, he follows the gray heron into the tower, and enters a fantastic world shared by the living and the dead. As he embarks on an epic journey with the heron as his guide, Mahito must uncover the secrets of this world, and the truth about himself. (from *IMDb*)

GAME WRITING

Baldur's Gate 3

Adam Smith, Adrienne Law, Baudelaire Welch, Chrystal Ding, Ella McConnell, Ine Van Hamme, Jan Van Dosselaer, John Corcoran, Kevin VanOrd, Lawrence Schick, Rachel Quirke, Ruairí Moore, Sarah Baylus, Stephen Rooney, Martin Docherty, and Swen Vincke

Gather your party and return to the Forgotten Realms in a tale of fellowship and betrayal, sacrifice and survival, and the lure of absolute power.

Abducted, infected, lost. You are turning into a monster, but as the corruption inside you grows, so does your power. That power may help you to survive, but there will be a price to pay, and more than any ability, the bonds of trust that you build within your party could be your greatest strength. Caught in a conflict between devils, deities, and sinister otherworldly forces, you will determine the fate of the Forgotten Realms together. (from *Steam*)

The Bread Must Rise

Stewart C Baker and James Beamon

You've been chosen as one of six contestants in the Great Godstone Bakeoff! Godstone, renowned throughout the twelve mostly civilized realms as the "city of a thousand bakeries," is not what it once was. The Queen Undying, a necromancer rumored to have a taste for human blood, has filled its streets with terror, while the robe-shrouded members of the Carb Freeon cult threaten bakers with impunity. And something is off with the City Council, a group of shadowy figures who nobody ever remembers seeing.

You're one of Godstone's top bakers, with a scrappy little business, a mysterious confectionary legacy from your late parents, and a former best friend who stole your recipes to make his own fame and fortune. You've got a lot to prove in this competition, and you'll stop at nothing to reach the top of the profiterole tower.

But everything changes when the Queen Undying herself appears at your bakery. The queen has forced you to become her newest thrall, helpless to resist her eldritch power. And, for mysterious reasons, she's commanding you to make her your baking assistant!

Exercise your breadcraft magic to turn the saddest soggiest-bottomed bakes into stunning showstoppers; sweet-talk the judges into giving you the win; or just put in good old-fashioned hard work. If you're not satisfied with just making bread rise, maybe you'll start making the dead rise, too: necromancy is powerful, and the Queen Undying's spells might be just what you need to complete that recipe...or to take down your rival once and for all.

Play up to the press, win the adoration of your fans, and navigate the influence of the Carb Freeon cult as you bake your way to fame! The farther you go in the tournament, the closer you get to learning the secrets of your own past, uncovering clues about your parents' life and death. And the closer you come to learning the City Council's shadowy plans for Godstone... (from *Steam*)

Alan Wake II

Sam Lake, Clay Murphy, Tyler Burton Smith, and Sinnika Annala

Alan Wake went missing in 2010. He was a bestselling writer based in New York City. On a vacation in the Pacific Northwest with his wife, Alice Wake, he came face to face with a force of supernatural darkness. It brought Wake's writing, a horror story, to life. He fought this dark presence and managed to banish it back to where it came from, a nightmarish dark place hidden under a caldera lake outside the small town of Bright Falls. Wake wrote an ending to his horror story and with that freed his wife from the darkness under the lake but became trapped there himself.

Alan Wake is not dead, although he has wished he was many times. For 13 years he's been a prisoner in the Dark Place, where his nightmares, his fears, and his stories manifest as reality around him. For 13 years, he has been fighting to stay sane and write a story that would change reality around him in order for him to escape. So far, he has failed. (from *Steam*)

Ninefox Gambit: Machineries of Empire Roleplaying Game

Yoon Ha Lee and Marie Brennan

Ninefox Gambit RPG is a tabletop roleplaying game of heresy and hard choices set in the tyrannical interstellar empire known as the Hexarchate.

YOU belong to one of the Hexarchate's six factions. YOU are entangled with a regime that can change the very laws of physics—at the cost of human sacrifice.

Will you...

CONFRONT your leaders, at the risk of being labeled a heretic and hunted down?

CHANGE the system from within, despite the chance that you'll be crushed by it instead?

COLLABORATE to preserve what you can, at the cost of your principles?

Assimilation is a fate worse than death. (from *Android Press*)

Dredge

Joel Mason

Captain your fishing trawler to explore a collection of remote isles, and their surrounding depths, to see what lies below. Sell your catch to the locals and complete quests to learn more about each area's troubled past. Outfit your boat with better equipment to trawl deep-sea trenches and navigate to far-off lands, but keep an eye on the time. You might not like what finds you in the dark... (from *Steam*)

Chants of Sennaar

Julian Moya and Thomas Panuel

Divided since the dawn of time, the Peoples of the Tower no longer speak to each other, isolated by fear or mistrust. It is said that one day, a Traveler will find the wisdom to break down the walls and restore the balance. Travel the endless steps of a prodigious labyrinth, uncover the truth and unveil the mysteries of this fascinating universe where ancient languages are both the lock and the key. (from *Meridiem Games*)

ABOUT THE SCIENCE FICTION AND FANTASY WRITERS ASSOCIATION

The Science Fiction and Fantasy Writers Association, Inc. (SFWA) was founded in 1965 by the American science fiction author Damon Knight under the name Science Fiction Writers of America with a charter membership of 78 writers. Today, SFWA is home to over 2,500 authors, artists, and allied professionals worldwide, and is widely recognized as one of the most effective non-profit writers' organizations in existence.

The mission of the Science Fiction and Fantasy Writers Association includes the promotion, writing, and appreciation of science fiction, fantasy and related genres and field; informing, supporting, promoting, defending, and advocating for writers of science fiction, fantasy and related genres; and to promote and defend the interests of writers in these genres within the publishing industry. Each year, SFWA assists members in various legal disputes, administers grants to SFF community organizations and members facing medical or legal expenses, and hosts the prestigious Nebula Awards at our annual SFWA Nebula Conference.

All authors can benefit from our Information Center and well-known Writer Beware® website. Between online discussion boards, private convention suites, and a host of less formal gatherings, SFWA is a source of information, education, support, and fellowship.

SFWA Membership is open to authors, artists, editors, and other industry professionals who meet our eligibility requirements. To learn more about SFWA or to apply for membership, please visit our website, www.sfwa.org.

ABOUT THE NEBULA AWARDS®

The Nebula Awards, presented annually at the SFWA Nebula Conference, recognize the best works of science fiction and fantasy published in the United States as selected by members of the Science Fiction and Fantasy Writers Association. The first Nebula Awards were presented in 1966.

The Nebula Awards are voted on and presented by full, senior, and associate members of the Science Fiction and Fantasy Writers Association. Categories include awards for outstanding novel, novella, novelette, and short stories, as well as for game writing, the Ray Bradbury Nebula Award for Outstanding Dramatic Presentation, and the Andre Norton Nebula Award for Middle Grade and Young Adult Fiction.

SFWA also administers the Kate Wilhelm Solstice Award, the Kevin O'Donnell, Jr. Service to SFWA Award, and the Damon Knight Memorial Grand Master Award, SFWA's highest honor for lifetime achievement in writing science fiction and/or fantasy.

Over the years, the Nebula Awards banquet grew to become the SFWA Nebula Conference, one of the premier professional development conferences for speculative fiction industry professionals and people aspiring to become one. It takes place each spring. For more information on the awards and the Nebula Conference, please visit the Nebula website at nebulas.sfwa.org/nebula-conference.

www.ingramcontent.com/pod-product-compliance
Lightning Source LLC
Chambersburg PA
CBHW032157190726

48289CB00007BA/2271